WHEN
THE NIGHTS
WERE LONG

BY
DUNCAN R. SMITH

Printed in the United States of America

Nickel City Books

First printing, 2021

ISBN: 978-1-7352779-2-2

Interior Design by booknook.biz

DEDICATION

I am greatly indebted to a supportive family and to a good number of brilliant teachers and professors, but I am likewise much indebted to an extraordinary group of close friends. Some friends date to my youth or college days, some raised their kids with Kathy's and mine, and some were made more recently. However, all of them have educated and buoyed me with their exceptional wit, their boundless compassion, their drive and careers, their well-knit families, their charitable enterprises, their keen insight and balance, their trust of science, their grasp of history and its lessons, their concern for those less fortunate, their constancy of affection and loyalty, and their unfailingly respect and love for those friends we've lost as the decades pile up.

I like to think that I have a good sense of humor, but don't think I was born with it. Rather, I think I was born with the want of one and developed mine to keep up with the sharp-tongued comics amongst us by testing it on an intelligent audience. As fun as all our gatherings are, our friends have also shared themselves and their experiences whenever I or my family encountered the unfamiliar or unknown. Having lived on both coasts and in-between, it's wonderful to know people who would hop a plane if I needed them – or vice-versa. Here's hoping that I don't "need" them but see them really often. As one friend put it, we should since "we're in the fourth quarter."

Here's to friendships that become lifelong once they are made, and here's to my friends who have enriched my life beyond measure:

My thanks and love.

CONTENTS

CHAPTER 1 1
CHAPTER 2 7
CHAPTER 3 11
CHAPTER 4 19
CHAPTER 5 23
CHAPTER 6 31
CHAPTER 7 35
CHAPTER 8 41
CHAPTER 9 47
CHAPTER 10 55
CHAPTER 11 65
CHAPTER 12 71
CHAPTER 13 79
CHAPTER 14 85
CHAPTER 15 93
CHAPTER 16 101
CHAPTER 17 109
CHAPTER 18 115
CHAPTER 19 121
CHAPTER 20 129
CHAPTER 21 139

Chapter 22 147
Chapter 23 155
Chapter 24 163
Chapter 25 171
Chapter 26 179
Chapter 27 189
Chapter 28 197
Chapter 29 207
Chapter 30 213
Chapter 31 219
Chapter 32 225
Chapter 33 235
Chapter 34 243
Chapter 35 253
Chapter 36 259
Chapter 37 267
Chapter 38 275
Chapter 39 283
Chapter 40 291
Chapter 41 299
Chapter 42 303

Afterword 309
About The Author 311

1

PANAMA CITY, PANAMA
MAY 14, 1995

One of the best things about his mistress, Hector Del Rosario thought, was that she didn't pray for him. His wife did pray for him, a bit too publicly, in the small cathedral that she favored. She was a country woman with family close by, a woman with little curiosity, and she and the children occupied a house of distinction in Cristobal, over on the Atlantic Coast. Hector's business was centered in Panama City, on the Pacific Coast, where he kept an apartment. And a mistress. The girl was currently stationed in an efficiency apartment.

Wednesday afternoon, during his lunchtime siesta, it was Hector's habit to skip lunch and visit his mistress. In preparation for just such a dalliance Hector had stopped by his own apartment for a quick shower, and now stood staring at himself, naked in front of his bathroom mirror, with much the same view as his mistress would soon have. The cologne that he splashed on his neck dribbled through his chest hair into the folds of his belly.

A lawyer and a businessman, Hector served as a director on the boards of a hundred-odd companies, and he was president, in a some-times-overlapping capacity, of as many as seventy companies. It was hard to keep track. The fact that he had no idea of what any of these companies did, if anything, didn't bother him, for he and his partner were players in the larger world of international finance. The shell corporations that he formed did business in the new capitals of money, the tax havens and resorts of the Caribbean, as well as the old capitals, New York City and its Gilded Age playground, Newport.

Hector and his partner had a thriving business handling the incorporations and subsequent paperwork of these companies. They were proud of their far-flung, if largely anonymous, client base, and they both considered such things as families in the country and mistresses in the city the just desserts of their labors.

A draft, blowing under the bathroom door and across his toes, surprised Hector. A door had opened somewhere in the apartment and had let a breeze, hot and moist, into his air-conditioned quarters. He frowned. His mistress must have found her way into his apartment, despite his strict orders to stay away. The visit was an affront, a breach of their working agreement, and he would have to be stern with her. She was inviting trouble, and she would have it.

Anxious as he was to settle the issue of territory, he caught sight of the bathroom's glass-handled doorknob turning and reached for a towel. With both hands holding towel ends and his back to the door, Hector was defenseless when the door burst open, when someone charged into the room, when he felt his head grabbed and snapped back, felt the tug of metal that tore across his throat. Voiceless, choking, Hector watched a geyser of blood spray against the bathroom mirror. His knees jammed into the iron sides of the bathtub as he was pushed against it. Toppling, his towel falling off, Hector felt oddly violated, to be taken like this in his own apartment, but then another sensation, a sharp and stabbing pain ripping through the ribs in his back, put an end to all feelings, as he tumbled to the floor, dead.

PROVIDENCE, RHODE ISLAND

A knife makes it personal, the cop was saying. "You use a gun and you might as well phone it in, long distance. But a knife, you gotta be real worked-up, one psychotic shit-bag, to wanta cut someone that way. What kinda animal does that?"

The cop had been the first police officer on the scene and now, at the request of the detective there, was showing Charlie Sanderson the apartment in the Providence neighborhood where the murder had taken place. A bank examiner who worked for the Office of the Comptroller of the Currency out of its regional office in Boston, John Stuart Robbins had been murdered with a carving knife that belonged to a set of knives at his lover's apartment. The killer, having punctured the victim's heart and cut his throat, had taken a few slashes at the victim's genitals. It was that last bit of gratuitous savagery that convinced the cop that the victim's lover had been responsible. Besides, the suspect and the victim were known to fight, loudly and frequently, and the forensics had found traces of amyl-nitrate as well as strong sedatives on a bedroom table.

Charlie took stock of the apartment. Save for the blood-soaked bedroom, the place was immaculate, spotless white walls showing off a collection of Cartier-Bresson photographs, a kitchen neatly outfitted with expensive gadgets. The detective was in the front hall looking through three paintings stacked against a doorframe. In the twelve years that Charlie had known him, Ray McClean had never fastened the top button of his dress shirt or raised the knot of his tie past the hollow of his neck, and he had an attachment to a corduroy sportscoat that superseded any question of season or fashion.

"What do you call it?" McClean asked Charlie, pointing at the series of paintings. "Three paintings in a row?"

"Triptych."

"If you say." McClean flipped through them; each was a portrait of a man, partially clothed, lying in a bathtub, apparently dead. McLean's eyes lit up with the opportunity for sarcasm. "Jesus, who's got this kind of wall space? This is what you want hanging over your bed? A series of dead guys in tubs?" He turned to the cop in uniform. "You said these were on their way to a gallery?"

"The suspect owns two galleries," the cop told Charlie. "One here, one in Newport."

McClean looked at Charlie. "Suspect says he woke up in a pool of blood, his lover dead beside him. Says the blood was drying, caking-up on him. First thing he does is shower. Washes up before he calls anybody." McClean checked with the cop before continuing. "The officer here has a theory. As I understand it, the gallery owner has these paintings lying around. He gets crazy last night, whacked out on a party drug, rough sex. Maybe he and the deceased fight a little, 'cause that's their history. Anyhow, at some point the suspect looks at these paintings and totally flips out."

Charlie looked at the paintings again, which seemed to be fashioned after Corot's masterpiece, "Death of Marat." There was, in their depiction of corpses, an evident delicacy: the bodies were partially clothed and propped up in the bathtubs; the blood was minimal. Charlie had a hard time connecting the paintings with the gory scene in the bedroom. "You talked to the suspect?"

McClean nodded. "I had him in a room for two hours, and I got nothing. You want to file charges, see if it shakes him?"

"Is he likely to run?"

"I don't think so. He did dial 9-1-1. Of course, his boyfriend's dead four or more hours by the time he called."

A State Attorney, Charlie rarely visited a crime scene, let alone on the day of a crime, but he and the detective greatly valued one another's opinions and McClean had asked for his. "What do you think?" Charlie pointed at the bedroom.

"It's all so cut and dried. Maybe a little too cut and dried."

"Gift-wrapped?" It was Charlie's term for a crime scene so convincing that it might be suspect.

"Maybe. Hard to imagine it isn't cut and dried, but I'm guessing the bloodwork on both the victim and the suspect will show they took a powerful stimulant – party drug – and then a powerful sedative. Is this their pattern? Does the sedative knock you out, or does it react with the party drug?" McClean broke off when he saw someone at the open front door, the frame of which had a band of police tape at chest level. "Hey," he called, "it's a crime scene. You can't come in."

"It's my apartment." Short and muscular, Robert Shure was wearing a linen suit.

"Right now, it's a crime scene." McClean identified the man in an aside to Charlie. "The suspect."

Shure turned to Charlie. "Who are you?"

"A State Attorney."

"I need a leash," Shure told McLean. "There's one on a hook in the hall closet. The neighbors have my dog."

"Hang on." McClean turned to Charlie and whispered, "What do you want to do?"

"Let's wait. I'm off to Newport, if you need me."

"Newport?" So am I," Shure said. "If I'm allowed."

Charlie was content to let the forensics on the case spend the weekend scouring the place. Something in the preliminary report, a line about the "scalpel-like incision" that had cleanly severed both carotid arteries, sounded peculiar. Did an enraged lover slash his loved one's throat with surgical precision? Charlie would have to talk to the medical examiner.

Outside the apartment, a few kids were gathered around a squad car and shielded their eyes from the mid-May sun, which flashed off the windshields of passing cars. Charlie fumbled for his sunglasses once he reached his car. If he hurried, he could avoid Friday afternoon traffic.

The drive to Newport would take thirty minutes, maybe less. He would be staying, for what surely was the hundredth time, at Four Winds, the Ocean Drive mansion now owned by Charlie's best friend, George Spaulding. The mansion wasn't quite what it once was, when George's great grandparents had built it back in the 1890s, but Charlie had been visiting the summer home since he and George were roommates at boarding school. George's grandmother had owned the house back then and had employed two caretakers year-round for the property, as well as a cook and a few maids who traveled with her when she abandoned New York City in the middle of May to take up an early summer residence in Newport.

Charlie circled south out of Providence and followed Route 1 towards Jameston. The smell of the ocean, salty and pungent, was everywhere in this quarter of Rhode Island; even in winter an invisible mist, rich with the hint of fish, could reach miles inland. Turning off for the Jameston Bridge, crossing the river, Charlie headed for the Newport Bridge and its long span across Narragansett Bay. Once past the harbor and downtown Newport, he drove straight to Ocean Drive, then west past Lily Pond.

Charlie felt his usual dose of apprehension and excitement as he neared the property. He'd spent, or misspent, enough of his own youth at the estate to have a history there: late nights, best friends, the love of his life. Forced to stop by a truck making an awkward U-turn, he imagined the sight of Four Winds, not yet visible until the next corner was rounded, but visible nonetheless to Charlie, who felt the sudden and oppressive crush of memory.

2

CHARLOTTESVILLE, VIRGINIA
JUNE 3, 1972

While their other classmates attended to the details of graduation, Charlie Sanderson and George Spaulding packed their cars and set off for Newport. The lead driver in the two-car caravan, George had no trouble piloting his year-old Corvette at speeds well over the legal limits. It was more work for Charlie, whose four-year-old Mustang was towing a U-Haul trailer full of George's belongings.

The sun was still up when they arrived at Four Winds and drove beneath the majestic canopy of elms that lined the estate's gravel driveway. As they neared the brick mansion, a huge Georgian structure that managed on first approach to hint at all its thirty-two rooms, the Mustang's tires kicked up a stream of pebbles that clattered against the metal trailer. Alerted by the noise of their arrival, George's grandmother walked out onto the front porch. Grace Botsford Spaulding was "Grace" to all those close to her, a group that extended to her grandson and a few of his best friends. Grace ignored George and Charlie, as they climbed out of their cars, and focused a critical eye on the U-Haul trailer. "Have you joined a carnival, then?"

The two boys were, as she often told them, as dear as anyone in the world to her. She greeted each of them with a long hug, concluding Charlie's by taking hold of his thick blond hair. "Haircuts? My treat."

Charlie laughed. "Are you okay?"

"Never better. I've had Hilda prepare dinner, but I didn't know when you'd be here or how many were coming."

"Half the world is coming," George said, "but they won't be here for a while."

Two hours later, the others began arriving. It was Graduation Day at the University of Virginia, and George had invited several of his and Charlie's closest friends to join them for a week-long celebration. The first to arrive were Lucy Daniels and Quad Shiner. Lucy was a firestorm, a tall and pretty brunette who'd transferred to the University of Virginia the moment that women were admitted; she was, as of today, a member of the first group of women ever to graduate from the college. Her fiancée, "Quad," was William J. Shiner IV and had never been keen on the nickname that George, having noticed the Roman numeral after his name, had stuck him with their first year at college.

Familiar with the mansion, Lucy marched through the open front door and found Charlie and George seated in the den. "You goddamn spoiled brats!" she started in on them. "You goddamn spoiled sons-of-bitches! I can't believe it! You skip your own graduation. You goddamn spoiled little shits!"

"What?" Nonplused, George attempted a grin.

Lucy noticed Grace in the room and blushed. "Excuse me, Ma'am, I'm sorry. But they skipped graduation. Like they're too good to go through something so dowdy and bourgeois with the rest of us."

"What's the big deal?" George asked. In George's family, and Charlie's as well, a college graduation was nothing special. The fact that someone was receiving a diploma was nothing to warrant assembling family members for a long and dull ceremony in a hot sun. George's father was at a resort in Tucson; his mother was in Florida packing for a trip. Had his parents been asked, they might have attended, but that missed the point. George skipped graduation because he could; he didn't need to be there.

"I would've come," Grace apologized. "But I wasn't invited."

"What's the big deal?" George repeated.

"It was hot," Quad conceded. "Damn almighty, it was hot."

"You, I can forgive," Lucy told Charlie. Everyone there knew that the ceremony might have been hard on Charlie, whose father had died several years ago, whose mother had recently succumbed to her long bout with cancer. People at graduation had endlessly grouped themselves for family portraits. "Still," Lucy added, "it didn't feel right without you two there." She turned to Grace. "Anyhow, it's really nice to see you again. Thank you so much for having us."

"We should eat," Grace said. "George may skip ceremonies, but he never skips dinner."

During the meal, two girls from Wheaton College showed up in a VW bus with mismatched tires and a graffiti-on-rust paintjob. The driver was Joe Turlik's girlfriend, the passenger an occasional date of George's. No sooner had the main course been served than Joe Turlik called from the bus station, in need of a ride.

A carload of other friends made it in time for dessert, at which point Grace handed out room assignments before retiring. Lucy was assigned the Chinese Room, named for its rare furniture and porcelain. Quad, Joe, and the other men were assigned rooms off by Charlie, in the servants' wing.

Well shaded by elms and sycamores, the servants' quarters stayed cooler than the main sections of the house. Last summer, working for a Newport law firm and spending the season with George and his family, Charlie had asked to stay in a suite of rooms there. When the summer ended, Grace had proclaimed the space, a small sitting room and sleeping chamber folded around a bathroom of its own, Charlie's apartment. It was his to do with as he pleased.

After suitcases were distributed, everyone gathered in the den, where the fully stocked bar was quickly under assault and George's stereo was blaring. Joe stood by an open French door and worked on a succession of joints, wheezing with each inhale and watching the drift of the smoke. George played a dozen LPs, the hours racing past.

By four in the morning, with the group beginning to disperse, Lucy had Charlie help her track down Quad, whom they found passed out on an upholstered bench in the cloakroom off the front hall. Unable to stir her lover, Lucy draped a coat over his shoulders, then let her eyes settle on Charlie. "Jesus," she muttered, "how is it you're the one without a date?" She was wearing the flimsiest blouse, all but translucent, the material clinging to her full breasts, her nipples poking into the fabric. Once or twice before, at middle-of-the-night hours such as this, Lucy had asked Charlie what might have happened if she'd met him first, not Quad. It wasn't a question that either of them had ever been comfortable answering.

"What's next?" Lucy asked.

Her hands slipped off her hips; her thumbs hooked the pockets of her jeans. It was not yet twenty-four hours since they had graduated, and the rules were all suspended. Anything was possible. Lucy was in a mood to take and be taken. Charlie knew that they could slip away, that a couple of hours wouldn't count, not tonight, not unless they wanted them to. And yet Charlie could read it on her. He could read it on her the same way that he felt it deep within himself. The hunger. A fling with Lucy wouldn't address what ailed them both, and he didn't want to address it, the loneliness that suddenly gripped him, so he took himself off to bed.

3

U p by seven, Charlie found Grace in the breakfast room, a large solarium attached to the eastern tip of the ground floor. The table was set with a tray of sweet rolls, two pitchers of orange juice, and a large jar of aspirin.

"Early to bed, early to rise?" Grace raised an eyebrow, then pushed her newspaper towards Charlie. "You take it. I hate the paper. This awful foolishness in Vietnam. They won't get you, will they?"

Charlie had drawn the number 192 in the draft lottery; George had pulled the number 203. It was unlikely that either of them would be drafted. "I don't think they'll get that high. Anyhow, I'd go before George."

"The military might do wonders for George. If only there weren't this terrible business of war."

"He'll be okay."

"It won't affect your plans, will it?"

"No." Charlie had been accepted at three different law schools and needed to decide which one to attend in the fall. Likewise, he had offers to work for two different firms over the summer, one in Boston, one in Newport. "I just have to make my mind up."

"Cholly?" It was her pet name for him, *Charlie* spoken through intentionally locked jaws, their private joke on the pretensions of a society that held little interest for either of them.

"Yeah?"

"You can always stay here, darling. You know that."

Charlie poured himself some orange juice and gulped it down, then grabbed a sweet roll. He started out of the room but slowed as he passed Grace and squeezed her shoulder affectionately. "Grace, you're a good shit."

"Charlie!"

"I mean it, Grace. You're a really good shit."

"Maybe I am, although it doesn't make me feel any younger when people use poor language in my presence. I gather it's supposed to."

"Yup." He turned for the door.

"Where are you going?"

"Swimming."

"Don't be so certain."

The estate was laid out on six acres of a small promontory that fronted the ocean. Hoping that an early morning swim would clear his head, Charlie cut through the gardens to the flagstone terrace of the pool, only to discover frigid water shooting out of pipes into a nearly empty pool. He headed for the shore.

The south side of the house faced the sea across an expanse of lawn that sloped down to the rocks, which dropped twenty feet to the crash of the surf. A lower terrace, a patch of ground eight feet above the high-tide mark, was accessible by climbing down the rocks. George's great-grandfather had cut stairs in the rock and installed iron handrails, but winter storms had long since eaten away the steps and the railings, and all that remained of the stone cutters' work was something of a bench, cut into the wall of the rock itself. Scraggly grass grew in the rough soil of what Charlie and George referred to as "the Women's Tee": the terrace was as flat as the tee area for a golf hole, and it sat closest to the "hazard" of the ocean, the way the women's tee might were the estate part of a golf course.

On his first visit to Four Winds, the summer after their freshman year at boarding school, Charlie had had to hunt for George and had found him on this hidden terrace. George's father was supposed to take the two boys golfing that morning but had forgotten and gone off on his own adventure. His father's golf bag on the ground beside him, George was busy knocking his father's golf balls into the ocean when Charlie joined him. "He won't even notice," George had said, offering Charlie his choice of clubs. George's father kept a large supply of second-hand balls and a carton of Marlboro cigarettes in his golf bag. "What a goddamn douche bag. Even if he noticed, my father wouldn't have the balls to say boo."

Intermittently taking a swing and sending another of his father's golf balls into the ocean, George christened the site "the Women's Tee" and stayed there long enough to sneak half a dozen cigarettes. Thereafter, the Women's Tee had been a favorite refuge of his and Charlie's, a place to dream up perfect girlfriends and plot their adventures.

Charlie scampered down to the terrace and sat on the bench cut into the rock. Though less than a third the size of this estate, the summer home that belonged to Charlie's family had a similar view. It was in Watch Hill, not far from Newport; Charlie's sister and brother-in-law spent their summers there. Ten years younger than his sister, Charlie had little in common with her and affirmatively disliked his brother-in-law. He preferred the company of George's family.

Some days, however, it was hard for Charlie not to think about his mother, who had loved to take afternoon naps in a lawn chair facing the ocean. He hadn't seen much of her the last few years, which was the way she'd wanted it, forever suggesting that he take a trip or visit friends rather than come home. She'd been angry, not just about her illness and the way it humbled her, and she'd insisted on keeping her distance. At first Charlie had thought that his mother was sparing him the pain of witnessing her debilitation from a slow, excruciating, unstoppable cancer, but he'd come to realize that his mother was sparing herself. She didn't want to confront her two children; she didn't want to deal with their loss. She refused their sympathy.

The distance did make it easier. One day the past April, not having seen her in two months, Charlie received his summons from a friend of the family: he'd better get himself to the hospital in Bryn Mawr; his mother had checked in again and would likely not be checking out. The suddenness of it all surprised Charlie, who'd been given none of the timetables. By the time he got to the hospital his mother was incoherent with the drugs; it took her two days to die.

Charlie gazed at the ocean, absently timing the rhythm of its swell, the progress of gulls tackling a headwind, the struggle of a lone lobsterman with a tangled line. Although Charlie waited until the sun had risen well overhead, none of his friends was up when he returned to the house. They started stumbling into the kitchen around noon and threw themselves upon the mercy of the cook, whose large breakfasts restored all of them, even Quad, to a state of readiness for the afternoon's party. A friend of George's had invited a bunch of people to her parents' summer place, a large colonial a mile down the road.

This property lacked an ocean view and turned its focus on the geometry of its gardens, concentric rings of flowers in the center of the circular drive at the front of the house, a rectangular maze of low hedges dividing the larger garden out back into careful mosaics. Arriving, Charlie grabbed a bottle of beer from a cooler by the front door, sat side-saddle on a stone lion, and thumbed through a magazine. He was still there when a small Mercedes - a well-polished maroon two-seater with the top down - pulled into the driveway and parked at the far end of a line of cars. A girl hopped out of the car, tucked the tails of a frayed dress shirt into her blue jeans, and started towards the house. Her figure was exquisite, her face tanned, with brown eyes that sparkled beneath dark eyebrows. She lingered at the bottom of the steps before climbing them and wandering inside. Charlie watched several other strangers arrive before he, too, moved into the house.

George was perched in a corner of the living room, where Charlie joined him and pointed out the beautiful girl in the frayed shirt. She was talking to George's date. "Who's that?"

"Talking to the witch?" George frowned at the sight of his own date, with whom he'd been feuding. "Julia Hoffman, I think. Her father owns half of Chile. Or used to. What with Allende." George continued the briefing. The girl belonged to a family of German ancestry, with some Spanish and English blood mixed in, who had long ago helped industrialize Chile. Members of that country's small power elite, they sent their children to American boarding schools and colleges. The family had fled to the U.S. soon after Allende took office, when their businesses were expropriated by the socialists. George presumed that the family was stuck in the U.S. unless, of course, something happened to Allende.

"I guess they got pretty well screwed over," George said, "although they rented the Beckman house for the summer. Her father, he knows everybody, not just Newport. Nixon, Rockefeller, Pell, of course, the Mellons. C'mon.."

George took Charlie over to the two women, who didn't stop talking. "God, you talk about conspicuous consumption," George's date hissed. "I mean, it's like this whole town must have this big royalty complex. Everything here's over the top. Wow, all this excess, and there's a war going on."

"In Newport?" George recoiled with mock alarm.

"Very nearly funny."

"All this piety," George complained, "from you, the queen party-hopper. Anyhow, you can't take Newport too seriously."

Anxious to interrupt their argument, Charlie smiled at Julia Hoffman. "What do you think?"

Julia looked at a huge breakfront on the near wall, the shelves of which housed a vast collection of miniature figurines of cats. "I guess the question is, how much do you really need?" Her diction precise, Julia had a trace of an accent that, subject as it was to a variety of influences, was hard to place. Certainly, it didn't sound Latin. "Isn't there the chance," she continued, "that less is more?"

Charlie stared at her. "You believe that?"

"Yes."

"Less is more?"

"It can be."

"And the Mercedes you arrived in? It's a two-seater, not a four-seater. So I guess you're making the big sacrifice and getting by with a little less."

"It's not my car."

"I .. didn't mean it .. like that," Charlie stammered.

"How did you mean it?"

"Uhh.. A joke? *Less* of one, not *more* of one."

"It's my brother's car," Julia admitted, letting Charlie off the hook. "Daddy would buy me one if I let him."

"You're Martin's sister, right?" George asked.

"Is he here? He's supposed to be."

"I haven't seen him."

Her brow furrowed with aggravation, George's date suddenly started off. George grimaced at Charlie, made a crook of a finger, hooked his own collar, and dragged himself after his date.

"So what do you think?" Julia asked Charlie. "This town. It's beautiful, but a little creepy. Some of the biggest mansions, turned into museums."

"They're cold, right?" Charlie also found it strange, the fact that some of the early mansions were such elaborate showcases of artisanship that the only way to preserve them was to turn them into museums.

"So?" Julia smiled. "Less is more?"

"I'm not the one to ask."

"Why?"

Charlie scratched his head. His life had been one of real privilege, as had Julia's, no doubt. "What I mean is, if you ask someone who has nothing, if you ask some beggar in Calcutta if less is really more, he's likely to laugh at the notion."

"Are you laughing at me?"

"Not at all."

As Julia studied him, Charlie's heart sank. She was uncommonly beautiful; she was looking for a simple conversation. He figured he'd blown it.

"I suppose." With a polite nod, Julia turned to greet a girl approaching her. The party dragged on for another few hours until somebody suggested continuing it at a bar in the harbor area.

Charlie gave Joe Turlik and his date a ride into town and parked near the designated bar. Inside, musical instruments were arranged around a stage, but the band was nowhere to be seen. Charlie was about to join some of the people from the party when he noticed Julia Hoffman sitting at the adjacent table. She grinned at his hesitation.

"It's okay." Julia tapped the chair that backed against hers. "You can sit. I'll buy you a beer. A big one. More, not less, right?"

"If you want.."

"I want to get this right. I understand your point. There are two kinds of silos, missile and grain, and some of them you want full. My point was: some things don't matter."

"What does?"

"Some music, some books, some people, some ideals. I'm working on my list - I want it to be long, but full of the kind of things you can take with you."

"When you die?"

Julia laughed. "When you travel. Things you can keep in your head, I guess."

Soon after Julia returned with the drinks, Lucy and Quad joined them. They talked for a while before the band started up, the keyboard player leading his group into a loud, extended version of "Light My Fire." Conversation was difficult, so they took the floor.

Charlie considered himself a good dancer; he was well-coordinated, limber, and could find the rhythm of most any song. Yet Julia's dancing was a revelation: her feet were quick, her hips lithe, her spirit one of joyful abandon. She cut loose to the music with a dancer's grace and a child's energy. Her habit was to end each song with a twirl, an arm extended and snaked across Charlie's shoulders, the delicate flesh on the underside of her arm tingling the skin on his neck.

When the band finally played a slow song, Julia slid in close and let Charlie steer her through a lazy two-step, the two of them shuffling back and forth on a corner of the floor. By the time the song finished she had her arms around his neck, and his arms were wrapped around her waist.

"I have a question," Julia said, pulling her head back from his. She glanced at his group of friends before continuing. "Are you ... seeing anyone?"

"Are you"

"I asked first."

"No."

Julia didn't volunteer her own answer. Instead, she placed her cheek back against Charlie's, and he was left to imagine her smile, which he hoped explained the shift of her jaw on his shoulder.

On the band's next break, Charlie bought a beer for Joe, who was standing nearby and flashing empty pockets that hung out of his trousers, then looked for Julia. He found her talking to some guy in a suit by the front door. The phrases that drifted to Charlie, as he approached, were French, not Spanish, the language of Julia's homeland. Julia noticed Charlie and interrupted.

"Wait. Martin, this is Charlie; and this is my brother, Martin."

"I was practicing," Martin said, extending his hand. "Julia's French is much better than mine."

"Martin's got a meeting tomorrow. With some Haitians. God, will that jerk be there?" Julia's lip curled with disgust. "Papa Doc?"

"I hope not." Martin made the sign of the cross. "Or there may be something to Haitian voodoo. Duvalier's been dead for a year. His son's in charge. Baby Doc. My meeting's just with some bankers."

"I'm going as a translator," Julia explained. "God, they don't speak true French, right?"

"The rich ones do," Martin assured her. "Except the meeting's really early. In the city." He looked at the door, then at his sister.

The jukebox started booming, so Julia leaned close to Charlie and shouted. "I'm sorry. If I didn't have this stupid meeting so early.."

Julia started to walk out of the bar with Martin but stopped and spun to Charlie. "Hey? Will I see you..?" She pointed at the floor, then at her watch, and mouthed some instructions. When she was gone, Charlie worried that he might have misunderstood. He thought, and dearly hoped, that the words had been: *Same time? Tomorrow?*

4

Charlie spent the next twenty-some hours trying, and failing, to convince himself that he hadn't gotten it wrong. His breathing remained a bit shallow until he was crossing the street near the bar the following night and saw Julia get out of a parked car. Martin honked a salute and drove off in his Mercedes, while Julia joined Charlie on the sidewalk.

"Thanks for coming," she said, taking his arm and walking beside him. "I wasn't sure if.."

"Me, neither."

"I made Martin wait. In case you stood me up." Julia's laugh was at her own expense, and it was perfectly contagious.

Charlie snuck a look at her, then another: she was more beautiful than he'd allowed himself to remember. The wind rustled her hair, a few locks trailing away from a slight widow's peak and sweeping across her forehead. Pale and soft, her lips were perfectly symmetrical, except for the tiny heart-top indent that centered the upper lip.

Inside the bar, Charlie found a large, unoccupied table and pulled out a chair. Julia silently counted all the empty seats and asked, "Expecting someone?"

"I couldn't get away without being grilled."

"Your friends are scared they'll miss a party?"

"Basically." They ordered drinks from a waitress whose blouse was a patchwork of McGovern-for-President campaign buttons, and waited for a song they liked, at which point Julia grabbed Charlie's hand and dragged him to his feet. They tilted chairs against the table to reserve it and danced until his friends showed up.

Lucy made it a point to sit at the table next to Julia, although Quad didn't much like the band and was soon arguing in favor of visiting another club. Charlie didn't commit to join his friends, who left to check out the other place. He and Julia danced a while longer, to slow songs that filled the floor.

With the crowd swelling around them, Julia grew weary of being bumped. "It's hot," she said, leading Charlie outside onto the bar's large front porch.

An empty lot across the street afforded them an unobstructed view of the harbor, where the reflections of lights played on the water like renegade neon, the beams sparking and rolling through hundreds of tubes cracked by the lapping tide. Charlie and Julia boosted themselves onto the porch's broad railing, her hand landing on his, her palm smooth and cool as silk. They stayed there, holding hands and gazing at the harbor, until a siren sounded in the distance, an odd shriek warbled by a stiffening breeze. As it faded, Julia squeezed Charlie's hand and grinned at him with a look of mischief and invitation. "Well...," she said, and stalled, as if she didn't know what to say next. "Any questions?"

Charlie took a moment. "Who invented lawn jockeys? And why did they do it?"

"That's your question?"

"I have others."

Watching the smile drift across Julia's face, Charlie was delighted to realize that he didn't need to postpone anything. He put his hand on her chin and dragged a fingertip along her lower lip, then leaned forward and kissed her. The kiss lingered, reverent one moment, playful the next. Free to breathe, they drank in the scents of each other, Charlie smelling like Ivory Soap and the sweet detergent that had washed his clothes, Julia scented by the floral hints of her perfume and by the seabreeze itself, which washed over them with hints of something damp and mysterious and earthy.

Charlie swiveled off the handrail and pulled her close while Julia brought her mouth back to his, her tongue darting forward and touching the tip of his tongue, their tongues caressing one another in lazy anticipation of a deepening kiss. Their embrace lasted until a tugboat noisily attempted to position a trawler in a narrow berth across the harbor. Its engines reversing themselves, the tug bobbed on the trawler's wake as the larger ship's bow banged against the dock's pilings.

Charlie and Julia walked down to a bench on the waterfront from where they watched the vessel, its ropes slung ship-to-shore, get tied down. Swept clean by the wind and the patchy high clouds that raced past a quarter-moon, the sky was brilliant, the stars too numerous to count. Julia raised her legs and sat Indian-style, her feet beneath her, her left knee spilling into his lap. Charlie put a hand on her thigh and was struck by the heat of her, her skin radiating its tan and warm with the stored energy of the day's sun.

"Lucy's a good friend, huh?" Julia asked.

"I guess."

"She is. She's very protective of you."

"I'm sorry. All those questions." In the bar, Lucy had quizzed Julia - about her plans, her family. Had her father supported the conservative government that Allende unseated? Would she return to Chile if conditions allowed?

"I like her for it," Julia said. "The way she looks after you."

Later, they strolled along the harbor, then drove to an all-night hamburger stand. They talked incessantly. Julia had wonderfully strong and well-informed opinions, especially about literature. She could support ideas and comments by referring to Spanish or South American novelists, none of whom Charlie, to his dismay, had heard of. Sometime about four, he drove her to the house that her parents had rented, where they sat in his car and talked until six in the morning, the moon long sunk, the sun rising over a row of trees and blinding them. When they finally did say goodnight, or "good morning," which was how they left it, they promised to talk later that day.

Charlie's head was spinning on the ride back to Four Winds. Thus far, a cynical streak had protected him from many of the vagaries and disappointments that dating relationships entailed. Now, Charlie wondered if something had slipped away from him, if this fetching and passionate woman had managed to reach around the hard part of him, had gotten around his guard and rooted herself in the soft, unprotected soil of his damaged heart. Charlie wanted control. He didn't get drunk, not like Quad, who could abandon all sense when drinking; he didn't sacrifice himself or his dignity to a joke, unlike George, who would offer himself up whole in the pursuit of some small amusement. Charlie was in charge, of himself and often of others, who turned themselves over to his big-brotherly care. But this morning he was out of control. He was excited and giddy and more than a little frightened. He could feel the hunger rise up within himself. It had been there for a damn long time, for longer than he could really say, only this time the hunger had a face to it, it had a sound and a scent and a touch to it. It had a name. Julia.

5

"Goddamnit, where were you?" Lucy was furious. Charlie was walking into Four Winds at eleven p.m., an hour after finishing dinner at her parents' house with Julia, who had spent the last three days with him. The only member of the group currently destined for military service, Quad was due to report for duty in forty-eight hours. He had a day left with the gang, a day left in a party that had already lasted a week, and Charlie had missed one of his last meals.

Charlie cajoled Lucy and tried to cheer up Quad, but by lunchtime the following day a distinct grimness had settled over Four Winds. Quad had to leave late that evening by bus for Norfolk, Virginia, for his formal induction into the Navy and a tour of duty that would begin on an aircraft carrier in the Atlantic; if his luck held, he'd avoid Vietnam altogether. Nonetheless, the group still sensed that they were being scattered into a random world and that they would have to work to prevent this separation from becoming irreparable, when up until now their friendships had been the simplest thing in the world: effortless, all but unavoidable.

Charlie helped George organize Quad's farewell dinner, then drove over to the house Julia's parents had rented. Not long after he arrived, Julia's father strode into the front hall like a cavalry officer - erect, confident, charging - but his confidence ebbed the moment Julia relayed a phone message. A ranking cabinet member in the Nixon administration had returned Mr. Hoffman's call: The Secretary could not help Michael Hoffman resolve his difficulties with the Chilean government. His cheeks caving in, hollow with the news, Michael Hoffman wandered off to a den. Tall and elegant, straight-backed as a ladder, Julia's mother followed silently.

Julia waited till they were gone. "I hate to see him like this. Weak. It's the one thing he never was." She explained that the Allende government had nationalized, which in her father's view was the same thing as stolen, his radio stations and copper-mining company; likewise, the bank that his family had long ago founded was now a "people's" bank. To legitimize these seizures, a government official had accused Michael Hoffman and his companies of criminal activity by "overbilling" the state on past projects. Although false, the charges effectively kept Mr. and Mrs. Hoffman in the state of exile which they had, in the beginning of Allende's reign, voluntarily undertaken.

"He won't discuss the charges," Julia said. "He thinks that to answer these charges is to dignify them."

Martin Hoffman's views on his homeland were distinctly different from his father's. Told of the phone call, Martin dismissed it and his father's recent support-gathering trip to Washington. "He thinks his friends in the States care much for his fortune. His friends like to be entertained in style, the same as he, which is the extent of their concern for his fortune. He's wasting his time. Nothing's going to happen by proclamation. Father thinks there's a way for him to be welcomed back into Chile, that the people will throw him a parade - The Return of the Capitalist - just because he never put a gun to the back of somebody's head. He thinks because he has nothing to forgive that he is forgiven. Nothing has changed since we left. He could go back, and he'd still be arrested for the high crime of having been rich."

"I think he'll manage to go," Julia insisted. "It's what he lives for."

"He'd have an easier time if he'd listen to me," Martin concluded, and left to change for dinner. He, too, would join them for Quad's farewell.

At Four Winds, when Grace announced the meal, she led everyone into the formal dining room. The household's two most valuable possessions were hung on the room's west wall, one on each side of the

24

high-arched entry. On one side, atop a sideboard, was a small Gains-borough portrait of a boy, the child looking savagely dandified and thoroughly frightened. On the other side, positioned over a matching sideboard, was a Charles Willson Peale portrait of George's great-great-great-grandfather, who had managed to preserve for posterity a look of dire, soul-wrenching constipation.

At her request, Charlie sat beside Grace, who thanked everyone for including her: she'd agreed to attend the dinner only when convinced that her presence was indeed wanted. She asked all the recent graduates what their plans were, and began with Quad, who puffed himself up.

"Well, when I'm through carrying the almighty cross of freedom and defending my country-"

"God help us," Joe interrupted. "I'm defecting."

As Quad pretended to spit-polish the sole medal on his uniform, Grace asked him, "Is this what you wanted?"

"Uhh..., I signed up with R.O.T.C. four years ago." Quad tried to cough the frog out of his throat and couldn't. He clasped his hands. "See, things looked a little different then. You know, do your duty, but don't be some dumb, dead grunt in the trenches. Be an officer, join the navy, see the damn world."

"And now?" Grace pressed him.

"Now?" Quad looked perplexed. "Now I go into one end of a tunnel and try to come out the other. At least the G.I. benefits will help if I go to business school. My dad's made it clear he's paid my last tuition."

It was Lucy's turn next. She was setting off for a job interview in New York the following morning. "I don't plan on being a Navy wife. Nothing to do but sit around and drink all day. Wait for your husband to visit. I need to do something."

When Grace's eyes settled on him, Joe mentioned that he'd been offered a job in the management training program of a large retailer of building supply materials. Joe's first assignment was in Arkansas, a place where he knew "no one or nothing," a place, he moaned, where "grass is something you mow, and moonshine is something you drink, and a Sunday drive is something you take on a goddamn tractor, .. if you'll excuse me, ma'am."

Charlie had decided to take the summer job in Newport; he didn't mention the proximity to Julia that the local job would allow. A year younger than most of the others, Julia intended to complete her degree from Smith College in the fall. And Grace knew about Martin's job with a commercial bank in Bermuda: he'd already asked her for introductions to potential clients.

Grace's attention fell upon her grandson. "Darling?" she badgered George. "Your plans? You did go to college?"

"Some choice. The University of Virginia or the University of Vietnam." George raised his hands to hold his grandmother off and allowed that he'd take a job when he found "the right situation."

"You could do something useful in the meantime," Grace suggested. "The Peace Corps or something."

"The Peace Corps isn't a Junior League hospital. Jesus, you don't volunteer a few hours. Besides, the people who join the Peace Corps..," George paused to search for the right pejorative, "they're so goddamn *earnest*."

Grace sighed. "It's a sorry world that scorns its few charities."

"I'm not mocking them," George said. "I just don't want to spend three years catching lice with them. Anyhow, I've got plans. There's this whole new arena. The investment banks know it. Money's moving across borders like never before. You've got to tap into it, manage it."

"Investments? You mean managing money?"

"Yeah."

"Well," Grace sniffed, "managing money - that's something this family hasn't done much of for a long time. We have a great deal more talent for spending it."

George humored his grandmother with a smile, then explained, "Look, money's going to move here. It's safe here. Think how much money's going to be packed out of Asia if Vietnam falls. The thing to do is to set up an office in Hong Kong, somewhere like that, go looking for accounts."

Presuming that George was merely parroting an idea that he'd gotten from Martin in an earlier conversation, Charlie wasn't really listening until he heard his own name. "I want to hire Charlie," George announced. "He can do the organizing, the lawyering."

"Charlie?" Grace looked at him.

"Don't ask me."

"This isn't your crackpot scheme?"

"God, no."

"Well, I think it all sounds silly." Grace picked up her wine glass and leaned towards him. "Doesn't it?"

Charlie didn't answer until George was preoccupied with other conversation. "I don't know. Honestly."

Grace took hold of Charlie's wrist. "I don't know anything about it. I can't imagine George does, either. He has no more sense than his father."

For all the time that Charlie had spent with George, he'd only met George's father on a dozen or two occasions. The man was a dreamer, laconic and preoccupied with half-fashioned ideas. Insofar as Charlie knew, George's father had spent the last several years and a considerable sum of money trying to form a cooperative to distribute Native American handicrafts. George got a lot of postcards from fancy hotels in the American Southwest.

When George left the room to get more wine, his grandmother leaned closer to Charlie. "I don't expect you to work for George. It'd be better if he worked for you. I want you to look after him."

"Sure."

Grace squeezed Charlie's wrist, her fingernails digging into his flesh, her eyes clouding with tears. "I mean it," she said. "Honestly. Cholly? You look after him."

Her request was simple. Charlie was closer to both George and Grace than to anyone in his own family. "Don't worry," he assured her, patting her hand.

Once the maid cleared away the main course, George distributed bottles of Dom Perignon, setting many newly uncorked bottles around the table. Lucy complained about the waste and asked for a glass.

"No glasses," George said, with mock affectation. "They're Venetian, and they're hell to clean."

Lucy looked at Grace, who had picked this moment to retire and was entirely unconcerned by George's extravagance. "Dear, I don't want to rain on your parade, but the house has seen far worse." Grace wished them all well, urged everyone to visit again, and excused herself.

When she had gone, Joe fished through his pockets until he found the stub end of a joint, then lit a succession of matches in attempts to ignite it. Oblivious of the others, who began to watch the prolonged charade, oblivious of his date, who was reverently offering a paper clip with which to hold the tiny remnant, Joe burned his fingers, scorched his lips, inhaled bursts of sulfur from numerous matches, all the while trying to raise the slightest spark from the gummy morsel of leftover marijuana. Finally, when a seed popped and sent an ember fluttering down his already tender lip, when his fingertips could stand no further singeing, Joe reluctantly returned the charred "roach" to his pocket and looked up to discover himself the object of everyone's attentions.

"You're a complete mushhead," Lucy said. "You're a goddamn world-class mushhead, but you're our mushhead."

Joe offered up a sheepish grin and raised a bottle of champagne. "Here's to us. The best. Don't any of you assholes go trying to forget. Goddamnit, here's to us."

Quad drank an entire bottle quickly and took large swallows from others. When the time came to leave for the bus station, Lucy said that she couldn't bear to say her farewell at such a forlorn place, so they took a walk down to the ocean. Charlie drove Quad to the station.

Quad could walk without stumbling, but he was torpid, unfocused. Worried that he might fall asleep and miss his bus, afraid that an argument between two apparent draft protesters and two guys in uniform might boil over into a fight that would sweep Quad, unwittingly, into the midst of it, Charlie sat with him until midnight, when the bus finally pulled into the station. Charlie squeezed Quad's shoulders and begged him to stay safe. Quad, flashing an impish V-for-victory sign, climbed on board the bus, which soon backed out of its stall and chugged off, slowly and loudly, into the darkness of a future as yet uncharted.

The party finally over, everyone left Four Winds the next day, except for Grace, George, and Charlie. With only two days left before his summer job began, Charlie made plans to spend them with Julia.

That evening, Charlie and Julia took a stroll along Cliff Walk. Cut into the cliffs, lined with beach plums and wildflowers and the sturdy stray grasses of the seaside, Cliff Walk traced the shoreline of many of Newport's Bellevue Avenue estates and provided an oceanside view of these palaces. Passing Breakers, the Vanderbilts' three-story stone palazzo, Julia paused and stared at it. "I know I could go see that," she said, "but I don't have any interest." Now the property of the Newport Preservation Society, the mansion was open to the public as a museum. What seemed odd to Julia was that one of the Vanderbilts still lived there, in a private apartment that the family had been allowed to maintain when title to the property was transferred.

"How awful," Julia continued. "To live in your own museum. It's like being a safari trophy, a stuffed lion. It's all so public. It's like being a prisoner. Of your past. Maybe I'd understand it if I were European." Julia turned to Charlie. "I don't need this, any of it. I mean, it's madness. I'm in town to be with my parents, but this kind of extravagance doesn't mean anything."

"What do you need?"

"I don't know. Somebody, maybe. Somebody, but not something, not someplace."

Julia took Charlie's hand, and they walked until they came to a private spot, where a ledge in the sandy soil provided them a comfortable seat. The view was to the south and east, a thousand miles and more of Atlantic waters swelling on a breezeless evening. The sun had set somewhere behind them, yet still fired the undersides of clouds with fierce pink and blue splashes of color, the cloud bellies hot with pigment, their tops gone dark and cool.

"If you were in charge of the world's only library," Julia said, "and it caught on fire and you could only get ten books, what would you save?"

"Ten?" Julia was fond of this type of question; Charlie knew that a prompt answer was expected.

"Be serious. Your library's on fire. It's your job to save ten books."

"I'd save ten I hadn't read. Long ones. Would that be selfish?"

"Probably. I don't know which ones I'd save. The job would be to save books written with real passion. I'd leave science out of it. That would be a different list."

"You think anybody's going to burn libraries?"

"You're spoiled. An American. It could happen. Except there are things, pure and passionate, things you can't corrupt. I'd save books that acknowledged that."

Moved by her conviction, by her solemnity, Charlie faced her. There were things that he'd acknowledge, things like the fact that she had become indispensable to him, necessary to any life which he dared to imagine.

"You know the song, 'Love the One You're With'?" Julia asked. Fond of the Stephen Sills hit, Charlie nodded, before she hummed a bit of the tune, then sang the key lyric. "*If you can't be with the one you love, then love the one you're with.'* See, I don't have any quarrel with that. It's fine. Except I can't do it. I'm not good at half-steps. If we make love, I won't be happy with half of you." She looked straight into his eyes. "And you won't get half of me. Because that's where we are, aren't we?"

6

Bedecked in medals and ribbons, the general made a formal withdrawal from the Hoffman household, bowing in Julia's direction and clicking his heels, shaking Martin's hand with unrestrained vigor, then issuing a quick farewell in Spanish to Charlie. When he was gone, Charlie asked Martin about his visitor. "Who's the Generalissimo?"

Charlie was still bristling at the way that he and Julia had been treated by the general's bodyguards, who hadn't allowed them into the Hoffmans' house until identification had been produced and reviewed.

"I'm sure his bodyguards' manners would be better," Martin responded, "if they'd had the opportunity to prep with you. You could have taught them proper English and all about the honor code."

"Martin?" Julia looked at her brother suspiciously.

"Well, it's an odd fit, isn't it? Honor codes in an age of guerilla warfare and chemical weapons. Charlie, your university's honor code is still very rigid, right? So what do you do if a student cheats? Do you have the poor kid expelled? He'd be drafted, wouldn't he? Off to war with the little cheat, let's hope he dies in the jungle, a Viet Cong trophy."

The University of Virginia's strict code had created just such a quandary for anyone who witnessed an honor code violation, professor and student alike, but Charlie didn't want to make Martin's argument for him. Julia came to his rescue. "Oh, please!" she scolded her brother, before turning to Charlie. "Martin likes to contrive dilemmas in the hopes they have horns."

Martin laughed and excused himself, without explaining the purpose of the general's visit; Martin was off to New York and Las Vegas.

"I'm not sure your brother likes me," Charlie said.

"My older brother! He's very protective of me. Don't pay attention. I don't." Her parents off on a separate trip, Julia suggested a swim.

The weather had turned to something more typical of early June, the air damp and cool, the sky gray. Fortunately, the pool was heated, a fine mist steaming off its surface, the diving board rising from the intricate herringbone of bordering bricks and floating out into foggy space. While Charlie and Julia swam, the water was warmer than the air, and the world went fuzzy in a haze of evaporation.

After the swim, they bundled themselves in towels and huddled in a poolside cabana, furnished with large wicker couches and chairs. Julia brought Charlie inside her beach towel and handed him the towel ends while she slipped out of the bikini top. Stiffened by the chill, her nipples stood erect on her firm breasts. Her hips were a bit bony, if beautifully delineated, her buttocks round and firm. She exposed all this by hooking a thumb into her bikini bottom and slithering out of it, the wet trunks slapping to the stone floor.

Charlie wriggled out of his swimsuit and kissed her, his lips slowly brushing past her mouth and down her neck and breast until they latched onto a nipple. He slipped his thigh between hers and stroked her backside, then pulled back to let a hand slide over her breast and rake her belly and circle her groin, there to double back and weave through the tight swirls of hair that centered the soft white flesh just beneath her tan line. Julia jumped at the contact and moaned at the pressure, a fingertip parting and slowly dragging through her.

Charlie steered her to the plump pillows of a couch, where she reclined. His hands massaged her neck, her shoulders, her breasts; his thumbs and forefingers teased her nipples. She rose to him, her tongue seeking his, as he dragged a hand down her belly and over a thigh. Julia spread her legs to welcome his hand, his finger curling and sliding inside her until it found its target, the light touch of which had her moaning. Excited, she pulled him on top of her, cooing with delight as he entered her. Charlie pushed all the way inside her and rested there, as if by some prolonged habitation he could lay claim to her, but he quickly abandoned himself to the bounce and collision of their bodies, the rub maddening, the rhythm corrupted by the anarchy of passion.

Julia held him in place long after he had finished, one of her hands on his muscular backside, the other on his neck. "Sweetie" she whispered. "Sweet, sweetie."

She combed her fingers through his hair, the roots dark as wheat, the strands light as pale gold, then traced a brow above one of his blue eyes. Her fingers glided over his cheekbone and around the arc of his chin. "I was afraid you'd be vain," she said, "when I first saw you."

They swam again and made love once more, before they dressed and took the long walk into town for lunch, following a country lane through a field of low heath and evergreens, the scent of which hung like a vapor, heavy and well-spiced. The world had never smelled newer or richer to Charlie. Julia stopped him once, as if to ask a question that was pressing on her, but she never found her voice. Overcome by a rush of emotion, she swept him up in a hug, clinging to him with a ferocity that asked the question that she hadn't been able to voice. Where the hell had he been all her life? It was Charlie's question, too.

That night, after a late dinner at Four Winds, they retired to Charlie's quarters in the servants' wing. Julia turned out the light in the bedroom and undressed by moonlight, rays of which wove through trees and reached the room with a crosshatch of beams that illuminated, however dimly, those parts of her body undarkened by the sun. Charlie marveled at the sight of her. Naked, she moved with childlike grace to the edge of the small bed and asked what side he wanted to sleep on. Charlie wasn't sure: he hadn't had anyone stay in his bed often enough to establish a pattern.

"We'll figure it out," Julia said, climbing under the sheet, falling asleep minutes after folding one of his hands between both of hers.

Julia spent every night that summer at Four Winds, although she and Charlie maintained the fiction that she was sleeping in her own room at her family's house. What Grace thought, when she found Julia in her kitchen in the morning, she didn't say. Julia's mother reacted in exactly the way that Julia predicted: she simply chose to ignore the obvious.

The month of June flew past. Charlie worked at the law firm, the monotony of his job broken by lunches with Julia, who'd found work at a bookstore two blocks away. Though she insisted she'd never been happier, Julia did mourn the homeland that she'd been forced to abandon, and she clearly longed to visit. She tried to describe for Charlie the violent majesty of the Andes, the rugged poetry of the coastline, the civility of the capital; she worried about the friends left behind and how their families were surviving the current economic difficulties. Despite Julia's beguiling descriptions of the country, Charlie sometimes felt threatened by Chile, its tug on her affection contrary to his own interests. Julia was extraordinary, heaven-sent, and the fear of losing her, even if only for a short visit, could rise in him like a rogue wave, swelling out of nowhere, threatening to capsize him.

7

As the summer wore on, Charlie discovered that first love is a pure and constant astonishment; he felt rapturous, even weightless, unbound by any simple gravity. Julia, too, treated every hour not spent with him as a stolen hour; they compensated for the hours spent apart by stealing them back at night, getting by on only a few hours sleep, making love with reckless abandon. Charlie was constantly amazed that his little bed didn't break, that their body parts didn't wear out, that someone didn't complain about the noise. It was a good thing that the cook, whose room was two doors from theirs, was stone deaf.

Come August, the Hoffman family received word from Chile that their ex-governess, Maria, was gravely ill. Julia frantically tried to phone her beloved former governess, but the telecommunications equipment in Chile was antiquated. Julia grew frustrated after a week of effort, without success.

"All my father can do," she complained to Charlie, "is lambaste the scoundrels in office."

"The world does love a scold," Martin said. He'd just returned from four weeks at his office in Bermuda and been asked to dinner, here on the back terrace of Four Winds.

"What would you do?" Julia asked sharply.

"I wouldn't waste my time whining about lost power." Martin thumped the wrought-iron table emphatically. "I'd speak to those who have it."

"Do you know them?"

"No." He leaned towards his sister. "Not yet." Martin suggested that she make a quick trip to see Maria, who was supposedly in a cancer ward of a Santiago hospital. Unlike other family members, Julia would have significant freedom while in Chile. Martin wanted her to contact two senators, both of whom held posts in the Air Force, both of whom were sympathetic to the claims of banished capitalists. Martin's hope was that the visit would establish a small beachhead for the prospective return of the Hoffman clan.

"My concern at the moment," Julia reminded him, "is Maria."

"There's someone else you could see," Martin said, speaking a name. "It's her old boyfriend."

"My god, how is he?" Julia laughed, and explained to Charlie, "He used to take me to dances. He graduated from Princeton a year ago and went home. He's very .. serious."

"Dull," Martin suggested.

"Dull," Julia acknowledged. "He's full of good intentions, but I'm afraid his only romance will be with politics."

"Romance? Politics?" Having sat at the table quietly, George was suddenly agitated. "We'll send him McGovern and Nixon. Let him find the romance. I finally get to vote, and it's a rodent election. A mouse or a rat. We get to crown something with a tail."

Charlie didn't discuss Julia's old beau again, but he was careful to make plans for the fall with her. That night, she decided to complete her degree at Smith by taking all her remaining courses that fall on Tuesdays and Thursdays, which would allow her to make the long commute from New York City. She'd live with Charlie four days a week while he attended Columbia's law school; he wouldn't need his car, so she could use it to commute.

The week before Labor Day, they drove down to New York City to find an apartment and settled on a large one-bedroom just above

East 90th St. Julia loved the amount of afternoon light that flooded the living room.

Two days after they got back to Four Winds, George returned from his own trip to Manhattan. All summer he'd been confident that his charm and his family connections would land him a good job; the trip and its brutal round of fruitless job interviews had been sobering. That night, unable to talk George into seeing a movie with them, Charlie and Julia returned to Four Winds late. George's Corvette was parked in the circle out front, but George was nowhere to be found until they crossed the back lawn and climbed down to the Women's Tee, where George sat on the weather-worn bench and stared out to sea. The wind was blowing hard, and he seemed not to hear his friends until they were beside him.

"What're you doing?" Julia asked, sitting next to him.

"I'm waiting."

"For us?"

"For my ship to come in." George nodded towards the dark Atlantic wilderness. "I think it's out there."

"You think?"

"Sure of it."

"What's on it?"

"Don't know. That's half the fun." George turned to Charlie. "You know what my father said? When I told him the interview process was mashing me into creamed spinach?"

"He offered you a job in the family business."

George laughed at their old joke, which he explained for Julia's benefit. There was no family business, at least not for the last thirty or so years. George's father had never, so far as his son knew, been gainfully employed.

Julia patted George on the leg and prodded, "What'd he say?"

"He said, 'Keep beating the drum.'" George chuckled, without evident bitterness, and repeated the gem of parental wisdom. "*Keep beating the drum.* Bang-bang, boom-da-da-boom. Words to live by, some of that old Spaulding wizardry."

"Why don't you go to law school with Charlie?"

"It's a little late." George waved off the prospect. "Anyhow, law isn't any fun."

"Why not?"

"Because somebody else made up the rules and you have to argue them. I'd much rather make up the rules."

"I keep looking for a small, corrupt principality that George can govern," Charlie said. "It's his destiny."

"To rule." George let his chest expand.

"To be a despot," Charlie corrected.

"And a damn good despot at that." George made a mock toast to the ocean. "Here's to despotism, nepotism, and a six-pack of all those other great *isms*."

"It's a good thing Charlie's your best friend," Julia said. "You're gonna need a great lawyer."

George put an arm around Charlie. "Great! He'll be working for me. Because lawyers don't make the real fortunes. I figure on being one of the rich guys who hires all the lawyers."

"A felon?"

"Well, not a *convicted* one," George said, poking Charlie in the chest, "or I'll have to find new counsel."

Three days later, on Labor Day, Charlie had the chance to introduce Julia to his sister, who'd invited them to Watch Hill, thirty miles west of Newport. Kate Sanderson Duval generally didn't call Charlie unless she needed something. She was joined at lunch by her husband, an arrogant, self-proclaimed "investor" whose mission, it appeared, was to lose what remained of the Sanderson family's money. Charlie had been eighteen when his father died. At his sister's urging, their mother had turned over the management of the family money to her son-in-law. As near as Charlie could tell, Bruce Duval was fond of leveraged bets on the stock market that he usually lost. Bruce had his stock phrases and standard excuses, his repertoire of "price corrections" and "market troughs"; he also had the skittish eyes and sweaty hands of a gambler on a losing streak.

During lunch, Kate produced mortgage documents that would, by virtue of a new loan, lower the interest payments due on the Sandersons' summer house. It was the first time Charlie had been told that a lien had been attached to the property, a twelve-room colonial which, in name at least, he owned with his sister. Charlie signed the paperwork. He supposed that his inheritance had been effectively squandered, and he didn't much care. He had enough money to get through law school. As for the rest of it, it was more trouble than it was worth.

After a quick lunch, Charlie took Julia on a tour of Watch Hill, quaint and picturesque, half the town looking as if it were staged for the snapshot on a New England postcard. Upon learning that his parents were buried there, Julia made Charlie drive to the tiny graveyard behind the Episcopal church, where two simple granite headstones marked the Sandersons' graves. Julia sat on a wooden bench in the shade of a nearby maple, and Charlie joined her.

He hadn't been to the cemetery since his father's funeral. The service for his mother had been held, at her request, at their home outside Philadelphia; Kate had arranged for the internment of the ashes here. Charlie let his eyes roam over all the headstones and monuments, over the thick grass and the ruptures that tree roots made in it, but his gaze kept returning to the cemetery's stone walls.

"Are you okay?" Julia asked, taking his hand.

"I guess."

Julia nodded at his parents' graves. "Do you think anything survives?"

"Light lasts. Some of the light that reaches us is older than the sun."

"I don't mean light. I mean people. What survives? What do you remember of your parents? Were they happy?"

"I don't know." Charlie could see that the answer displeased Julia, so he elaborated. "They were happy, just not demonstrably so."

"Did they love each other?"

"I don't know. I suppose." Charlie had never had much reason to ponder the question. He no doubt had loved his parents, but their relationships with their children had been distant.

"If I ever had children, that's something I'd want my kids to know." Julia's tone was accusatory. "Something has to last."

"Plutonium lasts. It's got a half-life longer than plastic."

"Jesus, Charlie!" Julia pulled her hand away. "Something lasts. Look around. Some of these monuments, these markers - they're more than two hundred years old and they haven't fallen over. Someone's looking after them. I don't know about any of the rest of it, but love lasts."

Julia gathered him in and held his head to her chest. His ear pressed to her skin, Charlie listened for, but couldn't hear, her heartbeat. Instead, he heard what he thought to be the faintest rush, the whoosh and churn of her blood. Slight as it was, the sound drove out all other noise. He closed his eyes and imagined himself suspended, afloat in her cradling arms.

The next day, each of them packed. Julia was leaving early the following morning for Chile; Charlie had to drive to New York and register for his classes. They postponed their goodnight as long as possible, but at midnight Charlie drove Julia to her parents' house. He cut the engine and let the car coast to a stop by head-high rhododendrons, the blooms long gone, where they sat in the Mustang with the top down and listened to the racket of the crickets, swelling like a chorus of cracked whistles from nearby thickets. They each had difficulty talking about the impending trip.

Julia kissed Charlie and promised to call in as soon as she had figured things out. The next time she saw Charlie, she said, they'd be at their apartment in New York. She opened the car door but turned back and threw her arms around him. "I wish you'd come. I wish you could come!"

"Goddamn it," Charlie muttered, a curse hurled at September, which had arrived, and at law school, the schedule for which was unforgiving. It struck Charlie how young Julia looked, the moonlight highlighting her brilliant features, her tears dulling the furious intelligence of her eyes, a ragged tie-dyed t-shirt looped in a knot around her waist. She seemed an odd envoy, too young for nursing duties in the terminal ward, too much a flower child for service as Martin's ambassador to the stray brokers of power in their homeland.

Julia clung to him for a while before she bolted from the car. They didn't say good-bye. There was nothing in their farewell - and Charlie would come to reexamine the moments endlessly - that forecast the difficulty ahead.

8

The next morning, Charlie drove to Manhattan, bought some second-hand furniture, and arranged to have the utilities at the apartment transferred to his name, only to discover that there was an eight-day waiting list for a phone to be installed. How would Julia reach him?

By the middle of the next week, settled in his classes and anxious for word from her, Charlie placed a call from a pay phone to the number he had for the Hoffman household in Santiago, but the long-distance operator was unable to put Charlie's call through and eventually concluded that there was a problem with the circuits. It took three more days before someone answered the phone at the Santiago residence. His English imperfect, the gentleman on the other end of the line promised to pass on a message: he would tell Julia that Charlie had called.

Once a phone was finally installed at his own apartment, five days behind schedule and fully two weeks after Julia had left, Charlie checked to confirm that his new number was listed with information, and he quizzed a resentful operator about the process. Suppose someone were trying to reach him from abroad? "Honey, you're listed," the operator insisted. "Whoever she is, she'll find you. If she wants to."

Desperate to know why Julia hadn't written or phoned, why none of his calls to the Hoffmans' American residences were being returned, Charlie contacted the Provost at Smith College, who knew no more than Charlie did. Julia hadn't shown up for any of her courses. After a dozen more tries, Charlie managed to reach the house in Santiago. The same gentleman who had picked up before answered, and Charlie demanded to speak to Julia.

"She has your message," was the gentleman's curt reply. Charlie tried again two days later and got a recording; an international operator confirmed that the line had been disconnected.

None of it made sense. Julia had planned to return within two weeks at the most. Was she staying longer to serve as Maria's nurse? Did funeral arrangements need to be made? Julia had laughed when Martin teased her about her old boyfriend in Santiago. Was a reunion with him possible? The specter of betrayal, unthinkable only a month ago, terrified Charlie.

Thus far, Martin Hoffman had ignored the calls that Charlie had made to his bank's headquarters in Bermuda. Prepared to leave another terse message, Charlie phoned again and was surprised when Martin came on the line.

"Charlie?"

"Where is she?"

".. Santiago."

"She hasn't called... For Christ's sake.."

"I'm sorry."

Charlie waited for Martin to continue and tried to imagine any other conclusion than the one that the prolonged silence implied. He had to struggle to find his voice. "Martin, I need to hear from her."

"So do I."

"What's going on..? I'll go see her."

"It's better you wait. Let things run their course."

"What're you talking about?"

Martin sounded irritated. "There's nothing you can do."

"Have you talked to her?"

"Briefly." Martin paused before continuing in a harsh whisper, "I'll try again. I'm doing what I can."

"I have to see her."

"I'll sort through it and call in a few days, let you know what I find out."

Martin didn't call back, but Charlie did. "Christ, Charlie," Martin said petulantly when he came on the phone. "The whole goddamn country's upside-down, that's the problem, she's caught up in it."

"What's that mean?"

"It means she may be there a while."

"Why can't she call?"

"Jesus, you'd have to ask her. Have some faith. Things may straighten themselves out. If you leave me -"

"You? You're the one who put her on the goddamn plane."

"Look. Give this a little time."

Nauseous, Charlie hung up and called the State Department to find out what restrictions, if any, existed for travel to Chile. A low-ranking duty officer explained that while the country was not on the prohibited list, like North Vietnam or Cuba, a current State Department advisory noted that Chile was beset by severe economic problems and social turmoil. Anti-government truckers were striking; middle-class housewives were marching in "empty pot" rallies. Travel at this time was not recommended. If Charlie chose to ignore the caution, he'd need a visa issued by Chile and should contact that embassy.

That night, Charlie drove straight to Washington, D.C., and was third in line the next morning when the doors opened to the Chilean Embassy. A few hours passed before he got a chance to speak to some minor official in a naval uniform who said that a request for a visa would be processed within three weeks. Three weeks sounded like an eternity to Charlie, but he didn't know what other options he had.

He spent those weeks all but sleepless, fighting a malingering intestinal pain, and called the embassy on the twenty-first day, only to be informed that his application had not yet been approved. Livid, Charlie decided to risk going without a visa: he'd beg, borrow, buy, and bribe his way into the goddamn country. But only a few airlines had connections to Chile, and agents for all of them were resolute: Charlie would need a passport and a visa. No airline would allow him on a plane without both.

By the middle of November, the weather was wet and chilly, and the subway cars stank of damp wool and synthetic rubber rain gear. Charlie hated the weather; he hated the city and its smells, the proximity of strangers on the subway, the odor of their clothes. He hated the silence of his apartment, the noise at school, the books he struggled to read.

At law school the Dean called Charlie into his office to discuss Charlie's disappointing academic performance. Was anything the matter? Told that Charlie dearly needed to get to Chile, the dean offered help: he'd have a friend who practiced international law look into the matter. Three days later, the dean summoned Charlie back to his office. Charlie's application for a visa had apparently been red-flagged but was being reconsidered. Charlie should hear something within a week or two.

Two weeks went by before Charlie received notice that his visa application had been rejected. Elsewhere in Manhattan people were making merry and preparing for Christmas. Charlie was shattered. Apparently, Julia had turned her back on everything and fled.

Charlie wanted to quit law school but didn't know what else to do. He stuck with it only because he couldn't bear the thought of having to confront the free time that would result if he dropped out. He dreaded Christmas and the godawful prospect of holiday cheer.

On Christmas Eve, Lucy stopped by his apartment. Her own wedding with Quad having been postponed till the summer, she was flying out that evening to spend the holidays with him. When Charlie answered his door, Lucy grabbed the waistband of his trousers, which were slack on him. "Goddamnit!" she hollered. "You must've lost ten pounds! Goddamnit, you start eating right!" She made him go to lunch with her and wouldn't leave the restaurant until he'd cleaned his plate.

By the new year, the pain hadn't much abated, although it had begun to feel like something else, like anger. Charlie was furious. Once in his life he'd abandoned himself, a mistake he wouldn't make again. The loss of Julia hurt even worse than the separate deaths of his parents. Hard as those losses had been, he'd managed to view them through the egocentric prism of youth: his parents were older than fifty; death was inevitable. Now, a little older himself, Charlie understood that no one ever really accepted the inevitability of loss, nor was there any comfort in doing so. What hurt the most about Julia's loss was that it wasn't inevitable: her abandonment carried with it the full weight of rejection. Charlie hadn't simply been cut to the bone; he'd been cored.

9

NEWPORT, RHODE ISLAND

MAY 19, 1995

Charlie Sanderson's beeper had been going off for several minutes by the time he reached the front gates to Four Winds. Once lined with magnificent elms, the long driveway was now bordered by Japanese Maples, an ornamental variety which hadn't grown much taller than twenty feet. The dwarf maples exposed the house and made the dusty gravel driveway seem more like a farm road than a grand entrance to a splendid Georgian property.

Charlie parked out front and hopped up the stairs, which like the rest of the house needed paint. He knew that George Spaulding and Joe Turlik were in a meeting; they'd join him when they could. As the Executive Vice President of a local bank that catered to small businesses and wealthy individuals, George had been instrumental in helping Joe get a job.

Charlie used his own key and passed through the front hall into a dining room that was eerily void of furnishings. Seven years ago, scrambling to climb out of debt, George's father had auctioned off most of the estate's antiques. The Sheraton table, chairs and sideboards were gone; the paint on the walls had yellowed, though whiter rectangles were still visible where the Gainsborough and Charles Willson Peale portraits had once hung. Six weeks after the auction, the creditors barely satisfied, Mr. Spaulding had suffered a fatal heart attack; the rumor, which hadn't gone away, was that he'd ingested a fatal quantity of barbiturates. "Chief One-Screw-Loose swallowed his tomahawk," was all that George had said at the time, refusing Charlie's sympathy, which was profound, and denying the anger, which Charlie knew to be real.

For all the repairs left unmade, Four Winds retained much of its charm. George now lived there year-round, although the cost of oil for the furnaces forced him to close off much of the house in winter. As recently as two years ago, Grace had stayed there briefly. However, her frailty and progressive senility now made such visits impractical; in her mid-nineties, she resided in a local nursing home.

Charlie checked his pager, found a phone in the kitchen, and called Detective McClean, who briefed him on the phone call that he'd just received from Robert Shure, the principal suspect in the murder of the Boston bank examiner. Suddenly emotional, Shure had called from the gallery he owned in Newport and asked to meet with "the guy at the apartment, the prosecutor assigned to the case." Technically, though Shure failed to appreciate the distinction, charges had not yet been filed.

The question for Charlie was, did he want to meet with the suspect. Charlie jotted down phone numbers and hung up. A conversation with a suspect without his lawyer present was nothing but a game of bluff. No evidence or admission gained from such a meeting would be admissible in a trial. Shure would try to determine what the police and prosecutors knew and what sort of ordeal he faced; in the process he might slip and reveal an unknown detail of the case.

Charlie considered the facts: that morning Shure's lover had been found dead in Shure's apartment; Shure had no alibi and had to have been present when John Stuart Robbins' throat was slit and his genitals slashed.

Curious, Charlie called Shure at his gallery in the Newport harbor and arranged a meeting. "Six o'clock sharp," Shure said.

The Velvet Hammer, a nondescript bar shoehorned into a space between much larger restaurants downtown, was easy for Charlie to find. He took a stool at the bar and studied the joint. The lighting was dim, the patrons male. His chest bare beneath a leather vest, the bartender slid a coaster at Charlie.

"What'll it be?"

"A beer. Draft. Thanks." Charlie assumed that Shure had picked the gay hang-out as some sort of test and figured that he might as well make himself comfortable. He also figured, correctly, that Shure would be deliberately late, thereby letting Charlie fend for himself a while longer. Another test. Charlie was ordering his second beer when a guy materialized at his elbow and inquired, "Sanderson?"

Robert Shure's linen suit was still well-pressed, but he had the air of someone who'd just been woken from a nap, an impression aided by his habit of constantly combing his short-cropped hair with the fingers of his left hand. "Want something?" Charlie asked, nodding at the bartender to conclude the offer.

Shure called out an order for a vodka, straight-up, and leaned towards Charlie. "Come here often?" It was an attempt at a joke; Shure's lips outlined a smile before settling into something else.

When the bartender set their drinks down, Shure knocked back a half-ounce of his vodka and put his glass on the counter. He took his time surveying the bar and its clientele before confronting Charlie.

"Make any arrests? While you were waiting?"

"No."

"Why not?"

"Why?"

"Isn't that what you do?"

"I'm not a cop. What do you do - other than act the martyr?"

Shure looked at Charlie's left hand before asking, in a voice that was quavering, "Ever been married?"

"No. You?"

"Is that a joke?"

"No. Your friend -"

"My lover."

"Your lover. How long did you know him?"

"John? Seven years. We were together most of the time. I won't pretend it was easy. He could be difficult. He never met a waiter he couldn't piss off."

"Did you love him?"

"That's a stupid question."

"Why?"

"I don't know what it means. Love. Are we talking about how much or how little we settle for?"

"Why settle?"

Shure forced a theatrical grin. "We're at that age, aren't we? Love? In the end, it's company – that's what it's all about, isn't it?"

"Sondheim." Charlie identified the source of Shure's last sentence, a line lifted from one of the composer's songs. "'*Company.*' Title song. I saw the musical when it was first staged in New York."

Shure's grin momentarily expanded. "Well, shit. A literate lawyer. You should go on '*Jeopardy.*' You all do."

Charlie took a sip of his beer before repeating his question. "Did you love him?"

"Does it matter? I know what you think. You think we're aliens." Shure nodded at his surroundings. "You think we'd have no goddamn trouble killing somebody we cared for."

"You tell me what to think. You'd had some fights, we know that. You two were alone in your apartment, you popped something -"

"Have you ever taken drugs? With a girl? When you were young?" Shure obviously realized that the police had found traces of amyl-nitrate in his apartment. "Did it make you feel sexy? Or did you want to rush into a kitchen and grab a knife?"

"There's no sign of anyone breaking in. Was anyone else there? Maybe another friend?"

"Do you need a third party there? In your bedroom? Does it take you three to tango? Or is it just us?" Shure swept his hand around the room to indicate the other patrons.

"It's just you. You're the one who took the party drug and probably a strong sedative."

"Says who? I mean, what're the police doing?"

"What should they be doing?"

"They should find out .." Shure broke off and put his palms to his forehead; he pressed hard before slapping the bar. "It doesn't make any goddamn sense."

"What's the last thing you remember?"

"We went out to dinner."

"Was this before or after you got loaded?"

"Who's to say I got loaded?"

"You don't remember a goddamn thing. You look at yesterday evening, and you've got an eight-hour gap. Christ, I hope you were loaded."

"That would make it easy for you."

"Have you blacked out before? You were loaded, right?"

Shure turned away and signaled to the bartender to refresh his drink. When he turned back, his face was drawn, his eyes haunted. "I don't know what I was."

"Is this a regular problem for you? Passing out?"

"Why would I answer that? It's a stupid question."

"Really? If you didn't kill him, who did?"

"You're the smart prosecutor. You tell me."

"Did he have other partners? John?"

"I don't think so. At least, not many. We had our rough patches."

"Did he have any enemies?"

"Waiters. He could be arrogant. He was tough on waiters." Choking on the memory, Shure coughed and fought back tears.

"Do you have any enemies?"

"Why would I?"

"Because you get wired and black out. Who the hell knows what you've done?"

"What've I done?" Shure's voice broke as he stared straight at Charlie; he wanted the answer, too. "You wake up, and there's so much blood it's like a gag, like something from a joke shop, a plastic turd. Christ! The blood's clotting and room-temperature, and I'm lying in a pool of it, and you fucking think I did this?"

51

Charlie turned his glass in his hands. He wanted to give Shure a chance to talk longer, to let the rush of emotion loosen his tongue. Whatever else he felt, Shure clearly felt victimized, but he seemed to ward off his despair by indulging his wrath, casting challenging glances at the other patrons. Once Charlie felt that he'd become the target of Shure's anger, he concluded the interview and left without obliging Shure, who insisted on knowing if he would be charged.

What an odd suspect, Charlie thought, walking to his car. Shure had adopted no poses during the interview: no cocksure defiance, no righteous indignation. The only role that he had accepted, as though he were accustomed to it, was that of the victim. However, if he didn't kill his lover, who did? The notion that someone - and a skilled professional at that - broke into the apartment and slit John Stuart Robbins' throat without leaving much evidence was a longshot.

Charlie grabbed a burger on his way back to Four Winds. It was after nine when George and Joe arrived, and the old friends were soon seated in the den, swapping complaints about strained backs and the cost of child support. George had an ex-wife and a nine-year-old boy in Florida; though he traveled a lot, Joe lived in Ohio with his wife and two teenage stepsons who, per Joe, could consume an eight-pound roast in one seating. Everyone made a few small wagers on the outcome of the next day's golf game and turned in early.

Not long after sunrise, Lucy Shiner met them at the Newport Country Club. An editor for a Boston-based magazine, Lucy had divorced Quad years ago; she'd come down to Newport to watch her seventeen-year-old daughter play in a softball tournament.

George led the golfers to the first tee and promptly sliced two balls out of bounds. By the fourth hole, the match had been abandoned, and no poor shot, of which there were plenty, escaped ridicule. Later that morning, although the skies threatened, Jennifer Shiner's softball team played its first game at a large park north of town. Charlie loved watching his goddaughter compete; quick and limber, Jennifer had inherited her mother's athleticism.

Charlie and Lucy had a late lunch and caught the afternoon game. With her daughter spending the night at a motel with her team, Lucy planned to stay at Four Winds and was bothered, upon reaching the estate, that the front flower beds were a tangle of weeds. "I don't know how he holds onto this place," she said. "The upkeep has to be brutal."

Charlie mentioned that the estate had been quietly offered for sale for more than three years and was now formally listed with a broker. The prospect depressed Charlie, as he knew it must George, losing a place that had been in his family for more than a hundred years.

"Jesus Christ, you're selling it?" Lucy asked, on greeting George. "Hey, maybe I could buy a timeshare. The Chinese Room, first week in August."

George grinned at the suggestion. "Plan B, darling."

"Will you sell it this summer?"

"Don't know. I'm trying."

"We have to get everybody here. Before it's gone."

"A reunion? You'll organize it?"

"If I have to. Except it won't be depressing, will it? A big party? With you selling it?"

George laughed. "For God's sake, I'd have sold it years ago if anybody made a decent offer. I mean, it'll break my heart when the place is gone - a death in the family. Hell, what am I saying? It's worse than most deaths in my family. We'll miss the house."

That night, George took Lucy, Charlie, and Joe to a new restaurant by the harbor in town. They'd finished their dinner when George excused himself and crossed the floor to greet a gentleman in a group that the maître d' was leading to a table. Joe stood up and gave a cautious wave to the person, whom he also seemed to know.

When the man casually approached their table, with George on his heels, Joe spoke his own name, "Joe," as if the reminder might be necessary. George handled the introductions from there. "These are my old friends," he said. "Joe Turlik, Lucy Shiner, Charlie Sanderson, this is Martin Hoffman."

Although Martin Hoffman paid little attention and nodded a polite, if distant, hello, his name did surprise Charlie, who hadn't forgotten Julia, though not for lack of trying. Long ago, on a wall of the den at

Four Winds, George had hung photos from the summer of 1972. They were little time capsules of style, of denim and beads and ponytails. In one of them Charlie and George flanked Julia. For a few years Charlie had deliberately avoided the photo, but curiosity and pride eventually got the better of him. Once in a while he wanted to see if the girlfriend was as lovely as he remembered; she was.

Martin conferred quietly with George before returning to his group, which the maître d' was seating. Two of the women in that group were matronly, their gaits confident and stiff. The other two women were younger, about Charlie's age; it was the last of them, a striking brunette, who caught Charlie's eye. She had not lost her figure to the sag of middle age, nor had her beautiful brown eyes, which darted over the group at Charlie's table, lost their luster. Charlie wasn't sure until he caught her looking at him, as if to ask the same question: Could it be?

Charlie felt lightheaded. He'd assumed, decades ago, that he'd grown a callus over the spot worn raw by Julia's abandonment, yet now, feeling the rub of coincidence, he sensed an injury that had never completely healed. Staggered by the strength of his reaction, he was unprepared to confront it. Aware of being scrutinized by George, Charlie pleaded fatigue and said goodnight. He had a chance, possibly, to answer a question that had long been left unanswered but presented with the opportunity he didn't know how or whether to proceed. As he left the restaurant, he saw the brunette squint at a blackboard that listed the restaurant's special dishes of the day. Julia Hoffman, if that was still her name, had reappeared.

10

PANAMA CITY

Brittle and off-key, the sound of the church bells drifted over the barrio like the distant twitter of a cheap car alarm, the notes distinctly tinny. The noise was a sorry summons for the faithful, a clamor not much preferable to that of the rooster that had been crowing since dawn out behind one of the nearby shanties. Eduardo Gutierrez hated the neighborhood's poverty; it was omnipresent, oppressive, depressing. It reminded him of his own youth, or what little there had been of it, a boy hustling trinkets to Canal Zone tourists, until his mother married a colonel and moved the family to the capital, a city of decent schools and small luxuries. Eduardo knew that the local church had had two of its bells stolen - signs were posted begging for money to help replace them - and yet he also presumed, with a resignation that he attributed to middle-age, that it would take the sorry little church an awfully long time to raise the money.

It was Eduardo's habit to go to church on Sunday morning. He would not go here, in his mistress's neighborhood; he would attend a service in the handsome Metropolitan Church across town where he would be surrounded by people like himself, people with money. The Saturday night stays at his mistress's cottage were complicated by his unwillingness to risk driving and parking his Mercedes anywhere in the area. The car would be easy pickings, stolen by morning, so he left it in his garage and commuted by taxi.

Sunday mornings Eduardo would say farewell to his mistress and head out to a nearby boulevard, where he could catch a taxi outside a small cafe. This morning, the heat already rising off the asphalt of the streets and turning the tar-coated alleys into flypaper, Eduardo kept his tie in his pocket, his collar unbuttoned; he was hot, and he didn't want to look too prosperous. Business had been good to him and his partner, but Eduardo hadn't heard from Hector Del Rosario in over a week. Perhaps this afternoon, when Eduardo drove his Mercedes out to the country to visit his own family, there would be word from Hector.

A cab was parked outside the cafe. Boldly emblazoned with red and yellow paint, the words "*MIAMI TAXI*" scripted on its doors, the cab sat idle, its driver reclining in the front seat. The cafe was not yet open.

Recognizing the cab as one that he had used before to make the same trip, Eduardo walked up, opened a back door, and climbed inside. The driver had a wispy mustache and skin as dark and rough as coffee grounds. With an indolence that bordered on insolence, the driver slowly sat up and turned the ignition key. Eduardo ventured a greeting that wasn't returned and mentioned the cross-town church, but couldn't be sure that the driver had heard, for he pulled out and sped south without managing the U-turn that would have pointed the car in the right direction. Two blocks later, the taxi still heading south, Eduardo repeated the name of the church.

The driver mumbled something and failed to change course until he turned down a rough-paved street which, Eduardo complained, didn't lead to a main boulevard. The street passed through a makeshift shantytown and dead-ended at an auto-graveyard, the whole lot an enormous scrap heap of automobiles so far beyond salvage that no one, even in a neighborhood this poor, had attempted their rescue. The cab swung through the open gates of the junkyard and started to circle, as if to turn around, but stopped next to a tall panel of the aluminum fence.

A curse of protest stuck in Eduardo's throat; the driver had turned and was studying him. Eduardo gripped his wallet, flung a door open, and jumped out the far side of the cab from the driver. He figured that he'd be safe if he could race back to the shanties. He'd toss his wallet aside for this highway-robber of a driver only if the driver caught him. Eduardo hadn't counted on the driver's foot speed, nor had Eduardo counted on an accomplice, another muscular man, this one mulatto, who appeared by the gates from behind a shell of a vehicle. Flinging his wallet off to the side in the space between the two thieves, Eduardo hoped to distract them long enough to escape, but the taxi driver ignored the wallet and tackled Eduardo to the ground. Unable to break free of the man's grip, Eduardo unsnapped his watch and shook it off into the dust; he would do this son-of-a-bitch's work for him.

Pinned by the driver, Eduardo saw the knife before he felt it, his whole head wrestled back, a furious stab at the back of his neck that drove into bone and severed cord, that left him fight-less before the fight had much begun. The fierce pain of the knife had extinguished itself, a blaze of fire snuffed like a candle, and Eduardo was free to concentrate on the tugging of his hair, the lifting of his head that exposed his throat. His hands should move there, should protect the throat, but he was senseless from the neck down. His limbs were deaf to all his furious commands, and his voice was silenced by the deep slice of the blade. He was not yet dead, but soon would be, when his body was dragged towards the trunk of a rusted-out sedan.

Joe Turlik had a question for Eduardo Gutierrez, whose law firm was clearly having problems with its phone lines. Joe had never met the Panamanian lawyer but had spoken with him multiple times about simple paperwork prepared for Joe and several of the corporations for which Joe worked. Although the legal documents were simple corporate boilerplate, Joe believed that Eduardo Gutierrez vastly overestimated his own comprehension of the English language and used poor software to translate Spanish into the English-scripted documents that Joe would have to sign. The grammatical errors now at issue, Joe figured, were consistent with those from previous documents, and any interpretation of them would be done in Panama, so Joe signed the documents and mailed the package.

NEWPORT, RHODE ISLAND

After her Sunday morning softball game, Jennifer hitched a ride to Providence with Charlie, who tuned in a radio station playing an old song, a rollicking display of keyboard and guitar virtuosity by The Allman Brothers. "Did you like them?" Jennifer asked. "This group?"

"I still do."

"Whatever." Jennifer unleashed a long sigh. "They're okay, I guess," she continued. "This guy I know, he's got their CDs."

"You got a date? For the party today?"

"That's what Mom asked. Are you spying?"

"Should I?"

"Charlie, you can't tell her. I get immunity or something. State's evidence. There's a guy who's going to be there. A freshman. I can't decide if he's a dickhead."

"Chances are that he is, if you're already wondering about it."

"The thing is, he's going through changes. Growing up."

"Really?" Charlie tried, but couldn't keep the note of cynicism out of his voice.

"I believe him. I have to give him the benefit of the doubt, don't I?"

"No." Charlie and his goddaughter had always maintained a strong and honest friendship; he saw no reason not to speak his mind.

"Didn't you ever give anybody the benefit of the doubt? Somebody you loved?" When Charlie didn't answer, Jennifer smiled slyly. "What about that woman you brought to Easter? She could use a little benefit of the doubt."

"I'll tell her - what? - that you've encouraged me to be charitable."

"Oh, shit, is she the one you're picking up? For the wedding reception tonight? Sorry."

"No, you're not."

"Okay, I'm not sorry. You know what she asked? Like she talked to me for two minutes, so like now we're best friends, and she asks me if you ever 'dated' Mom. I said I wasn't really sure."

"Why?"

"Well, you could have, I bet. You two are so close, you and Uncle George. Best friends. The three stooges. It's kind of queer."

"What're you dragging me into?"

"Nothing, nothing, nothing." Jennifer looked out the window at the green-gray puddles of a marsh, the silt and clay peeking through the windswept bristles of fat-stalked grasses that rolled towards the road like a wave. "This guy - who's at the party today. He says attachment and separation are two sides of the same coin, like love and pain; he says that's what scares him."

"He couldn't come up with better than that?"

"He's into the Oriental way of thinking - yin and yang."

"Or he's fucking overdosing on fortune cookies."

"He's very serious. And seriously good-looking."

"Why don't you stay at my house? Nobody will know you stood him up."

"He will."

"He'll survive."

Jennifer had stopped listening. It moved Charlie to watch her, her heart visibly rising within her chest on the swell of a deep breath. They drove the rest of the way in silence, though Jennifer's spirits had improved by the time they reached the Brown University campus. He dropped her off by a student union building, where two of her girlfriends were already waiting. When he got to his own house, a salt-box colonial on College Hill not far from the campus, Charlie checked his answering machine. A man had left a message returning Charlie's call; he identified himself as Milton Greene, the supervisor of John Stuart Robbins, the murdered bank examiner.

After voicing concern that the killer be caught, Greene responded to a few questions that Charlie and the detective had posed to his secretary. "Has it dawned on you," Greene asked, "that we don't keep public schedules for the visits an examiner is going to make? It's not exactly a sneak attack, but we don't notify a bank three weeks before a visit and make an appointment. We show up. That's the point. You asked for his schedule. I don't know about any surprises, but I'll get you what I can. He was rude at times - John. He had a sense of humor that gave him some license. Everybody feels the way I do. So call, if you want. We'll do what we can."

Helen Edwards was still in her bathrobe when Charlie stopped by her apartment to pick her up for the wedding reception in Newport. "You were supposed to tell me what the dress was," she scolded, closing the door behind him.

"God, I don't know. Sunday evening. It's a second marriage for both of them. Does that make a difference?"

"Should it?" Helen had been married and divorced twice and was, perhaps, reading something unintended in Charlie's analysis.

"I guess it's dinner."

"Buffet? Is it seated?"

"No idea. It's at the Yacht Club. The place can be stuffy, so it's probably sit-down."

"You could've called."

Charlie took a seat in an armchair. He'd offered to take her down Saturday to Newport, but she'd cited a host of errands and declined, probably because she'd felt uncomfortable the two times that she'd been in the presence of Charlie's old friends.

"You could've called," she repeated.

Charlie shrugged. He'd given her the phone number at Four Winds and suggested that she drive down early, if possible. He disliked arguments or scenes or whatever sort of confrontation that she was provoking. Women like Helen made everything difficult. She kept her distance, even in their occasional lovemaking, and resented Charlie for keeping his. She acted as if she wanted something robust and effortless, yet constantly threw up obstacles. Nonetheless, Charlie blamed himself, for he knew what Helen sensed, that it was hard for him to give effortlessly. The night before, he'd been in a restaurant and seen a woman with whom it had all come easily: simple to love, devastating to lose. Helen knew that she stirred few of these feelings in Charlie, and she was angry for it.

"You want me to call Lucy? See what she's wearing?" Charlie tried to sound upbeat, but Helen wasn't buying it. "C'mon, it'll be fun."

"Maybe we should just blow it off."

"The reception?"

"I don't know. Would that be rude?"

"Possibly. I could make an excuse." Charlie looked to see if his answer had satisfied Helen, but she wanted to be persuaded of the wisdom of the relationship itself, not just of the evening's date. He knew that he should say something more and couldn't.

In the end Helen decided that she might be coming down with something and really shouldn't go out, not on a Sunday night, and Charlie didn't offer to stay with her. He was grateful that it could end like this, without recrimination, a quiet expiration of a timid, tepid affair. Relieved, he drove straight to Newport and let a valet park his car at the New York Yacht Club.

Inside the main dining room places were set at ten ornately decorated tables for a hundred guests. The bride was an old friend who'd once gotten Charlie and George dates at her boarding school's prom. Her humor was wonderfully sarcastic and biting; Charlie found her new husband stiff and self-important.

George was on the patio, enjoying a cocktail, and grinned at the sight of Charlie arriving. George had long ago told him that, since neither of them had a brother, they served each other in that capacity. Charlie supposed that they had done just that, experiencing the consummate bond absent the sibling rivalry. Certainly, nothing in either of their lives had the constancy of their friendship, Charlie standing up as best man at George's two weddings, Charlie helping George pull himself together after both divorces.

George walked up to Charlie and leaned close in confidence. "God, you missed the service. I wish I had. They wrote their own vows - all this touchy-feely New Age shit." George had been one of the few guests invited to the ceremony held on board the groom's yacht.

George scouted the party for Helen. "What happened to your date?"

"Not coming."

"There's a guest. Uhh.." Tongue-tied, George pressed forward. "Well, you can say hello, I guess."

George steered Charlie into the dining room towards a cluster of people talking by the entrance. "I told her you'd be here. She asked."

As they neared the group, a woman stepped towards them tentatively. "Charlie?"

Voiceless, Charlie studied Julia Hoffman. She was still beautiful, her hair swept neatly off her forehead, her eyes piercing, her mouth perfectly proportioned. He put a hand in his pocket and fished for his car keys, something to anchor his hand, but he'd given the keys to the valet.

"You remember Julia?" George asked, backing away.

Charlie was expressionless and conscious of it. He wanted neither to display nor to dredge up any of the emotions that he'd struggled with upon her leaving, the fury and despair. He'd felt so weak then; he presumed that he should feel and act strong now.

"I'm sorry," Julia said. "I didn't know if you'd remember me."

"Yeah."

"I know it was a thousand years ago."

"That long?"

"Strange things happened." She tilted her head apologetically. "I sent a letter."

"A letter?" Two years after she'd disappeared, he'd received a brief note from her that mentioned that she'd been detained in Chile and was back in the States. The text of the "letter" would have fit on a postcard, and it explained nothing. At the time Charlie had begun dating another woman, but the real reason he hadn't responded was that he was still too angry with Julia.

"It doesn't matter," she said. "Are you okay? You're a lawyer?"

"For the state. A prosecutor. What about you? You work?"

"I rep for a manufacturer of office furniture. A regional manager."

"A family? Kids?"

Julia's eyes swept over Charlie's, as if to gauge his interest. "The short answer's 'no.' You?"

"No."

Charlie grew silent. It was hard for him to imagine a conversation with her that didn't address what happened all those years ago, and it seemed neither appropriate nor necessary to resurrect those skeletons now, particularly at someone else's wedding. After a long pause, Julia bridged the gap with a question. "You still come here? Newport?"

"Once in a while. I visit George."

"You live close?"

"Providence."

Julia nodded with recognition, then examined their surroundings at the yacht club. The room had a few good paintings of sailing ships and two intricate, miniature replicas of America's Cup winners. "Did we ever come here?"

"I hope not," Charlie replied. "I mean, it's my least favorite place in town. What is it about boats? People get around boats and start acting like commodores."

Charlie had to step out of the way as guests started to crowd into the room and to hunt for their names on place-cards. A woman, some sort of party planner in a taupe silk suit, aggressively circled through the celebrants and requested that everyone be seated. Another woman approached Julia and asked if she wanted to sit.

Charlie watched Julia signal for her friend to go ahead to their table. A slight flush rose in Julia's cheeks as she turned back. "I'm based here now. The East Coast. New York. If you ever want to catch up.."

Charlie recognized the effort in her offer. He didn't intend to be brusque, yet people were pushing through the archway where they stood. Confused, he excused himself and found his seat. Since his date hadn't come, no one was seated on his right; the woman on his left was either late or absent. When everyone else had sat, Charlie took his seat, but felt stranded, an outcast on a floating chair, where he dutifully waited until the wedding cake was cut. He didn't see either George or Julia when he left.

11

The First National Bank of Rhode Island was headquartered in an elegantly restored, three-story brick building by the Newport harbor. Among other duties, George held the title of Executive Vice President and functioned both as the bank's senior loan officer and as the head of its small private-banking unit. His third-story office was paneled with mahogany and furnished with antiques. Charlie was a favorite of George's secretary, Beth Spangler, who greeted him warmly as he strolled into George's office. The door swung shut behind him.

George waved hello from behind his desk, concluded his phone conversation quietly, and hung up. "You cut out early last night," he said. "How was it? Running into Julia?"

"I don't know."

"A ghost from the past?"

"What answer are you looking for?"

"None. Uhh, I gave her your phone number."

"Is this why you brought me here?"

"No." George's eyes darted to the closed door. "I need a favor."

"Sure."

"Off the record, okay?"

"Sure."

"Privileged."

"I'm not your lawyer." Charlie meant the comment as a simple caution, a reminder that their conversation was not guarded by an attorney-client relationship, but George looked hurt. "What?"

"We've got a problem. A loan. Technically, it's still a performing loan. Practically, it's another matter. We financed production for a film. Pretty much a no-risk deal with a fat fee. The production company pays the loan off when the film is delivered to the studio. The whole loan's guaranteed by the studio. The key word here is '*delivered*'. There's this argument going on, a lot of bullshit, between the producer and the studio as to whether the film has been delivered. The goddamn thing was finished four months ago."

"Why don't you get an entertainment lawyer?"

"I don't have anything budgeted. I don't need the scrutiny, not until I get a handle on it."

"What do you think?"

"The studio can't be happy with the film, which would explain part of what's going on. I don't give a damn, as long as the loan gets paid off. The numbers are huge."

"Who wrote the note?"

"We drafted it. It's mostly boiler-plate."

"You have a copy?"

"I'll get you one."

"You should get a lawyer, somebody familiar with federal banking laws. There might be an angle."

"I trust you."

Charlie raised a hand, a gesture to indicate that he'd give it a try, but that there were no assurances. George nodded a silent thank-you before muttering, "Christ, the people I'm dealing with on this. The sooner the better. I'll get a package to your house tonight."

Charlie hadn't reached his car before his beeper went off. That morning, a cleaning crew had found Robert Shure, swinging in a noose hung from the rafters of his Newport gallery. The police presumed that Shure, despondent and guilty, had taken his own life.

Uniformed officers surrounded the gallery when Charlie got there. There were no signs of struggle inside, where Shure had been lowered to the ground, his body in a stiff jack-knife on the rough concrete floor, the rope looped in careful coils beside him. No one had closed Shure's eyes, which looked bug-eyed, beleaguered. Stung by the sight, Charlie wandered into the alley out back and found a cop looking through Shure's car. Little was in the station wagon, except for a bag of groceries with a receipt that indicated the groceries had been purchased the previous day. Included among the items were a few cans of dog food.

Charlie pointed out the dog food to the cop, who was holding Shure's set of keys, one of which had a tag on it naming a dock in the harbor. Charlie accompanied the cop to the waterfront, where they had no trouble finding the boat, a 32-foot yacht registered in the name of John Stuart Robbins.

They heard the dog yelping as they boarded the boat. With evident distaste, the cop unlocked the padlock securing the hatch cover and extracted a pair of plastic gloves from a pocket. Down in the cabin, a Yorkshire terrier leapt at the ladder that led up to the deck and leapt again. Although the cop suggested that they wait for an animal control officer, Charlie climbed down into the cabin and picked up the dog, which whined and licked at his face.

"Damn things can bite, all unexpected," the cop warned, as Charlie brought the dog on deck.

To calm the dog, Charlie sat against the stern rail and held her in his lap. He'd owned a dog most of his adult life; his last one, a Labrador given to him by Lucy, had died a year ago. "Who the hell keeps a dog on a boat?"

"Some asshole cat-lover," the officer replied.

Charlie didn't bother to explain himself, but what he'd meant was that you had to be a little lost yourself to leave a dog on a boat. It saddened him that Shure couldn't provide better quarters for his dog than his dead lover's boat. Strays, every one of them, Charlie supposed.

After two hours had gone by without an animal control officer showing up, having walked and fed the dog, Charlie took her with him. He would relinquish her - her name was Roxy, per a tag on her collar - to whatever relative of Robert Shure's claimed her.

Charlie knew that when Ray McClean first heard of the apparent suicide, he'd hope that he could close the homicide case involving Shure's lover. Charlie also knew that the detective would buy into Charlie's notion: Shure's death was no suicide. On Friday, in their meeting, Shure hadn't seemed suicidal. Also, it made little sense that a man considering taking his own life would shop for groceries first. Lastly, there was the question of the dog. Wouldn't Shure have made arrangements for his pet before taking his own life? Charlie understood that he might be wrong on this point, that despair might be so all consuming as to blot out other concerns, but he stuck with his assumption. Shure's murder had been staged to make it appear a suicide. The case of John Stuart Robbins' murder hadn't been closed; the case of a second murder had been opened.

The terrier with him, Charlie was home that night when Lucy called. She was organizing a reunion for their college friends at Four Winds, the third weekend in June. "I'm having the dinners catered," she mentioned. "Maybe you and I can split the checks."

"Fine."

"I'm not sure what George can afford. I don't know what you know..?"

"Not much."

"C'mon, you're his best friend. Doesn't he talk to you?"

"About what?"

"Money."

"No."

"Is he paid well?"

"No idea."

"Jesus, how is it men never know these things about each other unless they're competing? Did you see his mail? This past weekend?"

"Why would I?"

"I was looking for a magazine," Lucy said. "But his table was clogged with bills. Past due notices. He'd opened two letters. Both threatened court action. God, how overextended is he?"

Charlie took a long breath through clenched teeth. "I don't know. He wouldn't want to admit it if he were."

"I hope he knows it won't kill him to get leveled out like the rest of us."

"Have you talked to him?"

"I'm chicken, too."

"Damnit..." The thought so depressed him, George in trouble with his creditors like his father, that Charlie couldn't talk about it. George had always lived well. He didn't hire twelve-cabin yachts for cruises through the Mediterranean or bid on Old Master paintings, but his life was not one of self-denial.

Glad to get off the phone, Charlie settled down with a book. He had nodded off, the dog beside him, when the phone rang again. Sleepy, he didn't recognize the voice on the other end, not even when she repeated herself. "Is this Charlie Sanderson?"

"Yeah."

"This is Julia." She sounded nervous. Or drunk.

Charlie sat up, tried to chase off his fatigue with a yawn.

"I know it doesn't matter, after all this time. But we didn't get to talk, and I don't know - I never knew - if I should set the record straight."

"What?"

"It wasn't what you thought."

"What're you talking about?"

"When I left. I don't have to go into what happened, but I didn't think it was fair you were so cold. You have no idea..." Flustered, she stopped in mid-sentence.

"You called? To tell me this?" Charlie remembered the phone call that he hadn't gotten, the apartment that she was going to share with him, the desolation that her disappearance had caused.

"Maybe you don't want to hear from me, or maybe it isn't necessary. I don't imagine there are old accounts to settle. I only wanted to set things straight."

Julia had regained her composure; Charlie was losing his. He held the phone like a projectile that he might throw. His life was orderly; he had control. He didn't want to address the question that he finally blurted out. "What're you talking about? Set what straight? Where were you? That's all I remember. Where were you?"

"Where were you?" She was firm without being vehement. "That was my question. I walked into a landmine when I left. That's the only way to describe it. I couldn't explain it in a letter, and I won't do it on the phone. But I had the same question. Where were you?" With a sigh of resignation Julia hung up.

12

A field manager for the Office of the Comptroller of the Currency, Milton Greene supervised a crew of twenty examiners, among whom John Stuart Robbins had been relatively senior. Charlie decided to accompany Ray McLean to downtown Boston to interview Greene. The detective drove, his unmarked sedan barreling up I-95 North, the interstate slickened by a constant drizzle. Although he acknowledged that someone else may have been responsible for the first murder and the subsequent "suicide," McLean stuck with his assumption that some fit of jealousy, a lovers' triangle, was at the bottom of it all. "It's love or money, it always gets down to that." McLean tapped the steering wheel. "Love and its flipside rage, or money, and I haven't figured a money angle."

At the regional field office of the OCC, at 150 Federal Street, they found Milton Greene's tenth floor office furnished with a cheap veneer desk and sagging fiberboard bookshelves - government issue. Greene didn't look anything like Charlie had imagined. It must have been the name and his guttural rasp of a voice because Charlie had pictured someone old, short, and bald. Greene couldn't have been more than thirty-five years old, and he towered over Charlie, a sweet-faced giant with bad posture and long hair. At McClean's request, Greene provided the victim's case notes and calendar.

"There are some gaps." Greene pointed at Robbins' desk-top calendar. "You can see when he was out with the team. After the initial visit, which is unannounced, there's follow-up, which is more freelance."

"Who decides? What the bank examiners follow up?"

"They do. Or we do. Obviously, with the loans we have classified categories. It's not as bleak as it used to be, three years ago. The capital requirements are tougher. You want me to get into that?"

"No." The detective had been staring out the window at the North End; he faced the supervisor. "Do these examiners always work in pairs? Or solo?"

"It depends. One guy can review a file or book a meeting."

"Who were Robbins' friends here?"

"I don't know."

"He have any?"

"He was acerbic. I think that was appreciated."

"'Acerbic?'" McClean scrunched his face up. "A wise guy? Acerbic? You appreciate that?"

"Yeah. At times. He could be funny when he wanted. But he could be a loner, too."

"People here knew he was gay?"

"I assume."

"Anyone mind? Anyone jealous?"

"Not that I know."

"Robbins? What'd he earn?"

"He was commissioned. I think a '12' on our scale. About forty-nine, five."

"He just bought a BMW." McLean rubbed his forefinger against his thumb, counting off imaginary dollars.

"It's not as if he's got a wife and kids," Greene replied.

"He owned a boat. A boat can cost more than a wife and kids. His parents have money?"

"I wouldn't know. He doesn't seem the type."

McClean picked up Robbins' desk calendar and slid it towards Greene. "You said there were gaps?"

"Time he hadn't accounted for. He could be sloppy. He was in New York a month or two ago. I figured he wanted to catch a few plays, but then he put his hotel bill in an expense report. Like the trip was business."

"Was it?"

"It's something I had to talk to him about."

"Isn't New York a different district?"

"There's another field office there. But he could follow up on a loan or account from here."

"How many banks are in your jurisdiction?"

Greene lifted a ledger off a shelf and handed it to McClean, who glanced at it and passed it to Charlie. The ledger listed about seven hundred banks throughout the New England area. A series of numerical codes were listed next to the banks' names, thirty of which were printed in bold type. Charlie skimmed that list until he came across one of the highlighted names: First Federal Bank of Rhode Island.

"What does this list mean" Charlie asked. "The ones in bold print."

"Banks recently reviewed," Greene replied.

"By Robbins?" Charlie tapped the ledger. "This bank in Newport?"

"Robbins lives – *lived* – in Rhode Island. We'd give him a lot of those visits. Convenience."

Once he got back to Providence, Charlie called George. He wanted to clarify a few terms of the film production loan and to discuss the impact on George's bank if the loan were classified as troubled.

"We won't even think about the loan failing," George said. "We'll take care of it before that."

"If there's a hitch?"

"There won't be. We'll deal with it. I just need to figure what those jerk-offs are doing out there in la-la-land."

"Did you see today's '*Journal*?'" Charlie had read an article in '*The Wall Street Journal*' on the perilous finances of the studio which had guaranteed George's loan.

"That's why we're moving quickly."

The streetlights were glowing when Charlie reached Julia's apartment building on the West Side of Manhattan. Hoping to make sense of their conversation the night before, he'd called earlier; a recorded message on Julia's answering machine had indicated that she'd be home that evening. The doorman called her on a house phone, and Charlie was invited up.

Julia opened the door to her apartment, saw Charlie, and slid the chain free of its latch. His rush of curiosity grinding to a halt, he stopped on the threshold. The idea that he had had, that a spur-of-the-moment arrival might induce a more forthcoming conversation, now seemed dubious.

She looked at him quizzically. "You can come in."

"You said we could catch up." Charlie stepped into the apartment. "We could go for a drink."

"Would a drink help?"

"Probably."

Charlie let his eyes wander around her living room. He was searching for a clue, an indication of the life she had, the person she'd become, but no photos were displayed. The furniture was traditional: nicely upholstered, carefully arranged, peculiarly antiseptic. Julia caught him looking. "I sublet."

"It's nice."

"It's okay," Julia corrected. "I bought a little farm in Vermont recently. As a getaway. The house needs lots of work, so I put my time into it."

"How long've you been in New York?"

"Four months. I was on the West Coast before."

"Did you like it?"

Julia nodded. "It's different. Maybe a little calmer. You ever spend time there?"

"Not really. Only vacations."

Julia started for her small kitchen. "You want anything? Tea? I might have wine..?"

"I'm okay. Thanks."

Julia lifted a cup of tea off the kitchen counter, took a sip, and put the cup down. "It was odd running into you. I guess I thought you'd have a perfect life. Maybe you do. And it's what I always assumed. You'd make this great life that anyone would be happy to share."

Charlie put a hand in a pocket and rolled the coins around. "I would've been easy to find," he said, trying to avoid any note of peevishness.

"Is that what you think?"

"It doesn't matter, you said so yourself."

"It does matter. I was arrested when I got to Chile."

Although Julia told her story dispassionately, Charlie was chilled by it.

The metal shutters were lowered when she got there, the Santiago mansion dark, but the cab driver's request distracted her. He wanted to be paid in American dollars, if possible, not worthless Chilean pesos, and his grin was hard to resist. Exhausted after several long flights and a seemingly pointless interrogation at customs, Julia was happy to oblige. She got out a ten-dollar bill, which took care of the fare and a tip, and let herself in.

The light switches inside her parents' home didn't work, the electricity shut off to their house, if not to others on the street, which were well lit. However, incidental light from clerestory windows in the reception hall let Julia explore the ground floor, and it was quickly apparent that the maid who was being paid to look after the property hadn't been by in months. The sheets that had been draped over the upholstered furniture were themselves draped with a thin coat of dust. A wall showed a large crack in its plaster, courtesy of a recent quake. Julia was heading for the pantry when a soldier appeared beside her, materializing out of shadows and announcing that she was suspected of drug smuggling and under arrest. He handcuffed her to a radiator when she protested.

Two days later, hungry and soiled and still chained to the radiator, she met a colonel, who was clearly in charge of the soldier guarding her. "I've taken up the study of physics," the colonel told his prisoner. "You might consider it. The history of physics, the whole purpose of the science, is to disprove everything about the world you know to be true."

"I don't think the joke was on me," Julia explained to Charlie, who was stunned by the remark, "and I had a year to think about it.

If there was a joke, I think he knew it was on him. But he never told me what he meant or why anything was happening."

"Forsaken," the colonel did tell her, about a month after imprisoning her, and angry with Julia for trying to escape. "You are forsaken, forgotten, alone. No one is coming. No one asks for you. No one cares. Where would you go? I am the only possible agent of your salvation."

If the colonel clarified little during his infrequent visits, the sergeant who served as her principal jailer occasionally tried to ingratiate himself with Julia by hinting at the colonel's motives: the colonel knew that Allende might fall, that the military might intervene; naturally, the colonel would want insurance in case Allende, who had appointed him to his current post, was removed from the presidency. The colonel's career was effectively finished if Allende lost power. Julia Hoffman, as the daughter of one of the nation's wealthiest men, provided the leverage the colonel needed; if all else failed, he could hold her hostage and negotiate the terms of her release with her family.

Besides fabricating evidence against Julia, the colonel had confiscated letters that she was ferrying from Martin to two opponents of the current regime. The letters, which promised financial support and cooperation if the opposition returned to power, would have been highly inflammatory to the prosecuting attorney and jurists that the colonel threatened to enlist.

"I couldn't understand the silence," Julia said. "I couldn't understand why someone couldn't do something, why you couldn't find me. I got so angry with you and with my family. It was only afterwards I found out what my family went through. They were told, right from the start, there was a strong case and I'd be convicted if anyone said anything publicly. Maybe they blamed you, maybe they thought I did have drugs with me. The penalties for drug smuggling were draconian back then."

"But your parents must've known -"

"Not at first. The colonel acted as if he were interceding - as their friend, not as my kidnapper. He said he'd hold me under house arrest, rather than in jail; he said he'd try to get the charges quietly dismissed. The colonel dragged it all out. Until, in the end, it was just a matter of money."

Two days after Allende died during the coup, almost a year after Julia had returned to Chile, she was handed over to her brother. It was Martin, not her father, who had overseen the wiring of two million dollars to a Swiss bank account. The colonel disappeared, presumably to a country where he had easy access to his Swiss bank account.

"You should've.." Charlie stammered.

"What?"

"I would have come."

"No. Martin and my family were told if anyone questioned my arrest or made it public, they'd start injecting me with the drugs I was accused of smuggling. After a month or two, I'd likely OD. There was other shit, too, that I was threatened with. By the time I finally got out of Chile, I wasn't anybody you knew. They kept me in a basement. You can't imagine what that did or how betrayed I felt."

"But-"

"I got so twisted. By the end I weighed ninety-nine pounds. I didn't want to see anyone, I didn't want anyone to see me. Especially you. You least of all. It was a year before I could write you a note."

"Why didn't Martin call? He knew how desperate I was to find you."

"He said he had contacted you at least twice. When I was back."

"He didn't. He didn't return my calls or my letters! He knew where I was and how to reach me."

Julie fought but couldn't hide her surprise. "I thought I had lost you."

"Damnit, Martin! Why did he lie about contacting me?"

"I can't imagine. Maybe he was worried I wasn't ready or you'd be totally put off by the wreck I was."

"Maybe he was embarrassed or ashamed. He sent you there."

Julie exhaled at length. "I can't go there. It was so long ago. He looked after me, he wanted me to get better, to give me some time."

"Martin?"

"Don't. He kept me going."

Overwhelmed by the savagery of what had befallen her, Charlie couldn't speak. On the one hand, he felt strangely unburdened of what had been a crushing rejection; on the other hand, he felt a renewed sense of loss, as if he might again need to vent himself of the fury and despair that had consumed him years earlier. He tried to take his cue from Julia's composure: she had long ago made peace with a wound that he had long nursed.

"I figured you'd have written me off," Julia admitted. "I figured my life had gone inside out and I couldn't ruin things for anyone else. I figured you'd have found someone else. I even half-hoped it."

Julia mentioned that Martin had taken her from Chile to Miami, where she became co-dependent with the therapist who treated her. They had daily sessions, they dined together three times a week, and he finally tried to substitute another therapist so that he could pursue her. She had sent her brief note to Charlie months beforehand. "God, it was a five-alarm wake-up call. 'Co-dependent?' With him? I decided I had to work, I had to free myself from anyone, from Martin and my family and their money. I worked hard. A lot of travel. It's one of the reasons I'm now in New York. Less travel."

"God..." It was all Charlie could manage.

"It was chaos, the first year. Out of my control. I was a zombie. It's how I got through it."

Charlie had felt powerless when he lost her; he felt helpless again, hearing of injuries that he couldn't spare her. Julia's detachment, the way she calmly discussed her misfortune, disturbed him. Had some of her extraordinary fire been extinguished? Or had she healed? Charlie wasn't sure. He was only certain that she still had appeal beyond her beauty, a strength and mystery to her that captivated him. He had the sense that he was standing next to a well which he had fallen into once before. He knew if he fell in again, he might never get out.

13

S tuck in court all day, Charlie didn't arrive at Four Winds until
seven-thirty, when a dozen of his old friends had already gathered in the den for cocktails. Joe Turlik's wife had been unable
to come at the last minute, but Quad's wife, Erica, was there, helping
organize dinner. Charlie found Quad huddled with Joe and quizzing
him about his job. "So your role with these clients?" Quad waited for
Joe's answer, then continued, "You're an account manager?"

"Sort of," Joe said. "I press a little flesh. Do some corporate stuff."

"Such as?"

"Details, paperwork, a lot of small tasks."

"Do you place money for them? Recommend money-managers?"
Quad ran a large bond portfolio for an insurance company in Hartford
and rarely passed up the chance to hustle new business. "If you do,
you should meet with us. We -"

"It's simpler than that." Joe paused to take a gulp of wine. "What
we do is have them structure things right. You know, watch the tax
angles, facilitate investments. We're a facilitator."

"What the fuck is that?"

Joe laughed at Quad. "God, you're an old lady! Fit to be retired.
Me, I'm just waiting my turn, ready to do the bump-and-grind for
anybody with heaps of money." Joe stopped himself, as if he might have
been indiscreet. Anxious, he looked around the room until he spotted
George, whose attention was held by his date for the weekend. Joe

took another swallow of wine. "Boy, I'll tell you - these global types, they're a little wacko."

Lucy interrupted by joining them. "No shop-talk."

Joe took Lucy's empty glass from her. "Let me freshen that."

Quad watched Joe head for the bar, then turned to Charlie. "His job? Do you know what Joe does?"

"Not exactly."

"I don't think he does either."

"It's his birthday." Lucy frowned at both of them. "Not that I'd expect you'd remember."

"How do you do it?" Charlie asked.

"I not only own a calendar, I actually look at it."

"Amazing."

"I bought him a present. You two can chip in. But first, get everybody moving. It's dinner-time."

Once the plates for the main course had been cleared, the dining room went pitch black as Lucy flipped off the lights. A violet glow flickered from a side table and slowly suffused the room with unnatural light that transformed everything into lavender and phosphorescent lint.

"My God, a black light! How long's it been?"

"Where in hell did you find it?"

"Joe!" someone else hollered, familiar with Joe's fascination with "black" lights during his college days.

Lucy flipped the room lights back on and unplugged the black light, which was stuck like a candle into a birthday cake. "To our original mushhead," Lucy said, raising the tubular light in a toast.

At Lucy's insistence, Joe stood up, while the other guests sang "Happy Birthday." Lucy presented the black light to Joe and announced that she had another gift for "Popeye the Sailor Man." The joke, which everyone understood, was that Joe had recently been forced to do some yachting with clients: Joe, who hated boating, who claimed to have once gotten seasick on a dinghy ferrying him from a dock to a yacht. Although not expensive, the watch was all tricked out with fancy dials, with a chronometer and a depth gauge and an inset face that displayed Greenwich Mean Time.

Joe kissed Lucy, then threw an arm around Charlie. "You guys, you're the goddamn best. No one better. Never will be."

The party continued in the den, where George had to reattach the cables from his turntable to his receiver before he could play his "oldies". Thumbing through the dusty LPs, George conducted a rapid-fire "pop quiz": what was Iron Butterfly's hit, what was the first song on The White Album, what group played last at Woodstock?

Lucy sifted through another stack and called out the artists, each name eliciting exclamations of delight: James Taylor, Joni Mitchell, The Kinks, Laura Nyro, Simon & Garfunkel! When the music began, Lucy dropped onto the couch next to Charlie and slumped against him; the dog Charlie had brought for the weekend curled up in her lap. "You remember the first time we were all here?" she asked.

"Late spring. Quad got arrested for speeding on the way back."

"Jesus, what a memory!" Lucy shifted her weight. "Do you think a good memory is a blessing or a curse?"

"I don't know."

"I remember everything, Charlie. Everything. I don't like it. I remember the way I felt. Unstoppable. I figured I'd be a publisher, not just an editor. I figured I'd be an owner. You, too. The world was ours."

"You mean it isn't?"

"We got screwed somehow. I didn't figure we'd live this long and work this hard and still be chasing a future."

Roxy repositioned her chin in Lucy's lap. Charlie extended a hand and scratched the dog behind her ears. "The trick is to sleep eighteen to twenty hours a day and take a couple of walks."

"You never feel disappointed?"

Charlie smiled. "It's not a question I ask myself. I can't. Maybe when I'm middle-aged--"

"Oh? And when do we get there?"

"When we grow up. And not one day sooner."

"It's our children who'll wind up feeling cheated. All we've given them is rock 'n roll, and they'll outgrow it before we do."

Roxy stirred at the faint sound of doorbell chimes and jumped to the floor, barking. Soon, a waiter on the caterer's crew appeared in the doorway and asked, "Is Mr. Spaulding here?"

George got to his feet, cleared his throat, and spoke to the young man in tones of haughty displeasure. "Son, Mr. Spaulding retired for the evening. With a couple of co-eds. I do rather hope you're not planning to disturb him."

"Uhh.." The waiter put his hands in his apron pocket and stared at his feet. "No, sir. Except, uhh.. there's visitors."

"Alright, alright," George said, marching to the door. "I shall fetch Mr. Spaulding myself. Damn tough luck for those co-eds." As he left the room, George called over his shoulder to Lucy. "Keep the candles burning, darling."

"God." Lucy glanced at a wall clock, then at Charlie. "Do you think we'll last till midnight?"

"No idea."

"I don't remember the last time I stayed up till midnight."

"That's depressing."

"Maybe we should stay up. Something wonderful might happen."

"An epiphany?"

"Midnight epiphanies? Wow, my favorite kind."

"I don't think we've drunk enough - for an epiphany."

"Just enough for a hangover, right? Anyway, you should get to bed early. You've got a date tomorrow."

"And?"

"I'm not saying anything."

"Like hell." Lucy's comment was the same one that she'd made when Charlie first told her that he'd bring Julia to the gathering.

"Okay. I think it's nice you run into her after all this time. But I can't help wondering. It seems, at some point, Julia could've figured out where you were. Why now? Maybe there's nothing to the question, maybe it's the way her life has unfolded. It just seems odd. After all this time."

"You think?"

Lucy shrugged. "Is she still the same person?"

"Are we? Twenty-some years later?"

"Yeah. I think we are, at least you and me. We're pretty much the same, except now we need a little bran in our cereal."

"I don't know."

"It has to have an impact, doesn't it? What happened to her, kidnapped, like poor Patty Hearst. God, Charlie, imagine, if you can." Lucy's eyes blinked away the threat of tears. "I can't. Too catastrophic."

"What're you saying?"

"I don't want you surprised or hurt. And maybe I'm a bit jealous. Me, with nothing in the wings except this flake I didn't invite. I reach this point in my life – no date this weekend, a boss I barely tolerate - and the best thing I can say about my life is that it's not unsuccessful. A goddamn double negative. God, Charlie, there are days I just feel.." Lucy hunted for the word, "undiscovered. Undiscovered, you know?"

"You? 'Undiscovered?'" Charlie squeezed her hand. "Nonsense. You're a classic. A Broadway hit, always in revival."

"'*In revival?*' Good God, Monsignor, are you trying to talk me in from the ledge or off it?" Lucy raised her lips in a wry smile. "The hell with it," she said, turning her attention to the music. Someone lifted the phonograph's needle and hand-placed it into a scratchy groove, and the hoarse-voiced poetry of Bob Dylan swept through the room like the anthem it had become. "*Like a Rolling Stone.*" Unable to restrain herself, Lucy closed her eyes and sang along, a chorus of other off-key, dry-throated patriots joining her.

For all the alcohol poured and the memories shared, the party never gathered much steam. When Charlie decided to turn in, Lucy was asleep on the couch in the den, Roxy curled up beside her. They looked so comfortable that he didn't disturb them; he turned out a few lights and headed upstairs.

Charlie was asleep when more late-night visitors showed up at the mansion, but the dog heard people arriving and trotted into the front hall. Roxy kept her distance, growling ferociously, barking and baying at the strangers, even after the door to the office had been closed behind them and Lucy had stumbled into the front hall to collar her.

Lucy carried the dog to Charlie's room, where she explained that something had set Roxy off. "She was a little frantic or didn't like whoever showed up," Lucy said, closing Charlie's door behind her and going down the hall to her room.

14

On Saturday, a fierce sun quickly burned off an early morning haze. While Quad and his wife toured several of the Newport mansions, the others participated in a makeshift golf tournament. Everyone was back at Four Winds by mid-afternoon, when Julia drove up in a Jeep with Vermont plates. Charlie met her on the front porch.

"I was trying to remember this house," she said, peering into the front hall. "Do you stay in that room in the servants' wing?"

"No. They never rewired that part of the house. I usually bring my computer."

Julia smiled. "What about the pool? Is it still unheated?"

"George added a heater, but it doesn't work."

Charlie took her on a tour of the grounds. As they crossed the back lawn, Julia asked, "Is it there? That terrace?"

Having survived the high seas generated by winter storms and end-of-summer hurricanes, the Women's Tee was little changed. When the surf was rough and the tide was in, a big wave could spray anyone there, which was what happened to Charlie and Julia moments after they climbed down. Julia laughed and used a sleeve to dry her face. "Is that a race?" she asked, squinting at the horizon.

Charlie had to squint, too, and made out a cluster of similarly sized sailboats. "I guess."

Julia watched the race for a while, then let her eyes sweep over the lawn behind her and the house. "How's George?"

"Fine."

"Will it kill him? If he can't hold onto this?"

Charlie didn't remember telling her that George couldn't afford to keep the house. Was it that obvious? His instinct was to protect his friend. "George? This place is too big for him."

"My father lost much of what had been his. His businesses. His own father's ranch. It was terrible for my father. Very personal."

Charlie waited, but she seemed to have spoken her piece. Another wave kicked up a rooster's tail of water, which fanned out towards them. They scrambled up to the lawn, got a leash, and took Roxy on a walk.

Of all his friends, Charlie was most concerned about Lucy. Her reception of Julia would set the tone for others, and Lucy was waiting on the porch when they got back. "Welcome to the reunion," Lucy said, smiling at Julia and clasping her hand. "We're gonna smoke virgin joints and raffle off face-lifts later."

Lucy made a few other jokes about chemical peels and swimsuit competitions in which the winner was the one who didn't get caught in public wearing one, but she was distracted by the arrival of Martin Hoffman. Martin carried a basket full of ice and champagne up the front steps, greeted everyone with polished smiles, and disappeared with George into his office.

At dinner, Charlie and Julia wound up at a table with Joe, who was leaving early the next morning for a flight to the Cayman Islands and worried about getting enough rest. He forgot about his slumbers, however, when a deejay showed up with hundreds of old records, and the tables were pushed aside for dancing. All the twenty celebrants there marveled at the music, how much of it had retained its immediacy, how compelling it remained. Charlie danced once with Quad's wife, twice with Lucy, and quite a few times with Julia.

George cut in on Charlie at one point, whisking his hand in a gesture to shoo Charlie from the floor, then grabbing Julia's hand and launching her into a jitterbug twirl. George paused long enough to shoot a dance instructor's smile at Charlie, a toothy and loathsomely self-confident smirk that suggested that if Charlie, the pupil, would pay better attention to George, the master, then Charlie too might be a swell. With a little faux ballet, George swept Julia up in an exaggerated tango. Charlie was pleased, if surprised, by the way George and Julia were so comfortable with one another. If they had run into each other over the years, George certainly hadn't said a word about it to his best and oldest friend.

Restored to Charlie, Julia danced a while longer until, pleading fatigue, she left the party. Charlie walked her to her car.

Out front, she glanced at all the vehicles gathered there. "It's pretty remarkable," she said. "Your friends. You get together. After all this time. It's great luck, to be able to do that."

Julia's look, distant if wistful, made Charlie wonder at the enormity of what she had lost. She opened her car door and turned to face him. "Thanks for including me."

"Sure."

"Hard to imagine, isn't it?" She waved a hand at the house, as if to pay homage to the way their lives had intersected years earlier. Julia suggested that he call and drove off.

Charlie was the only one awake the next morning when Joe left for his nine o'clock flight to Miami, with connections to Grand Cayman. Joe said he'd booked the trip late and dreaded having to fly on a small commuter airline over Cuba. He was old enough to remember the mayhem created by the Cuban missile crisis; it felt stupid, he told Charlie, to bisect Cuban airspace, with or without Castro's permission.

GRAND CAYMAN ISLAND

Joe landed on Grand Cayman without incident. After collecting his luggage, he hailed a cab and headed for the harbor. The cab traveled west alongside a tranquil turquoise bay before passing through George Town, the thriving capital of the Crown colony. The island's prosperity never failed to amaze Joe, the island not much more than a sun-bleached sandbar made prosperous by its status as a tax haven, almost six hundred banks clustered on an island with only thirty-five thousand people. The principal business of the island was sheltering large sums of money from the confiscatory raids of high-tax governments elsewhere: business was good.

Once again bound for a meeting on board a boat, Joe was making his fourth trip to the island in ten months. It was the worst part of his job, the shipboard meetings. He hated being out on the open water, hated his unshakable dread of the ocean. The people with whom he met - Joe assumed that they were owners of the holding companies and offshore trusts that employed him - preferred to conduct meetings on their yachts, no doubt because remote locations helped keep the conversations private. These were people who had their yachts periodically swept for bugs.

Joe heard the wail of sirens, a crescendo rising from the waterfront, before the taxi stalled in a traffic jam abreast of the harbor road. Some catastrophe - a slew of red lights blinking and flashing, a few ambulances crunching past on the gravel of the road's shoulder - had turned the normally sleepy waterfront into a war zone. When five minutes had passed and traffic hadn't budged, the cab driver got out and ambled forward to investigate. Minutes later he was back with a report: a capsized trawler had been towed into the harbor; more than a hundred bodies had been discovered in the ship's cargo hold. "Dem Haiti folk, mahn! Dey jump on anyteen' dat float," the driver said, before suggesting that Joe would make better time walking.

Joe paid the fare, slung his suitcase over his shoulder, and walked around the barricade and the drowsy policeman who was stationed at the entrance to the harbor road. Spectators were everywhere, crowding the end of the breakwater, perched on the roof of a supply store, scaling the pilot's cabin on a sport-fishing boat. The capsized trawler had been towed to a cargo dock at one of the piers, where lines from hydraulic lifts had been attached to it and dozens of emergency workers were scurrying about. Drawn to the scene, unrestrained, Joe approached the cargo dock until he got an unobstructed view of the temporary morgue. Twenty corpses, just disgorged from the boat and grotesquely swollen, were laid side by side. The disarray was such that it was impossible to tell who, if anyone, was in charge, but a man in a uniform was yelling at one of the lift operators, whose winch was raising the stern of the boat. Suddenly, with a great metallic groan, the trawler shifted, the stern rising seven feet, the bow dipping a proportionate amount, a huge wave splashing the dock, the emergency workers leaping out of the way of the whipsawing cables, curses howled the length of the ship while the boat rocked and settled into a new and tenuous balance. A few portholes were now visible along the waterline of the capsized vessel's stern. Joe saw it the same time that the crowd did, the instant that a low gasp rippled through the bystanders. Rigid with death, its fingers spread in a last appeal, an arm was stuck out of a porthole; in his struggle to avoid drowning a man had been trapped, an arm crushed and pinned as the boat rolled and uncountable tons of water pushed against and through the porthole.

The stink of death was unavoidable, the chemical reek of decay unscrubbed by even a slight breeze. There were no survivors. The talk was that there may have been a mutiny, hundreds of desperate people crammed onto a boat supposed to be manned by a crew of seven; the trawler was presumed to have capsized in a storm three days earlier. Bodies of other victims were floating up on the beach at Spanish Bay. No one understood why the ship, terribly overloaded with its cargo of boat people, would have steamed due west from Haiti rather than north, but bystanders speculated that the captain must have intended to circumnavigate Cuba, risking a long passage to Florida in hopes of avoiding the Coast Guard dragnet.

Next to Joe, a woman was weeping, all the while whispering a prayer for those who had drowned. Joe had never had much sympathy for the Haitians. True, it was a nation that had been plundered by its rulers, but its peasants had ravaged the republic too, the hillside forests cut and burned for the pennies that charcoal cubes brought, the rootless topsoil left to wash into the ocean, the black magic of voodoo given the stature of science, the people breeding so frequently in the midst of unspeakable poverty and disease. Now, confronted by the sight of half-starved victims and stunned by the realization that these men and women had voluntarily undertaken a terrible risk for a modest chance at bare survival, Joe began to understand their plight, the ineluctable and godawful horror of it. When Joe was a boy, he had often sung a hymn in church for sailors lost at sea. Joe wished that he could remember the words, the haunting tune, that he could hum some prayer for the poor souls laid out like cargo on the dock, but the hymn was lost to him.

It was a bad omen, this shipwreck. Anxious, Joe hustled away from the drama unfolding there and hurried for a pier a hundred yards away, where pleasure craft and sport-fishing boats were tied up. He found the cabin-cruiser that would ferry him to the day's meeting and stepped aboard, but didn't recognize the skipper, a guy not much more than half his age. The skipper was curious about what Joe had seen: had Joe learned anything about the tragedy or had the chance to discuss the tragedy with the harbor police? Joe pointed to his new watch; he hadn't had the time to discuss anything with anyone. The skipper ordered two deckhands to cast off and had Joe put anything in his pockets, especially his phone and wallet, in a small safe: the standard precaution for the meetings.

The boat quickly steamed out of the harbor and turned north, Seven Mile Beach visible off the starboard bow, until they lost sight of land altogether. After an hour or so, when they still hadn't rendezvoused with the yacht, the skipper cut his engines and the boat slowed into an aimless drift. Puzzled, Joe stood up as the two deckhands approached. One of them, a mulatto, was holding a length of lead pipe that had been used to prop the cabin door open.

"Where's the boat?" Joe asked.

The darker-skinned deckhand hunched his shoulders in response, while the guy holding the pipe circled aft. Joe kept an eye on the man beside him and started for the cabin. He heard the rush of footsteps from behind, the mulatto attacking and swinging the lead pipe. Joe ducked, but the pipe smashed into his right shoulder, shattering the clavicle, and driving him to the deck. He raised his left arm to protect his head from the man with the pipe, who swung again, this time connecting with the left forearm, a bone-breaking blow that left Joe screaming.

Joe rolled onto his back and kicked at his attackers, who seized him. They yanked him to his feet, held his broken limbs in excruciating armlocks, and dragged him to the rail, where a knife's blade flashed with the sun and a sharp, tugging sensation tore through the fingers of his right hand. The pain exploded, momentarily obliterating his consciousness. He felt himself lifted and tossed overboard, his eyes reopening upon his body's impact with the water. Bobbing to the surface after breaking its plane, flailing with his legs, Joe heard the boat motoring off and tried to collect his thoughts, which had been scattered by the attack. After he had kicked off his shoes and begun treading water, he found himself thinking of his friends, who had been steadfast and supportive all these years. Charming and generous and clever, they had surprised Joe all those years ago by sweeping him up into their tight-knit group. They never seemed to have suspected, as Joe did, that he might not quite belong. His friends were his one real accomplishment. He didn't think of his wife, who would somehow take this unnecessary treachery as a personal betrayal. Instead, he imagined George, who had provided him this job when he was desperate for work. He would warn George, if only he could. Yet the pain was unmanageable, his broken bones jarred by the slightest motion, a fire lit in the stumps of his severed fingers; the pain would, Joe realized, force a quick surrender to the fate which he understood to be inescapable. He would drown, within minutes, the weight of clothes that he could not shed tugging him into his wet, miserable destiny.

15

Silent throughout the meeting, George picked at the skin flaking off the back of his hands. He was flanked by Charlie Sanderson and Nick Boorstein, a lawyer whom Charlie had rounded up. Also well-versed in entertainment financing, lawyers for the studio and the producer, as well as the producer himself, sat across the table from George in the plush conference room of Boorstein's midtown office.

Although the producer continued to insist that the final cut and answer print of the film had been delivered, the studio's counsel argued that certain contractually required edits for a less-violent TV version were as yet unmade, that the film was thus technically undelivered, and that the studio was not as yet obliged to honor and fund its takeout guarantee. "Where's our TV version?" the counsel kept asking.

"You think this piece of filth is ever gonna play on TV?" The man asking the question, a lawyer for the producer, had flown in from the West Coast for the meeting.

"Your client's the producer."

"He wants his name taken the hell off it."

"So?"

"You couldn't show any of it, not on network. So all this stalling around is accomplishing … is stalling the fuck around."

The meeting dragged on and ended with no real conclusion; the only thing that the lawyers agreed upon was that the director, who hadn't bothered to attend the meeting, had created a mean, spiritless, sexually graphic film. The bank's problems were the bank's hard luck, it seemed.

When the others had left, George asked Charlie and Nick Boorstein for their view of things. George looked so desperate that Charlie didn't want to tell him what he thought, but Boorstein didn't spare him. "First off, you have to understand that Multimedia Group is going under. They don't want this film, they hate this thirty-four-million-dollar piece-of-dirt, but it's all beside the point because it's all gonna wind up in bankruptcy court. So you gotta figure out what to attach and how to do it quickly."

"You don't think they can work through this?" Charlie tried to sound hopeful.

"Unlikely."

"Can we attach their planes?" Charlie knew that when making the deal, George had repeatedly been ferried to and from California on one of the studio's luxury jets.

"I doubt they own them. My guess is they mostly lease and whatever they own is leveraged to the max."

"If it comes to it," George said, "we're gonna have to take the film."

"You don't wanna do that either," the lawyer said. "You want anything other than the goddamn negative, which is what you're likely to end up with. If the film were releasable, it might be different, but no one wants to distribute this."

"Why not?"

"To start with, I hear the heroine's bedroom looks like a museum of sex toys. Just what America wants in its heroines, a curator of a dildo collection."

"How could the goddamn director do this?"

"He did it," Boorstein said. "And I doubt you can fix it. What you gotta hope for is a turnaround by the studio, a cash infusion, its credit line made real again."

The fingers of his right hand stepping through a lazy box-step, George remained at the conference table after Boorstein left the room. Charlie kept him company but felt heartsick. He surmised that it would be difficult for George's bank to take a loss as large as the one it now faced.

George had made the loan, a lucrative one for the bank, at a time when the studio had secured a two-hundred-million-dollar credit line. The bank had made three similar, if smaller, production loans before. Never had there been a problem; never had there been an indication that the studio's Japanese financing might one day evaporate.

"Jesus," George said, spinning his pen on the table. "Jesus, I wish the goddamn Rangers were in town, I wish they were playing."

George and Charlie had been to countless hockey games when they were younger, when George could use his father's membership in the Madison Square Garden Club to get great seats, even at the last minute. But it was July, and the heat and humidity were fierce outside the office building.

Charlie took George to lunch at a restaurant across the street. "Here's the thing," George complained over a beer. "No one feels sorry for you if you started with something. It doesn't matter if you're blindsided. If you started with money and lose it, if you had all the advantages and tumble, the world writes your sorry ass off. Only first they gotta get their laughs."

"That's not true."

"It is. There's this special contempt for the once rich. I probably felt it myself for some fallen prince. What kind of idiot - other than my father – can't hang onto his fortune? How hard is it to put money into a good stock? You know why my father never invested in McDonalds? Undoubtedly because he never ate at one. The dumb, spoiled son-of-a-bitch. But nobody gets it, the way money consumes itself trying to toss off income. They just think you're a schmuck who was too dumb to buy Microsoft, Amgen, Disney."

"Are we?"

"Fuck, yes."

"George, it doesn't matter."

"It matters. It's all going to land at my feet."

"The bank?"

"Well," George said, without conviction, "we've got some time."

"Then what?"

"The lid comes off." George lifted his beer for a quick sip, then stared at Charlie. "It's okay. I've taken precautions."

With a bravado that rang false, George waved his hand to change the subject. Charlie let it go, but on the ride back to Providence he called Quad at his office. He understood the world of banking much better than Charlie.

"Do you know if the loan's performing?" Quad inquired. "I presume it is, at least technically, or this might already be academic. So there may be time."

"How much?"

"Probably until the next audit, whenever that is."

"What then?"

"The bank examiners look pretty hard at any loan guaranteed by MultiMedia."

"And?"

"I don't know the bank's balance sheet, what kind of write-down it can withstand. But off the top of my head, it's a large loan for this bank to be making. I don't know how somebody puts a value on this loan. How do you value some crappy movie?"

"What about George?"

"If a bank has to reorganize, somebody's gonna take the fall."

"It's not fair."

"No. But damn George. Honestly, with his background, you'd think he'd know better than to get sucked in by Hollywood cash and flash."

George was right, Charlie thought. The world does reserve a special contempt for the newly fallen. Even Quad couldn't see fit to spare him.

Charlie checked with his office and returned a call from Ray McClean, who informed him that in the two months prior to his death John Stuart Robbins had written fewer checks than normal and hadn't used his credit cards at all. "Generally, he's pretty busy with those cards," McLean explained. "You wonder if he's using cash and where he got it. He's not depositing cash in a bank, he'd be too smart for that, but they did find five hundred bucks hidden on his boat. Exactly five hundred. A few bucks more, and I figure it's not an emergency stash. I figure it's dirty. But my figuring won't figure without more cash."

Julia had also called to invite him to a piano recital at Carnegie Hall. A few days later, Charlie drove to New York and arrived at her building before Julia did. The doorman had instructions to give him a key. Charlie rode the elevator in silence, stepped into a vacant hall, and let himself into her apartment. The stillness of the place bothered him, the space radiating its emptiness, an uncluttered sublet with rented furniture. He wanted to find something of Julia - a scattered stack of books or a cache of old perfume bottles - amidst the prim and neat surroundings, but Julia had said that she was putting her time and money - herself, Charlie supposed – into her place in Vermont.

A pair of speakers was hung on the living room wall; Charlie traced their wires to a hall closet where he found a stereo and hundreds of CDs. He flipped on the CD player to see what she'd been listening to. Handel's "*Water Music*" had begun playing when Julia rushed into her apartment, intending to change clothes, but the music brought her up short. "Do you like this piece?" She tilted her head at the speakers.

"Yes."

"It's a favorite of mine. Maybe *the* favorite. There was a time when I listened to it almost daily. It's so buoyant. Is that a bad word for it?"

"No. It's lovely."

"I think it's the horns, the way they make it into this glorious processional. The horns are so upbeat, so joyful. Like a waltz. It's a piece without any hidden sorrows. You know the history of it?"

"Not really..?" Charlie hadn't seen Julia so animated and wanted her to continue.

"Handel wrote the suites as a concert for the king. They first performed it on barges that floated down the Thames. I used to imagine myself on one of those barges, floating through the countryside. I needed something to lose myself in - after I got back. Music - certain suites, horn concertos, they could do the trick. I couldn't handle Beethoven, not for a while."

Julia dressed for the recital and reappeared, holding a small envelope. "These are Martin's tickets. He has tickets to everything and is very generous with them."

The recital featured a newly prominent German pianist and opened with a few Chopin's etudes. Charlie didn't dislike them, but the music had always struck him as a pianist's test for piano students, as pieces inaccessible to all but the instrument's true aficionados. After a contemporary piece and a brief intermission, the recital concluded with a pair of popular Mozart sonatas. This music was irresistible. Julia slid her arm over the armrest and held Charlie's hand, her grip childlike and firm, the contact sustained throughout the two sonatas. Charlie was moved by her touch; he couldn't remember the last time he had been in a theater and held hands with a woman.

Charlie stroked the soft and supple skin on the back of Julia's hand with his thumb. Her fingers, which he traced with his own, were drier, the skin creased by fine wrinkles, the tip of the forefinger callused by a pen or pencil. Her little finger, in a habit that she seemed to indulge unwittingly, moved in conductor's arcs with the music.

Julia continued to hold his hand on the cab ride home. Her eyes turned to the rush of street signs and stray headlights. Oblivious to his musings, she quietly hummed a Mozart tune until the cab dropped them off outside her building. She had an appointment early the next morning; he was due in court. They said goodnight with a hug.

It took Charlie almost three hours to drive home to Providence. Exhausted, ready for bed, he glanced at his answering machine. It blinked, indicating a new message.

"Charlie? .. Charlie? .. Shit." The recorded voice, crackling with static, took a moment to recognize. "Mayday, Charlie, we're going down. Losing altitude."

The voice belonged to George, who paused - Charlie imagined that he could see George taking a sip of a cocktail. There was a rattle, the handset bumping against something, before George resumed. "Rumor is, a Dutch bank may lower the boom on MultiMedia. They must want everybody to crash and burn. Or maybe they'll try to ride it out. Anyhow, I'm on this plane to the Bahamas. Jesus, how gauche.

It's not even season, except for hurricanes. A busman's holiday. Like my goddamn future, right? ... This may take a while. Shit, somebody'll work up a lather. Look, I'll call in a week or so, if I haven't fallen off any tall buildings, and let you know where I'm camped out."

16

A week passed with no word from George, although Beth, George's secretary, reported that he had been through the office and was headed back to the Caribbean. "Does he have something going on down there?" she asked Charlie. "Some chick who took her last husband for a hotel chain or two? How come the divorced guys I meet are so broke their shoes need resoling?"

That night, Charlie was asleep when the phone rang. He woke to the thought of George on the line, calling in the middle of a late-night escapade, but it was Lucy. "Is it too late?" she asked.

"Would it matter?"

"No, but it's good form to ask. Hey, did you hear from Joe's wife? I got the strangest call."

"What?"

"I guess Marion hasn't heard from Joe in a while. I gather he goes off on these trips, sometimes for a couple of weeks, but he generally checks in. She asked if I knew where he was. Don't you think it's strange she calls me?"

"Why?" Charlie barely knew Marion Huntley, although both Lucy and he had attended her and Joe's wedding.

"We're not close. I guess she calls me because I'm a woman. I think she suspects they're up to something. Like it's some sort of boys' trip. Take the clients gambling and whoring in the tropics. God, does anybody do that anymore?"

"I don't know."

"I thought they closed Havana forty years ago."

"It doesn't sound like Joe."

"Joe? If you got him drunk enough, he'd curl up with a side of bacon. I'm sure Marion knows that. But would George? Hire hookers?"

"No."

"I can't see George with a call girl. Great breasts, bad teeth, bad grammar."

"He wouldn't be comfortable. It's not his world."

"He'd take clients to Bailey's Beach. Let the club put them and their arriviste pretensions in place."

"No." It disappointed Charlie that so many people, even George's dearest friends, misjudged him. "It isn't the privilege, the prestige, that George cares about. It's the wall."

"The wall? What? If you're born a snob -"

"You need a wall to hide behind. You've got everything to lose."

"That's a novel take. WASP terror? I'm not sure Joe would get it. Listen, if you hear from him, tell him to call home."

Off the phone, trying to imagine what trouble Joe might get into, Charlie recalled an incident from college. Their first year, Joe, Charlie, George, and Quad had all joined the same fraternity. With the Vietnam War raging, the hazing of fraternity pledges had begun to be considered a vulgar indulgence for young men lucky enough to have college deferments. Hell was war, it was the body bags and torched hamlets on the evening news; it was not to be confused with fraternity pranks. Thus, Charlie's class of pledges was the last in its era to suffer the indignities of "hell nights."

A "hell night," such as it was, concluded with a two-hour ordeal of push-ups and insults and headfirst slides through puddles of 40-degree rainwater. Before those activities commenced, each pledge was given a pick-up spot and told to wait there from ten p.m. until such time as the brothers fetched him. The spot designated for Charlie was the grave of a former fraternity cook, so Charlie spent three hours - from ten p.m. till one a.m. - hanging out in a graveyard. The town's Black graveyard.

Charlie, of course, didn't follow the brothers' instructions to the letter, since the pledges had been told to wait in their designated pick-up spots with a paper grocery bag, uncut, over their heads. He was certain that none of his fellow pledges would actually be stupid enough to wear the paper bag. He was wrong.

When Joe Turlik was picked up by the fraternity brothers assigned to him, he was found seated on the floor in a corner of the filthy men's room at Charlottesville's bus station. The walls were covered with pornographic cartoons and homophobic insults. In the three hours that Joe was there, dozens of people had been through the place, but Joe hadn't seen any of them. He'd kept a paper bag over his head.

"Jesus, you want to get arrested?" George had scolded, once he heard of the bag being faithfully left in place. "They don't expect you to wear it. They sent you there 'cause it's where the cops go bust the poor homos."

The memory stirred others, with Joe's role often that of the gullible sidekick. Charlie slept fitfully. He woke in time to meet with the realtor hired to sell Four Winds, who was at his door at eight a.m. prompt, dressed for an audience with royalty: high neckline, low hem, short heels, plump pearls. Charlie was listed as an alternate contact, and the realtor had some questions about negotiating in George's absence.

"There's a possible offer on the estate," she explained. "I'm getting some of this second-hand. From a buyer's broker. But it does raise a question. Does George plan to pay off any shortfall? If the sales price doesn't cover the loans on the property?"

"I don't know." Charlie doubted that George would be able to put much money into the transaction.

"I pulled a copy of the title report. I wanted to see what the buyer was getting at. I sensed .. Well, maybe you should see it." The realtor took a copy of the report from a folder, handed it to Charlie, and stood by expectantly while he skimmed it.

The estate was much encumbered. The realtor expected Four Winds, its age and size working against it, to sell for something "in the neigh-borhood" of three and a half million dollars. The title report indicated that significantly more was owed on the property. At least four million dollars had been loaned by an offshore lender; a quarter-of-a-million-dollar credit line, once unsecured, had been attached by the First Federal Bank of Rhode Island. Lastly, there was a mechanics' lien for fifteen thousand dollars, which had been placed five months ago by plumbers who had done extensive repairs.

"What do you think?" she asked.

What Charlie thought was unprintable. Any prospective buyer for the property, if he got wind of the title report, would react in one of two ways. Either he would presume that the property was hopelessly burdened and walk away, or he would smell the blood and circle. Clearly, the realtor was aware of the jeopardy. Rather than discourage her, Charlie reminded her that the extraordinary property had never been on the market before: she had a unique opportunity. He was glad for the distraction of his own work.

Charlie got home that evening to good news. He'd canvassed numerous summer festivals before finding "Water Music" on the program at Tanglewood, and a friend had come by tickets for a performance on Saturday night.

"You got tickets!?" Julia whooped, on learning of the concert. "Oh, God, that's wonderful. Really!"

"I'm in White Plains on business Friday. I can pick you up early Saturday."

"Great."

"We could spend the night near Tanglewood, but I'd have to find a room or two."

Julia was amused by the offer. "*Find* a room? Or two?" When Charlie was slow to reply, Julia continued, "Are you always this awkward?"

"I hope not."

"What would you normally do?"

"Get a room, see what happened."

"Then do that."

On Saturday, they arrived in Lenox in time for lunch. The grander hotels long since booked, Charlie had reserved a room at a bed-and-breakfast six miles out of town. After buying provisions for a picnic, they spent the afternoon checking out a shop full of old and rare books.

They got to Tanglewood early, the grounds not yet swarmed by concertgoers, the approach of twilight leaving the surrounding woods still, the occasional sound of a musician tuning an instrument escaping the orchestra's shed like birdsong. Julia spread a blanket towards the back of the lawn area that faced the open rear wall of the Kavenitsky Music Shed. Behind them, a finger of water cut between the roll of densely wooded hills; beside them, along the edges of the broad manicured lawn, a set-designer had hoisted square-cut sails, which flapped gently on the stir of a breeze. As darkness fell, as torches were lit to backlight the rugged and ancient sails, as a few long oars were raised and made visible, the set designer's genius became apparent, for here was the illusion of barges, the lot of them made ready for a royal summer night's cruise. Although their tickets entitled them to excellent seats inside the concert hall, Julia wanted to sit outside, to imagine herself on a barge on a river, the guest of a king and his orchestra. Her only regret was that, unlike the premiere, when King George so liked the piece he had commissioned that he had the orchestra play it three times, there would be only one performance of "Water Music" tonight.

Once the music began, the billow of the mock sails created the illusion of a slow drift, with the trills and chirps of wildlife spilling out of the woods like an echo from a Thames riverbank. Enrapt throughout the performance of "Water Music", the crowd cheered wildly at its finish, rowdy as a ballpark crowd.

The night was overcast, the sky low, the air damp. The lively performance of another Handel piece for the English king, "Music for the Royal Fireworks", concluded with actual fireworks, a small arsenal of green and red clusters that burst in the air and traced fluorescence on the embers' descent through the moist air.

"That was incredible," Julia murmured, once they reached his car. "Really incredible."

They drove to the bed-and-breakfast, where a couple of other guests were gathered in the inn's living room. Julia had a glass of brandy, Charlie a glass of port, before they retired to their room, a chamber crowded by its four-poster bed. An antique washbowl was perched precariously on top of a small writing desk, its legs uneven, its wood well-hollowed by worms. An old print hung cockeyed on the wall.

Julia let her eyes sweep the room's cozy charms before opening her overnight bag and sorting through it. She turned, when Charlie touched her, and brought her lips to his, kissing him passionately, then breaking off to turn out the lights. She undressed by starlight, tossed the covers aside, and lay on the bed. He slipped out of his clothes and joined her on the cool, crisp sheets. Anxious for the touch of her, he ran his hands over her shoulders and breasts. Her flesh was soft, her skin hot to the touch, her nipples large and quick to swell. His hand slid down the side of her ribcage and paused on her abdomen, but she lifted her hips to encourage his hand to continue its descent, and so it did, into the press of her thighs. Julia sped things along, spreading her legs and wrapping one around him, eager to have him inside her.

Well aware that he'd lost this woman once before, Charlie would have preferred more control, would have liked some surrender of hers to precede his own, but he was overcome by the heat of her embrace, and wondered exactly the same thing that he had when they'd made love all those years ago: was it possible that the temperature of some women, from their skeleton to their skin, was permanently higher than normal, was such an idea scientifically credible, or was it a boyish notion? Charlie let go of everything, even his curious idea, as her hips swallowed his and his release flooded into her.

Charlie nodded off with her in his arms, but had a hard time sleeping. The heat seeped out of the attic into the close room, and he woke in the middle of the night and opened a window. A quarter moon was visible through lacework clouds. Having put her nightgown on sometime in the night, Julia had kicked the sheet off and lay on her side, one knee drawn to her chest. Charlie stretched out beside her and drifted in and out of sleep, waking at dawn to find Julia staring at him. She extended a hand, brushed it across his cheek, then intertwined her fingers into the close-cropped hair on the back of his head.

"You have to let this grow a little," she whispered, squeezing her fingers to make flat rows of short blond bristles.

"You'll have to clear that with my barber," Charlie replied, pretending to be worried. "He's an ex-Marine."

"He doesn't like long hair?"

"It's not that. He just doesn't believe in confusing a customer with a lot of choices. He thinks the world went to hell the moment men started going to hair salons instead of barber shops."

"Did it?"

"I don't know. I think you're in trouble the moment you start keeping that kind of list: *the-world-went-to-hell-when.* Personally, I don't understand the logic of aerials on skateboards, but you won't hear me complaining that *the-world-went-straight-to-hell-when.* If you complain like that, you'll soon find yourself listening to talk radio and talking back."

Julia smiled and bent over him, lightly kissing his eyebrows. She dragged the sole of her foot along the outside of his calf and kissed him again, this time on the mouth. Charlie stroked the back of her neck, then let his hand drop into the scoop of her neckline, his hand cupping a breast, his thumb lazily circling a nipple.

Julia lifted the nightgown to her waist and sat astride him, slowly exciting herself while exciting him with the rub of her hips. He was patient when she straddled him, the rhythm and tug geared to her pleasure, but her frantic climax encouraged his. Breathless and flushed, Julia laughed when it was over. "Charlie. Charlie! When was the last time you started a day like this?"

"Long time."

"Is it too early for breakfast?"

"It's six."

"Six?" She shook her head incredulously. "Let's go for a walk."

Julia disappeared into the bathroom to take a shower. Her back to the glass door of the stall, she didn't hear Charlie enter the room and hunt for his toothbrush, only to be struck by the sight of her. Her limbs were beautifully proportioned and delineated by small muscles, her breast and buttocks still firm, and she revealed part of her face when she used her fingers to sweep water from her hair. She was lovely.

Julia didn't see him until she turned off the water and spun to open the shower door. Startled, she turned away, then composed herself with a shake of her head and turned back. She yanked a towel off its bar and cloaked herself in it.

"What?" Charlie wondered.

"You were staring."

"Yes."

"There's a story."

17

The road, which ran along a riverbed where a trickle of water coursed through exposed rocks, was overhung with a tangle of branches, a dark arch that would lighten to pale, luminescent green as the sun rose and filtered through the foliage. Julia walked down the shoulder, her sneakers crunching on a thin layer of twigs and rotting leaves, and told Charlie more of the horror that had been her return to Chile. She had been denied the use of any razor for her legs or underarms, on the theory that she might try to cut her wrists with one – or the wrists of the sergeant who became her principal jailor. Any time Julia needed to use a bathroom the sergeant insisted on watching her. If she showered or bathed, the sergeant would stare at her and occasionally unzip his pants, masturbate, and suggest that she join the "fun." Frightened that she would be violated, Julia would remain in the tub or shower until the sergeant finished masturbating. "He just stared and stared," Julia said. "I felt so dirty."

Charlie was doubled over by the story. He had to stop walking, had to put both hands on his knees and fight off the dizzying sensation of having been kidney-punched. His work exposed him to the occasional brutality, but Julia's ordeal struck him as particularly senseless and savage.

"I'm okay," Julia insisted. "It was like a cave-in, like finding yourself buried in a tunnel, but I got out."

"Jesus."

"Let it go."

"I can't. Did anybody find them?"

"It's the first thing Martin did. After he got me out. He went after them. The colonel got away; he had the money. Not the other one. He was still in the service. Martin tried to tell me, he thought it would make me feel better, as if what I cared about was revenge."

"What did Martin do?"

"He had someone else do it. Some ranking officer. The sergeant was taken care of. '*Disappeared*.'" Julia steadied herself with a slow breath. "I didn't want to know what happened; I didn't want anybody else to know. I felt so filthy, so hateful."

The bluntness of the word shocked Charlie. *Hateful*. Nothing in his experience of Julia allowed him to imagine her as hateful. It was something close to what he had felt, at her abandonment of him, but not a state of mind that he could associate with her. The word made him consider the dichotomy that he had to master if he were to continue to see her. Julia was one-part old lover, one-part stranger.

"It's behind me," she said. "It wasn't easy, but I got past it, and that's where I want it left."

Charlie felt the weight of her eyes studying him, to see what had registered. They walked a little longer before returning to the inn for coffee and muffins.

After breakfast, they headed north on Route 7, which wove through the rich Berkshire forests, down the main streets of small hamlets and past the near-suburban sprawl of Pittsfield and Williamstown. By the time it hit the Vermont state line, the road had briefly rejoined the wilderness.

They followed Route 7 a few miles further until Bennington. It was here, four miles west of town, that Julia owned a farm. Whitewashed and green-shuttered, the house sat atop a grassy slope, long uncut, that ran down to the road. More mud than gravel, the driveway bisected two small pastures, one of which was surrounded by white posts and plank rails. A piled-stone fence ran along the road. New copper pipes and sheets of drywall were stacked by the front door, which was secured by a loop of wire.

"You know what they say about the seasons here?" Julia asked, scraping dirt off a heel on a scrap of lumber left on the porch. "The four seasons in Vermont? There's early winter, winter, late winter, and next winter. God, you haven't heard that?"

"I thought there were two seasons. Snow and mud."

"Be careful. I love this place."

The workmen had Sunday off, but their craftsmanship was evident everywhere. Charlie was particularly impressed by Julia's redesign of the house. Two small parlors, their interior walls removed, bordered the center hall and staircase. A powder room was squeezed beneath the stairs. Most of the work had been done at the back of the house where three small rooms were refashioned into a large kitchen, a window-seat disguising a large firewood box, a fireplace refaced with an antique mantel. A back door led through a mudroom to a turnaround for the gravel driveway, now overrun by clumps of clover and thistle.

Near the driveway, partly hidden by a thicket of woodbine and ivy, a pair of storm doors led down to a large cellar, which could also be reached by steep wooden stairs that descended from the back door of a hall closet. Exploring, Charlie found an old cache of coal in a corner of the basement, an ancient shovel sticking out of the pile, the handle long-dried, light and brittle.

On the second floor the windows in the front bedroom looked over the hardwood-studded hills to the Green Mountains. Charlie rejoined Julia there and picked up a rusty hinge, discarded on the floor. "When'll the work be done?"

"By the end of October."

"How often do you hope to come up?"

"A weekend or two a month. And Thanksgiving, Christmas, most of July. Imagine how beautiful it is in the fall."

Julia took Charlie around the sixty acres of her property and showed him a long-abandoned brick kiln that she had found in the woods, a spindly shoot of a sumac growing through the middle of it. "I adore this," she said, using a sneaker to flatten some weeds that engulfed the base of the kiln. "My ruin."

"The world passed this way."

"And moved on," Julia added. She knew that Vermont, with its dwindling population, once played host to twice as many settlers, who had forged hard lives from the rocky soil and the hostile climate. Many of their descendants had ultimately picked up and left for richer fields and gentler climates. Julia craned her neck to survey the stands of beech and birch and pine, the second- and third-growth forests that had reclaimed the farmland. She clearly loved the simple poetry of her land: it had been colonized; it had rebelled.

After lunch at a bakery in town, they browsed through antique stores and came across a two-hundred-year-old music stand, the carved base and delicate scrolls cut from gleaming walnut. Julia spent a while admiring its rich patina and intricate flourishes. Charlie knew that he was overpaying, but wanted it for her, for her farm.

They returned to the farmhouse and put the music stand inside. After locking up, Julia stalled by his car. "Do we have to go back?"

"Well.."

"I'm not ready. Couldn't we stay a couple more days?"

Charlie happily agreed to her proposal. They had no trouble booking a few more nights at the bed-and-breakfast, and checked into the largest suite, its huge iron bathtub set on claw-and-ball feet beneath a corner skylight. Their stay extended through most of the week, and each day the routine was the same. They took a long walk or jogged in the morning, then drove to Bennington to check the progress of the work on Julia's farmhouse. They spent the early afternoon at the inn reading, the late afternoon making love. At dinner they sampled the local restaurants.

On the last day of the trip, they made love in the afternoon heat, the lovemaking turning frenetic at the prospect of a final opportunity. Charlie adored the way Julia abandoned herself, caution gone in favor of a fierce concentration on touch and grip and stroke, restraint melting away in the stifling heat, their bodies slick with perspiration.

Afterwards, once she had collected herself, Julia startled him by laughing. He could imagine the joke, the two of them acting half their age and thankful that the adjacent room was unoccupied, the spirit lusty and libertine, the sex wildly uninhibited and very much the province of younger lovers. Intimate as the moment might have been, Charlie was worried by her laugh. She was, at some level, in control of herself and of the moment; he wasn't sure that he was.

They packed their suitcases with the extra clothes they'd been forced to buy and drove back. Once home, Charlie reclaimed Roxy from his friends next door and checked his answering machine, which he had been doing remotely. He hoped to hear from George, but none of his calls had been returned. However, Lucy had left a recent message, so Charlie called her.

"Jesus, what a week," she groaned, at the sound of Charlie's voice. "I was in Providence Monday. I met some specialist at the University hospital. My father. The cancer's back, it's moved into the bone."

"Oh, God, can I do anything?"

"No. No one can do much, not really. Maybe we got a remission, but it's all run away from the doctors now, they're useless. They can't even control the pain. You weren't there, were you, when your mother went through it? I swear it's awful, the pain can shatter him. Goddamn it." She paused to blow her nose. "Did you know George approached him?"

"Your father?"

"Daddy told me George talked to him. Asked him to become a customer of the bank."

"When?"

"A little while ago, I guess. I don't think Daddy's done anything about it, but I bet he was flattered, getting recruited. Have you heard from George?"

"No."

Charlie kept Lucy on the phone a while longer; he dreaded the second call that he had to return. Before making it, he listened again to the new message left on his machine. The voice was panicky, frightened. "This is Marion Huntley - you know, Joe's wife?" she'd begun. "I can't get hold of George, maybe he's with you, I want him to call. Joe's supposed to be back more than a week ago, I can't imagine, maybe you know something from George. You got the number - if you could call, please. Okay?"

Marion Huntley picked up on the second ring. "I don't get it. Joe's never checked in at his hotel, he never got there. Darn it, it's all wrong, it's all bad, I knew it since he first started talking to George, working with some clients down in the islands. Who are these people?! I know it's all wrong, and I don't know where he is. If you don't know how to help, tell me who can, 'cause George is in the Bahamas, too, isn't he? Please, Christ, tell me who knows how to find them. Where are they?"

18

The next morning, Charlie contacted a friend at the U.S. Department of Justice who promised to bring the State Department in if necessary and to circulate a Missing Person Report to two dozen police forces in the Caribbean. By late Monday several responses had found their way to Charlie's desk. The morgue in Nassau had two unclaimed John Does, both WM, one presumed to be in his twenties, the other elderly. Elsewhere in the islands there were other white male corpses, unidentified, but only a report from the Cayman Islands offered a possibility.

A sport fisherman on Little Cayman, running a few tourists offshore for bonefishing, had pulled alongside a well-decomposed body two days ago. The fisherman had hooked the body, tied it onto his transom, and taken it into port, where it was put on ice in a spare fish locker. Authorities from George Town were scheduled to pick up the corpse today and transport it to the capital. The fisherman's radio transmission had been transcribed into the report forwarded:

"An ankle's all swole up like a melon. His eyes missing, his hair full of filth. He got a watch on: Lugano, it say."

Lucy had given Joe a Lugano watch.

The first plane that Charlie could book left from Boston early the following morning. He arrived on Grand Cayman during a lunch hour squall, the propellers from a departing plane driving horizontal sheets of rain under the umbrellas that the airline provided. By the time

Charlie's taxi dropped him at the Royal Cayman Police headquarters in George Town, the storm had quit, and the sun was steaming the sidewalks dry.

Young, plump, a ridgeline of acne along the bony expanse of his forehead, John F. Kennedy Gagnier was the constable assigned to Charlie. Jovial and chatty, he immediately mentioned that the initial F. in his name didn't stand for anything, except possibly ceremony. His mother boasted of having met the former American President when she worked as a chambermaid at a Jamaican hotel.

On the ride to George Town Hospital, while Gagnier breezed through a short history of local life and legend, Charlie's stomach started to convulse, the cramp rising through his ribs to his throat. Having dealt with plenty of medical evidence in his career, Charlie had assumed that he could get through it, this identification of a corpse, with businesslike dispatch, but he was trembling when Gagnier led him from the police car to the basement of the hospital.

"It's beam to beam, all full up," the constable apologized. "Standin' room only, you'd say. Since the damn boat of Haitians went upside-over." Ahead of them, empty gurneys lined a wall beside a broad door covered with steel plate.

Inside the morgue the air-conditioners rattled their screws loose and dripped puddles of condensation on faded blue linoleum. Charlie had to choke back his nausea. The room stank of formaldehyde and of something else, of something charred, as if flesh had caught fire. Gagnier waved over an orderly.

"Get us the body from Lister Cay," he said.

The orderly hunted down a gurney and wheeled it into the hall, where the light was better. Charlie followed, his hands shaking at the prospect of touching the sheet covering the corpse or the chart tucked under the blackening feet. Gagnier tugged at the sheet and let it slide to the floor. The eyelids had been closed and sagged into hollow sockets, the body's skin was puffy and mottled, and the stomach was grotesquely distended, but it was possible to recognize Joe, who had distinctively long earlobes and a chin that jutted well forward of his narrow-lipped mouth. A watch was on the left wrist, its crystal cracked and clouded; its band dug into swollen flesh. Charlie could see that it was the watch Lucy had given Joe.

Gagnier handed him the coroner's report and read the chart over Charlie's shoulder. The coroner had noted the broken bones and missing fingers but concluded that death was from drowning. "You wonder he's on that Haiti boat?" Gagnier asked. "Like a captain they throw overboard."

Charlie handed back the chart and leaned against a wall. On the ride over, Gagnier had mentioned that an inquiry into the death of this John Doe was unlikely. The island's resources were strained by an investigation into the boat disaster; also, there was a question of jurisdiction since the man had probably drowned in international waters. Gagnier presumed that Gulf currents had "streamed" the body into the Little Cayman bay.

"You know him?" Gagnier had trouble sliding the chart beneath the feet and jammed it under a heel.

"Hard to say." Charlie wanted time to think. George was somewhere in the Caribbean, in trouble himself. Charlie could see no advantage in acknowledging the death of Joe Turlik, whom someone had wanted to dispose of.

About to wheel the gurney back into the morgue, the orderly jerked his head to pull Gagnier aside, who soon rejoined Charlie. "Well, then," Gagnier said, with the hint of embarrassment. "The orderly says he had a visitor this mornin', a grandmum from Haiti, poor thing, pointin' out her two grandboys. Misery enough for many lives, and she got no money to bury 'em. She was here when they brung this one in. Says the water demon got 'em, them missing fingers, says it's the work of the *Macoute*. '*Demons*,' she says. '*Tonton Macoute*.' You ever hear of such a thing?"

"No."

The constable drove to the police station, where he brought over an inspector, an older man with pink skin and a wrinkled gray suit. "Poor excuse for a visit," the inspector said, extending a plump hand to Charlie. "You weren't able to identify our fellow?"

"No. Maybe someone else can fly down at some point. Is there a deadline? For the ID?"

"How long do we hold bodies? That's your question? For quite some time, I suppose, if it's a suspected homicide. But this business about the Tonton Macoute eludes me."

"Why?"

The inspector frowned and said that the old lady probably had it wrong, since the Tonton Macoute hadn't been active, to his knowledge, in almost two decades. These much-feared Haitian secret police had done their hellish work under the cover of night; their midnight brutalities - kidnapping, torture, rape, murder - were often ascribed to voodoo demons. The elite officers of the secret corps helped several families retain power in Haiti, most notably the Duvaliers. The inspector mentioned that he had once been asked to investigate the drowning deaths of two popular opponents of the then current regime. Both men had disappeared from their homes in the middle of the night; both bodies turned up offshore. One of the men had been mauled by a shark; along with a sizable chunk of flesh ripped from the hip and a gash torn in a leg, several neatly severed fingers were missing from one hand. A shark could have torn a hand off, but no one believed that a shark was capable of the surgical precision required to detach three fingers below the knuckles. The other body turned up days later; that corpse was missing two fingers.

"There were other trademark tortures," the inspector said. "But I suppose this was as awful as any, have your fingers cut off, then put overboard. Bleeding shark bait. I saw Papa Doc once, gambling in Nassau, surrounded by his entourage, the lot of them acting like soiled royalty. You knew which ones were his police; they were the ones who didn't gamble."

Charlie thanked both officers and walked two blocks to a car rental agency. He had phoned the local hotels on route to the island. Three days ago, George Spaulding had failed to arrive at the Grand Hyatt; his pre-paid room was still being held. Charlie drove out to the hotel, where the lobby was empty, beset by an offseason hush.

Charlie used a house phone to call the front desk and asked if there were any messages or mail for George Spaulding. "Yes, sir," the clerk responded. "Will you be checking in?"

"In a few minutes."

Charlie tried his luck. The clerk at the reception desk asked if Mr. Spaulding intended to leave the room charges on the credit card that the hotel had on file. He did. Charlie registered by forging a signature and claimed the mail and room key. He found his way to George's room, where he turned down the covers and rustled the sheets. Charlie didn't have a plan, but he wanted to create a decoy, to delay whatever was unfolding in the hopes that he could find George before the people who killed Joe did.

One of George's letters came from an address in Panama and contained an invoice, written in Spanish; a second letter was a typed notice about a dinner being postponed: time and date were listed, not place or people. A four-day-old fax from George's secretary at the bank had been folded into an envelope by a hotel employee: it relayed several phone messages. The last piece of mail was a large manila envelope with no return address. Charlie didn't recognize the stamps, which were denominated in dollars, or the postmark, which was smudged. Inside this envelope were copies of five bank account statements, all established at a George Town bank and held in a variety of names:

Metallica Minserra, Ltd.
JayDee Trust
Island Principal Management Trust
Global Panamanian Finance
Rumson Cay Development, Inc., SA

Charlie consulted the map provided by the rental agency as he drove to the address listed on the bank statements for Cayman International Maritime Bank. When he got there, he couldn't find the bank; instead, there was a small cottage, with a manicurist's shop occupying most of its floor space. Charlie circled the block twice before finally approaching the cottage, where a side door admitted him to a tiny room filled with mailboxes. The bank, if that's what it was, was a mail drop.

19

Charlie tried to picture Marion Huntley, whom he remembered as having the demeanor of the once cheated, a mouth that hung open with the expectation of disappointment. He'd seen her laugh, but rarely when she was in Joe's immediate company. She must, Charlie supposed, blame Joe for something; there'd be no chance to settle it now.

Haunted by the desperation in her voice, Charlie had decided to break the news to her in person and had booked a flight to Chicago with a connection to Dayton, Ohio. It was early Wednesday morning, not yet three full days since they had spoken, when he pulled up outside a house on Willow Lane. Joe and Marion's house.

While parking in the shade of a curbside tree, Charlie felt a rush of guilt; he'd never visited. He sat in his car, sapped by fatigue and unable to gather himself, until Marion Huntley walked out a side door of her house and got into a sedan parked in the driveway. Charlie scrambled out of the rental car and hurried up the driveway. She had only backed a few feet before her car jerked to a stop: Marion studied him in her rearview mirror for several long moments before letting her head slump to the steering wheel. She was crying when she got out.

"Charlie? For God's sake, ... Charlie?" She held up a hand to stay his approach, to give him a chance to bear any other news than what she feared, the fury slowly crawling across her face. "Goddamnit," she bawled.

"I'm sorry."

"Goddamn him. Goddamn all of you!" Weeping, she climbed the steps to the side door and had trouble with the key, which Charlie took. He unlocked the door and escorted her into the kitchen, where he stood helpless, while she sobbed into her hands. Finally, the sobs subsiding, she paced the room until she turned on him, an accusation resonant in her tone.

"Charlie, where did you find him?"

"Grand Cayman. He drowned."

"What was he doing?! Do you have any goddamn idea?"

"No."

"Three years ago, George calls, and Joe just goes leaping off, says he gonna help manage a few offshore businesses, says these businesses need an American on the board. Or a trustee. Goddamnit, you tell me, Charlie. You know Joe. Do you think he's a trustee?"

"I don't know."

"If you had a trust, would you have him be your trustee? You're damn right you wouldn't. Goddamnit, tell me what he's doing."

"When'd you talk to him last?"

"Three weeks." Marion started to cry again. "Three weeks, he said he'd be a week or ten days. Where is he, did you see him?"

Charlie explained that the body was in the Grand Cayman morgue. The next of kin would have to sign paperwork authorizing release and transportation, but Charlie hoped, if it were okay with Marion, to leave the body unclaimed a while longer. There might be a better opportunity to find out what happened if Joe's disappearance were unacknowledged, a better chance of finding George.

"I won't do it for George," Marion said. "But Joe can stay there, goddamn him, always so anxious to please. I told him I didn't care if he worked at a preschool. I earn enough. But not Joe, he was always so goddamn worried about measuring up to you guys."

Stung by the remark, Charlie stared at her. "Why?"

"Because he worshipped you. You and George, all your old money and goddamn family portraits. George, who bailed him out, with Joe acting like a damn leper, grateful for any job. He was jumping at anything, ready to march anywhere, after his business failed."

Charlie sadly remembered the story of Joe waiting for hours in a bus station's squalid bathroom with his head encased in a grocery bag, the only pledge who had obeyed such silly commands. Marion was right. Joe was the perfect foot soldier, too trusting and too insecure to question his orders. He wouldn't have gotten into trouble for failing to follow an order; more likely, it was an order that he had followed or a client he could identify that had gotten him killed. Charlie fumbled for a pocket notebook, while Marion paced the floor and filled him in on Joe's previous professional difficulties.

Seven years ago, with money from a severance package, Joe had bought the Mid-Atlantic franchise of a now defunct distributor of office supplies. Besides investing everything he owned, he signed personal guarantees to borrow more money, all of which he eventually lost. When Marion married him, aware of his looming bankruptcy, she insisted on maintaining separate accounts. The house remained her separate property, a precaution that proved wise when Joe was forced to file.

"Even his old pension money, from before, it got sucked in. He still owes taxes, that's the way it's going to end, I guess, him still on the hook for taxes. I never did a joint tax return, I guess that looks smart now, right?" Marion used her sleeve to brush away tears.

"His new job?"

"Christ. What'd he tell you?"

"That it was mostly 'client contact.' Whatever that means."

"George knew some investors or something. Joe worked for them."

"You meet any of these clients?"

"No."

"Did you see his payroll checks?"

"He didn't get them. He was paid fees. No withholding. Everything by wire. He's got an office here."

Marion led Charlie to the basement, where an office had been fashioned in a corner of the unfinished space. There were lamps, a desk and two chairs, file cabinets, a phone, a shredder, and a combination answering-machine-fax. The desk contained a safe, hidden behind a side panel, which Marion removed. "I don't know why he needed to lock these up," she said, opening the safe and pulling out a stack of papers. "They're just forms."

Marion handed him the stack of blank wire-transfer authorizations. "Sometimes money needed to be wired between accounts," she continued. "Ten, twenty thousand, or a helluva lot more. He could do that from here, by fax."

"To where? Where'd the money go?"

"I guess to other bank accounts. I had to send some for him."

"Why?"

"Remember last summer? Your whole gang was off playing golf in New Jersey. Joe called up in a panic, clients needing transfers, so I faxed them for him. I forged his signatures. I got good at that in the bankruptcy proceedings. There was stuff he couldn't look at, let alone sign."

"Is there a list? Of the accounts he worked on?"

"If there is, he kept it with him."

"Did he keep copies? Of the wires he sent?"

"Everything wound up there." Marion pointed at the shredder. "But I kept copies. Of the ones I sent."

She and Charlie returned to the kitchen, where she found what she was looking for in an over-stuffed drawer, a paper-clipped pile of eight copies. Seven of the money transfers were outgoing, sent from First Federal Bank of Rhode Island to banks in New York City, Boston, and California. The last transfer directed that money be wired from an account at Cayman International Maritime Bank, in the name of Rumson Cay Development, to another account in the same name, this one at First Federal Bank of Rhode Island.

In George Town Charlie had seen a bank statement for Rumson Cay Development. "Anything else?" he asked.

"No. I've been looking everywhere. There's not even a file in the computer, I opened 'em all. But I figure if Joe could sign those," Marion pointed to the wire authorizations, "he must be signatory, right? On the accounts? Joe could send money anywhere."

"Did he?"

"He wouldn't steal. Is that your question?"

"No. But he can move money around. Something he did, something he knows. There has to be a reason."

"Why him? It's not fair." Her shoulders shook as she wept again.

When she had stopped, Charlie explained the problems with jurisdiction. Joe had arrived on Grand Cayman and may have visited other islands. He was thought to have drowned in international waters, a circumstance that complicated any chance of a prompt investigation. If they acknowledged his death, Joe would be swept aside, which was where someone wanted him. Marion agreed to go along with Charlie's plan. They'd leave Joe in the Grand Cayman morgue until they discovered more about his recent doings; by proceeding as if Joe were alive, there might be a chance to find out who knew that he was dead and who was therefore likely involved in the murder. Only the stepchildren and a couple of Joe's closest friends would be told the truth.

"My boys were stand-off-ish when we first got married." Marion looked at the refrigerator, where magnets pinned a few photos of her sons. "But they were getting closer. Joe wanted that."

She comforted herself by making lists: clothes she'd give away, authorities she'd eventually have to notify. She was preoccupied with details when Charlie left.

He quickly telephoned Quad, who was stunned into a long silence. "Somebody beat him up," Charlie said. "Threw him off a boat."

"Goddamnit.."

"What was his job? You heard his spiel. As far as I know, all he was doing was signing checks or wiring money."

"It's one thing to deal with corporate customers," Quad replied. "It's another to sign their checks. Joe may be an officer. Think about it. After his bankruptcy, Joe's judgment-proof. I used to have a cousin who'd be the front-man. A law firm would use him. He'd be the sole officer and director for these little start-ups, companies formed to shepherd some little project along, so if the companies got sued or fell behind on payroll deposits, the creditors or the government wouldn't have much recourse. My cousin was the dummy in the window. Penniless. Of course, he'd sign a lot of side-letters that were kept private. He spent six years trying to get a teaching credential, couldn't hack it, and suddenly he had seats on more corporate boards than Warren Buffett."

"The foot soldier in a general's uniform."

"What's George up to? Did you know he knew Martin Hoffman?"

"No. When I asked why he hadn't told me, he said Martin had steered a lot of business to George's bank and insisted on a low profile. George said he never asked about Julia because he had never forgiven her for 'abandoning' me."

"Does Lucy know about Joe?"

"I haven't told her yet."

"You better."

Lucy's reaction - she moaned wretchedly into the phone - was even stronger than Charlie had anticipated. "Not now, don't tell me this!"

He heard a rattle and bang, the cord pulling the phone off its perch and onto the floor, then the light *thunk* of the phone being replaced. "God, the phone's walking off the counter," she resumed. "Joe would get this, he'd know how you wake up one morning and the phone has become your goddamn enemy. Lately, the phone rings, it's my father's oncologist, it's Jennifer calling to tell me she's doing something, staying on the line just to argue even after I've conceded. Joe would understand. He doesn't know how to be glib; he hates the fucking phone. Remember that telemarketing campaign he tried? Joe of all people. Christ, Charlie, how?"

"I'm not sure."

"What about the funeral?"

"Not yet." Charlie told her that Joe's death was to remain a secret for a while.

"I feel sick. God, what's George say about all this?"

"I don't know where he is. He's in trouble, too."

"You have to find him."

"I'm looking."

"God, Charlie. God Almighty, tell me what I can do. But find him."

Charlie got off the plane at Logan by 3:30, hoping to beat the weekday traffic out of Boston, but work on the expressway brought everything to a standstill. He didn't get to Newport until after six.

Since George's bank was closed, Charlie drove to Four Winds. The driveway was strewn with leaves and small branches, blown down by a storm that passed through a day earlier, the tail end of a Caribbean hurricane unfurling in a New England downpour.

Charlie let himself in and made a cursory tour of the mansion. He half-expected to find George in the den, in full retreat from whatever was bearing down on him, the stereo pumping out a ninety-decibel barrier, yet the room was quiet. A stack of George's newspapers, *Boston Globes* and *New York Times*, lay next to a coffee table littered with empty Diet Pepsi cans. Charlie checked the office off the front hall. Empty, the drawers in the large desk were open, the desk seeming to tilt with the weight of its yawning drawers, the whole room thrown out of kilter. On the desktop was a phone with a built-in answering machine; Charlie had left half a dozen messages in the last few weeks. Hitting the replay button, searching for some trace of any message, he found none.

Two richly upholstered Queen Anne chairs bracketed a window, which overlooked the driveway. He took a seat in one of them. Outside, with the light failing, the shadows enveloped unkempt gardens as the grounds surrendered to the sounds of the night. Charlie knew that George, somehow connected to Joe's trouble, would try to get word to him. George would, at some point, try to make his way here, to Four Winds.

Charlie must have drifted off to sleep, for he found himself startled by the sound of the doorbell, the house dark, his neck cricking from its jerk to attention. On his way to the front door, he noticed a walking stick in an umbrella stand, the knob a heavy silver-plated hound's head. It was, if needed, the only weapon within reach.

As he unlatched the lock, Charlie caught a glimpse of women's shoes through a leaded glass window beside the door frame. Julia was standing on the step, clearly relieved when she saw him open the door.

"I didn't know where you were. I called Lucy. She said you'd come here." Julia stepped inside. "She said there might be trouble."

Her eyes, searching his, asked the question, which he was too exhausted to answer. He was pleased, if confused, by her company.

He didn't quite understand why she had rushed to find him here; he didn't know what she knew or ought to know. He had no idea what jeopardy, if any, they themselves were in. "What is it?", she insisted.

20

They spent the night rummaging through the house, searching for some trace of George and his trouble. In the wainscoting that ringed the dining room, a secret panel opened to a shallow vault where the Georgian silver used to be hidden during the winter months when the house was unoccupied. Except for a few chipped and cracked vases of no particular value, the vault was empty; nothing, either there or elsewhere, provided a hint of George's whereabouts or doings.

Around three a.m., Julia stretched out on a couch in the den and fell asleep. Charlie curled up on the floor beside her and caught a few hours of sleep, though he was awake by sunrise. He was at the First Federal Bank of Rhode Island when it opened. A woman stationed outside George's office, unfamiliar to Charlie, acted surprised when he approached and asked for George.

"He's not here."

"We've got a meeting."

"Not on the calendar." She pointed to a large, loose-leaf calendar on which the day was crossed out.

"Where's Beth? His secretary?"

"Well, I guess if she was here, I wouldn't be temping for her, would I?" The woman treated him to a smile of punishing insincerity.

"Is she sick?"

"Don't know."

Charlie nodded down the hall to the bank president's office. "Is he in?"

"His secretary isn't here yet." She glared apprehensively at all the buttons on her phone. "Uhh, you want me to buzz him?"

"Not necessary."

Charlie had forgotten the president's name, but a plaque on the door listed it: Anderson Wells. Well-mannered and avuncular, he greeted Charlie warmly. "You're George's friend. You were at his party last winter? Lots of fun."

"Right." Charlie shook Wells' hand, then gave him a business card on which the insignia of the State Attorney General was prominent.

"What can I do for you?"

"I thought I'd find George."

"He's on vacation, isn't he?"

"He told me he was on bank business."

"Not to my knowledge. Not in the Bahamas, isn't that where he's off to? If we had business there, I'd take care of it myself, preferably in the winter."

"I have some questions."

"Maybe I can help."

"I'd like a list of all the bank's accounts."

"Really?" Wells winked. "So would the competition."

Charlie tried a bluff. "This is what I discussed with George."

"We don't keep simple lists, per se, except as part of broader data, profitability reports, things like that."

"There must be ownership forms for each account, signature cards."

"I'm sure there are. And there are significant consequences for releasing that information, but if you help me a little, tell me what you're looking for..?"

"I'd like to see activity reports, transactions for some of the accounts, like Rumson Cay Development."

Wells cocked an ear; he looked genuinely stumped. "Who?"

"Rumson Cay Development."

"They have an account?"

"Yes."

"No kidding? I'll take your word for it. I'm fairly new here myself. George has his bailiwick. I tend not to pay attention unless somebody wants a loan. Are they one of George's clients?"

Charlie shrugged; he didn't want to let on how little he knew. "I've been talking to George," he said. "About certain loans."

"So have I." Wells' face reddened. "But George - I don't know what you know, but you're a close friend, aren't you? George's personal affairs – it's not my place to discuss them, yet I think we all sense some difficulty."

"Really?"

"Well, it's not my business."

"He talked about it with you?"

"Not with any candor."

"I talked to George yesterday." Charlie watched for the slightest flinch, the smallest gesture of surprise; there was none. Instead, falling back upon his unfailing courtesy, Wells offered Charlie coffee and promised to grant what favors were within his reach.

Unwilling to leave town empty-handed, Charlie drove by the club at Bailey's Beach, then by the Newport Country Club. George sometimes left papers at both places. Long familiar with Charlie, attendants at the clubs opened George's cabana and lockers. The cabana was empty save for some well-worn plastic glasses and lawn chairs, whereas the locker at the country club was overstuffed, two pairs of golf shoes crowding the floor, clothes spilling off hooks, two visors and a box of golf balls anchoring a sheaf of papers on the top shelf. Beneath an incomplete application for a personal loan, Charlie found George's recently expired passport.

The heavily stamped passport revealed a plethora of trips that George had never mentioned to Charlie. Along with numerous stamps from Caribbean republics and Crown colonies, there were stamps from Singapore and Indonesia, from Panama and half a dozen other Central and South American countries. The stamps provided an itinerary, however sketchy, of George's life over the last ten years. Charlie was shocked by the number of overseas trips.

He pocketed the passport and drove to his office, where he asked one of the younger attorneys, a woman fluent in Spanish, to translate the bill from the Panamanian law firm. Sent to N. B. Trust c/o a Cayman Islands address, the bill totaled over five-thousand-dollars; the main charges specified were for "research corporate name & file incorporation documents," "draft & review articles of incorporation," "process articles, S.A.," "conduct inaugural meeting w/ appropriate records," "Directors' fees, as agreed," and "miscellaneous expenses." Missing from the invoice was the name of the new corporation for which these services had been performed, though the name of the law firm, Del Rosario & Gutierrez, and its address were prominent.

Charlie didn't collect Roxy from the neighbor's until twilight. The dog rushed forward at the sight of him, leaping on his shins and muddying his trousers, then picking up a flattened soda can and racing around the yard, making mock offers of the can and cantering away, taunting him with a toy that she had no intention of sharing. The dog's adaptability amazed Charlie; for her part, Roxy didn't let him out of her sight, sleeping on his bed, assuming a watch on the back porch Friday morning when he headed off to the criminal courts building.

When he got home that evening, Charlie flipped his computer on and logged onto the Internet, looking for information on some of the places that George's passport indicated he'd visited. A recent article on The Bahamas, from the travel section of a Sunday supplement, was by a writer who didn't think much of recent developments:

> "The day-trippers from cruise boats, disembarking by the hour, and the conventioneers, rushing off to try their luck at the slots, have robbed the islands of their tropical mystery, of their status as a warm-weather hideaway for British aristocrats on the lam from social scandal and Canadian oil men fleeing the tax man..."

Another article, published a few months earlier in a business magazine, discussed the Cayman Islands:

".. a British dependency with Swiss-like bank secrecy laws, very much the Jersey/Channel Islands of the Americas. The banks provide a full array of sophisticated services, from trust management to currency straddles and implementation of offshore tax schemes. Grand Cayman attracts a great deal of business and functions as the clearing house of the Caribbean..."

George had been forwarded legal bills from Panama; one report seemed to typify the several that Charlie read:

"The return of the Canal to Panama, by year end 1999, generates undue optimism and undue suspicion. The widely rumored Japanese intercession is improbable... Noreiga remains in prison, but his cabal of thieves is active, many of them in the drug trade, Panama something of a warehouse alongside a worldwide distribution network. The legitimate economy is expanding..."

Unable to find much recent information on Haiti or anything about the Tonton Macoute, Charlie posted a few questions in a travel forum. He was interrupted when Jennifer used a hidden key to let herself into the house. With her boyfriend at a summer session at Brown, she'd been allowed to spend the weekend in Providence on the condition that she report to Charlie's house no later than two a.m. each night.

"Hey!" Jennifer dropped her suitcase and hugged Charlie hello in the front hall. "Mom says I have to tell you that you're my *'approved housing.'*" She raised an eyebrow expectantly. "So? There's a story or something?"

"Your mother didn't explain 'approved housing?'"

"She gets depressed when she talks about ancient history and her role in it. I figured I'd ask you."

"A very, very long time ago," Charlie began, "our first year in college, visiting women had to stay in 'approved housing.' Elderly women in Charlottesville would rent extra bedrooms to college girls of *good charactah an' upbringin'*."

"Bad Southern accent."

"Curfew was midnight. These ladies would lock up their houses, have one last Mason jar of sherry, and toddle off to bed. One time, when your mother was late, your father and I had to boost her through a side window."

Jennifer smiled mischievously. "Are you going to leave a side window open for me?"

"You've got a key. Don't take advantage, okay?"

He took her suitcase upstairs. When her date picked her up, Jennifer answered the door and handled the introductions. Her date made the kind of remarks to Charlie that hinted at coaching: was it true that Charlie was a prosecutor, what did he think were the "ascendant" law schools, was Charlie too disenchanted with the "tawdriness of elective politics" to consider running for Attorney General himself? The guy made every effort to show himself not to be the self-involved, conceited jerk that Jennifer's accounts of him had made him appear.

Julia arrived for the weekend as Jennifer left for the evening, and glanced in the den, where a screen-saving pattern was flickering across the monitor. "Your computer's on," she told Charlie.

He joined Julia, who walked to the keyboard and tapped the space bar; the screen reverted to a map of the Western Hemisphere, the background graphic of the Internet's *search* engine. "Going somewhere?"

"Have you spent much time in the Caribbean? Or Central America?"

"Not really. A trip to Jamaica. And a convention some years ago in Haiti." She shuddered at the memory. "The poverty was overwhelming."

Charlie decided not to burden her with the details of his own trip to Haiti, but had no trouble recalling them. In the late-Seventies, a girlfriend had booked a trip with him to an exotic resort on the outskirts of Port-au-Prince. Bored at the hotel, Charlie had gone sightseeing, only to be set upon by a horde of juvenile beggars. To elude the children, he had tossed money onto the sidewalk and hurried through several alleys to a different street, only to encounter another child. This waif couldn't have been eight years old, but at the sight of the tourist he wiggled his finger, stepped into a collapsing doorway, and clapped his hands. A tall girl appeared, her hair clumped in tight little knots, her white party dress badly stained. The boy grabbed the teenager's arm, spun her around in the doorway, and bent her over while pulling up her dress. She was naked beneath the garment. Her legs were rail thin, her backside a couple of bones. The boy pumped his hips, in case there were any question about what was being offered; the girl held her position without protest. Revolted, Charlie returned to the resort, there to be scolded by his companion for leaving the hotel's plush grounds. He had entirely forgotten the woman; it was the tableau in the doorway that he remembered, one malnourished child selling another. A boy pimping his sister. Haiti. Unspeakable deprivation.

"Charlie?" Julia said, breaking his reverie, then looking at the map of the hemisphere. "What are you looking for?"

His eyes met hers, but he couldn't answer. He couldn't shake the image of the girl in the doorway, he couldn't fit George into any scheme that trespassed on the well-frayed fringes of the Third World, and he wasn't prepared to involve Julia in something which he had no real grasp of. He hadn't yet told her about Joe Turlik.

"I brought food," she said, a bit stiffly. She left the room, heading for the kitchen.

Besides dinner, Julia had brought a bottle of wine and a CD of several Handel symphonies. The music was pure distraction for Charlie, who was exhausted by his tumultuous week. He and Julia listened to the CD twice and went to bed early. Her nightgown bunching around her waist, Julia slept with one leg saddled over one of his, her face turned to him. The familiarity of her light embrace, the fact that she could sleep while touching him, charmed Charlie, who was more accustomed to women who sought their own side of a bed. Julia's head slid sideways and found its way to the corner of his pillow.

Charlie woke at 5:30, slipped downstairs, and turned his computer on. Someone had responded to his query, a writer in Omaha who identified himself as a Marine:

"You asked about Haiti and the Tonton Macoute. I only heard of them once, right before my tour ended, when a police officer in Arcahaie got arrested and needed protection from the townspeople who'd have torn him to pieces if our "peace-keeping" troops hadn't taken him to a federal jail. The people said that about him. It scared them. Tonton Macoute. The craziest thing about Haiti is the police. They're all rotten. In Cite Soleil, the cops won't leave their station at night. Not even for a car accident. They won't go out, they won't answer the phone, and the only time they patrol is if they got Marines with them. A lot of the Caribbean guidebooks don't even describe the country anymore, our own Sec. of Transportation lists their only real airport as unsafe. God help those people when the Marines leave. You wonder where the money is hiding because the country is too poor to believe. 20% employment (not <u>un</u>employment!!), the gutters are the sewers, the kids have stick arms and swollen bellies. My belief is Haiti should hand itself over to the Marines, no one else can possibly run it. The Marines built most of the roads for the island, sixty years ago, which have been let ruin. Maybe we could do it again.

"If you visit the place, and I sure as heck wouldn't, you ought to carry your own blood. Hope this helps."

Why had George gone to Haiti? His passport documented two trips taken within the last seven years.

At the sound of Julia's voice, Charlie turned off his computer and started towards the kitchen but stopped when he heard Jennifer sullenly make her point. "Mike's always got a reason ready."

"Like what?" Charlie caught a glimpse of Julia setting a coffee mug on the breakfast table while looking to Jennifer for a reply.

"Like *I'm* not ready for the relationship *he* imagines. It's such a convenient excuse. But I see him the way he could be. I see the potential."

"You're not buying stocks. I wouldn't invest for potential."

"I don't know what I should expect." Jennifer pouted. "He says I'm chasing romance at the expense of passion."

"Are you?"

"Should I?"

"Hard question."

"He says he wants *passion*, it's like he puts the word in italics."

Julia looked doubtful. "I think you're in trouble the moment he starts distinguishing between romance and passion. Which isn't to say there might not be a distinction. But you're way too young for your relationship to founder on it."

Jennifer pulled at her hair before asking, "Do you think it's real, him and me? Or are you one of those adults who's gonna tell me it's only infatuation? I mean, what do you feel? When you're in love? What was it like when you first met Charlie?"

Julia's smile was tentative. "I guess it was a runaway train, that's the only way to describe it. I don't mean 'a train wreck'." Julia considered her choice of words. "I mean unstoppable, effortless, thrilling."

Jennifer snorted her approval. "Swept off your goddamn feet! Way to go, Charlie." Enchanted, catching a glimpse of Charlie, stuck outside the doorway by his own reluctance to interfere, Jennifer asked, in a voice loud enough for him to hear, "Did you ever love anybody else like that? Like Charlie?"

21

Charlie? Don't stand out there and eavesdrop." Jennifer signaled him to come into the kitchen, which he did. "I was being nosy. I asked if she ever loved anybody the way she did you."

"I heard. She doesn't have to answer."

Jennifer faced Julia. "I want her to. What's the answer?"

"Not exactly."

"What the heck does that mean?"

"It means I was really screwed-up when I got back to this country. Weak. A wreck. Charlie knows the story. I lived in Miami for well over a year and saw a therapist pretty much daily. I knew he began to love me and would act on it if I saw another therapist, but he was my crutch. We became so co-dependent. It felt completely necessary to me, but it wasn't love. It was sad, really. One day I decided I didn't want to be dependent on anybody. Not my therapist, not my brother and his money and him trying to take charge of me. I wanted to be independent. So I worked. Hard. I sell office furniture to big companies and firms. There are twenty-five other people in the regional office I run."

"Do you make a lot of money? Six figures?"

"Jennifer! Jesus!" Charlie scolded.

Julie laughed. "Most years my bonus hits six figures."

"God! Can I work for you when I get out of college?"

"I won't still be doing it. There's been so much travel, which is okay, but it gets in the way of anything else. I have a year left on my contract. I'm thinking of becoming a teacher."

"That's a change."

"Work at something you enjoy," Julia said. "And find someone to race home to."

"That's what I need. Someone to race home to. Lose this guy. Right, Charlie?"

Charlie poured himself a cup of coffee. "I'm staying out of it."

"But that's what you think. Put him on a bus. Dump City."

"I'm staying out of it," Charlie repeated.

"Is it fun?" Julia asked. "When you're with him?"

"Not really. He's got a way of being upset half the time, so you're always trying to figure out what you did wrong. It's not a 'runaway train', it's a trial."

Julia squeezed her hand. "You can do better."

"Yeah, maybe," Jennifer deferred. "But not today."

As Jennifer left the kitchen, Julia's eyes trailed her a while before she picked up her cup of coffee and took a sip. "Charlie, you should've had a child. You'd be a lovely father."

"I think I would be," he admitted. "It's one of my few conceits that've survived."

She put a hand on his waist and slowly finished her coffee. After she had departed for a meeting and Jennifer had gone off on her date, Charlie called the Newport Police Department to request extra surveillance of Four Winds in the weeks ahead. Next, Charlie tried phoning George's ex-wife, Lisa Calvert, who lived in Boca Raton. He hoped that George might have checked in with her, his second wife and the mother of their nine-year-old son, but the message on her answering machine was unchanged from the one Charlie had heard when he'd tried to reach her six days earlier. She was probably traveling on business; most likely, she had her boy with her. Her inclination to take the boy along on business trips, even during the school year, infuriated George.

Charlie got Ray McClean on the line and discussed the possibility of using Interpol to track George down. "The thing is," the detective cautioned, "the best way to do it would be to charge your buddy with something, so maybe he lands in jail until you get him out. But some of the shithole jails down there - and the corrupt cops - I don't know he's safe. You ever tried to get a stolen car back from Mexico? From their police? I got a friend, his Jeep's found four days after it's lifted, a checkpoint just over the border, only the chief of police down there winds up hanging onto it. Drives the frigging Jeep like a company car. It took the goddamn insurance company three months before they'd agree to write the damn thing off. So I'd be real careful what I set in motion."

Charlie had locked up his house and was waiting outside when Lucy stopped by on the way to visit her seriously ill father. Curious about what Mr. Daniels might know of George's bank, Charlie had offered to accompany her.

"I'm glad you're coming," Lucy said, once they were on the road to Connecticut. "I dreaded going by myself. Plus he'll be happy to see you, if he's lucid. The drugs they've got him on..?"

At Lucy's urging, her widowed father had sold his house in Atlanta and moved to New England to be close to Lucy and her sister and their children. Shortly after he'd arrived, he was diagnosed with a fast-spreading cancer.

"God, I made him move up here. Then this. I need some good news, Charlie, something to cheer him up. Or me."

"I think Jennifer's going to break up with that guy at Brown."

"Really?"

"Julia pretty much suggested it."

"Julia?"

"She and Jennifer were talking this morning."

"It'd be such a lift if Jenny dropped him. I wouldn't have to worry about her getting hurt. Besides, that boy is such a throwback. Prima facie evidence that all men are pond scum. Except you and George."

"Exception noted."

"Is there any word?"

"No."

"What is it, Charlie? What's George gotten himself into?"

"I don't know. He's in default on his mortgage. And he introduced Joe to something, somebody, offshore. Which is where George went - offshore. Plus, he's got problems at the bank."

"Have you talked to Julia's brother?"

"Why?"

"Martin and George are pretty thick."

"Martin's firm may do some work for the bank."

"Martin doesn't work for George, not the way George treats him - half deferential, half joking. It's not like George to be deferential. It's more likely the other way around. Martin in charge."

"Did you talk to Martin?"

"Not about any of this. Can't you ask Julia?"

"I guess." The prospect of questioning Julia about her brother unsettled him.

Lucy picked up her purse. "I need a favor," she said. "You have to forget you work in law enforcement."

"Just don't confess to a multiple murder."

"Look what I got." Lucy reached into her purse and extracted a small plastic bag filled with two tightly wrapped joints and a tiny pile of greenish-brown buds. The scent of the marijuana, unpleasantly herbaceous, seeped out of the bag. "I'd forgotten what the crap smells like," Lucy said, cracking her window open. "It smells like a stable weed. I got it from the woman in the office next to mine. She's got a brother with AIDS, who takes it medicinally, if not legally."

"Your father knows you're bringing it?"

"No. I don't know if he'll try it or if it'll cut the pain."

Charlie had a hard time imagining Holton Daniels, a very thoughtful and dignified gentleman, smoking marijuana. "Does your father have the right kind of music?" Charlie asked. "In case he gets really stoned? *Ten Years After*? *Led Zeppelin*? Some *Deadhead* stuff?"

"Very funny. See, that's why I had to bring you. You won't let it get too weird; you won't let me get too depressed. I wish we had George with us. He'd help break the ice, you know how irreverent he can be, the guy who farts in chapel when it's all getting a little too Pentecostal."

Lucy and Charlie reached her father's house by noon and went straight to a room on the ground floor, which had been set up as a sick room. The rented hospital bed backed up against a built-in bookcase lined with leather-bound volumes, the gold-leaf lettering of their spines making an odd backdrop for the skeletal forms of IV racks. Lucy tiptoed to her sleeping father and kissed his forehead, which glistened, dew-like, with perspiration.

Charlie was struck by how the man had withered; his arm, draped over the bedcovers, was pale and thin and much bruised by the recurrent punctures of IV needles. As if obliging his guests, Holton Daniels soon stirred and blinked his way to a smile at the sight of his daughter, suddenly hovering. He tried to sit up, grimaced at the pure agony of movement, and managed to position his back upright against a bank of pillows that Lucy plumped for him.

"Did it rain?" Mr. Daniels asked. Staggered in their drift across the Connecticut hills, clouds had begun to gather and now darkened the mid-day sky.

"Not yet," Lucy said.

Mr. Daniels flapped a hand to wave hello to Charlie, who gestured back.

"You need anything?" Lucy asked. "A drink, some lunch?"

Mr. Daniels shook his head.

"Daddy, let me ask you something. Didn't you say George talked to you? About his bank? What was that? A sales pitch?"

"He knew I sold my company."

"Were you interested?" It was the first time that Charlie had joined the conversation. "In his bank?"

"His bank?" Mr. Daniels grinned. "Out of my league. They have special interest rates for personal checking accounts with over a million dollars. Whoever heard of such a fool thing, leaving that kind of money in a demand deposit?"

"Major league shopper," Lucy supposed.

"Nouveau show-off," Mr. Daniels concluded. "George said the bank's trust department uses a New York outfit to manage the investments."

"Did he mention the name?" Charlie asked. "The company in New York?"

"I don't think so. But they'll do everything for you, pay your bills, whatever you need. I'm not that spoiled or rich. I can manage my own money. Government'll take a bunch of it anyway. Not long now."

"Daddy," Lucy objected. "I don't care."

"I do, but there'll still be plenty left for you. And your sister." He closed his eyes and rested a moment. "I said I'd think about the bank. Didn't want to turn down George. A favorite of mine. Something Southern about him - heck, that's a mixed blessing, right?"

Mr. Daniels shifted his weight but was struck by a wave of pain that sent a shudder rolling from his knees to his chest. Gritting his teeth, he fought back the attack and the urge to give it voice.

"Christ, Daddy, you're unplugged," Lucy said, looking at the IV holders and dangling lines, none of which were attached to her father. "What're you taking?"

"Nothing. Not in the morning. My head clears." Mr. Daniels struggled to get his breath. "The nurse comes at one."

"Then humor me on this. I brought something." Lucy got her purse and brought out a joint, thin as a swizzle stick and neatly compacted.

"Is that what I think it is?" Mr. Daniels protested. "You had your mother try it. The summer you graduated." He turned to Charlie. "My wife didn't feel anything. Just dizzy. She ate four brownies and threw up. Doesn't sound like a lot of fun to me."

"It's supposed to help with the pain," Lucy said. "What do you have to lose?"

Mr. Daniels looked to see if Charlie might object and thereby spare him, but Charlie's expression, genuinely sympathetic and equally at a loss, convinced him that it would be easier to acquiesce than to argue. "Open a window, then," he grumbled.

Lucy raised a window and placed the joint in her mouth. She spoke through clenched teeth. "I haven't done this in so long. It may be strong. Think of it as one of those Lucky Strikes you used to smoke when I was little."

It took a second match before the tip glowed and Lucy's loud sucking filled her lungs with acrid smoke. She passed the joint to her father, who took it warily. He attempted to inhale, but choked, the smoke repelled with violent hacks that shook his slender frame. Coughing herself, Lucy rubbed his back while Charlie poured a glass of water.

It was a minute before Mr. Daniels finally stopped coughing. "Haven't smoked in thirty years," he apologized. Wheezing, he added, with a little pride, "The cigarettes didn't get me."

Exhausted by the attack, he soon nodded back off to sleep. Lucy helped herself to three extra hits from the joint before extinguishing it in the soil of a bedside plant. She was in the kitchen making sandwiches when the nurse arrived. Tall and wiry, the nurse strolled into the bedroom to check on her patient but stopped short of the bed. She sniffed the air and its cloying chemical residue, then glared at Charlie.

"An experiment," Charlie explained. "Something for the pain."

"Whose? His? Or hers?" The nurse tipped her head towards the kitchen.

Charlie felt obliged to defend Lucy. "His."

"He handles it pretty good," the nurse said, also inclined to stick up for someone. "Some people, they quit, just to stop the pain. Not him."

When the time came for Mr. Daniels' bath, Lucy kissed him goodbye and promised to visit next weekend. As Charlie sped back towards Rhode Island, Lucy let her seat recline all the way back and whispered, "I don't want to cry. That's my goal this weekend." She closed her eyes and kept them shut.

Excited by their return, Roxy rushed into the kitchen to greet Charlie and Lucy, then doubled back and fetched the sofa pillow that she'd been playing with in the living room. Charlie had shut the dog in the kitchen, where she could use a dog-door to get to the backyard; he had a hard time understanding how Roxy had escaped. Jennifer had expected to be gone all day. Had Julia returned, she would have changed out of her business suit into the blue jeans that hung over the back of a chair in the master bedroom. There was no evidence of anything being disturbed, yet if the latch to the kitchen door hadn't slipped - and Charlie didn't understand how this could happen - then someone had been through the house while he was out.

22

J ulia was back by the time Charlie set off for Newport; Lucy accompanied them after repeated assurances that she was welcome.
Charlie planned a short trip. Two days earlier, impersonating
George, he'd called American Express and Citibank Visa, provided
account and social security numbers, and asked for recent statements;
he hoped that he could track George by the location and type of his
charges. Those statements should be in the day's mail, and Charlie
wanted to retrieve them before anyone else had a chance.

A fog was settling as they reached Four Winds, a seaborne haze
that would thicken within the hour and steal the twilight. Lucy and
Julia set off on a walk while Charlie entered the front hall. The mail
- catalogues, a few bills, a host of stray solicitations - lay scattered on
the floor beneath a mail slot in the door.

Charlie sorted through the envelopes. The statements from American Express and Visa had arrived, as had the phone bill, which listed
an assortment of numbers dialed in Jamaica, in Panama, and in the
Bahamas. There were also repeated phone calls to various numbers in
New York City and Miami. It would be harder with the out-of-country
calls, but Charlie knew that if he waited till Monday, he could have
Providence Police run ID's on all the domestic listings.

George's American Express bill revealed a charge posted ten days
earlier for airline tickets; no charges had been reported since. His Visa
bill also showed no activity since the card had been used, at a bank in

Nassau, for a cash advance of two thousand dollars. The outstanding balance on this card was perilously close to the listed credit limit: George was somewhere in the Caribbean, where his cash and his credit wouldn't last long.

Charlie put the bills in a pocket and checked George's office. On his last visit he'd stuck a sliver of a Post-it across the bottom edge of a desk drawer and the slide-rail that supported it. The drawer hadn't been disturbed. Charlie looked through the other drawers until, distracted by the murmur of conversation, he caught a glimpse of the two women outside.

Lucy and Julia were approaching the water garden, or rather to what was left of it, the water garden having long ago fallen victim to faulty plumbing and poor drainage. The only surviving element of the original landscaping was a low stone bridge, not more than two feet high and fifteen feet across, that once traversed a pond and its lily pads. Now it lifted the garden path above the crabgrass and weeds that had overgrown the basin.

Charlie raised the window to hail the women but held back. Unimpeded by stray noise, the drift of their voices reached him with extraordinary clarity.

"Remember the summer after college?" Lucy asked.

Julia took a moment to study the small bridge and the weeds that surrounded it. "There were rosemary bushes over there, right? The bees were fierce."

"What I remember, the weekends I'd visit, Charlie'd be sleeping by the pool, his back all scratched up by fingernails." Julia pulled back, as Lucy quickly added, "I'm not trying to embarrass you. I thought it was great. I wanted something like what you two had."

"Why didn't you date Charlie? After your divorce?"

"Not that I didn't think about it, but one of us always was seeing somebody. Or on the rebound. I guess our friendship grew around that question. We're so close. He's my safety net - it's hard to risk that."

"Are you worried? For Charlie?"

"Should I be?"

Julia puts her hands in her pockets; she spoke haltingly. "I didn't think he'd want to see me at first, not after what happened. I was angry, too. It took a few years to turn the corner."

"And now..?"

"Who knows? I'm holding my breath. And you're still looking out for him."

"He's important to me. So, yeah, Charlie's family to me. George, too." Lucy paused, then swept a hand to indicate the grown-over water garden. "George brought me here. When I came here to tell him I was divorcing Quad. I was terrified - it was worse than telling my family. I figured Charlie and George would try to talk me out of it, they'd be loyal to Quad. They wouldn't know what his drinking was like. I figured I'd lose both of them. They were my best friends, too."

"Charlie's very fair."

"I didn't know what he'd think. That's why I came here first, so I could try to change George's mind if he was opposed, and George could help with Charlie. I got here, and Grace had some bridge party going on, so George took me for a walk. He knew something was up. When I told him I was leaving Quad, George didn't say anything at first. He took me by the hand and led me here." Lucy walked onto the low span of the stone bridge and pointed out the two-foot drop. "He took me to the middle, acting very solemn, and pushed me to the edge. He told me to jump."

Lucy smiled at the recollection. "He sounded really stern when he said it. *'Jump.'* Of course, he jumped with me. It felt great, jumping. We landed on a lily pad or something. I hadn't known if he'd understand, but of course he did. He hugged me and asked, 'What the *goddamn hell* took me so long?' I was so relieved. I knew if George understood, Charlie would. God, the fact they supported me - you can't imagine how much that mattered."

"Where is George?"

"No idea."

"He doesn't talk to you?"

"Not about everything. He probably spends more time with your brother."

Julia's back noticeably stiffened. "I wouldn't know."

Charlie hated the turn in the conversation, the swelling undercurrent of suspicion; he hated his acquiescence in an eavesdropping that, briefly, had been accidental. He closed the window and locked up the house. By the time he got outside, the women were walking towards the bluff, their forms evaporating into a fog that leeched the color out of them. Shadow-like, they disappeared in the gray mist. Charlie went to the garage and slid a door open, a wheel squeaking horribly through the rusty overhead rail.

The garage could house four or five cars, but no one had ever, in Charlie's experience, kept a car inside it. The first floor was cluttered with obsolete gardening equipment, an old two-cylinder tractor, several rotary wheel-driven mowers, and hundreds of stacked plastic pots. The smell, slightly sweet, was of evaporating gasoline and oil-based lubricants. A stairwell on the side of the structure led to a caretaker's cottage on the second floor.

As he climbed the stairs, Charlie noticed the faint outline of footprints on the dusty, wood risers. He pushed through the unlocked door, which was wedged into its sagging frame. Uninhabited for twenty years, the apartment was filthy, except for a patch that Charlie spotted on the bottom of the kitchen sink. Recent use had rinsed the patch free of its grime. In one of the bedrooms, he found a few empty Diet Pepsi cans and a pizza delivery box. A loaded rifle was leaning against the sill of a window that faced the mansion. Charlie recognized the gun: George's boyhood .22. Whenever George had last been through Newport, he'd spent the night here, clearly aware of the jeopardy that he was in.

Outside, Charlie rejoined the women by his car. They rode in silence back to Providence, where Lucy got into her car and drove off. Jennifer returned late that night, and Charlie woke to greet her. He woke again at five a.m. to a half empty bed and found Julia looking at the view of the city from a window in his den. Seeing him in the doorway, she crossed the room and swept him up in an embrace. In the crush of their ribs a tremble escaped her chest, a sob.

"What?"

"Nothing."

"What?"

"I don't know exactly. A little night terror. I guess I don't want it to go wrong."

"It won't."

"You won't let it?"

"No."

"Say it."

"I won't let it."

Julia tilted his head and brushed his forehead with the sweep of a slow kiss, then yawned and asked him to lie beside her on the couch, where she folded herself inside his arms and dosed off. The dog joined them. Once he heard the thump of a delivered newspaper, Charlie got up, brewed coffee, and scrambled eggs.

By late afternoon, Julia was gone, back to New York. Jennifer also left, though it was Charlie and not her boyfriend who put her on the Amtrak to Boston.

A break came Monday courtesy of a police sergeant, who'd had the phone company supply copies of George's bills. The sergeant researched the account names and addresses for the long-distance numbers that George had dialed from home. Among the many calls to Manhattan, George had made dozens to Gramercy Capital Management, a firm with an address on East 74th Street.

Charlie wanted time off to check this and any other lead that developed, so he stopped by the Attorney General's office Tuesday morning. A longtime friend of Charlie's, Peter Vicari was bent over his desk, carefully rubbing out a dull spot on the toe of a shoe. "I liked this building better," he said, "when there was a shoeshine stand right inside the entrance instead of a metal detector."

"Me, too."

"Is that a bad thing? Have somebody else shine your shoes?"

"I don't know."

"You busy?"

"Yes."

"Is it a case?"

"Not yet. I don't know if it will be. A lot of what's happened is out-of-state, out-of-country."

Vicari looked vexed. "Then why..?"

"Because George is missing. You met him. Another friend of mine is dead."

"I'm sorry. What..?"

"I don't have a handle on it."

"We're not the police."

Charlie dismissed the objection with a wave of his hand. "I need time off."

"I want you to take this other-"

"File for postponement. Give me a month."

Vicari yielded with an exaggerated sigh. "Take as little time as possible, okay? We'll cover what we can."

Charlie nodded his thanks and started out, but Vicari called after him. "It's not indefinite - your leave."

Charlie worked late into the night preparing his caseload for the hiatus. The following morning, he drove to Manhattan to investigate Gramercy Capital Management, the company with the number that George had repeatedly called, and arrived on the upper East Side at lunchtime. The traffic was so slow that he parked several blocks away and walked to East 74th Street.

Gramercy was housed on the third floor of a brownstone, the front door of which was operated by an intercom. Charlie scanned the building's directory and wrote down the names of the other tenants before the sound of an elevator, descending to the first-floor landing inside the small lobby, chased him off the front steps. He took a seat across the street on a bus stop bench and watched to see who entered or exited the building.

Fifteen minutes later, a cab double-parked outside the brownstone. Charlie saw a woman step out of the cab, rush up the steps, and announce herself over the intercom. He shaded his eyes from the sun as the woman turned back towards the street. Purse in hand, Julia Hoffman returned to the cab and left the rear door open as she took a seat inside. Shortly, Martin Hoffman left the building and hurried to the cab, where he joined his sister.

Charlie ducked into a storefront's recessed doorway and watched, in the clear reflection from the door's polished glass, as the cab slipped past. Once it was out of view, he walked to the nearest intersection. He intended to cross the street again, to sneak into the brownstone and to look around, but he felt disoriented. There was likely a simple explanation for what he had seen, but at the moment he trusted nothing, not even himself.

23

The suspicion dogged Charlie, an Iago barking on his heels. *Why her? Why now? What about the brother?* Charlie thought of Patty Hearst, the captive turned by her captors, the heiress become accomplice to the very people who had held her hostage. Kidnapped, she'd been kept in solitude, then thrown the bone of her kidnappers' radical politics. Charlie didn't know what snapped, didn't know what tricks confinement and brutality played on the will, but Patty Hearst had, at some point, surrendered herself. She had converted to the fiery religion of her jailer, the rebel warlord who stationed his once preppy recruit on the front lines of class warfare. Whether or not she had fully reclaimed herself in the years that followed, whether or not all that had been lost to the Symbionese Liberation Army was youth, Charlie couldn't guess.

Julia's captivity had been different. Julia had been held much longer and had been thrown no lifeline, no revolutionary dogma to espouse, no chance to appease her captors, who had given up on revolutions. One, a colonel wise to intrigues inside and outside the armed forces, wanted only money; the other, the sergeant guarding Julia, wanted her. She had had no sermons, no chance to cross-over and lock arms with the enemy, and her terror must have been all the more absolute for her complete isolation.

Julia barely talked about the year that she had spent imprisoned, though she had told Charlie about a game that she played in her shuttered room, where days could blend into an incalculable night. At a point, she didn't know when, she started to count the days till spring, as if the season's arrival might herald a change. Having lost track of the month, not caring which hemisphere she was in, she began counting the days until an equinox. Any equinox. She kept careful count, but reluctant to let the number swell she started the count over every time she reached nine. She refused to count as high as ten. Charlie couldn't tell if the game indicated extraordinary resilience or a total breakdown; he couldn't tell what she might have lost or what she owed her brother, whom she credited with her rescue.

Charlie called Julia that evening and asked, with what struck him as poorly feigned nonchalance, what she'd been up to, where she'd been. She mentioned a difficult customer, a crisis in an order; there was no mention of her brother until Charlie specifically asked how Martin was. "Good," she said. "I had lunch with him."

Julia volunteered little else: either she had everything to protect, or nothing. Her rendezvous with her brother may have been a simple family luncheon - not in the habit of visiting his own sister, Charlie couldn't gauge other people's family ties - or it might signify something more. Either way, he couldn't explain George's extremely frequent phone calls to Martin's office.

Charlie spent the night trying to wrestle himself to sleep, but kept imagining Julia, the unperfumed scent of her, the sound of her voice, the heat of her body. He couldn't focus on anything else, not even George and his troubles.

He rose early, the sun trying to break through storm clouds, and tracked down Ray McLean. His hair wet from a thundershower and gleaming under the fluorescent lights of the public cafeteria in the criminal courts building, McClean was sitting on a plastic chair at a long, otherwise empty table. Waiting to testify in another case, he poured sugar into a large Styrofoam cup of coffee as Charlie approached and took a seat. "Damn stuff," the detective said, stirring the coffee. "Not supposed to drink it, damn prostate's the size of a grapefruit."

"When's your trial?"

"Sometime this morning. They're in chambers. Anything new? On your friend?"

"No."

"Your friend's a banker, right? You thought about him running money? Customer comes in, says he needs a little help getting some invoices paid, a lotta offshore vendors."

"I don't think George would.."

"I don't think any of us knows what we'd do, enough money's put on the table. Besides, it's innocent. A customer - you don't know much about his business except he's got money going overseas - he has you turn the cogs. Nothing fancy, he's got paperwork for all his transactions."

"Money laundering," Charlie interjected, "we'd turn it over to the unit at the Justice Department."

"What about your other friend, the one who drowned?"

"Joe? I keep thinking it's simple. Wrong place, wrong time. He probably didn't know much except someone he shouldn't have."

"It's just a thought, money-laundering."

"It's money-something. Joe in the Caribbean, pushing dollars around."

McLean took a sip of coffee and put the cup down. "Another item. This bank examiner, Robbins. You were right. He did visit your friend's bank, First Federal Etcetera, back in March. An official visit with another examiner, so maybe it's nothing, the stink of coincidence."

"What 'coincidence'?"

"We turned up cash in his BMW. Five grand. Somebody in the lab found it. Real money this time, not an emergency stash for a boat trip. This shit is cash with a history."

"Goddamnit." Charlie pushed himself away from the table.

"Sorry." The detective offered a sweet, crooked smile. "I know you don't want it to snowball, get away from you, but I think that's the first angle we check. The examiner, it doesn't have to be any bank in particular, but suppose he notices a cash trail and wants a piece. Drug money, cartel customers, something on that angle."

"Christ."

"Meantime, I ordered up copies of Robbins' phone bills. You want me to see who he called, check it with your friends' bills, see if the examiner ties into anything?"

"Yeah."

The day plodded along, Charlie grateful for the small scale of Providence, all the federal and state offices lumped within the same square mile, the trek from one agency to another manageable, if futile. The Rhode Island Secretary of State was gone on what turned into a three-hour lunch; the workers at the state income tax office had no employment records for any of the entities named on the Cayman Island bank statements.

Frustrated, Charlie phoned Quad at his office. He'd remembered, during his sleepless night, a long-ago conversation in which Quad had outlined a nearly perfect money-laundering scheme used by a bank in Manhattan that catered to the jewelry trade. Upon receipt of a shipment of diamonds, a wholesale diamond merchant wired payment to an offshore dealer and resold the diamonds to another merchant, the transactions all supported by a paper trail. Well-documented as they were, the transactions only lacked one thing: the diamonds themselves, which didn't exist. Quad repeated the details of the case but interrupted himself.

"Wait a second, hold the train.." Quad's fingers could be heard drumming his desk. "Hell, George's bank might be laundering money, but generally you have to handle cash. Cash is a bitch to handle. You'd have money flowing out. We got evidence of cash? Phony invoices, gold bullion, import-export?"

"Not that I know."

"Also, the bank's not international."

"So?"

"Look at Citibank. They have offices and private bankers all over the world. They got embarrassed in Mexico, helping the President's brother or someone with the fortune he plundered, flowing money through foreign offices and trusts."

"First Federal has a trust department."

Quad snorted with disdain. "God! Not a real one. They're a custodian. They don't even manage the money in-house. I mean, hell, who's going to invest the money? George?"

"Why not George?"

"Jesus! He doesn't even have an MBA or a CFA." Quad was cocky about his own MBA. "Who'd give him money to run? I told him, years ago, to go back to school, get an MBA, not box himself in."

"Maybe he was happy."

"Maybe he was comfortable. Didn't want to get too far from the country club."

"Goddamnit, can you stay on point? The bank?"

"The bank would have to split trust fees with any group that manages the money. Maybe the big customers want that. Everything under the same roof, at the same bank. Of course, the trusts are off the balance sheet. They won't be directly impacted if a loan sours."

"What will?

"The bank itself. And the deposit accounts that get frozen if the government steps in."

"George's bank? What do you know about it?"

"It tripled in size the last five or six years."

"So it's doing something right."

"One would think."

Charlie fought back his temper. "Help me here, will you?"

Quad described other schemes that had imperiled small banks in recent years. Though he tried, Charlie couldn't make the details of these schemes fit the specifics of George and Joe's lives. George was credited with attracting customers and swelling his bank's deposits; it was his job, apparently, to bring and to keep his clients' money onshore, not to ship and cleanse it offshore. As for Joe, Charlie had a hard time picturing him involved in complex, multi-tiered transactions.

Charlie caught up with the Secretary of State late that afternoon and didn't get home till evening. Not yet enveloped by the mist descending on College Hill, his house sat high on a corner of Prospect Street, every window a lookout on the river and the city beyond.

Julia had arrived before Charlie. Her appointments the rest of the week were in southern New England, and she could reach them more easily from Providence than from New York. She was feeding Roxy when Charlie entered through the kitchen door and tossed a file folder on a counter.

"Where were you?"

"All over."

"Providence?"

"I went to the state banking commission – to see if anyone filed a complaint against George's bank."

"And?"

"Nothing. Every other bank has at least ten complaints on file, most of them pure crap, but First Federal is different. No complaints on record. The clients must love it."

"You doubt that?"

"How would I know?" Charlie opened the refrigerator, grabbed a bottle of beer, and popped off the cap. "You want anything?"

"No."

Charlie took a sip from the bottle, then another, before setting it down. "I got the Rhode Island Secretary of State to help. The banks file annual statements. Jesus, it was hard to unravel. George's bank is owned by a corporation, most of the stock of which is owned by another corporation, those kind of layers, more peels than an onion."

"I don't understand." There was an edge to her voice.

"It takes a while to get to the bottom layer, to find out who owns it. It turns out your brother, or some group he controls, owns most of it."

"A bank?"

"You don't know this?"

"Martin's investors," Julia replied, "they own different kinds of things. They own the land under some malls and a lot of other things, too. It's not my business, and I don't keep track. But it would surprise me if Martin wanted to invest in a bank. It was hell for my father. When he finally got his bank back from the socialists, Martin was very scornful."

"Why?"

"Because the socialists had saddled the bank with terrible loans, because my father willingly assumed the loans along with control of the bank. My father went down with his ship – Martin was bitter about it."

"Your brother, or people he knows, own First Federal."

"So?"

"So maybe somebody knows where the hell George is."

"Ask Martin. God, Charlie, if you've got a question, ask it. Don't bait and cross-examine me."

Julia stalked out of the room. She said little the rest of the night and stayed up later than Charlie, who heard her pacing in the kitchen before he drowsed off.

He woke to find Julia asleep beside him, curled up in a tangle of covers. She was undisturbed by the dog, which had found its way into the room and was jumping around the bed for attention, or by the phone call, a wrong number that he had to hurry back from the bathroom to answer.

Charlie sat down beside Julia and pulled the blankets away from her face, brushing the hair from her brow: her skin was damp and cool to the touch. Alarmed by the absence of a response, he pressed his fingers into her chest just beneath a shoulder and found her pulse, the beat slow, no quickening to the touch. Her only reaction was a slight whimper that rose out of her depths and surfaced, like an air bubble.

Charlie sorted through Julia's toilet bag in the bathroom and discovered, among the odd medications and ointments, three large vials. One contained melatonin, an herbal sedative available over the counter. The other two held prescriptions: Seconal and Halcyon. The sleeping pills mocked his concerns about how she might have changed or what she had lost. What had her ordeals cost her? Thousands of hours of sleep, to start with.

Charlie checked the dates on the prescriptions: both were months old; both bottles were mostly full. Whatever Julia had taken, she'd been using it very sparingly. He returned to the bedroom and shook the mattress, then spoke her name loudly. She didn't stir.

24

Charlie grabbed one of Julia's legs through the covers and pulled it. The muscles in her leg stiffened, then relaxed as she rolled onto a side. She lifted her chin as her eyes fluttered open and murmured, "Don't worry. No appointments till this afternoon."

"You okay?"

"Couldn't sleep."

"Took a powder?"

"Damn things knock me out."

Charlie stroked her cheek until she dropped back off, snoring lightly. He showered and was in the kitchen when McLean called. The detective had put John Stuart Robbins' phone bills alongside George's. Several times the murdered bank examiner had dialed a number in Manhattan that showed up on George's long-distance charges. "All I got so far," he told Charlie, "is an address for the phone number. No name."

"What?"

"580 Park Avenue. You know where that is?"

"Somewhere in the East Sixties, I guess. You want me to check it out?"

"Yeah, if you can. Get a fix on it."

Off the phone, Charlie sped across Connecticut and cruised into Manhattan. He found a parking lot on East 66th St., a few doors west of Lexington. The building in question, a real Park Avenue dowager, was several blocks away: twelve stories of graying marble and arched windows. Its gilt numbers were posted on a large canopy over ornate doors, which two doormen in full livery guarded. Residential, the plush co-op was named after its address. **580.**

The foyer featured limestone floors and oriental rugs, Louis Quatorze chairs and ormolu tables, and a high-walled reception desk just inside the front door. Flanked by a phone operator seated at an ancient switchboard, a clerk raised his head expectantly at Charlie's entrance. Charlie looked for a row of mailboxes, a list of residents, an intercom, anything that might indicate who lived in the building. The clerk at the counter coughed politely, a gentlemanly come-hither; his muscles strained the seams of his crested blazer.

Approaching the counter, Charlie noticed a room behind it where two men in chauffeurs' caps were sitting on a bench. A lounge for the help.

"Sir?"

"I'm supposed to meet someone here."

"Does *Someone* have a name?"

"My partner. For a meeting. This is 580 Park Avenue?" Charlie grinned sheepishly. "I lost my memo but I've got the phone number." Charlie fumbled through his pockets and produced a piece of paper. "Let's see. 242-5800. That must be the switchboard..?"

"Yes, sir."

"If I can check a directory?"

"Sir?"

"Maybe I'll remember the name. The meeting was for ten. I can't stand them up. You got a phone list?"

The reception clerk looked at the operator. She had a phone list, but Charlie wasn't likely to get a copy. No names were displayed anywhere in the lobby. A call made to any of the units, if it was made to the central number, was impossible to trace past the ancient switchboard. The residents enjoyed a very concrete anonymity.

The clerk stepped out from behind the counter and squared his broad shoulders in the passageway. "You got the right address?" he asked.

"Positive. Maybe you can check with the garage, a valet there. Anybody who might've parked my partner's car. A red BMW. Maybe a valet knows where my partner is."

The clerk delayed a moment before walking through a door at the rear of the lobby. As soon as he was out of sight, Charlie turned to the phone operator and leaned over the counter. "Hey, maybe you could patch me through."

"Huh?"

"I think it's 9-B, is that the right unit?" Charlie saw the phone sheet pinned to the side of her switchboard. Encased in plastic, it listed names and extensions for each unit. The operator recoiled as he stretched well over the counter and took hold of the sheet. He pulled the tack out, put the sheet on top of the counter, and tapped a name at random. "Here. Try this one."

The operator frowned at Charlie and his poor manners, then stood up and disappeared into the employee lounge behind her, where she muttered something to those present. Charlie folded the phone list and stuck it in a pocket. He was a block away before he stopped to look at it. The names listed were family names, some Hispanic, some French, a few Asian. Robbins had called at least one of these people. So had George.

Charlie called McLean and grew impatient waiting for him to pick up. "Charlie?" the detective finally said. "Where..?"

"On Park Avenue, near 580. It's a co-op."

"That was quick."

"The phone number we have is the building's switchboard."

"You get anything on the residents?"

"A list of names and units – for the house phone. I'll send it over."

"I just got off a call. Buddy of mine. N.Y.P.D. Knows the address. Says the building's a bit of a legend."

"It's swank. I can go that far."

"He says the place is known - unofficially, this is - as 'Miami North.' A place with a Latin flavor, nothing migrant about it, rich people from south of the border. He says he took a complaint once from somebody there. The Honorable P. C. M. J. Cervantes, some fucking stack of initials. Supposedly he once sat on Paraguay's Supreme Court - who the hell knew they had one?"

Charlie finished the call and cut over to Madison Ave. He was crossing 68th Street when he made up his mind and continued to the brownstone on 74th. There, he was buzzed through the front door and took the stairs to the third-floor offices of Gramercy Capital Management. A receptionist looked up as he walked into a small anteroom.

"Is Martin here?"

"Mr. Hoffman?" She lifted her handset. "He knows you?"

"Charlie Sanderson."

She punched a button and repeated the name. Less than a minute later, Martin entered from a rear door. "Charlie! You staying at Julia's?"

"Actually, she's at my place." Martin stared at him curiously, so Charlie added, "I was in town. An extradition. Thought I'd say hello."

Martin escorted Charlie back to his office. The largest room on the floor, the office fronted the street with broad windows, the bright sunshine highlighting the prismatic streaks left by a window-washer.

Charlie sat in a chair by the desk, on which he noticed a blank piece of stationery. Lifting it, he read its letterhead. "'*Gramercy Capital Management?*' What, you manage money?"

"We're small. Conservative." Martin took his seat behind the desk and picked up a pencil. "Why? Are you thinking of establishing an account?"

"I don't have enough money to worry about. People like you or George, you've got high minimums for your accounts."

"How is George?"

"Fine, I guess."

"I hear he's on a trip. Anderson Wells told me. You know him? The president of the bank? The board brought him in about six months ago."

"You sit on the board?"

"No." Martin waited a moment, then continued. "Although, as you probably know, I own most of the bank's stock."

Charlie did not "probably know" until yesterday about Martin's controlling interest. He couldn't imagine why George had never told him, and he was irritated that, by revealing the information quickly, Martin had stolen any thunder that Charlie had been hoping to use to his own advantage. Martin knew that George was missing, and certainly understood that George's whereabouts was the real reason for Charlie's visit.

"Your clients?" Charlie asked. "Do they own the bank, too?"

"Not our clients. It'd be a little racy for them. They prefer CDs, index funds, a little real estate. No, with the bank there's a shell company involved, but I own most of it. I try to be discreet about my investment."

"Why?"

"When you manage other people's money, they don't want to think you're too busy managing your own." Martin sighed with exaggerated patience. "Besides, Newport's an anachronism. Old money is still revered. One reason why Anderson Wells was hired was his background. He's comfortable around old money."

"You're not?"

Martin smiled at the challenge. "I'm a money manager, not a banker. Jesus, Charlie, you know these people. The bluebloods want tried and true. Wells worked for the private client group at Morgan, did a stint at U.S. Trust."

"How's the bank working out? They refer you business?"

Martin shook his head. "That's not the point. The bank's separate, an investment of mine. I stay completely out of it, let the bankers run it. It was small when I bought it, well located. It turned out George was there. A few key personnel."

"Is that how you knew Joe?" Charlie's tone was casual, but his choice of the past tense was deliberate. He wondered if Martin knew that Joe was dead and, if so, how he knew. Joe's body still lay unclaimed in the Grand Cayman morgue.

"Joe?"

"Joe Turlik. He works for the bank, right?"

"George's friend?"

"Yeah."

"I don't think he ever worked for the bank. You could ask personnel. Or George. Or Joe." It sounded like an afterthought. "Ask Joe."

"George treated me to certain confidences. About the bank. Maybe I should let him brief-"

"I'm worried about George," Martin interrupted. "He's done a few things - some of the people he's borrowed money from. That's my concern."

"Why?"

"He refinanced that estate of his, didn't he? How'd he do that, how in God's name did he borrow - what? - millions of dollars, with his income? How'd he get that loan?"

When Charlie failed to reply, Martin threw his hands up, surrendering to his own question. He swiveled to the credenza behind him and sorted through several large envelopes. "Did Julia ask you to pick up her package?"

"She didn't know I was coming."

"Didn't know?" He spun his chair back around to face Charlie. "You can take this to her. If you don't mind." Martin tossed him a sealed manila envelope.

Charlie caught the package, heavy enough to contain a variety of documents. "Sure."

"How is she?"

"Fine."

"She's sleeping okay?"

Unnerved, Charlie forced a smile. "You think I shouldn't give her a pot of coffee at bedtime?"

"She has trouble sleeping sometimes, doesn't she? With what she's been through. Christ, what they did. To beauty like hers." Martin paused to take a sip from a bottle of water on his desk. "When I got her out of Chile, she looked like a prisoner-of-war. The worst moment of my life, seeing her like that. I asked her to let me call you. She wouldn't let me. Maybe I should've called you anyway..?"

"Why didn't you?"

"I don't know. I was shaken. The worst heartache. She was the most important person in my life. I wanted to get her well."

Charlie wanted to change the subject. "It was a long time ago."

"She's still the most important person in my life."

It irritated Charlie that, by staking his own claim upon his sister, Martin took control of their meeting. Flustered, Charlie left the office minutes later. The day before, Julia had complained that he was cross-examining her. Today, he doubted his ability to cross-examine anyone. Martin had produced information, at least the information that could be procured easily, moments before Charlie had asked for it, as if Martin were a chess player, one move ahead.

Outside, his head clearing, Charlie thought about the inconsistencies in Martin's statements. Martin claimed to take a "hands-off" approach with the bank, but that didn't explain the frequent calls that George had made to Martin's office. Secondly, Charlie didn't buy the notion that "old money" was particularly revered anywhere anymore, even in Newport; a superheated global economy had created trillions of dollars of new money, a sum so colossal that it surely dwarfed all other distinctions.

Charlie headed west, towards Central Park. He wouldn't have noticed the two men across the street, except that they were sitting on the same bus stop bench that he'd occupied several days earlier when he'd spotted Julia in the taxi. Both men rose as Charlie turned onto the sidewalk. A block later, pretending to read a billboard, Charlie looked across the street. Half a block behind, the two men stopped and checked out a storefront. Their dark faces were well hidden by their caps, one a bicycling cap, the other a sport fisherman's cap with its long brim.

Charlie hurried south when he reached Fifth Avenue. Six blocks later, he slowed, put his nose to a window of a chic clothing store, and then entered, circling behind a rack of cashmere overcoats and a table covered with silk scarves. It took several minutes, but one of the men from 74th St. appeared in the window on Fifth Avenue, lazily sauntering past the store. Half a minute later, the second of the two men appeared, pressing his face against the store front window till the bill of his fisherman's cap buckled. Charlie got a good look: his cheekbones were high, the whites of his eyes were pink with ruptured vessels, his sparse mustache had a gap in the middle of it, and his dark skin was pockmarked.

Charlie crouched between racks of clothes and retreated to the back of the store, where a red *EXIT* sign marked a doorway that led to public phones and restrooms. Down that corridor, beneath another *EXIT* sign, a door was posted with a placard that warned *"Fire Exit Only!"*; a waist-high handle would, if depressed, release the latch. Charlie picked up one of the wooden coat hangers that were scattered on the floor and inserted the hanger's metal tip into the latch, which popped open. Either the door wasn't wired to the fire alarm, or the wire of the coat hanger closed whatever circuit ran through the latch, for the door opened soundlessly. Charlie slipped out into the alley behind the building and didn't let go of the hanger until the door pinched his fingers. The hanger clattered to the ground as the door closed, but no alarm sounded.

Charlie sprinted north down the alley, ran four blocks over to Third Avenue, and turned south. He kept running till he came to the garage where he had left his car. After paying the cashier and receiving an exit token, he rode an elevator to the fifth level, then descended the staircase to the fourth level and hustled to his car. Only when he had driven to the West Side and merged with the light traffic on the Hudson Parkway did he believe that his pursuers, if indeed that's what they were, had been shaken.

25

She was sitting at her desk, the paperback that she was reading disguised by a file folder, a pen suspended over the folder as if notes needed to be taken. The part in her blond hair exposed a thin pink line of sunburned scalp. Engrossed by the book, George's secretary went suddenly pale as she heard, then saw Charlie standing beside her desk.

"God, Charlie. You could announce yourself."

"Good book?"

Careful to leave the pen as a bookmark, Beth closed the file folder around her book. "You heard anything?"

"What've they told you?"

"Just that George isn't back. It's got Mr. Wells all fried. I guess if an officer disappears for a while, a bank has to check itself, make sure nobody's embezzled anything, is that ridiculous?"

"You think?"

"They made me take a few days off. Jesus, here I had a run-in with Linda in personnel. Bitch? A major bitch, and where's George when I need him?"

"You keep his phone sheets? Message pads?"

"We don't use those. We use the little pink pads." She let her voice rise in a sing-song pattern. "*While-you-were-out*. Single sheet."

"So who calls? Who leaves messages?"

"Joe leaves a lot. You know him, right? Joe Turlik?"

"Who else?"

"You. You call a lot. You and Lucy. Other than that, people call from everywhere. Most use his private line."

"Whom does George call?"

"He makes his own calls. We have a trunk line."

"His mail?"

"Nothing."

"His desk?"

Beth pinched the bridge of her nose, releasing her grip after a slow breath. "Christ, you can look through his office. I already did. There's nothing there."

"Does he have a safe deposit box?"

"Two. I got a key for one of 'em. He puts business stuff in it."

"What's he keep in the other?"

"Personal stuff. I know he put a copy of his will there. He made some changes a few months ago."

"Who drafted it?"

"Purtzman, some name like that. I got it on my Rolodex."

"Call the law firm. Tell them George can't find his files. Have them send over copies of anything they've done the last few years."

Beth nodded, then whispered, "You're scaring me, Charlie."

"Get me everything you can. A list of his appointments, copies of files, everything."

Charlie heard Anderson Wells call out to his secretary and started down the hall. He waved at Wells' secretary and strode into the office, where Wells sat behind a vast partners' desk.

"Hullo?" Wells was visibly put off by the intrusion.

"You have a chance to talk with Martin?" Charlie walked right up to the desk; his tone was breezy. "Did he call? Martin? After I saw him this morning?"

Puzzled, Wells shook his head. Charlie shrugged and continued, "I had a chance to talk to George."

"When?"

"We discussed some of the bank's problems. The loan to Metromedia."

"That's a problem. We're working on it. Is that where George is? Sitting on the sidelines, waiting for the storm to pass?"

"You think George would sit it out?"

"I wouldn't mind sitting it out. Except first, what I'd like to do, and George too, I bet," Wells harrumphed, "I'd like to cut off the balls of everybody at Metromedia, put those balls in a skillet, sear them over high heat, and feed the pan-fry to the crows. These people, they're just the worst sort of scum."

"That's the bank's position?"

"That's my position. They're twisting everything."

"So what're you going to do?"

"Maybe we'll lay some of the loan off. Syndicate it."

"Sell it? How?"

"Entertainment lending. Everybody knows it's lucrative, wants into the business."

"Not your end of it."

"For your bloody information we're negotiating right now with a Latin American group. George got the ball rolling. This is a world in which you can trade or sell any kind of paper, especially if it's connected to the movie business. We'll work something out."

"That's what George thinks?"

"I'm damned if I know what George thinks," Wells said, his face reddening. "He could tell us if he were here."

"What George thinks is that he's in the line of fire. And if he is, I wonder if you are."

Wells didn't flinch. He had the look of an aging university professor, interrupted mid-lecture, struggling to remember exactly where he had left off. He concluded their short interview by requesting that Charlie keep him advised of any developments.

When Charlie got to his own office, he faxed Ray McLean a copy of the phone list from the co-op at 580 Park Ave; the police might make something of a name or two on it. The Attorney General had left a message, so Charlie stopped by his office and was greeted effusively, a hug concluding with a pat on the back.

"Nice vacation?" Vicari asked.

"Expecting a postcard?"

"There's a motion we need to respond to." Vicari grimaced apologetically. "I hate to bother you, but it's been your show."

Charlie oversaw all the state's significant litigation and knew that Vicari didn't trust anyone else, even himself, with certain cases. "Sorry," Vicari said, handing him a thin set of documents.

"I'll take a quick look, draft something," Charlie promised.

"I owe you one. Any luck finding your banker friend?"

"Not so far."

"Anything we can do?"

"I wish there were."

"What about the Justice Department? If it's banking? Can they use *RICO*?"

"The scope of *RICO* is broad, but the definitions aren't. They'd need to establish a pattern, a conspiracy on our shores. Whatever the hell's flying around, it's all coming in under the radar."

"Jesus, can't you turn this over to the police? You're not trained as a peace officer."

"No kidding. God, have you ever been followed?"

"'Followed'?"

"I think people followed me this morning. In New York. I can't prove it, but whatever my friend George tripped over, it's real, and it'll swallow him if I don't find him first."

"Christ." Vicari punctuated the protest with his hand, a "slow down" gesture. "There's nothing the police can do? I realize a 'Missing Person Report' is going to gather dust."

Conjuring as it did images of lost children on milk cartons, the term "*missing persons*" disturbed Charlie. The term also upset George's ex-wife. She reached Charlie later that day, shortly before sundown. Back from a long business trip, Lisa Calvert became hysterical at the suggestion that George was missing but composed herself long enough to complain. "He's months behind on support, I really wish you'd get on him, he listens to you, Charlie. Although this – week after week - it's a long time for him not to call. It's clockwork, mechanical, *the call to the kid*. God, their phone calls, they're so strained. He and Walt aren't that close, it's just George desperately doesn't want to disconnect, you know? Like his father. Let me know if you find out anything, okay? Swear to God, Charlie, you'll let me know."

Drained, Charlie limped home late that evening. A rich soup was in a pot on the stovetop, ready to be reheated. He found Julia upstairs, stretched out in the deep iron bathtub of the master bathroom, her head resting on the tub's broad lip. "Lazy day," she murmured, barely opening her eyelids. "My afternoon appointment cancelled."

Charlie sat on the edge of the tub and ran his fingers through the hair bunched on her head: it was damp and silky to the touch. Happy for the silence, he closed his eyes, too. He didn't open them until Julia leaned forward to unplug the drain, letting half the water drain before she spoke. "Somebody called. Beth? Is that her name? She's getting you a package."

Julia stood and dried her shoulders with a towel. Her flesh was pink, mottled by the scalding soak; her face was flushed. Heavy with the water that dripped from it, her pubic hair hung in wiry braids.

Charlie held her arm while she stepped out of the tub. After she had dried herself on the mat in front of him, he slid his arms around her and put his head to her chest, a cheek pressed to a breast. What he wanted was the warmth of her flesh; what he didn't want was conversation, noise, stress. Julia held his head to her for quite some time before laughing. "Charlie, I just had a bath."

Content, he let his head cling to the perch of her bosom, which heaved slightly on the intake of each breath. Julia slowly pulled back, raised his head, and put her lips to his. It was a teenager's kiss, entirely mischievous and arousing, her tongue pushing into his mouth. Apparently, she had misread his intentions and assumed that he wanted to sleep with her. She put a bathrobe on, but left it open and untied, and had him strip in the bathroom.

She led him into the bedroom and onto the bed, where she coaxed him on top of her. Charlie would have been happy to remain in their cozy mount, the hips rocking delicately, a slow cradling of desire, everything else in the world subordinate to the lovely heat of their embrace, but Julia brought her ankles close to her buttocks, her hips rising and locking him in a purposeful grind, her fingernails dragging down his back with encouragement.

Julia held him in place long after he had finished, her legs wrapped around him. Slipping from her, Charlie rose and dressed. She held her knees to her chest and lay on the bed a while longer, while he warmed their dinner.

Downstairs, fetching plates, Julia noticed the manila envelope that Charlie had ferried from her brother's office in Manhattan. A mailing label identified the package's source: Gramercy Capital Management. Julia looked at Charlie, then tapped the parcel. "Where'd you get this?"

"New York."

"You saw Martin today? You went to New York?"

"Something came up."

"Really?"

"I dropped in on Martin when I was there." Though he tried, Charlie couldn't make himself sound convinced by his story, or convincing.

"Why?"

"The bank. George."

"What about George?"

"I don't know. But I think your brother might."

"You think Martin does? God, Charlie, George could be in any kind of trouble. Haven't you figured that out about George? It's like he's wandering in somebody else's dream."

"How?"

"It's his family. It's the dream-world they lived in. God, do you remember the meal his grandmother cooked?"

Charlie did remember the meal. The summer that he and Julia had spent together at Four Winds, they'd arrived one weekday evening and found Grace tearing the pantry apart, hunting for various utensils and pans. The cook was sick. Though Grace could have taken them to any of a host of clubs or restaurants, she was determined to cook the menu that had been planned.

Grace had graduated Phi Beta Kappa from Wellesley College, had served on the boards of numerous charities and schools, and had won enough bridge tournaments to be designated a Life Grand Master. She was an extremely intelligent and accomplished woman, and though she was hopeful of proving otherwise, she did not know how to cook. The meal's menu was ambitious for a novice, and the food that she prepared - she was the first to admit it - was awful.

Shaken by the failure, Grace endured George's good-natured teasing at the dinner table, the tone only souring when she reminded her grandson that he wouldn't enjoy the luxuries that she had. "This will all pass," she had said, sweeping a hand to indicate the mansion. "It'll all pass, or somebody else will get a turn at it. Which is fair, I suppose."

"Thank you, Grandfather," George muttered. He'd recently discovered that his grandfather's will provided that the bulk of his fortune would ultimately be left to his alma mater, Yale, and thus not to his grandson.

"He wanted to leave something behind," Grace explained.

"They can name a goddamn chair after him. What exactly was his field of study at college? Polo?"

The memory was still vivid to Julia, who recalled Grace's humiliation at the meal she had served, who hadn't forgotten George's bewilderment at having been schooled as an heir, with every expectation of wealth, only to find himself without it.

"What's your point?"

"George is great, but at times he's lost. You refuse to see it."

"George is doing okay."

"Is he? You think he was prepared? For this world?"

"You were?"

"I was eleven when I was sent off to a boarding school in this country. You grow up in a hurry."

"And Martin? Him, too?"

"Leave him out of it."

"He was prepared for this world?"

"He's my only family. Leave him alone. You can do that much, right?"

Charlie didn't answer; he simply avoided her eyes, while she picked up the package from Martin and waved it at him. "Goddamnit. Don't run around behind my back, then come home and take me to bed."

The prospect of mutual betrayal, each of them distrustful of the other and possibly duplicitous, could no longer be ignored. Conscious of her pain, Charlie stuttered. He would, were his tongue agile enough, reweave what had just passed between them and fashion something free of the snares of distrust. He would allow the language of their bodies - her body clinging to his half an hour ago - to plow under this agony of words. But she turned away from him. After dinner, she made a point of packing her suitcase; she'd be gone by morning.

26

For one brief moment, the plane tipping a wing into the prevailing Pacific breeze, the isthmus was visible, as were two oceans, the Atlantic turning gray with the shadows of retreating storm clouds, the Pacific a distant glitter under a late afternoon sun. Other bodies of water - lakes, bays, gulfs, channels, slices of the canal itself - splashed the jungle below with varying shades of blue and green. Its forests steaming with evaporation from a recent rain, the tiny republic of Panama lay between mountains, which climbed to the north and south.

Charlie had never had occasion to ponder, until he saw the rugged terrain of the Canal Zone from the air, what an extraordinarily improbable undertaking the construction of the canal had been. Having decided to visit Panama the day before, he'd had to buy his tourist card on the plane. Along with it, the Ministry of Tourism provided a short history of the territory, long a crossroads to conquerors, explorers, and prospectors.

It was Beth who'd started him on his voyage south. Three days earlier, she'd met Charlie after work. She'd snuck several packages from one of George's safe deposit boxes out of the bank. "You keep 'em," she'd told Charlie. "Damned if I know what any of it means."

Inside the packages were a variety of Spanish-language documents that a friend translated: notably, there were corporate minutes for half a dozen Panamanian corporations, all of which gave blanket approval for transfers of money between a Panamanian bank, Banco Centro, and a bank in the Cayman Islands, Maritime International. The six Panamanian corporations all shared the same address in Panama City; Charlie recognized the address as identical to the one on the legal bill from the firm of Del Rosario & Gutierrez. An officer had signed authorizations for each corporation: Hector del Rosario, identified as the president, had signed documents for four companies; the signature of Eduardo Gutierrez appeared on two other similar documents. Charlie hoped to interview the two men and to investigate a recurring address on a batch of bank statements.

As the plane descended, Charlie caught sight of tankers lined up at a Canal lock, then spotted several small airfields, one a U.S. military base, the other a commercial facility for local traffic. On route to Tocumen International Airport, the plane circled east of Panama City, which sprouted irregularly around a bay. The city looked like a poorly sown crop: nondescript high-rise condominiums and offices sprung up randomly, as the city sprawled along the Pacific coastline into the southern hills.

A colleague of Ray McLean's had warned Charlie about the city. "Wild place," he'd cautioned. "Not as poor as some of the towns in Panama, where your wallet has a life expectancy of an hour. But the city's too poor to have all those high-rises, you know? I swear half of 'em are empty. Luxury units the owners pretend to rent just to launder their own fucking money."

Charlie woke to the sound of traffic outside the hotel, tires squealing into corners, every intersection contested. After breakfast, he descended to the ground floor, passed a few gamblers sauntering into the lobby from the hotel's casino, and headed for the street entrance. Outside, a cabbie at the front of the taxi line hit his ignition and cruised forward. Slouching in his seat, tipping the bill of his cap down, the driver pulled up next to Charlie; the words "*MIAMI TAXI*" were brightly painted on the vehicle's doors. A light rain was smudged by rapid strokes of well-worn windshield wipers and obscured the driver's dark, pocked face.

Charlie turned to the doorman, who was about to open the rear door. "Wait. I had the concierge hire a driver. Roberto."

The doorman nodded and whistled at the fourth cab in line, which jumped into traffic and jerked to the curb, ahead of the others. Its driver leaned across the seat and yelled at Charlie. "Mister? Sanderson? You want Roberto?"

Charlie tipped the doorman and was seated in the back of that taxi. "Mister," the driver said, treating his passenger to an infectious smile, "you call me Robert. I speak English plenty good."

"Robert?"

"Robert. I live in Dallas four years. You live in Dallas ever?"

"No."

"Crazy place. Everybody wanta ride a bull and drive a pickup. Hey, you drive a pickup?"

"No. I don't ride bulls, either."

"Good. Me, if I rich, I drive a Cadillac. Leather, air, automatic everything. Don't need no tow package."

"Right."

"Where we go?"

"Two streets." Charlie handed him a list of the addresses.

Robert looked at it and frowned. "You wanta see the bridge? Canal? Rain forest? Golden altar?"

"Maybe. Later."

"You don't take no bus. You need a guide." Robert adjusted the rear-view mirror so that he could study Charlie in it. "*Fulo.* You know this word?" Robert tapped the mirror, an instruction for Charlie to look at himself in it. A *fulo* was apparently a blond foreigner.

The narrow frame of the mirror gave Charlie a glimpse of Robert's face. His eyebrows suggested Asian bloodlines; his brown leather skin looked African. Three gold teeth figured prominently in the grin that he flashed. "I hired you for the morning," Charlie reassured him. "But I need to check out those places."

Robert hit the gas and forced his taxi into the heavy traffic on Avenida Balboa. The first place on the list was the law firm of Del Rosario & Gutierrez, located in Casco Viejo, where the city had been relocated after it had been sacked by the pirate Henry Morgan. Some of the buildings in Casco Viejo dated to the late seventeenth century;

all of them showed the wear and tear of the tropics. Exposed wood was pitted by rot; rusty iron balconies overhung narrow cobblestone streets. Though the rain had stopped, water gathered in foot-wide holes where stones had been dislodged by torrents of run-off. The profusion of spindly antennas atop faded tile roofs only added to the neighborhood's impression of colonial grandeur gone to seed.

After squeezing his taxi into a row of double-parked vehicles, Robert pointed down a side street to the first address on the list, a four-story building that sat fortress-like behind high walls topped with embedded shards of broken glass. Charlie slipped out of the cab and walked to an archway that led through the building's thick adobe walls to an interior courtyard, but a locked iron gate barred entry. A sign said that the gate would open at ten.

With twenty minutes to kill, Charlie returned to the main street, flashed his watch at Robert, and strolled towards a cluster of open-air stalls in a nearby plaza. Robert abandoned his vehicle and followed, hovering protectively as Charlie sat on a seaside bench. A few hundred feet away, the tide retreated, leaking through the rocks at the base of a breakwater.

An Indian woman crossed in front of Charlie and stopped next to the low wall of a broken fountain. Very short, she had to step on the wall in order to unroll a sheet on which she had pinned her collection of *molas*, elaborately embroidered panels that depicted a variety of colorful scenes. The sight of her peddling her merchandise reminded Charlie of the time that he, George, and Lucy had vacationed in Mexico. His second divorce finally concluded, George had booked the trip to celebrate. "Maybe in Mexico I won't feel so goddamn poor," he'd said.

One afternoon, sitting on an otherwise deserted beach down the coast from Cancun, the three of them had been approached by a young Mayan woman. Extremely tiny, the woman had a precarious hold on a package kept under her arm. As she neared the tourists, the package stirred, a baby's head now visible, while the woman fished through her pockets and found a well-used toy, a cone-shaped clown with its round head on a string. Attempting to demonstrate its use, the woman flicked the head, but failed to catch it with the rim of the neck, then held the toy out towards George.

"Golly," George joked. "Native handcraft. If the Mayans lived in Taiwan. I'm sure my father could've given us an informed goddamn opinion." George's father had died the summer before, and George demonstrated no intention of forgiving him. George held up his wallet to the woman. "I'll give you two dollars for it."

"I'll give you twenty," Charlie offered. One of the woman's eyes was pink and swollen half-shut; a fly buzzed at a scab on a sore under her nose.

"Thirty," George bid.

"Thirty-five," Charlie countered.

"Forty, and that's my final offer." George yanked two twenty-dollar bills from his wallet and handed them to the woman, who seemed unfamiliar with the denominations. She pushed the bills into the bottom of a string purse and extended the toy towards George, who refused it. The woman started off but slowed and waved at George.

Charlie split the cost by stuffing a twenty-dollar bill in George's pocket, while George watched the woman retreat and wondered, "Do you guys think I'd do better with someone like her? Someone who doesn't speak the same language. Hard to fucking argue."

"George, she's way too short," Lucy teased. "Four feet tall. You'd never have sex in the shower."

"Huh?"

"You have to be the same height, or it doesn't work. Sex in the shower. Isn't that what every guy wants? God, what's so great about having sex in the shower? Soap everywhere you don't want it."

"Who the hell are you dating?" Charlie wagged a finger at Lucy. "And what the hell's he doing in the bathroom?"

"If we lived here," George swept an arm to indicate the rocky shore and the encroaching jungle, "we wouldn't get many hot showers. Could you guys do that? Chuck it all? Live here?"

"Too isolated." Charlie tossed a stone into a tidal pool. "And too many bugs. The cockroaches? They're baby armadillos. I'm afraid to step on them."

"I'm serious," George said. "One day we might retire to a place like this. All of us half broke, stretching *el dolleros.*"

"George." Lucy opened her eyes wide with disbelief. "I have a hard time picturing you spending your sunset years at a trailer park in Guadalajara."

"Anything's possible. Although maybe I won't have to. I'm finally getting stock options."

"Yeah?"

"At the bank. A new regime. A new contract. Maybe that'll be my windfall."

George had never mentioned his stock options again. Sitting there in the square, thousands of miles from Rhode Island, Charlie regretted his neglect: he'd been too delicate to press George for details of his financial problems, and he'd never been interested enough to inquire about George's terms of employment. George had gotten stock options when the bank changed hands - when Martin had purchased it - and the bank was now much larger. If the bank survived its difficulty with the troubled loan, the options would have real value. Charlie made a mental note to try to discover what they'd be worth.

In the distance, a cathedral bell struck the hour: the office building should open. Charlie intended to pose as a potential client and to question the lawyers by taking his guide along as a translator. They reached the offices of del Rosario & Gutierrez by climbing an exterior staircase to a private second floor patio, where a row of five doors led to each office in the suite. A plaque, with the law firm's name on it, hung over the center door.

Charlie peered under the half-pulled shade on the door's window and cursed. The office had been quickly evacuated. Empty file drawers hung open; a desk and a table had nothing but scraps of paper on them.

"Mister..?" Robert signaled Charlie over to the adjacent door, which swung open when Robert pushed it. The wood around the latch had been splintered by a chisel.

Charlie used a corridor at the back of the suite to check the rooms, all of which had been emptied of everything except large pieces of furniture: there were no chairs, no phones or other electronic equipment, no documents. All that remained were empty filing cabinets, cumbersome bookshelves, and the oversized desks that anchored the bigger offices at each end of the suite.

Charlie searched for the slightest lead, anything that might give off a little information. Robert pushed ahead and whistled him into one of the large offices. Standing by a massive, intricately carved desk, Robert held up the end of a phone cord that had been severed mid-line. Whoever took, or stole, the phone equipment had cut the line in his haste.

"Who was here," Robert said, "they gone now."

"When's the mail delivered?"

Robert smirked. "You want mail, you get a box, an' you hope nobody steal it."

Robert went downstairs to find the janitor, while Charlie rummaged through the cabinets. He found nothing, not a single slip of paper.

"Lawyers up there," Robert said, when Charlie joined him in the courtyard. "One is dead, the janitor says. Cut up. Police thinks his girlfriend done it." Robert made numerous stabbing motions, then shuddered and dropped a hand in front of his groin to demonstrate where one of the knife wounds had been lodged. Senor del Rosario had been dispatched in much the same fashion as John Stuart Robbins, the New England bank examiner.

Charlie had one other lead from George's safe deposit box, statements from a bank in the Cayman Islands that listed a Panama City office. Robert shook his head when he looked at the address. "Mister? This? *Dogshit*." Robert dropped his mask, the cheerful tour guide suddenly becoming a driver of his own property, careful to calculate the risk to it. He consented to the drive only after the promise of a big tip, and made Charlie tilt a baseball cap over his face for the ride. They were going into the heart of El Chorillo. One of the city's poorest slums, the neighborhood had sustained the worst damage in the American invasion in 1989; tourists, especially Americans, were at risk here.

Stopping as infrequently as possible, rolling through red lights, avoiding the often-flooded underpasses, Robert drove to a hilltop crowned by a school, an outpost among dilapidated tenements and shanties. Behind steel-link fences capped with concertina wire, girls in blue uniforms raced about in improvised games as a nun stood guard. Across the street from the school Charlie saw a single-story structure that had huge numbers painted across its front wall, displaying the address that they were looking for. The words, "*POST OFICE*", were printed on a sign by the road.

"Damnit." Charlie realized that the bank's so-called "office" was nothing more than a mailbox inside, that this was not a place where a foreigner was free to snoop around. Robert double-parked, while Charlie hurried inside, the cap bent over his eyes. Large mailboxes lined an entire wall, at the far end of which a lone attendant lounged behind a well-fortified teller's cage. Charlie found the box in question - it was full of mail - and made a show out of checking an adjacent box that was empty, before leaving.

"A mail drop," Charlie explained, climbing back into the taxi.

"You want mail?" Robert picked up one of the bank statements, then studied the building. "I need a key. For the box."

Charlie dug his wallet out of his pocket and handed Robert a hundred dollars.

"A bigger key."

Charlie gave Robert another hundred dollars. Charlie had no idea how much of the money Robert kept for himself, but two minutes after he entered the mail drop, he emerged carrying a cardboard box full of mail.

"Mister," Robert cautioned Charlie, "after today I never seen you."

On the ride back to the hotel, Charlie opened several of the envelopes. Bank statements from the Maritime International Bank made the flow of money clear. Money moved from Panamanian corporations to trusts that were established in the Cayman Islands and from there to accounts at the First Federal Bank of Rhode Island. Copies of documents for several trusts listed the trustee as Joseph Leonard Turlik - Joe had always hated his middle name.

When they got back to the hotel, Robert waited as instructed, not far from the other cab parked out front - the "*MIAMI TAXI*", back at its post. Inside the lobby, near the doors to the casino, a crowd of tourists watched the police interrogate a suspected pickpocket. Charlie was convinced that the smartest thing to do was to return to Rhode Island immediately. Someone had already covered his tracks in Panama. Wherever George was, if he were still alive, he was somewhere further down the trail.

27

Charlie and Julia hadn't spoken in several days, both of them glad to put a little distance between themselves and the awkward conclusion to their last gathering. Before the return flight from San Juan, Charlie called from the airport and managed an exchange of messages. Julia would be back from a business trip by mid-afternoon and suggested that he meet her at her apartment, since his plane landed at Kennedy.

A taxi ferried him from the airport to Julia's apartment, where a doorman had been instructed to provide a key. Charlie rode the elevator in silence, stepped into a vacant hall, and let himself into her apartment. The stillness bothered him, the sublet space radiating its emptiness. He didn't much like her meager tenancy of the place; he didn't want to find himself once again abandoned.

Charlie walked into the kitchen and helped himself to a Diet Coke, then noticed the manila envelope on the counter, the one which he'd brought from her brother. Various papers and pamphlets stuck out of the end that had been torn open. He hated the prospect of snooping, but he couldn't explain the secrecy that had veiled Martin and George's business relationship nor the circumstances that surrounded his and Julia's reunion.

Charlie removed the documents from the envelope and skimmed them. In response to Martin's inquiry, a letter from an associate commented very favorably on Julia's well-funded pension plan. A separate statement detailed her growing stock portfolio. The rest of the package's contents were course catalogues from Manhattan colleges, with a focus on education.

Charlie reassembled the papers and put the envelope back on the counter. A dismissed indictment, he thought, as he laid down on a couch. He woke to find Julia sitting beside him, tousling his hair. "Wake up," she said. "It's three in the afternoon."

Charlie rubbed his eyes open, while she picked up the plane ticket that had fallen out of his pocket. She examined the receipt. "Panama?"

"Wild goose chase. I figured George had been there." Charlie shuffled his feet to get the blood flowing and put his head in his hands until he'd considered what to do next. "You feel like driving?"

"It's raining."

"Is it?"

"Where do you want to go?"

"Newport. I want to check the house." He sensed her reluctance. "I can rent a car."

"You'd fall asleep at the wheel."

They fetched her car from the garage. Charlie slept while Julia drove; he didn't wake until they were stuck in a line at a toll booth just north of the Newport Bridge. Stirring, Charlie looked at Julia: he vividly remembered crossing this bridge when they were young, a post-midnight romp, both of them unable to long abandon the touch of one another.

The traffic thinned out by the time they got past downtown Newport. It was September, and the tourists were mostly gone. At Four Winds a boxwood hedge, its trunks withered and speckled with disease, grew alongside the road. Running the length of the hedge's glassy green foliage, a flower bed once had fronted the road with a variety of white blossoms. Only the lilies-of-the-valley survived, their season over, the rain hammering their waxy leaves, which drooped towards muddy puddles.

Once inside the mansion Charlie sorted through the mail. Among the magazines and catalogues was an alumni bulletin from the University of Virginia, with a cover photo of Thomas Jefferson's Rotunda as a backdrop for protesting students. The lead article promised a definitive encapsulation, by a classmate of George and Charlie's, of the turbulent "Strike Semester" of 1970. Were he there, George would have laughed at the writer's presumption: George was too much of a cynic to appoint anyone a spokesperson for himself or his generation. "Everything got inside out," he'd once remarked of the era. "Christ, was that goddamn fun."

Charlie found Julia in the den, flipping through George's collection of records and CDs. She spoke without looking at Charlie, who filled the doorway. "You know what George told me? At that reunion? He said his first wife took almost all his old records. Well over a thousand LPs and 45s. I guess he had a great collection."

"Yes."

"He said she didn't even like much of the music, she only wanted it so he couldn't have it. Wasn't she the one who wanted the divorce?"

"It didn't make her any less angry."

"Why?"

"Because that's how people are when it doesn't work out."

"Are you mad with me?"

"I'm mad with George. He's gotten himself into something, only this time I don't know if I can get him out."

"Well, I'm mad with you."

"Why?"

"Because it scares me, you running down to Panama. Noriega, thugs like that."

"Noriega's in an American jail. 'Pineapple Face'. That's what they call him down there."

"Let somebody else go. You're a prosecutor. If you've got anything-?"

"What if I do?"

"Can't you go to the police?"

"It's not that simple."

"Why?!"

"Because there are issues of jurisdiction. Because I'm looking to keep George out of trouble, not get him in it. Maybe the same could be said for your brother."

"You think Martin's in trouble?"

"Yes. I think I was followed when I left his office. It wasn't simply me they were watching."

"Does Martin know?"

"No. And he doesn't act as if he's in trouble."

"Would you help him? If he needed it?"

"I don't know. I'd help you. Can we leave it there?"

Julia threw up her hands and moved to a windowsill; she dragged a finger through a layer of dust. "How long do you want to stay?"

"Not long."

"Let me know when you're ready."

Charlie checked the office. There were two new messages, both from the realtor, who said that an "unidentified" buyer for the estate was "worried" about possible problems. The realtor wondered if George, or Charlie on George's behalf, wanted to review the copy of the deed of trust that she'd procured from the county recorder.

Charlie called the realtor and gave her his fax number at home, then set off through the house. Upstairs, the loud flapping of a window shade, spinning itself into a tight coil, led him to the two-room suite in the servants' wing that once had been reserved for him.

"I didn't remember it being so small," Julia said, when Charlie joined her in the small bedroom. She stretched out her arms and glided, in three full steps, from contact with one wall to its opposite. "This room must've shrunk. It was the center of the world."

"I didn't stay here after you. A single bed. The mattress is probably made of horsehair - God knows it's old enough."

Julia looked at the narrow radiator, flecked with peeling silver paint and listing a bit to starboard under the window. "Do you remember the morning they turned the heat on?" It had been Grace's habit to turn on the heat, an antiquated boiler pushing steam heat through rattling pipes, in late August. "The middle of the night. I'd never heard such a racket. I thought guns were going off."

"1972. The war at home had finally begun." Charlie touched the frail fabric of the bedspread; the contact sent up a cloud of dust.

"Sometimes I think about our summer here. Incredible. I never imagined I'd get the chance to visit again."

"Why?"

"I didn't know what I'd be willing to risk. I lost everything for a while, not just you. I didn't expect we'd get another chance." She straightened a doily on top of the bureau before continuing. "But I don't understand what's happening. Why hasn't George called you? Wouldn't he do that?"

"You'd think."

Julia looked out the window; rain swelled and spilled out of clogged gutters on the west wing and splattered on the brick terrace below. "He'd call, or he'd come here. He's never let go. It's his castle, his '*home-free*,' isn't that what you call the safe place in a game of tag? He'd come here if he could."

The rain had stopped by the time they got to Providence. A copy of the deed of trust was waiting on the fax machine; the mortgage, which allowed for two years' worth of interest to accumulate until the debt totaled over four million dollars, was held by the Royal Bank of Grenada. The realtor had underlined the amount and put exclamation points around it: she didn't understand how such a large loan had been obtained four years ago, in the midst of a real estate slump. Jon Levitz, Esq., of Cranston, had notarized signatures and supervised the processing and recording of the deed.

The next morning, Charlie met Levitz at his office behind his home, a converted garage that smelled of disinfectant and of mildew that had not been wholly eradicated. Levitz wore wrinkled trousers held in place by olive green suspenders and reading glasses set low on his nose.

He'd already retrieved the file for the loan which Charlie had inquired about. "It was a big one. That I remember."

"Who hired you?"

"I don't remember the name. George Spaulding referred me. See, sometimes I do a little work for the bank."

"George's bank didn't make this loan."

"Yeah. The guy who hired me was some loan broker. Kind of seedy. Some guy from the Caribbean, acted like nobody ever made a loan before: *do I appreeshut, mahn, de loan fee gotta be paid wid a ca-sheer check?"*

"What was the loan fee?"

"It was ten percent! Paid out of loan proceeds. You're an attorney for the state, right? Is that usury? Ten percent for a mortgage, just the fee, and a goddamn lender willing to finance it."

"You remember who got the fee? The broker's name?"

"The file would have it. Very slick guy. Talked about his brother, who I think was a government finance minister. His brother had to sign off on the loan. Why else would some bank down there hold this mortgage? See, that made me uncomfortable, 'cause technically I'm representing this foreign bank. They hired me."

"You didn't object at the time."

"Is that a question?"

"Did you object?"

Levitz puffed himself up. "I did advise the client a second appraisal might be a good idea. Of course, the loan fee was steep, a nice bit of skimming. But hell, the borrower consented."

"Why would George do that? You have any idea?"

Levitz winced. "You're a friend, right? Mr. Spaulding's father had used the property as collateral. Even though the mansion wasn't his, he got old Mrs. Spaulding to let a loan be secured to it. Killer terms. Ultimately, the holder of that note tries to foreclose. George Spaulding is, my view here, a real gentleman. He didn't want to let the place go like that, some asshole muscling in, trying to foreclose on his grandmother. I think he figured real estate would turn around, and he'd sell it, or keep it if his business was good. Funny thing, huh? George Spaulding bails the family's summer mansion out from his dead father's killer loan, but he has to sign a killer note to do it. He keeps the house, but even the trust officer for his grandmother didn't cut him a break. Always fun to do business with your family, right?"

The story grieved Charlie: George crushed in the vice of family. Charlie had to concentrate to think of his next question. "You do any other work? For the loan broker?"

"Hardly."

"What about for the bank? In Grenada?"

"*Hardly.*"

"You didn't file the notice of default?"

"They asked me to file the notice. But I don't want any part of that. Foreclose? George Spaulding's a hell of a good guy, plus he sends me business."

"Who asked you to file?"

"Somebody from that bank." Levitz opened the file and fished through it. "Let me give you what I got."

The loan broker's address, four years ago, was a local hotel; no other address or phone number was listed. However, Sebastian Frank, the Deputy Minister of Finance for the Republic of Grenada who'd had to approve the loan, shared the same last name as the loan broker, Gifford Frank, who'd profited handsomely by the fact that George had been unable to refinance the mansion through conventional channels. George's gamble, that he could sell the mansion for enough money prior to falling behind on the loan, had backfired.

"Well, damn," Levitz said, as he paused to pull another document from the folder. "I'd forgotten this." He continued while he made a copy of the letter for Charlie. "A bit of fluff. Padding for the file. A letter of introduction for George Spaulding, written from some office in Haiti. Not a letter of credit, which would mean a whole lot more. This is kind of a reference, '*Mr.-Spaulding's-known-to-us-as-an-upright-substantial-individual*.'"

Charlie left with a copy of the brief letter, which was written on behalf of an investment company in Haiti and addressed to the Royal Bank of Grenada. He tried to phone the Haitian company, but its phone number was long out of service and no new number was listed. He considered, and rejected, the idea of a quick trip to Haiti. The "investment company" had vanished, and air-travel to the republic was greatly limited by the reluctance of major carriers to fly there.

Two phone calls to the Royal Bank of Grenada convinced Charlie that he would get no real information over the phone. His calls were shuffled from one secretary to another; the last secretary with whom he spoke promised to "try" to deliver a message. Likewise, a call to the Ministry of Finance was unreturned; no one seemed much concerned that the mortgage on George's house, now in default, had been made from funds in the general pension account of government workers.

Charlie couldn't tell what jeopardy the loan and its circumstances created, but the answer, if it existed, involved another trip. Julia showed up that evening at Charlie's, with the intention of spending several nights. Her response, when told of the troubled loan and his prospective trip, was simple. "I want to go."

"I don't know what I'm getting into."

"You're willing to risk it."

"That's different."

"Why?"

"Because it's George."

"I want to help."

"Then call your brother. See what he knows."

"God, you're determined to involve him. Martin works for people with money. The same could be said of your sister. She's an interior designer, right? Are her clients rich? What does that make her?"

"She's not missing."

"Charlie! I don't pay attention to Martin's business. It doesn't interest me. If you're asking me if he could look the other way if he had to..?"

"It'd be one thing to close your eyes and ride the bus. It'd be another to drive it."

"For God's sake.."

Charlie wasn't yielding. "Call him."

28

"D o you want to record the call?" Julia asked, grabbing a wall phone in the kitchen. "Pick up another phone and listen?"

"No."

"What are your questions?"

"George borrowed money from some bank in Grenada."

"Is that so strange?"

"Yes. Who put him in touch with these people? This isn't Household Finance, a Chase Manhattan mortgage. You don't get flyers in the mail. How the hell does he meet people who make such a dubious loan?"

"You think Martin knows?"

"You can ask."

Julia angrily punched in a phone number and hung up at the sound of an answering machine. She tried a second number and held the phone far enough from her ear so that Charlie, eight feet away, could hear Martin's voice. "Hello?" The receiver buzzed with the static from a cell phone.

"It's Julia."

"Where are you?"

"At Charlie's. I'm trying to spare the two of us a trip."

"What's up?"

"George. I guess he borrowed money."

"Charlie knows about this. Is he on the line?"

"No."

"He's not with you?"

"Not at the moment." Julia looked at Charlie. "He went to get cash. With his bankcard."

"He wants to travel?"

"I'm going with him. Grenada."

"Grenada? Are you crazy!?"

"George - some loan."

"Why's that your concern?"

"I'm helping. I want you to help. If you know anybody we should talk to..?"

"I don't interfere with George. I'm sure he can solve his own problems. But, Jesus, I'd stay clear of Grenada. What do you know about the place?"

"What do you?"

"I know it's more Third World than First. It was run by some psychotic for decades, a Marxist with a thing for UFOs."

"You did business there?"

"Castro did business there. There was a coup, another maniac in charge, before Reagan sent in the troops."

"Is it safe?"

"If you're rich .. and if you know the right people to bribe. Jesus, that's what they sell down there - justice and bananas."

"Do you know anybody?"

Martin paused. His voice turned gruff. "Why would I?"

Charlie could see the tears welling in Julia's eyes, the tremor in her hands, but she kept her voice steady. "Why would George?" she asked.

"Christ, what are you meddling in?" Martin changed the subject. Julia didn't cry, not audibly anyhow, until she was off the phone.

Under other circumstances, the airplane trip might have been fun, Charlie and Julia buoyed by anticipation of a three-day vacation, two lovers anxious to deplane into the steam bath of September in the tropics, but George had been missing for at least four weeks. Exhausted by a sleepless night, Julia slept on the flight to Miami, while Charlie tried to imagine a tactic that would gain him an audience with the

Deputy Minister of Finance, who trafficked in dubious loans of his own government's money. The threat of a subpoena, issued offshore, would certainly be ignored. Ultimately, all Charlie could hope for were candid answers to certain questions. He wrote them down on a legal pad:

(1) Had anyone other than the deputy minister approved the loan for the mortgage?

(2) Who was the loan broker who made out so handsomely on the transaction? Was he the deputy minister's brother?

(3) With the loan in default, what steps were being taken to foreclose?

(4) Had any other loans been made to friends or clients of George Spaulding?

(5) Who introduced George to the Deputy Minister of Finance? The letter from the Haitian firm was unsigned.

This last question most intrigued Charlie, who doubted that George's jeopardy stemmed solely from a delinquent loan. Certainly, the loan might prove an embarrassment, but the process itself, inflated fees being skimmed off the top while a foreign bank made large loans secured by American real estate, seemed tailor-made for the repatriation of tarnished dollars.

At the airport terminal in Grenada, sheets of jasmine hung over a fence like laundry on a line, the smell mingling with the odor of airplane fuel, vapors from which rose from spilled puddles of it. High clouds drifted past a scorching sun. The back of Charlie's shirt was damp by the time he had climbed down the portable ladder and crossed to the aluminum-roofed baggage claim. A taxi driver tried to relieve Charlie of his and Julia's suitcases before leading them to a rental car agency, which delivered on its painted promise of ICY AIR CONDITION AUTOS.

The road from the airport was lined with young palms and untended skeletons of industrial buildings, half-built or half-demolished and hard to tell which. Almost always in view, the ocean tumbled onto a long beach with sand so fine and white it could have been refined. Charlie passed the turn-off for his hotel and drove into the capital city, St. George's, where he found the Royal Bank of Grenada on a prominent street corner. After Panama City and its high-rises, after the bustle and commerce of Grand Cayman, St. George's seemed a sleepy relic of the early Sixties, quaint and strangely inert, as if the town had surrendered itself to the languor of its lower latitude. There were few pedestrians; traffic plodded and played to the rhythms of unseen bottlenecks. Only the buses looked new.

They took a quick tour of the town and doubled back to the hotel. Built on a rise overlooking Grand Anse Beach, guest cottages were scattered around grounds overrun with flowers. Charlie and Julia's cottage was equipped with its own private plunge pool. Mosquito netting, bunched like a canopy, was suspended over the king-size bed.

No sooner had they been shown to their room than Charlie was busy working the phone. He first called the government office of Sebastian Frank.

"Mr. Frank is in meetings," the Deputy Minister's secretary announced when the call was finally put through.

"It's a matter of some urgency. Confidential. I'm sure he'll want to discuss it with me privately."

"If you care to leave a message-?"

"I can call back tomorrow."

"The minister will be at Parliament."

"Will his brother?"

"Pardon?"

"His brother."

"Which brother?"

Charlie had her attention; he mentioned the first name of the loan broker. "Gifford. With the loans. I'm sure the minister will know what I'm talking about."

"The minister's schedule -"

"He needs to talk to me. I'm down here from Rhode Island. Attorney General's Office. I'm sure he's anxious to help."

"Can you give me your name again?"

Charlie's next four phone calls were to senior officers of the Royal Bank of Grenada. None of them took Charlie's call, although each of their secretaries was given a lengthy tease about troubled loans and the prospects of investigation and/or litigation in the United States.

With nothing to do but wait, in the hope that someone felt like talking, Charlie and Julia changed into bathing suits and walked down to the ocean. The shoreline dropped off gradually, the water's color slowly deepening from turquoise to cobalt. Julia was soon bobbing in troughs between waves. Anxious for the exercise, Charlie swam a quarter mile offshore and struggled with the currents on the way in.

The sun low on the horizon, they returned to their cottage and rinsed themselves free of sea salt by diving into their private pool. They left their swimsuits on the terrace, wrapped themselves in towels, then stepped inside.

Julia's eyes swept over everything: the sunset striped by tilted blinds, the room's cozy furniture, the bedcovers turned down by a maid, Charlie's gaze. "I wish..," she said. "I wish we could go off the clock. Just us. We could have the world's longest sundown."

Charlie put his arms around her and brushed the wet hair from her forehead. He felt the stress in her shoulders, the stiffness in her back, so he made a couple of drinks, rum on ice liberally splashed with a passion-fruit concoction from the mini-bar. She drank her glass quickly, on her feet, her tension still apparent in the tuck of her shoulders. Charlie unhooked their towels, led her to the bed, and had her lie belly down on the crisp sheets. He massaged her neck, his fingers sliding over the soft skin on the back of her ear lobes. His hands worked the knots out of her shoulder blades before his thumbs traced her spine down to the base of her back, where his palms circled through the delicate hollow there. The flesh of her buttocks softened to the knead of his knuckles, but her thighs stiffened with resistance. The calves were more pliant, the heels of his hands rolling up and down their curves, the bottoms of her feet curling to the unexpected touch.

He turned her over and concentrated on her legs, sliding his hands up them, stroking everything, the bone of the knee, the supple skin inside her thighs, the pale crease between leg and abdomen. She reached out to touch him, but he wouldn't let her, so she lay there, no longer still, yet not fully excited. Wanting more of a response, he rolled her back onto her stomach and worked his hands along her ribcage, her waist, the contour of her hips, then traced the crease of her buttocks with his thumb and spread her legs, a hand slipping beneath her, a finger inside her, while his other hand rubbed circles into the base of her spine. Her body writhed to the odd tug, the press of a hand, the touch of a finger. When she turned to face him, he fondled her neck, her chest, her abdomen, before the fingers of one hand parted her and the fingers of the other hand played there, the pace unhurried, the delicate stroke gradually becoming firmer. Julia let go of everything but the rhythm. Her hands grabbed the sheets as the pace quickened, her back arching as her hips shook and a violent shudder stole through her. She had little chance to compose herself, Charlie pushing inside her and driving hard into her fierce contractions, holding off till she peaked again, then lying on the bed until the heat, flesh pressed to flesh, got to both of them.

A minute or two later, her breath restored, Julia laughed and gave a playful slap to Charlie's butt. "It's not a contest."

Charlie realized that she meant the sex, her orgasms. "If it were? I mean, who's counting?"

"Both of us."

Dinner was wonderful: a breadfruit vichyssoise, highly seasoned fish, mangos and a mild cheese. They stayed at their table - on the edge of the hotel terrace with a splendid view of the starlit surf - well after the meal was finished. The restaurant closed at midnight, and still they sat there, measuring the slow shift of the heavens with the makeshift sextant of two treetops. Scents of vanilla, sage, and nutmeg drifted in from the island's lush interior. With several of the island's spice farms a short distance upwind, the air was pungent as cheap cologne.

The wind picked up, driving in the storm and pelting them with odd debris, a bug blown off-course, sand churned into a miniature spout. Julia checked their bottle of wine, now empty, and sat in Charlie's lap. She kept a hand on Charlie's neck as she watched the rush of clouds blot out the stars.

Only when rain began to fall did Julia lead Charlie back to their room, where the rain rustled the roof with soft notes of steel-drum music. Charlie slept like the drugged and woke to the sound of chambermaids looking into his room.

"Maybe a little later," Julia told the maids, who withdrew with polite apologies.

"What time is it?"

"Eleven. They brought breakfast at nine." Julia nodded to a table, where a tray was laden with a basket of rolls, a platter of fruit, and a pot of coffee.

"It's pouring," Charlie grumbled. Sheets of rain slapped the roof.

"There's a tropical storm. Not yet hurricane strength, but it's not moving off into the Atlantic either."

"Some holiday."

"No one's called. I checked with the front desk."

After a quick breakfast, they drove into St. George's and spent an hour at the public library researching the government's constitutional powers. Though the republic's constitution had been much rewritten in recent years, the Deputy Minister of Finance still had broad latitude and little supervision in administering loans.

Equally alarming was the broad range of criminal charges that a debtor could face. A contact at the U.S. State Department had cautioned Charlie about the fates of Americans held in Caribbean jails: "Due process is a joke. It can be months before we hear about an American in jail. Half the time, the charges are pure shit."

Not far from the historic Fort Frederick, with its own view of the harbor from Richmond Hill, stood Longley Prison. Any male foreigner incarcerated in Grenada would be held there. Anxious to rule out the chance that George had shown up to renegotiate his loan and been jailed, Charlie drove by the site and found a building that looked like an enormous chicken shed tucked on the edge of a cliff. There was no prison yard, no guard tower, nothing but a long structure streaked with rust and encased in barbed wire. Though the rain had tapered off, muddy water streamed through countless narrow gullies down a steep, fragile cliff.

The road to Longley Prison ended in a cul-de-sac, well posted with signs that forbid parking. Julia offered to wait with the car while Charlie checked inside.

A passage through a thick cement wall led to the well-fortified reception area. Two guards, sitting in an elevated cage, fanned themselves with stacks of advertising circulars and watched Charlie, who loosened his tie as he approached. The heat was crushing. One of the guards slid a short-barreled rifle aside, leaned towards the bars, and flashed a smile full of perfectly white teeth.

"Any Americans?" Charlie inquired.

"With the embassy?" the guard wondered.

Charlie nodded. He saw no reason to correct the guard's assumption that he worked at the American embassy. The guard reached under a counter and handed an application for a visitor's permit to Charlie, who completed it quickly. After a perfunctory review, the guard motioned Charlie towards a pair of steel doors, where another guard, a giant of a man, frisked him; the guard's hands were the size of baseball mitts.

"Who you want?" The guard's voice was high and soft.

"Americans. I'm looking for one."

"No' many. Come see."

The guard punched in codes and led Charlie through a series of sliding doors and down a central corridor that bisected a long cell block, with two tiers of cells on each side. Sunlight angled into the cavernous space from windows tucked under the roofline, while overhead fans stirred the close air without managing to clear it. The stench was overpowering: fungal, fecal.

Cell after cell was crowded, oftentimes four men jammed into a space with two cots stacked on a narrow wall. Charlie supposed that the prisoners must take turns sleeping, while their cellmates shuffled in place or slumped on the floor. The less crowded cells seemed to harbor the sick, one prisoner retching constantly, two others madly babbling in their shared quarters. Some of the prisoners, upon spotting Charlie in his well-tailored suit, had proposals:

"Hey, Mistuh Gennelman, Suh, you tell my goddumb wife.."

"Pretty boy! Ain't you a struttin' cockatoo.."

This jail might not be hell on earth, but it was only a few degrees north. Charlie was terrified by the thought of George – or anyone else he knew – imprisoned here, out of the reach of his help. Outspoken and sarcastic, spoiled beyond such humbling, George wouldn't last long in Longley Prison. He'd take general exception, and in doing so publicly, he'd incite personal violence.

At the conclusion of his brief tour, Charlie was greatly relieved that George wasn't languishing in any of the cells. The jailer, however, checked out Charlie's expensive suit and ridiculed the idea that a friend of his might have been incarcerated for any length of time in Grenada.

"He got money, doan he?"

Charlie gave the guard some cash, a description of George, a phone number, and a promise to pay a substantial reward upon delivery of any information. Once back at the rental car, Charlie had to shut off its air-conditioning; the sudden chill was too abrupt.

Julia suggested a walk when they'd returned to their hotel. The rain had quit, the clouds massing themselves on the southern horizon, but the beach was littered with the shriveled carcasses of Portuguese men-of-war, stranded by the wind and tide, fried by the equatorial sun.

Julia climbed a dune and looked out to sea. "What would you have done?" she asked. "If you found George today? Would you pay a bribe to get him out?"

"You want to hear me say it?"

"I want to know what the rules are."

"There aren't any rules. This island's a free-for-all."

"I don't think he's here. We're way out on the edge of nowhere. Twelve hundred miles to Haiti. This morning, outside the lobby, somebody tried to sell me smuggled cigarettes. It's small-time, isn't it? How does George fit into that?"

"He doesn't. But he was here several years ago. And he got a loan nobody in his right mind would make."

"Suppose someone owed him a favor? Suppose that's all the loan is?"

"A four-million-dollar favor. You have to wonder what he did to deserve that kind of favor."

That evening, their room phone rang twice, but the caller hung up when they answered. When it rang again in the middle of the night, Charlie picked up without answering and heard the caller whisper something - it sounded like French - before hanging up.

29

It didn't take long for Charlie to confirm that he, and possibly Julia as well, had attracted attention. The following morning, the two of them were at the Finance Ministry when the doors opened but were delayed by a security guard. Ultimately, they gained admission to an antechamber, where they were ignored for several more hours. Charlie settled for sending his business card to the Deputy Minister of Finance; beneath the embossed insignia of the State Attorney General Charlie wrote the words "will call later – your brother Gifford is worried."

The next stop was The Royal Bank of Grenada. An armed guard was stationed by a row of tellers, but there was no one to prevent Charlie from wandering through several other floors and collaring the bank's Executive Vice President outside his corner office. Charlie thrust a photocopy of loan documents into his hands.

The banker gave Charlie a withering stare. "You're the American? Making all the phone calls? Goodness, sir, do you think it's our only problem loan?" The Executive Vice President expanded his chest. "We are a substantial institution."

"Great. I'm sure your loan committee can explain-"

"The loan committee meets on Thursday afternoon. I will discuss this with them."

Charlie left with a promise that his questions would be addressed two days hence. Julia had secured a cash advance on a credit card and was waiting for him in the lobby near the glass doors that led to the parking lot.

"Any luck?" she asked.

"I'll find out Thursday. I'm not optimistic."

"Somebody's been checking out our car."

"Who?"

"I don't see them now. At first I thought they were going to break in."

Charlie signaled to the armed security guard, who approached. "Would you mind escorting her to her car?"

The guard smiled and nodded. Charlie handed Julia the car keys. "Drive around front."

The guard opened the door for Julia and followed her to the parking lot, where she got into the rental car. Charlie slid alongside a wall of windows to a corner of the building. On the other side of the windows, not ten feet away, a man slipped around the corner and lowered the bill of his fishing cap. He watched Julia back out of a parking space, then swiveled his head to track the guard's lazy saunter to the back door of the bank. Dark and roughly pitted, the man's face was unforgettable. It belonged to the guy who had followed Charlie in New York City.

Charlie saw the man gesture at someone sitting in the driver's seat of a small blue van, the engine of which came to life with a burst of smoke. While Julia drove towards the side street, the van circled through the lot. The man with the fishing cap took hold of something inside his windbreaker and turned to the windows. Charlie was already moving, hurrying to the other entrance.

The bank fronted Church St. Charlie burst through that door, darted between traffic, and was waiting on the far corner when Julia pulled to the curb. She slid into the passenger seat and pointed him to the driver's side.

Charlie jumped in and jerked the car back into traffic. He headed north, slowing on his approach to the few traffic lights, speeding up at the last moment, hoping to be the last vehicle through yellow lights.

"Who are they?"

"They were in New York a few weeks ago."

"What?"

"They followed me, or they were sent."

"Why?"

"I was set up." Charlie explained how he had been spoon-fed the information about the loan on Four Winds. Some "unidentified" buyer had voiced concern. Although the loan might be in default, it probably had little to do with the trouble that George was in. Charlie had been deliberately sidetracked, and now there were two men in a blue van five cars behind theirs.

Julia looked over her shoulder. "What do they-?"

"Can you open the map?"

"The police?"

"Won't help. They'll hold us."

Julia spread a map across her lap. The road headed north along the island's western coast until Sauteurs, where it looped back to the south and east. It was at Sauteurs, in 1651, that the last band of Carib Indians had thrown their wives and children off the cliffs, then leapt to their own deaths, rather than surrender to enslavement by the French. That spot had been known as Leapers' Hill ever since: Charlie had no intention of allowing himself to be trapped there.

At the tiny town of Gouyave a road cut inland towards the lush, low mountains and rose to a volcanic lake, then split into a fork and split again before reaching the eastern coast and its road. It was the only route that offered pursuers any chances at wrong turns. At the intersection, liana vines draped themselves around a cluster of signs. Charlie careened around the corner and was fifty yards down the new road before he saw the sign that warned FLOODING AHEAD. He pulled a hard U-turn on the muddy shoulder, raced back to the coast road, and edged the car forward until oncoming traffic was obliged to stop. Once on that highway, speeding back towards St. George's, Charlie had to slow for two goats, which stumbled onto the road and lingered, before finally trotting after a bag of litter that blew into roadside brush.

In the rear-view mirror Charlie spotted the blue van, also south-bound now and not more than a hundred yards behind, as it darted around a three-wheeled pick-up. Charlie drove hard, passing vehicles at every chance, but approaching town he felt, then heard, the recurring flap of a deflating tire. The men in the blue van must have punctured a tire and created a slow leak. Worsening, the tire's flap grew louder; the hubcap flew off near Market Square in the center of town.

Charlie steered for the harbor and limped the rental car halfway into a parking space, the trunk stuck out in traffic, the tire completely flat. He and Julia jumped out of the car and ducked down a flight of wooden steps to the trash-strewn quay that bordered the harbor.

They stayed low and close to the wall as they ran past several piers. Tourist boats sailed from a few of them; a huge yacht was moored at another. A sign on a dilapidated dock promised BOATS TO HIRE. Beside a tiny shack, eight motorboats were strung together, one line tethering all of them to a floating dock. The attendant at the shack eyed Charlie and Julia suspiciously, both of them sprinting up to him in business clothes and wanting to hire a fishing boat with only a few hours of daylight left.

"Fishin' bettah in the morn'," the attendant warned. He looked south: the sky was unnaturally dark.

Charlie handed him his credit card and requested the most powerful motorboat the man had. The attendant kept the card and a photo i.d., and led them down the ramp, where they scampered across five boats to reach a twenty-four-foot Sea Ray. Just aft of the bow, a canvas roof covered the wheel, the controls, and the electronic gear. While the attendant untied the boat, Charlie climbed into an adjacent boat and fetched two spare tanks of gasoline, as well as a Styrofoam cooler which had several bottles of water left in it.

The attendant put a key in the ignition, issued a quick set of instructions, and nodded at the narrow entrance to the harbor. "An hour, no more. Git in 'fore the storm."

The attendant hopped into the adjacent boat and cast the Sea Ray off, a strong shove helping ease it out of the crowded slip. Charlie caught sight of the blue van, double-parked on the far side of the harbor, and hit the power. The boat was well in violation of the harbor speed limit by the time it hit the chop of the ocean, which crowded through the breakwater. The boat lost speed as the propellers bounced out of the water, so

Charlie cut the power and steered north by west, a course diagonal to the swell of the waves. Fifteen minutes later, the island had grown small beneath an enormous sky that was filling with thunderheads.

Charlie turned the wheel over to Julia and examined the main gas tank. "Charlie?" Julia had to shout to be heard over the roar of the motor. "How far can we go?"

"A hundred miles, maybe two if the weather holds."

"Where's that get us?"

"I don't know."

The boat's hull was shallow for the height of the waves and the pitch of the ocean, so Charlie had Julia further reduce power and angle the boat along the line of the swell. For two hours, as it grew dark, the boat kept its bow forward in the rough sea. With the wind at their back, the swell slowly subsided and the sea grew calmer, although the southern sky exploded with electricity, lightning flashing in lateral arcs or bolting into direct hits on the horizon.

The static made it difficult for Julia to tune in a station on the boat's radio. Unfamiliar with the marine bands, she picked up a variety of weak AM signals: French patois, lilting island Spanish, a hint of the BBC and its Oxford English. Finally, she tuned in a clear station, a news broadcast entirely in Spanish. In thirty- to fifty-word bursts, the announcer raced through the stories, all but a few simple phrases ("*dos haciendas a Isla de Margarita..*") incomprehensible to Charlie.

Julia paid attention. "It's from Venezuela," she determined, pointing at the radio. "He says the weather is next."

Though the reception faltered, Julia made sense of the report: the news was good. The tropical storm had lost strength and was drifting into the Atlantic; its winds no longer approached hurricane strength and it posed no further danger to Venezuela - which meant that the Caribbean had been spared as well.

With its overlapping signals, its multitude of stations, and its various languages and dialects, the radio illustrated what a crossroads the Caribbean was. For centuries these waters had been home and hideaway to all sorts of rogues, "low tech" and "high tech" pirates. Charlie couldn't understand how Joe and George had come to traffic here.

Shortly after increasing his own boat's speed, he spotted another powerboat, this one sleek and deep-hulled, an ocean racer. The boat barreled out of nowhere and continued west. None of its lights were lit, nor was it likely that its occupants could see the Sea Ray. The speed and violence of the boat's course made it apparent that the driver was engaged on his own flight, the boat consumed by its spray as it launched off and crashed through waves. Someone was running something somewhere, and according to the charts posted in the Sea Ray's makeshift wheelhouse, it was a long way to anywhere if the boat continued west. The powerboat vanished into the darkness.

Thus far, Charlie had only briefly lost visual contact with the chain of small islands that constitute the Grenadines. He was unfamiliar with much of the boat's electronic equipment, and two loose wires hung from the instrument that he presumed to be the transponder. Unable to rely on his own navigational skills, he didn't want to lose sight of land altogether, nor did he want to be caught weaponless on open water come daybreak. At the moment a small island, seemingly uninhabited, was a few miles off the starboard bow.

The boat headed north along the chain of islands and their occasional landmarks: the beacon of a lighthouse, a tall volcanic outcropping, a series of lights strung up at a beach hideaway. It was hours later, sometime near dawn, when Julia thought she heard a helicopter. Once Charlie cut the boat's motor, the roar of the aircraft was unmistakable, the flap of its blades adding percussion to the unmuffled drone of its engine. Though it couldn't be seen, the helicopter circled a mile off the stern of the boat before it darted into the distance.

The running lights of another plane, flying so low that Charlie first thought it was a boat, were visible off the coast of a larger island a few miles ahead. The plane disappeared behind a hill as it reached the shore. Five minutes later, a second plane, this one a commercial jet, took off over the same hill, its jets cutting crisp gray trails through the early morning light. Stronger than it had been in days, the sun was rising. Not much more than a liter of water was left, and it wouldn't last long in the morning heat.

30

According to the plastic-encased charts, the island was St. Vincent. The descent of an old Cessna towards the same hill confirmed the existence of an airport not far inland. Charlie followed the coastline north till he rounded a rocky peninsula and found a slew of boats moored in the lee of a bay. Numerous skiffs had been dragged up onto the beach.

Charlie gunned the motor and aimed for a vacant patch of sand. A hundred feet from shore, he cut the power, then quickly yanked out the cotter pin and raised the propeller-shaft of the outboard motor. Tossing off giant pinwheels of spray, the propeller blades slapped across the water line moments before the bow crunched into the sand and the boat ground to a halt. A lead line in hand, Julia jumped overboard and held on while Charlie stepped out. Together, they tried to drag the boat farther onto the beach, without success, so they tied the boat to an iron ring that anchored two adjacent skiffs.

They crossed the sand, climbed to the beach road, and put their shoes back on. Minutes later, a mini-bus pulled onto the shoulder, and a uniformed driver opened the door for them. Aware that the driver was measuring the prospect of a fare, Charlie held up his wallet and asked, "You going by the airport?"

The driver looked over his shoulder at his sole passenger, an elderly woman sleeping soundly in a back seat, and waved them aboard. After a short ride, he dropped Charlie and Julia at the E. T. Joshua Airport.

Inside the terminal, several commercial airlines had counters, but only one was staffed. Per the schedules posted on the grids, the next flight to leave the island didn't depart until noon. The only sign of activity was out on the tarmac, where a fuel truck and several workers were gathered around a two-propeller plane that was painted with the words LINDBERG BAY CHARTER. A middle-aged man in a windbreaker, Bermuda shorts, and sneakers - no shirt, no socks - was directing the activity.

Charlie stepped around an unmanned security station and continued towards the gentleman in the windbreaker. The man's face and legs looked perpetually sunburned, dark red patches of half-scorched, half-peeled skin. He kept an eye on Charlie, who was also ragged, his suit filthy, his cheeks unshaven, his shoes stained by salt water.

"Charter?" Charlie called out. "Where can I charter a plane?"

The pilot of the plane being serviced, the gentleman took all their remaining cash and flew them to San Juan, where they could connect to Kennedy Airport. Before that flight, Charlie left a message on Ray McLean's voicemail, then phoned Beth at the bank.

"Charlie?" Beth lowered her voice and whispered into the phone. "I got more stuff. From George's lawyer. I mailed it to you on Monday."

"How're things there?"

"Busy. Crazy. Lots of meetings in Mr. Wells' office."

"Who's at them?"

"Don't know. They look like bankers, ties perfectly knotted, except they got accents and Italian shoes."

"What kind of accent? French? Spanish?"

"Some Spanish; some British. What do people from Bermuda sound like?"

"Is there anything else you can get for me? Lists of George's accounts, names of his clients."

"I'll try. But, shit, it's gotten real strange around here. They're watching me."

Charlie hung up and turned to Julia. "Your brother's bank - everybody's jumping around like crazy."

"I don't know about the bank. But Martin tried to talk us out of going. He'd never do anything to hurt me."

"Suppose it's bigger than him?" Charlie handed her the phone. "Maybe he thinks he's still in charge. You need to warn him."

Julia's hands trembled as she dialed Martin's office. She didn't leave a message and called his cell phone instead, leaving a message on its voicemail. "It's Julia," she said. "Can you meet me tonight? About eight o'clock. A rendezvous?"

Julia clicked off the line and turned to Charlie. "He'll know what that means. There's this little restaurant near where he keeps his boat. '*The Rendezvous*.'"

At Kennedy Airport, no luggage to claim, Charlie and Julia found his car where they had parked it, at the end of an aisle in one of the lots. Charlie examined it for evidence of sabotage: there'd been a recent case in which a disgruntled supplier put a pound and a half of plastic explosives on the underside of an ex-client's fuel tank. Set off by vibrations from a passing truck, the blast disintegrated the car and tore a six-foot-wide hole in the second floor of a parking garage.

Long unwashed, Charlie's car showed no obvious sign of having been tampered with, nor could Charlie see anything stuck to the undercarriage. He kept Julia at a distance while he unlocked the passenger door and leaned across the front seats to flip the release for the front hood; the engine looked the way it always did to him, a block of greasy attachments and hard-to-identify parts, none of which were clean enough to suggest recent tinkering. Once the car started without incident, Charlie motioned Julia into the passenger seat.

The sky had turned rust and gold, the sun setting through the filter of autumn leaves, by the time they reached Groton. Martin docked his boat in Stonington, five miles east of there, and was fond of stopping at a restaurant, just off Route 1, on the drive back to Manhattan. Charlie turned off the highway by the harbor and followed Bridge Street inland, crisscrossing the narrow side streets till he found the well-lit restaurant in a stretch of darkened industrial buildings. He parked the car down the street and kept watch, while Julia took a table inside.

Martin didn't show up until nine o'clock, the few streetlights casting dim rings of fluorescence on well-buckled sidewalks. He must have parked around the corner because Charlie first spotted him in the rear-view mirror. Martin stopped when he noticed Charlie, slouching behind the wheel of the car, and crossed the street towards him.

"Julia's inside," Charlie said, as Martin opened the curbside door and ducked into the passenger seat.

"What's she want?"

"She's worried."

"She needn't be." Martin took a moment to study Charlie's dishevelment, the wrinkles in his suit, the stubble of his beard. "Jesus, whatever you're up to, keep her out of it. For that matter, you stay out of it."

"Martin, I've got two homicides in Rhode Island. I bet I could find twenty cases of bank disclosure violations."

"You're an attorney for the State of Rhode Island, correct? You need me to tell you how many bank disclosure laws the state has? Zero."

"Is that why you picked Rhode Island? For the bank?"

"You have no jurisdiction. You're meddling, you're way over the line."

"We all crossed the line, Martin. If I knew where George was-"

"If you find him," Martin interrupted, pausing to kick the dashboard, "you can ask him what the fuck he was thinking, a thirty-four-million-dollar loan, with every guarantee imaginable except one that holds up."

"Is that it? The loan? He screwed up, didn't he?"

Martin considered the charge and retreated. "Maybe it's just bad luck. It's George's curse, isn't it? But it doesn't matter. George works for the bank. The bank'll get through this."

"Nobody gives a damn about your bank. Except you."

"The bank'll get through it."

"It's past that! Joe Turlik's dead. So's a local bank examiner and a lawyer or two in Panama. I don't know about George, but someone's running around, trying to erase everything."

Martin was visibly taken-aback. He looked down the street at the red script of the restaurant's neon sign and spoke haltingly. "This doesn't make sense."

"Help me."

"Things will straighten themselves out."

"Martin! You think they won't find somebody else who's clever with money? If you know something, anything, I can protect you."

"You can protect me?" Martin's ironic smile slowly faded. "Charlie, nothing's going to come of all this."

"Somebody's nervous. Somebody sent people after me in Grenada. It made no difference that Julia was with me. You think they'd have spared her?"

"Are you crazy?" The flush spread through Martin's cheeks. "Keep her out of this!"

"I wish I could."

Julia watched him approach her table. Charlie knew that she was looking for a hopeful sign from him, a nod, a smile, an indication that things were okay, but his expression masked little. Julia was crying by the time he sat down in the restaurant booth beside her.

"I spoke to him," Charlie said.

"Why didn't Martin come in?"

"I couldn't persuade him." Julia bent forward at the news, gripping the sides of the table for support. Charlie gave her a while to compose herself before taking her hand in both of his. "He wants you to slip away, go somewhere safe. Maybe your farm. He said not to worry, he'll get word to you."

"Where is he?"

"He promised he'll be careful. He said he'd take his boat out for a while, lay low, let things sort themselves out."

"His boat? God, what if they catch him on it?"

"Maybe he thinks they won't expect him to use it, or that he can outmaneuver them. He's buying time." Charlie shook his head doubtfully. "I think he believes he can get control of things, keep himself and his bank out of harm's way."

"Can he?"

"I don't know. I don't know how much time there is."

"What about us? How much time do we have?"

"A day or two before someone figures out we're not in the Grenadines."

They ordered food for takeout and ate in the car, reaching Charlie's driveway in Providence before midnight. The curtains in his house were drawn and the blinds closed. Charlie had left a few lights on timers, but judging from the glare in the windows, every light in the house had been turned on. Someone was at the house.

31

Next to the back door the green light on the security system panel was lit; the alarm had been switched off. Charlie slipped a key in the lock and cracked the door open until he saw Jennifer, watching television from her seat at the breakfast table. The dog was sleeping by her feet but perked up at the sound of people entering.

"Where were you?" Jennifer scolded, swiping at Charlie's soiled suit. "God, you look like something the dog dragged in."

"When did you get here?"

She stood up and turned the television off. "Last night. I was freaking. Every time I call Mr. Wonderful," Jennifer nodded her head in the direction of the Brown University campus, "I get his answering machine. Like he's screening his calls. Which is to say me. So I had to investigate."

"Is he?"

"No. The asshole's not around." Jennifer gave a purposeful, exaggerated yawn, as though she had tired of the project of reforming a part-time boyfriend. "So I came here. I picked up Roxy from your neighbors." She leaned towards the dog and nuzzled her.

"It's not safe here." Charlie's eyes swept the room and the view of the back yard. "Crazy things going on."

"Is that why Dad's flipping out?" Jennifer turned to Julia. "Did you know my dad's an alcoholic? He's been sober a long time. Until recently."

"He's drinking?" Charlie asked.

"Dad thinks you can't tell. He acts extra polite, eats all these breath mints. Christ, how dumb is that?"

"Where is he?"

"At his house, I guess. Hey, is this what he was like when he used to drink? He gets sappy. Not mean or anything. Just sappy. It's disgusting. The other night, he started mumbling, telling me how great it is to be young. Like I need to be told this? You should see him with Mom. Lately, he just stares at her."

"Does it matter?" Julia wondered.

"Yes! It's so lame. What's he hanging on to? To someone he loved once? It's pathetic. Why can't he let go? Wouldn't you?"

"I don't know," Julia said. "Talk to me when somebody has turned you inside-out."

"Hey, I'm waiting. I could use a little excitement. Dad, too? Is that it? Lately, it's like he's all worn down."

Charlie walked to the phone, picked it up, and started dialing. The phone rang four or five times before it was answered. Quad, on hearing Charlie's voice, took a deep breath and asked, "What's up?"

"I had the same question."

"Any word on George?"

"No."

"Oh..? Not good. I'd prefer .. another answer." Quad's tone had the strain of deliberation to it: Charlie was certain that he'd been drinking. Quad coughed into the mouthpiece and added, "Wish I could help."

"You can. It's not safe here. At my house."

"What?"

"I can't explain. But Jennifer's with me."

"Jennifer?"

"Julia, too. I thought we'd come over."

"Now?"

"An hour or two."

"Jennifer's there? School's started."

Quad's protest, tendered meekly, was the only obstacle that he could think to erect. Charlie ignored it and got off the phone quickly. He sorted through the mail, making certain to collect the large manila envelope that Beth had sent, and took it with him.

Quad and his second wife, Erica, lived west of Hartford, in Farmington. Jennifer rode with Julia, who had her own car; Charlie and the dog followed in his. It was late when they reached the house, the modern home a stylish testament to Quad's success.

Before Jennifer could knock, her stepmother opened the door and led her in. "Your dad's gone to bed. He was grumbling about your school having started, blah-blah-blah, so I just sent him up."

"He's asleep?"

"Hit the bed like a landslide. You'd need a bulldozer to move him."

Jennifer put a hand on Charlie's shoulder. "You'll be here in the morning?"

When he nodded, Jennifer kissed him on the cheek and headed towards the back stairs. "Your bed's all made," Erica called after her, then turned to the others with a frown. "You could've given more notice."

"You want us to stay at the inn?" There was an inn half a mile down the road.

Erica took a while before shaking her head apologetically. "No. I made up the beds. Besides, the inn wouldn't let you keep that dog."

Roxy continued to squirm in Charlie's arms until he set her loose on the floor. "Poor thing. She's spent more time at the neighbor's than at home."

Erica, watching the dog trot off to explore the house, spoke wistfully. "At least she knows what's up. Right, Charlie? You come in here - goddamnit, it's past one. Joe and George are missing. William's really upset." Erica never used Quad's nickname.

"Is he drinking?"

Erica's eyes shifted from Charlie to Julia and back again. "It's not for me to point fingers."

"Jennifer told me."

"She said that?" Erica tugged at the stray ends of her brown hair, which had been twirled by nervous fingers into tortured curls. "God, I sent him to bed. I didn't want Jennifer to see him. I guess that was silly. Shit, he hasn't brought the booze home. He'd be worried about me."

"How long's it lasted?"

"Two weeks, maybe. Hard to know. It's the sly kind of drunk. Glassy eyes. I don't know if he knows I know. It's so silly. Me, an alcoholic, same as him. Like I don't know all the goddamn tricks."

"Has he said anything?"

"We've kept kinda quiet. Charlie, if you get a chance.."

"I'll talk to him in the morning."

"Maybe you can figure this out."

Erica bid them goodnight and headed upstairs. Julia followed Charlie to the guestroom but didn't speak until the door was closed. "I feel sorry for her."

"Erica?"

"She's on eggshells. She wants you to confront him so she doesn't have to."

"Is that so terrible?"

"She's hoarding her suspicions. I don't want you doing that."

"Okay."

"It's not okay, damnit! You don't trust me. You never told me Joe Turlik died."

Charlie put a suitcase on the bed and fumbled with the latch. "Who told you?"

"Jennifer. On the ride tonight."

"Damnit, Jennifer's not supposed to know."

"And me, Charlie? I'm not supposed to know?"

"I don't want anyone to know. That way, if I find someone who does know, I know he's involved."

"Not anyone, Charlie. *Me*. You didn't want me to know."

"I didn't want you involved. I want you out of it, clear of it, safe."

"You could've left me out of it. You didn't have to call me, see me."

"I did have to see you. I spent years of my life waking up every morning with the same goddamn questions. '*Why did she leave? What did I do wrong?*' I was bitter. I held onto it so long."

"You think I didn't lose? God, I worked so hard and ran into men who wanted to be in complete control and hated how hard and long I worked. Or you've been there, right? You're pushing thirty, and your big question for a prospective date, subtly broached, is, 'Have you ever been married?' A lot of wonderful people made bad choices, yet all the divorced present as victims, and they mostly have baggage. Charlie, there won't be a future if you can't let go of the past."

"And George? Martin? Do we let go of them?"

"No, not yet."

"It's Martin, it's his bank."

"Maybe it is Martin," Julia conceded. "But it doesn't matter because if you don't trust me, I can't be with you. It's too painful."

Julia stared at him until she was sure that he understood her terms: he would trust her, or he would lose her. Charlie felt, at her ultimatum, a slow unburdening: the discarding of suspicion, a recovery of purpose. He took her in his arms and held her until Julia finally broke free, disappearing briefly into the bathroom. She spent the night curled up on one side of the bed, the covers tossed aside. Her breathing had the rhythm of a child's recovery from sobs, each inhale hampered by a series of small fractures.

Unable to sleep, Charlie opened the envelope from Beth, pulled out a copy of George's will, and struggled through its opening sentences: "*I, George R. Spaulding, being a resident of Newport County, Rhode Island, declare that this is my Last Will and Testament. I hereby revoke all previous..*"

Charlie hated the document and its humorless declarations. Formal and final, the language denied George and his considerable charm. A will was an abomination, Charlie thought, more legal extinguishment than loving farewell; this one had been drafted a year ago. Skimming through it, he noticed that he was named the executor of the estate. What money George had after a settling of debts - and Charlie doubted there would be much, if any - was to be put into a trust for the benefit of George's child.

Much of the will's language was standard until a series of bequests was detailed. A few rare books were donated to the St. Mark's library. Quad and Lucy were each left long-admired paintings. And Charlie, as the executor, was instructed to "hand deliver" one hundred dollars each to "my distinguished and worldly friends":

01575722(170678NYT)

01540562(050182BG)

01566913(290392NYT)

01599208(141191WSJ)

01592228(061282NYT)

01588362(221288NYT)

01526577(090492WSJ)

01579921(310391NYT)

01596485(020479NYT)

01568943(251193NYT)

01511902(020191BG)

01559056(281090BG)

Charlie played with the numbers, reversed them, tried to assign alphabetical equivalents to the digits and their combinations, and got nowhere. Whatever George meant, the list in his will was intended as a potential indictment from the grave. A precaution. That was what George had said: he'd taken a "precaution." If Charlie could decipher the list and its code, he might make sense of George's jeopardy. He might find George - if he weren't too late.

32

Charlie barely slept. He tried to imagine what Martin would do, adrift on his sailboat, but his thoughts kept turning to a yacht race from long ago when he and George had been drafted to crew for the father of a fellow student, the father a besotted and hopeless skipper, the son all of fourteen years old and an unbearable perfectionist, the race on the ocean course already lost by the first buoy, where the yacht dropped its spinnaker overboard. The sail quickly filled with tons of water, anchoring the boat despite the stiff breeze, while the father and son screamed at one another, bawling hysterically, refusing to acknowledge that their boat trailed the field by half a mile at the first buoy and that the dropped sail had cost them time, but not standing.

George had had the right response to nautical disaster, unlike Charlie, who worked feverishly to wrestle the errant sail aboard and aloft. With the boat underway again and the father and son continuing to howl never-to-be-forgiven recriminations at one another, Charlie found his fellow crew member aft. George had stripped to his boxer shorts and was stretched out across the rear deck, baking in the midday sun. At the sound of Charlie approaching, George cocked an eye open and shaded it with a hand; his other hand was busy fishing sugar cookies out of a box. "Do be a dear," George had said, in Grace's most regal tones, "and fetch me some jam."

It was what Charlie loved best about him: George *knew*. He knew how silly all of it was, every last pretension of Newport society, the yacht race with the son threatening patricide to the skipper and keel-hauling to his friends, the mutinous crew, the clubs and debutante parties and Social Register jockeys. George knew, and he hung on because nothing else was quite as amusing or addictive.

Charlie woke to that memory, George refusing the role of the shanghaied cabin boy. Daylight rimmed the blinds with thin ribbons of gray phosphorescence. Charlie rose quietly and slipped into the kitchen, where Quad was pouring a cup of coffee. Quad handed him the full cup and got another one for himself.

"You want milk, anything in your coffee?" he offered.

"No thanks."

"When'd you get here?"

"Last night. Jennifer and Julia are with me."

"Here? Great."

"I told you last night we were coming."

Quad retreated from the accusation by spreading a newspaper across the counter and looking through it, but he couldn't keep his feet still. He shuffled back and forth and flipped through sections of "*The Hartford Courant*" without settling on a story.

Charlie could feel the hunger and felt crowded by it, Quad pacing the kitchen, restless as a caged fox. The hunger didn't seem so specific that Quad couldn't dose it with caffeine. He gulped coffee and sweated, ellipses spreading under the arms of his dress shirt, but the fever was on him, and the itch of it, his constant motion unconnected to a function, rattled Charlie, who finally erupted.

"Goddamnit!"

Startled, Quad looked at Charlie. "What do you want?"

"I need you to look at something."

"Maybe lunch, if I'm free."

"If you're sober."

"And..?"

"I need you sober."

"Charlie, you did your duty. Gave me a talking-to all those years ago. Had the guts to speak up. Few did."

"It's not why I'm here."

"Thank Christ. I get free lectures. The whole AA network."

"What about Jennifer? What's her network? AA has one for the kids, too, right?"

With a determinedly casual air, Quad put his coffee cup on the counter. "You're in my house."

"I told you. I need you sober."

"I've been sober for fifteen years. That's not an accomplishment you undo in a week or two."

"Isn't it?"

"Fuck you. Jesus, what're you doing here?"

"George put something in his will. I want you to look at it."

"His will?" Quad batted his eyelashes and raised his voice coquettishly. "Am I mentioned?"

"Yes."

"C'mon. I was kidding."

"He leaves you that painting you always loved."

Quad put a hand on a table to steady himself. "I'm not ready for this."

"You think I am?"

Quad stepped towards the doorway and listened to the stillness of his house, the whine of water running through a distant pipe, the murmur of faint conversation, before facing Charlie with a look, at once endearing and heartbreaking, of childlike bewilderment. "You know what Lucy said? About Joe? She said she was glad it wasn't me who went first. Why would she say that? Some kind of idiot consolation?"

"She must've meant it. Maybe it's that simple."

"No ulterior meaning? Good. We can stick with the superficial. It always worked for me." He poured himself yet more coffee and fought the steam for a slow sip; relenting, he granted Charlie a smile.

"What the hell is it?"

"Don't really know." Quad rubbed the back of his neck. "Lately I get stuck sometimes. I can't explain it. Maybe it's Joe, damn him, dying in some muddle. Or maybe it's my life. You know how you look back on your life, and you wonder what it is that you didn't know, and what the fuck you might've done if only you'd known."

"Isn't there a song about this? 'If-I-knew-then-what-I-know-now.' Crosby, Stills & Nash? Bob Seeger?"

"It isn't Lucy, that's not what I'm talking about. It isn't our marriage I miss. What I miss about her is she had sex like she meant it." Quad lowered his voice and looked towards the doorway. "For Erica it's a fucking accommodation - literally."

"You've been married twelve years. This is a surprise? Two of your best friends are missing or dead, and this is what your 'drunk' is about? Boring sex?"

"Shit.." Tongue-tied, Quad flipped both middle fingers at Charlie, the gesture intentionally juvenile and placating. "Look, asshole. One thing about being a recovering alcoholic is you don't risk losing control. No wild afternoons in bed, no all-nighters, you can't stick around the office on St. Patrick's Day. Dismiss it if you want, but that's what I miss. George, obtuse as he can be - he'd get it, only for him it's not crazy parties, it's money. He's starting to feel his age and his looming impoverishment, and it scares the shit out of him. It's what makes him vulnerable. It's what you choose not to notice about him, how desperate he is for everything he once had. He doesn't want to get old, goddamnit, not without putting up a fight."

"And I do?"

"I don't know." Quad ground his knuckles against the countertop's tile. "You don't have my issues. The last year with Lucy? Jesus, we had a kid, and I have to look at photos to imagine it. That year vanished."

"You think everybody doesn't reach an age and start counting his mistakes?"

"What about George? You think he's counting his mistakes?"

"I think he's running for his life."

"I can't count his mistakes. Except his biggest one. Which was imagining the world's rulebook was written by you St. Mark's boys."

"That's a tired refrain. I'm really fucking sick of it."

"What about Joe? What would Joe think? He didn't get himself into this shit."

"What're you saying?"

"George brought him into something. That's what I'm saying. I'm saying George isn't all victim."

"There are lines he wouldn't cross."

"You think?"

"And friends he wouldn't abandon."

"What about Joe? The hell with your notion! What happened to Joe? Did Joe screw up? If he did, if he was in trouble, what'd George do?"

"He'd stand by him. You belittle all the boarding school shit. Well, that's the only code George left school with. He saw his parents on occasional holidays. His friends are his family."

Quad pressed his fingers into his forehead, then traced his eyebrows as his hands relaxed; he concluded the gesture by offering Charlie a look of genuine contrition. "See, that's what I think, goddamnit. George wouldn't save himself and feed Joe to the sharks. But that's why the odds of finding George are so goddamn slender."

"For Christ's sake, help me. George gave us a clue. In case he disappeared. There's a list of numbers in his will. I want you to look at it. You know about banks, loan acquisition, offshore money."

"Offshore money? It can be an extraordinarily complicated game."

"George must have brought some of it to his bank."

Quad's eyes fled the room, settling momentarily on a bird feeder in the backyard, before returning to Charlie. "Today could be difficult. I need to get cigarettes."

"I'll go with you."

"You don't trust me? Jesus? House arrest?"

"My car's blocking yours."

They drove to the nearest convenience store, where Quad bought a pack of cigarettes and returned to the car, apologizing as he lit a cigarette. "You go to an AA meeting, and everybody smokes. Drives you goddamn bonkers unless you have one. Only time I smoke."

Back at the house, they set up at a table on the covered porch. Charlie pulled George's will out of its manila envelope and showed Quad the list of twelve numbers that began with 01575722(170678NYT).

"He fingered something," Quad said. "I mean, it proves George isn't innocent. He knows who'd be after him."

"At some point, money moves through Panama to the Caribbean, but I don't know where it's from or where it ends up." Charlie pointed at the numbers. "Unless it's here."

They played with the sequences. Unable to make sense of the numbers and letters in parentheses, Charlie and Quad hunted for progressive or algebraic patterns that might formulate words or more recognizable data. They spent an hour at the task, all the while looking for a word or a name to emerge. At ten o'clock, after they'd emptied the pot of coffee and exhausted many prospective correlations, Charlie called the bank and asked for George's secretary. He was told that she was on vacation.

Quad turned up a listing for a *B. Spangler* in Jameston. Beth answered their phone call, her voice rising with delight.

"Charlie? How-?" She suddenly snorted with suspicion. "Hey, did the bank give you my number?"

"No. What's up?"

"Yesterday afternoon, they told me I had to take time off, at least till George returns. I'm owed five weeks of vacation, but they're making me take it. That was my cushion in case of severance."

"Who told you?"

"Linda. In Personnel. She said it was bank *policy*. The asshole. Like you got some kind of policy for executives who disappear and their secretaries' vacation pay."

"Listen to this number. 0-1-5-7-5-7-2-2. It's followed by more numbers."

"There were eight numbers, right? Starting with 0-1-5. Those are George's accounts. His clients. You notify him if there's a problem or anything. You go right to him. Nobody else."

Charlie looked at Quad, who was listening on a second extension, and asked, "How big are these accounts?"

"I don't know. I might be able to find out."

"You ever talk to any of the account owners?"

"They don't call the office. A secretary or assistant, someone in New York. She phones sometimes, I don't know what about."

"These account numbers? They're for checking accounts?"

"Yeah, but they could be connected to trust accounts. I only know 'cause George had me do some deposit slips once. *Large* deposit slips. Mega-bucks."

"There's a second set of numbers in parentheses. 1-7-0-6-7-8-N-Y-T. That mean anything?"

"A license plate? Nah, too many numbers. I don't know. Nothing to me."

"Can you get back into the bank?"

"If they don't fire me. Can they do that? Let me go if George doesn't come back?"

"Not necessarily."

"I'll get a lawyer if they screw with me. Everybody's been worried, this bad loan we're not supposed to know about, so naturally everybody does. Now everybody says the bank'll be okay."

"The sale of the loan is going through?"

"Must be."

Charlie was incredulous. "Who's buying it?"

"You want me to find out? I'll call Edie - she sits next to me. Hold on."

The sound of Beth's double click was followed by the crackle and static of call holding. It was two minutes before she came back on the line.

"Charlie, I got a name and number. From Edie. She says Mr. Wells is faxing a bunch of documents and talking to Banco de Sud. Other banks are involved, but that's the lead bank. The correspondence is addressed to the bank President, Quentin Casillas. I got a phone number for the bank."

Charlie wrote the name and phone number down, then cautioned Beth. "Listen, everything's coming unglued. I don't know if you're safe. You should stay with a relative."

"Charlie, I'm not worried about me. But if anyone hurts George, you tell me who, and I'll scratch his fucking eyes out."

Quad pointed at his phone when Charlie hung up. "George should marry her. A goddamn scrapper."

"Yeah. But explain this to me. George makes a big loan that's in trouble. Then, when he's gone, the bank unloads it. How do they get rid of it when George couldn't?"

"It's not easy. It's supposed to be arms-length. The bank examiners will check out any transaction that takes a shaky loan off the books."

"I have a dead bank examiner. He covered Rhode Island and had a lot of cash when he died."

"Christ."

"I also have a dead lawyer. Panama. Formed a bunch of shell companies and trusts."

"You better move quickly. The accounts George named in his will? They can be closed. At the moment the trouble with the bank's bad loan might prevent that - capital requirements and so on - but once the bank is free of its bad loan, the accounts may disappear, too."

"Shit."

Quad slipped a cigarette out of the package and tapped the butt end with a fingernail, tamping the tobacco away from the hollowing tip. The only matches that he had been able to find were foot-long wooden ones, which were used in the living room fireplace. A flint patch on the top of the match box had long ago corroded, so Quad struck a match by dragging it across the tile floor. Exposed by the tightly packed tobacco, the end of the cigarette paper flared as the blue flame hit it. Quad smirked at the folly of it all, a twelve-inch match igniting a three-inch cigarette.

Erica knocked on the doorframe before stepping onto the porch. Her relief apparent, she watched Quad tug on his cigarette, one poison substituted for a stronger one. "Don't bring that crap inside," she said.

"Where's Jennifer?"

"Getting dressed. I'll give her a ride to school." She stared at Charlie. "If someone can stay till Don Beaume gets here..?"

"I can stay." Charlie recognized the name; Don Beaume was a mentor of Quad's at a local A.A. group.

Charlie turned when Julia walked onto the porch and acknowledged her with a nod, then picked up the handset of the phone. "One more call," he mentioned, punching in a number.

Ray McClean was brusque when he came on the line. "Charlie? Where the hell are you?"

"Near Hartford."

"What? You got frequent flyer miles about to expire?"

"Listen. There's this guy. His bank is helping First Federal bury a bad loan."

"So what?"

"So it's a hell of a favor. It's a loan John Stuart Robbins probably reviewed. I'm trying to tie him into it."

"You better tie our dead bank examiner into it. We got nothing happening in Rhode Island, nothing to prosecute, no business in any of this, except him buying the cemetery."

"He'd visited First Federal. Maybe he figured something was suspect, maybe he was bought off."

"A chain of 'maybes'. If I bring you this case, you'd throw my ass out of your office."

"I want you to run an i.d. for me," Charlie said. "Quentin Casillas. He runs a foreign bank. Banco de Sud."

"Is that a name we've seen? Casillas? At that co-op? Park Avenue."

"'Miami North'?"

"Yeah. The posh place. Let me get the phone list you sent. Wait.." McLean could he heard rummaging through drawers, slamming them shut. He came back on the line with a drawn-out, "Yuu-up. He's on the phone sheet. Must own a unit. I don't know where he's based, but this dog's got himself a hydrant in Manhattan."

"I have a phone number for his bank. 0-1-1. That's international. Then 5-6. Then a 2. Then 7-5-7-7-0-0."

"Okay."

"See what you get on him. Get Justice or Interpol on it if you can. I'll call you, maybe end of the day." Charlie hung up.

"The name you mentioned?" Julia asked.

"Quentin Casillas. Some banker. I don't know where."

Julia put her coffee cup down; her hand was shaking.

"You know him?"

"The phone number?"

"What?"

"I know the country code," Julia said. "And the area code. They're for Santiago, Chile."

33

Lucy's phone call to Quad's house postponed the argument. Jennifer refused to talk to her mother, who settled for talking to Charlie. "What the hell's going on?" Lucy demanded. "Everybody's got to be there? One of those asinine reunions with Roman numerals. Woodstock *Quad*?"

"Long story short," Charlie said. "It's not safe at my house."

"Longer story shorter - it's Jennifer's fourth week of classes."

"Erica's taking her."

"Tell her not to write Jennifer any excuses."

"Where are you?"

"Work. I don't know what happened to the rest of your jobs." Lucy cleared her throat. "So what am I missing? Jennifer? She's okay?"

"Yes. She's not the kind to humble herself for long."

"Her father? How's he?"

"Verdict's not in."

"Christ, Charlie, I can't wait for the new year. This year sucks."

"I want you to do me a favor. The Federal Reserve has a district headquarters in Boston. Don't you know someone-?"

"He doesn't work there. He sits on the District's Board of Directors."

"Call him, okay?"

"Charlie! I had three dates with him and saw no evidence of life. I never invited you to join us: you'd have tried to make the best of it."

"Lucy, I need this. Get the name of the District President. Say there's evidence a Rhode Island Bank is disposing of a loan illegally. Set up a meeting for me. I'll give them details in a couple of days."

"You have details?"

"I'm looking."

Charlie got off the phone to hug Jennifer and Erica goodbye, then headed into the guest room, with Julia following. She watched as he grabbed his small suitcase and stuffed his toiletries bag into it.

"Charlie?"

"What day is it? Wednesday?"

"Thursday." She moved towards him. "What're you thinking? You'll go to Chile?"

"I've got nowhere else to look."

"You're chasing shadows."

"Goddamnit, that's all there are. All I can do is run around with a shovel and see what they're trying to bury."

"You think someone will talk to you?" she said incredulously. "This man Casillas?"

"You know him?"

"He knew my parents. He sent flowers to the church for my mother's funeral."

"Would he talk to you?"

"Probably."

"Freely?"

"Not a chance."

"What about Martin? Does he know him?"

She thought hard for a moment before answering. "I suppose."

"Christ!" Frustrated, Charlie threw the last of his belongings into the suitcase.

"Damnit, you don't understand the risks."

"I'll manage."

"Goddamnit, it isn't your America, Charlie. You grew up in this one. They don't speak English in the other America, or boarding school French. They have different rules, and it doesn't matter who's in charge - there are always people who're above the law."

"It doesn't-"

"I went once for a short visit, and it was a year before I got out and a couple of years before I let anyone touch me. I went, and nobody could get me out. You couldn't get into the country then. How do you know you'll get out now? At least I speak the language."

"I wouldn't dream of asking you to go."

"Charlie, I visit every few years. You don't know the country, you don't know Spanish." When he failed to respond, Julia switched tongues, the vowels emphatic, the pace quickening. "*Senor, cuantas veces ha pasado tiempo en un carcel? Que drogas tiene contigo? Usted da apoya a los radicales?*"

"C'mon. I don't know what you said. I'll have two beers - *dos cervezas, por favor.*" Charlie conceded with a sigh. "What?"

"I asked how many times you'd been in jail. What drugs you were smuggling. If you supported the radicals. You think the police don't ask those questions?" Julia took hold of his arm. "If you go, I'm going with you. It isn't just George in trouble now. It's Martin, too."

The route south detoured west because the day's last connecting flight to Santiago left Los Angeles at four-thirty, local time, that afternoon. A delay caused a mad scramble at LAX, the two of them sprinting through terminals and hurdling luggage, racing to a gate where an airline agent rushed them down the jet ramp. Full, the plane pulled away shortly after Charlie and Julia had boarded. Charlie had a seat towards the back of the plane. Julia was seated much farther forward.

The passenger next to Charlie kept his eyes closed during take-off and didn't open them until the plane's climb had leveled off and he could finally release his furious grip on the armrests. He stared out the window a while before speaking softly. "Just made the plane?"

"Yeah."

"I'm not a good flier." The man laughed nervously and told stories about his misadventures while traveling. Charlie added his own anecdotes, during which the passenger slowly relaxed, especially once he'd been served a beer.

He had poured most of that beer when he asked, "Where you going?" Their flight stopped in Bogota on route to Santiago.

"Chile."

"On business?"

"Yeah. You?"

The man smiled quizzically. "Chile. A reunion, I suppose." His voice, with its trace of a Spanish accent, was more elegant than his clothes; he was dressed like a professor, a skinny tie centering an ancient sportscoat, crumpled khakis bunching up in his lap. "Have you heard of Villa Grimaldi?" he asked.

"No."

The man shrugged and looked away, prepared to let the subject drop. "What?" Charlie persisted.

The passenger bent forward to the carry-on bag tucked under the seat in front of him and retrieved a photocopy of an article, which he handed to Charlie. The article described efforts by a victim rights organization to maintain Villa Grimaldi as a memorial to those who were tortured and murdered during the reign of the Generals who overthrew Allende. A nineteenth-century estate known for its Carrara marble statues and rose gardens, the Villa had been used as a prison during the mid-Seventies by the National Intelligence Directorate. Suspected political opponents were brought there, several hundred of whom died or "disappeared." Thousands more suffered brutal interrogations, most of which began with prolonged electric shock.

"Were you there?" Charlie asked.

The man poured the remainder of the can of beer into his plastic cup. "For two days."

"Why?"

"I was looking for my brother. A professor of history. A prominent leftist. I went to see if they had him at the Villa. I share my brother's name, so they detained me. I was covered with electrodes - this pain you don't forget."

"They let you go?"

"Luck." He spread his hands open in apology, as if his good fortune had been purchased with someone else's catastrophe. "I was engaged to a diplomat's daughter. Her father went to the government."

"And your brother?"

"He'd gotten away. To San Francisco. I followed him there. You Americans have a very funny government. They support the Generals and give amnesty to those who don't. My brother, myself. Once, I taught English in Santiago. Now I teach Spanish in Palo Alto. I have a few days' leave to attend a ceremony at the Villa."

"Your brother?"

"He won't return. He forgives nothing."

"What about you?"

Equivocal, the man tilted one shoulder, then the other. "The people of Chile have spoken. They prefer moral ambiguity to economic chaos - you can't force this on them without their acquiescence. Maybe it's the Catholic choice, bread on the table, wrongs addressed in the confessional. The economy!"

"It's booming?"

"Yes. This is something we're doing well. Unlike politics. I once revered Allende. Poor man, to be a martyr to socialism, in a century that renders you a footnote. Now I admire the other Allende. Do you know her?"

Charlie's shoulders hunched with uncertainty. The schoolteacher leaned into his bag and rummaged through it before he produced two paperback versions of a novel, "*The House of Spirits*", by Isabel Allende, one version in Spanish, one in English. The author was the niece of Salvador Allende, but had lived in California for a long time, a circumstance which pained the schoolteacher, who could excuse his own exile but not that of a talented writer. "A country should never lose its Elgin Marbles," he lamented, handing Charlie a paperback. "The translation is so good the students cheat and read it."

Charlie opened the English version and was immediately enchanted; the language was rich and dense, heady as a subtropical garden. Charlie had nodded off by the time the plane landed in Bogota, where he used a telephone in the airport to phone Ray McClean.

"I got a limited bio here," McClean began. "General Quentin Casillas. Never retired. He's president of a private bank now and a reserve military officer. Which, according to the boys at Justice, is interesting, since the Chilean military had itself granted amnesty for all the crap they pulled. Casillas ran the military's bank for years: payroll, procurements. He did resign that position."

"It'd be a hell of an opportunity," Charlie speculated, "if you were inclined to graft."

"His reputation is okay, but a name or two show up with his. A colonel. Javier Leopoldes. He was forced to resign from the army. Damn unusual unless you're a monster. He had a high post in DINA. You know what that was?"

"Yeah." Several pieces Charlie had read, including the article on the Villa, mentioned the National Intelligence Directorate (DINA), the soldiers responsible for Villa Grimaldi and other acts of terror designed to quell opposition to Pinochet's reign.

"Leopoldes is on the Board of Casillas's bank. Which is odd, you gotta figure there's shit in somebody's bucket if he lands on the Board, but I don't know what we can do about it."

"Casillas must owe a favor," Charlie interjected. "His bank is helping First Federal."

"So?"

"So I'm trying to slow things down."

"And me?" McLean wondered. "My job in all this?"

"Buy me some time. You remember the guy we spoke to? At the OCC? Call him. Tell him to examine the loan the bank is unloading. Ask for a review. Throw an anchor on it."

"We're off base, Charlie. It's beyond a stretch. I'll make the call, but that's it. We're way the hell out'a line. I mean, what do you think you're gonna accomplish in Chile?"

"I don't know. I won't stay long enough to get in trouble, but I'll pester the bank president. Hit his office with a blizzard of initials. OCC, FDIC, FRF, make them think every American banking bureaucracy is curious about the loan they're willing to assume. I want these bastards looking over their shoulders."

"Charlie!" McClean spoke sharply. "You want the sum total of what I know about Latin America? Here it is, goddamnit, the sum total. You fuck with anybody in the military, and you're the one who better be looking over your shoulder."

Boarding the flight to Santiago, Charlie switched seats to sit beside Julia, who gave him the window seat. The plane was taxiing towards the runway when Julia touched his arm and asked, "How long do you plan to stay?"

"Not long," Charlie said. McClean's caution was still fresh on his mind. "Two days if we're lucky."

"So tomorrow morning..?"

"You call the bank, use your Spanish. Act like a prospective client. Let's find out what we can about the bank, start there."

Julia nodded, then lifted her purse from the floor and fished through it for a vial of aspirin. She took two tablets, which she swallowed without the benefit of fluids, and curled up with an airline blanket.

Thirty minutes after take-off, the sky had long since gone dark, the light on a wingtip dulling the radiance of stars that otherwise would have burned brighter, the plane holding at thirty-seven-thousand feet and sinking beneath the equator into an unlit hemisphere. Below the plane, in the view that the window afforded, the world was black as a forest floor at midnight. Nothing glowed; no shape announced itself, the Andes flattened, the Pacific an ocean or a puddle, the western half of a continent untracked and uninhabited. This was, Charlie realized, a flight that George must have taken. His expired passport was cluttered with stamps from republics on this, the other side of the world.

34

The plane landed at three in the morning at a modern airport that belied the heart-of-darkness passage of the flight, though Julia flinched at the sight of two soldiers on patrol, their carbines slung loosely over their arms, the tasseled berets snug on their heads. After Charlie and she had cleared Customs, a taxi sped them into town. Save for the Spanish on the billboards, they could have been in Switzerland. Snow capped the moonlit mountains to the east, which lay behind dazzling skyscrapers like discarded packaging. The streets were immaculate.

At the hotel, a sparkling new Hilton, a reception clerk sneered as he reviewed their passports; an unwed couple was sharing a room. The clerk's reaction reminded Charlie of what Julia had said of her homeland, that for all the upheavals of the last quarter century the principal politic was religion, a fairly inflexible strain of Catholicism.

Early Friday morning, Charlie contacted Banco de Sud and posed as an American bank examiner, using a fictitious name and seeking interviews with the bank's key officers. Julia played the part of his Spanish-speaking secretary and was concise in her request: the American bank examiner was puzzled by a prospective transaction involving the purchase and possible syndication of a suspect loan from a Rhode Island bank. Would the officers, especially the bank president Quentin Casillas, be free to meet with the examiner today or tomorrow? The secretaries for the bank officers were invariably circumspect: the officers' schedules were crowded; the examiner should send a written query.

Julia spoke with the bank again, this time to secure an interview for herself with a private banker. At noon, she visited the main branch of Banco de Sud and was directed to a plush third floor reception area, there to be met by a short gentleman in a perfectly pressed gabardine suit. Alert, thorough in his answers, the private banker courted Julia and the several million dollars that she claimed to have – billions of Chilean pesos, he noted. He gave detailed answers to her questions. The bank did have certain deposit accounts denominated in American dollars. The bank had a growing international presence with branches in most South American capitals. No, the bank did not have offices in Panama or the Cayman Islands; no, the private banker regretted to inform the potential client, the bank could not provide management of or access to offshore trusts, but he would be happy to research a referral. Claiming to be impressed, Julia thanked the banker and left.

Outside, as she recounted her meeting, Charlie surmised that there might be a connection between the principals, Quentin Casillas having the bank he ran assist in a bail-out of a bank owned by Martin Hoffman, but there was no obvious involvement by Banco de Sud in the offshore money schemes that had swept up Joe Turlik. It was true that Quentin Casillas owned a Park Avenue co-op, title to which was likely held by an offshore entity, but the threads of that circumstance were unlikely to lead anywhere quickly, at least not quickly enough. There on the sidewalk, the mist slickening the paving stones, the clouds funneling inland and bunching over the basin in which the city was built, Charlie felt the tug of his gathering desolation. Cold, he wondered if it would snow.

"What now?" Julia asked. They were standing on the broad Alameda Libertador Bernardo O'Higgins, a block down the avenue from Banco de Sud.

"I don't know."

"There's somewhere I want to go."

Julia hailed a taxi and directed it to San Michel, an old cemetery located on the north side of a hill where plane trees, soon to bud, would shade rows of elegant headstones and statuary come summer. She led Charlie down a central path through the graveyard, past a few enormous Gothic crypts that honored the nation's founding fathers, and stopped by a large block of white marble, the size of a minivan. The monument was elaborately sculpted; bands of intricate frieze edged the top and bottom of the marble slab. "My parents," Julia said. Deep letters chiseled out their names and dates.

Julia did some housekeeping, sweeping debris from the top of the marble, before speaking. "My father died a month after my mother. It was his most romantic gesture."

"Did he order the stone?"

Julia nodded. "He didn't live to see it. He never should have come. His homecoming, like mine, was awful."

"Why?"

"To begin with, he never liked the military. To him they were riffraff. He always referred to the coup as 'the restoration;' his little joke. It was his empire he expected to be restored, but the rules had changed. He got desperate, I think, with the chances he took."

"And you?"

"I wanted none of it."

"Does Martin visit?"

"I doubt it. He'd want people to visit him."

A gust of wind blew past, trailing a little city noise, unmuffled motorcycles and construction equipment. Julia was crying when she continued. "I don't blame Martin. He's done everything for me, been everything to me. He never could've imagined what would happen; he never would've allowed anything to hurt me. But it was his business that got me attention and in trouble all those years ago. So what do I make of that?" She brushed away tears on the sleeve of her coat, before concluding, "All I know is there are knots you can't untie. And Martin..? I have to do what I can to help him."

Charlie worried at the tangle of his own allegiances. He had come to Chile to find his oldest and dearest friend: George was family to him, a knot he couldn't untie. And yet Charlie knew he could never leave the country without Julia. He was bound to her, too.

Low on the northern horizon, the sun broke through a swollen bank of clouds and gleamed off the Hoffmans' block of white marble, which stood like a rebuke to the darker stones around it. Julia completed a little grooming, repairing a patch of sod cut by a wheelbarrow tire before she faced her parents' headstone and whispered several phrases in Spanish. She turned to Charlie. "Okay. I've told them my secrets."

"And me?"

"I don't keep any secrets. Don't you, either."

Once they had left the graveyard, the taxi driver was instructed to head back to the hotel. Along the way the energy of the city proved contagious. Charlie wished that he could visit Chile under other circumstances: the people he glimpsed from the taxi seemed brisk, happy, confident; theirs was a New World expanding.

The taxi was traversing a neighborhood of apartment buildings when they passed a post office with a banner hanging over its Neoclassical facade. Striped with the country's colors, it read:

15-10-88 "..la paz y la democracia.."

Charlie swiveled his head for a second look at the banner. "It's a quote," Julia explained. "From ten days after the plebiscite."

"The plebiscite?"

"It was held the fifteenth of October. 15-10-88. General Pinochet failed to get a majority. It ended-"

"Damnit." Furious that he hadn't broken George's code sooner, Charlie fished through his pockets for a copy of the addendum to the will. Each bank account number was followed by six more numbers in parentheses, to which were added two or three letters. The first number on the list was:

01575722 (170678NYT).

Each six-number sequence within the parentheses fit the pattern of the banner. A date was given in the European fashion: day/month/year. If Charlie's hunch was correct, something that happened on the 17th day of the sixth month of 1978 would provide significant information about account #01575722 at George's bank.

"A library?" Charlie asked. "Can we go to a library?"

Julia translated the request for the driver, who returned to the Alameda and dropped them off at the imposing Biblioteca Nacional. Inside the huge building, Julia got directions and led Charlie to the reference section.

"What're we looking for?"

"We have dates," he said. "Something about the dates has to give us detail about the accounts. There has to be a connection – an event, a place, a name, something."

"Something? Or someone?"

"Someone. George's 'worldly friends.' That's the language in his will, as if he were going to leave money to his 'friends.' To people who tie into these bank accounts."

A librarian showed them to a terminal at which they could review back issues of local newspapers. Julia fished through two boxes of microfiche before finding a reel that included the date June 17, 1978. She skipped forward until she found the day's newspaper in question and skimmed through its pages in search of something remarkable, of someone notorious, but the news was overwhelmingly bland. No article would or could have offended a censor.

While Julia checked other dates, Charlie moved to an old-fashioned card catalogue and, with the librarian's help, searched through it. Starting with a name he knew, he turned up numerous references to Quentin Casillas. Articles about him were categorized by date and publication:

31-07-95 *L'Opinion*
04-11-93 *Santiago*
20-03-89 *Viva!*
23-10-88 *B.A.T.*
06-12-82 *N.Y.T.*

The fifth reference matched a number on George's list, which was accompanied by the letters *NYT*.

01592228 (061282 NYT)

The New York Times. Per the catalogue, there was a front-page article about Quentin Casillas in *The New York Times* on Dec. 6, 1982. If George was singling someone out, in the case of each account, for Charlie's benefit, account # 01592228 at First Federal was owned or controlled by Casillas, the subject of the article printed Dec. 6, 1982. The account ownership was certain to be obscured by an otherwise impenetrable foreign trust or corporation, as was the ownership of Casillas's Park Ave. co-op, but a look at the newspaper in question would confirm that General Quentin Casillas was the principal subject of the article; it would confirm that a past Director of the military's bank had money secretly stashed in a Rhode Island bank.

Charlie's question about whether old issues were stored on microfiche embarrassed the librarian, who apologized profusely in her halting English. Regrettably, the library's collection of foreign newspapers, or of any newspapers critical to the reign of the Generals, was woefully inadequate, although complete back issues of prominent periodicals like *The New York Times* were now on order. Before the year was out a decade and a half of imposed silence would be shouted down by a chorus of free journalists and their work.

Julia joined them and looked through the catalogue's list of Spanish-language news articles on Quentin Casillas. "Can I read these?"

The librarian disappeared into the stacks and returned several minutes later with four binders filled with newsprint gone yellow. Julia sat at a table and flipped through the pages, while Charlie analyzed George's addendum.

George's list noted other dates as well as two more publications: BG and WSJ. *The Boston Globe* and *The Wall Street Journal*: they were newspapers that George read, or reviewed, daily. Anxious to search their back issues, Charlie would need to return to the States. He killed time by scrolling through microfiche files and trying to make sense of the headlines, until Julia groaned.

"Oh, God," she whimpered. She pushed herself away from the table. "Just once I'd like it not to go all to hell."

"What?"

Julia looked at the newspaper in the binder, then at Charlie. Her voice cracked under the strain. "This article." She pushed the binder away. "It's about a meeting of bankers. In Haiti. Casillas had run a bank there during Allende's reign. Casillas returned to Haiti in 1976. To attend this goddamn conference."

Charlie turned the binder so that the full-page article in a Santiago newspaper faced him. He couldn't read the text, but the photos were plentiful. Three shots of rural Haiti, highlighting the extreme privation, were juxtaposed with three shots of the conference, prosperous bankers discussing the country's languishing economy. One photo was given significant prominence: five men were standing on a stone terrace overlooking a distant sea. Three of the men were clustered together and smiling at the camera; Charlie identified each of them by struggling through the Spanish-language caption: General Quentin Casillas, in uniform, a Director of the Armed Forces Bank of Chile; Cesar Palliz, Chairman of the IMF Banking Advisory Council for South America; and Jean deVillieres, Minister of Security for the Republic of Haiti. Off by himself, striking a Napoleon's pose, was Jean Claude Duvalier. Baby Doc. Still in his twenties. Chubby and arrogant, he fixed his stern eyes on an off-camera nuisance. Lingering in the background between Duvalier and the others, a fifth man wasn't identified, but Charlie had no trouble recognizing him. Martin Hoffman.

"Goddamnit." Julia pointed at the old photo of her brother. "Martin's their banker, isn't he?"

"I can't prove it."

"But he's their banker. He's the one they've used."

"Yes." And someone Martin knew in Haiti had also played a central role.

"Christ." Julia doubled over on her chair, her tears streaming off her cheeks. Concerned, the librarian rushed off and returned with a glass of water. Julia fought long and hard for her breath until she was finally able to take a few sips of water. "Can we help him?" she asked.

Charlie thought of Joe Turlik, a bloody hand thrashing in agony and bewilderment, loyal to the end, beaten and drowned. George had hired Joe; Martin had hired George. The blame stopped somewhere. "I don't know."

"Can't you do something?" Julia pleaded. "At least in the States?"

"I don't think Martin's worried about American justice. He's worried about losing his money and his bank, he's worried about the people he's done business with, he's worried about standing trial elsewhere." Charlie pointed at the photographs of Haiti. "It's probably what everyone's afraid of - a jail in Grenada or Santiago, a goddamn kangaroo court in Port-au-Prince, island justice."

Julia closed her eyes and didn't open them until Charlie helped her out of the chair. He held her to him, her chest shaking against his, until she was calm.

Back at the hotel Charlie called Beth Spangler at her sister's apartment and asked if she could slip into the bank and discover names and balances for the accounts specified in George's addendum. "I'll try," she promised.

"If you can," Charlie added, "try to find out how many of these accounts Joe Turlik signed on."

Next, Charlie had Julia phone Quentin Casillas's office. She left a message that Charlie dictated: Julia Hoffman, Martin's sister, would arrive in Chile in a day or two and wanted a quick audience. Martin worried that things were moving too quickly with the troubled loan, thereby gaining attention. Martin wanted the process slowed down.

Charlie and Julia would be flying out of Chile late that afternoon. When he stopped by the hotel's reception desk, a clerk handed Charlie a fax from Ray McClean:

"Charlie: Took a look around your house, found it tacked to the door, hope you're watching your back."

The second page was a grainy black-and-white reproduction of a photo, taken from a distance, of Charlie and Julia sitting at a beachside restaurant in Grenada.

35

T he fatigue was mind-altering, a mild hallucinogenic. In the
past eighty hours, Charlie and Julia had spent thirty-five hours
on planes and been in and out of four time zones and seven
airports. Now, she slumbered in her airplane seat, slumped like a soft-
spined creature, her breathing broken and nasal, the hack of her cough
failing to wake her, while he tried to collect his thoughts.

Their plane landed in the rain, settling like a gull on a beach, its
wing flaps up, its speed scrubbed until it dropped onto the runway
and waddled into its loop, back to the terminal. Seated in the rear,
Charlie waited till most of the passengers had deplaned before rousing
Julia. She struggled to wake, a hand shielding her eyes, an involuntary
spasm rippling through a leg.

"Hartford," Charlie announced.

Julia slept on the short drive to Quad and Erica's house; once
there, teetering on her feet, she accepted their offer to spend the night.
Though Quad invited him to stay, Charlie wanted to keep going. The
Brown University libraries would be open late, if necessary.

Upon reaching Providence, Charlie drove past his house: nothing
looked out of place, a hose still coiled on the porch beside the front
door, a neighbor laboring to rake wet leaves. Charlie continued up
Prospect St. to the top of the hill, parked at a meter by the ornate iron
gates to the campus, and headed for Rockefeller Library by cutting
across The Green.

The ivy there had gone brown, a shade darker than the muddy red brick of the Georgian halls to which it clung. Charlie watched an errant frisbee fly past and strike a tree. Made lively by its lithe and busy youth, The Green swept him back to the University of Virginia and his final year in college, when Joe, George, and he had been walking across the Alderman quadrangle. George had nodded at the handsome building that anchored the expanse of grass and asked Joe, "Jesus. What's that building? Chemistry?"

"The library!" Joe replied. It bothered Joe that he worked hard for his grades, which were no better than George's, and George barely worked at all. "Fuckin' A, Almighty! You're telling me you've never been? In four years?! It's the goddamn library!"

Unfamiliar with the word, George cupped an ear. "The what?"

"The library! If you'd ever researched a paper.. Oh, cut it out. You've been." Joe turned to his other friend for corroboration. "Charlie?"

Charlie looked doubtful. "George doesn't believe in papers that require footnotes. Too stifling. Prefers original thought."

"Original thought," George agreed. "Don't fuck it up with something that's been published."

Joe was prepared to surrender the point until he caught sight of George's smile. "Okay, goddamnit." Irritated that he'd bitten, Joe pointed at the Alderman Library, where a good collection was made special by private rooms that preserved many of Thomas Jefferson's papers. "You've been," Joe insisted. "First year. Orientation. They took us on a tour."

George shook his head. "Didn't go. I was sick. Right, Charlie?"

"You were hung-over."

"I was bedridden."

"You guys!" Joe whined. "A goddamn tag team."

With Joe still thrashing on the hook, George fed him more line. "A library? Hey, maybe I should go see if they've got old issues of '*Playboy*.'"

"That would be the barber shop," Charlie corrected. "If you ever got a haircut—"

"Goddamnit!" Joe interrupted, grabbing George by the shirt. "You've been. You've been, you've been, you've been!"

A coed inside the Rockefeller Library directed Charlie to indices for periodicals, with which he made short work of the addendum to George's will. Within two hours he had identified, through old newspaper articles, seven of the people whom George had associated with various accounts.

In no particular order, the list included Colonel Miguel della Carsa, once the Chief of Staff for Noriega and lately the Commissioner of Panama's Canal Management Board. Teng Seeh, a brother-in-law of Suharto, Indonesia's long-term Prime Minister, was mentioned in a *Times* article on that nation's oil business; as Chief Justice of the nation's civil courts, it was his job to adjudicate disputes among the oil companies over their franchises. The *Boston Globe* wrote up the Honduran National Police governed by General Jose "Jim" Jimez, whose force had the appearance of being lax on cross-border drug traffic.

J.C. Romero was the former Minister of Finance in Grenada; his name was familiar as the presumed owner of a co-op at "Miami North". Cesar Palliz got his due from The *Wall Street Journal,* which noted that all World Bank development loans to Uruguay and Paraguay were being distributed by a bank he controlled. A long-time Prime Minister of The Bahamas, Teddy Jenks had retired to his modest government pension and his warehouse of rare and fast autos.

One name proved difficult to identify, till Charlie dug past the first page of that day's newspaper. A front-page article in the Business section discussed the attempts by Manhattan cooperatives to restrict ownership to preapproved buyers; the growing use of foreign trusts and corporations as "owners" of local real estate had greatly complicated the weeding-out process for many co-ops. A lovely unit at 580 Park Ave. had been sold to an entity presumed to be controlled by Jean deVillieres. Mr. deVillieres, the story reported, had long headed Haiti's notorious secret police.

George's list comprised, exclusively, foreign civil servants with a preference for secret American bank accounts. Charlie called Beth Spangler, who was bursting with her news. "Goddamn, these accounts, there's like millions in each of them. I got numbers for you."

Charlie arranged to meet her in Newport and didn't get to Four Winds till after dark. He left his car on a public access road, descended to the shore, and followed it over wet, jagged rocks half a mile north. He had ripped his trousers by the time he climbed onto the Women's Tee, from where he snuck around the mansion to the garage. The side door creaked with the wind, the noise of it a cover for the squeak of his footsteps. Everything in the second-floor garage apartment was exactly as he'd last seen it, the mess in the sink, the gun leaning against the wall. Charlie checked the load of bullets and took the .22 with him.

The grounds and house were quiet as he moved about the property, staking a new position every few minutes. By nine o'clock he had a good view of the front gate. Right on schedule, Beth's dilapidated Nissan turned into the driveway and flashed its high beams, then backed onto the road and continued north. No one responded, visibly or audibly, to the intrusion of the Nissan: either no one was watching the estate or that person's blood ran colder than Charlie's.

Heavy rain had made the gravel driveway soft and pliable, but Charlie didn't notice any new tire tracks. He hurried to a hedge that served as a northern property line. Beth would make her way across the neighbor's property to the other side of this hedge, where she'd been instructed to wait until she'd been assured that everything was all right. As Charlie crawled under a thinning section of the hedge, his jacket caught on brittle branches, which snapped off. Flushed, a small animal made its getaway, bursting through the neighbor's garden.

"Shit!" Beth was twenty feet from the commotion. She jumped again at the sight of Charlie, rising from the bottom of the hedge.

"Goddamnit, Charlie."

"Sorry."

"*Shitdamnfuckshit.*" She composed herself with another string of run-on curses before handing him a few sheets of paper. "Okay. It's better than good. I went into the bank today, said I had to talk to the head of operations about reassignment. I told him George's filing was for shit, I better get it cleaned up, so he lets me go through everything. Then, when he chats me up, he's showing off, saying the really big money is in the trusts, not the checking accounts. He says the checking accounts are the 'small potatoes.' He's one of those guys who think the smell of somebody else's money is gonna stick to him, is gonna make me hot for his sorry ass. *Right*."

Beth had balances for nine checking accounts, all of which were titled in the name of offshore trusts or corporations, all of which held between four and eight million dollars, all of which George's addendum connected to a former civil servant of a foreign state. Joe Turlik had authorization to sign on each of the accounts.

Charlie accompanied Beth to her car. "You're sure you're safe at your sister's?" he asked.

"Totally. My brother-in-law works out of the house, so he's like always around. He's really sweet, but he's fat as a Buddha and no one to mess with."

"I gave you the number for Detective McLean. Call him if anything comes up."

"What about you? Where will you be?"

Charlie had to think for a moment. "I don't know. I'll try to keep you posted."

After Beth drove off, Charlie circled back to the garage apartment and slept there. He left the windows open in the hope of hearing someone arrive. He wanted to engage the enemy, to confirm that they were still hunting George. If they were chasing him, then George was alive. The idea that Charlie had had earlier, that the estate was no longer being watched by the same people who were tracking him, was too painful to long consider. He wanted action.

Barn swallows had found their way under the eaves into the crawl space of the garage's attic. Their noisy exit at dawn woke Charlie. He grabbed a quick shower, carried the rifle down the shore to his car, and headed for the Connecticut border.

Charlie phoned Gramercy Capital Management from the car. The receptionist was cordial, but useless. She didn't know when Mr. Hoffman would be in and was referring all Martin's calls to his voicemail.

In Stonington, Charlie stopped by the harbormaster's office to pick up a diagram of the various docks, then checked Martin's slip, which was empty. The nearby Coast Guard station in Mystic had nothing in its logs to suggest any recent mishap with a yacht, although a duty officer mentioned that rough weather was expected. "High wind, mostly," he told Charlie, "and big swells out of the southeast. Already had a tanker run ashore in the Carolina islands."

If Martin was on his boat, in a holding pattern offshore, he had about two days left before he'd need the shelter of a harbor. "I wouldn't want to put in at an island in the Sound," the officer added. "I'd want my yacht in a mainland port, the north side of a breakwater."

It was midafternoon when Charlie used his cellphone to retrieve the messages from his answering machine at home. Lucy had called with the name of the President of the District's Federal Reserve Bank; she'd done as requested and solicited the president's help in setting up a meeting. Five times the line had gone dead with the sound of a hang-up before any message was recorded. The last call had been made late the night before. The woman was short of breath, each word expelled into little huffs of shock. It took Charlie a few moments to identify the speaker: Lisa Calvert, George's ex-wife, calling from Florida.

"Charlie..? Charlie, you better call. Oh, God. Oh, Jesus, the police are here. They found him. That's what they think. Oh, my Jesus, they found him."

36

Charlie spent an hour trying to reach Lisa Calvert at her home in Coral Gables before declaring an emergency and having an operator interrupt the series of calls that was tying up the line. "Charlie?" Lisa burst into tears at the mention of his name. "Oh, shit, I've been holding it together. Goddamnit."

George had been found several miles off Nassau. He had drowned, apparently by becoming entangled in the main sheet of a small sailing boat and falling overboard. His legs were twisted in the rope, which was dragging his body in the slow wake of the pilotless boat. Rented weeks earlier, the boat carried such few provisions - barely enough for a lunchtime outing - that the Bahamian Police had ruled the death an accident, a mishap on a day's cruise, though they were puzzled by the fingers that George had lost. The police theorized that the fingers had been severed by a stay as the victim was swept overboard.

The Bahamian police had transferred the body to the morgue in Dade County, because George's only identification was a key in his pocket from a Miami motel that he frequented when visiting his son. The motel owner had suggested an identity and knew that there was an ex-wife in the area. Contacted by local police, Lisa Calvert had gone to the morgue to identify the corpse.

"Oh Jesus, Charlie. Jesus-Jesus-Jesus, what's he doing on a boat by himself?" She started sobbing, her speech interrupted by violent bursts of tears. "I can't tell Walter – how am I supposed to tell him? He's still waiting, waiting for the magic between him and his father. For the connection. George, too. He kept imagining something brilliant with his kid. Oh, God, Charlie, and now? Maybe you can take care of things on that end. I called the mortuary in downtown Newport. It's Goldman's, right? They're flying the body there."

Desolated, Charlie focused on the details. George would never rent a boat, especially a sailboat. Like Joe, George had been set upon by a son-of-a-bitch with a knife and a penchant for incapacitating his victims by slicing off several fingers. Charlie wanted, more than anything else, to find the bastard responsible, but his rage and grief were held in check by duties to perform. A plane carrying George's body would land in two hours at Warwick Airport.

Charlie drove to the mortuary in time to ride with the young man driving the hearse to the small airport, where the casket was taken to the cargo facility and inspected by the hearse's driver. The sight of the temporary casket nauseated Charlie: fashioned of industrial cardboard, the narrow box was full of Styrofoam pellets and the stiff nylon of a coroner's body bag. George might find the humor in it, but Charlie couldn't: his best friend packaged like computer parts.

Charlie had made the short drive from Warwick to Newport a hundred times or more, never once in such silence, the driver's sweet *tsks* of concern ticking off the seconds, monotonous as a clock. Seated in the front of the hearse, Charlie longed to turn the radio on. George would want music, jokes, a party. He'd remember the last time the two of them had ridden inside a hearse: some upper-classman had bought a used hearse, put a mattress and a *bong* in the rear, and ferried Charlie, George, and another first year student down the road to a women's college for a raucous evening. It wasn't an anecdote Charlie could tell; the driver was too young to appreciate the details, the hearse pulling up at a club in Roanoke and spilling out four Yankees with hair hanging to their collars, and four demure Southern girls from Hollins College, none of the eight students welcome this particular evening at the Thunderbird Club, redneck night, a band named The Confederates hooting up a little white pride, the good-old-boys feeding their courage long-necks and itching to kick the conceit out of any Yankee, their good-old-women sporting honest-to-God beehives and reserving their special scorn for the college girls, prim and preppy in their size 6 dresses, and not one of them ever spread-eagled in the backseat of a Dodge Charger. One woman stirred up trouble, flirting shamelessly, sticking her tongue out at Charlie until her boyfriend exploded, threatening serious fuck-all if he didn't get some goddamn r-e-s-p-e-c-t. Under cover of that quarrel, the students left the club, only to spend the evening meandering around Roanoke in the hearse, finally finding their way to the hilltops, to the giant electric star there, the pride of the Star-City-of-the-South. They got back late for the Hollins College curfew: the security guards acted like East German troops patrolling the Wall. Sober enough to drive the 110 miles home, Charlie fought the persistent understeer all the way back to Charlottesville, the hearse buckling and swaying like a boat, while the other three slept in the casket compartment, though a half hour short of town George forced his way into the front seat, crowded out of the back by a simple lament, his attraction to his date that evening not reciprocated, George stung by the failure, the long, long night ending on that note of loneliness.

The drive to the mortuary finished as it began, with an apologetic smile from the driver. By the time Quad got there, about ten p.m., the undertaker had begun his work. Charlie and Quad followed an assistant into the laboratory, where George's body was stretched out on a stainless-steel table perforated by drains and hose nozzles. Quad's knees buckled at the stench of chemicals which elsewhere in the building had been perfumed into flowery disguise.

Roughly scrubbed, and paler now than the rest of his discolored flesh, George's face was the subject of the undertaker's current attentions. Quad halted his advance by the door and pointed, his motion half-spastic, his voice breaking. "God Almighty! Oh, God, who does something like that?"

George's right hand, wrapped in an elastic bandage, lay outside the sheet; a stiff little finger protruded from the fist, as though a teacup might be elegantly hoisted. The nubs of other fingers, all missing, poked into the tight bandage. The undertaker stepped aside as Charlie crossed to the steel table and ran his hand across the cool, rubbery flesh of

George's shoulder. Matted down by a gel, the hair was wrong: George never would have taken that much trouble with his hair, nor allowed a stylist's grease to slick it into place. Charlie put an arm under George's head, used both his sleeves to brush off the gel, and cradled George's head as long as he could stand it. He mentioned that there were no burial plans as yet and hurried out.

Charlie joined Quad on the street. A friend of Quad's was there, ready to drive him back to Hartford, with no stop for a pick-me-up on the way. Charlie reclaimed his own car and headed to a nursing home near the harbor.

The entrance to that facility was off the visitors' parking area; at this time of night a security guard sat at the reception counter. As the door opened, the guard signaled the visitor to approach.

"Grace Spaulding." Charlie choked on the request. "It's important."

The guard picked up a phone and dialed the nurse on floor duty. "A visitor for Mrs. Spaulding." The guard listened a moment and hung up; his tone was reproachful. "She's awake. Shouldn't be. You know the way?"

Charlie walked down the hall to an enclosed staircase, which he climbed to the second floor. It had been four months since he visited, a period that might have shamed him had it not been more than a year since Grace remembered his name or given much indication of recognition.

The floor of the corridor glowed with the low wattage of night-lights recessed in the baseboard. Familiar from his other visits, a nurse waited for Charlie outside the open door to Grace's room. Most doors on the corridor were closed, although the gurgle of an oxygen mask could be heard behind several of them. The sound of a muffled newscast drifted out of Grace's room.

"She likes her radio," the nurse whispered, escorting Charlie into the room. "Mrs. Spaulding, you got a visitor, honey."

Grace turned her head in the general direction of the door. "Who's there?"

"It's Gloria, dear. Doing the nightclub shift. You might want to turn your radio down. You got a visitor."

"Oh? I'll turn the radio off, is that right?" Grace slowly leaned to her bedside table, fumbled for the power switch, and clicked it off.

Charlie was stunned by the sight of her. She had lost at least five pounds since he last saw her, and this from a frame that had little to spare. He guessed that she didn't weigh ninety-five pounds. A chair and a walker were next to her bed. Staggered, Charlie made his way to the chair.

"We play bridge sometimes," the nurse said. "Except it's half a pinochle deck."

Grace turned to Charlie as he sat beside her. "I can't remember the cards... Is that silly?" Her voice, delicate and frail, posed the last question as an apology. Ninety-four years old, she knew that memory had failed her, and it embarrassed her.

"You two have a visit," the nurse said, ducking out the door.

Grace extended an arm towards Charlie, who took her hand between both of his. Fearful of hurting the brittle, exposed bones, Charlie rubbed the back of her hand with a finger. He could feel the throb of her pulse; her heart was beating extremely fast. Grace smiled at the contact. "Who is it?"

"Charlie."

"Charlie?" Grace struggled with the name. "I've known several Charlies. My first tea dance, the boy who took me, otherwise forgettable. I do like the name. There was another boy. I think he's grown now. I don't remember. Is that silly?"

It was the last phrase, the apology again, that struck Charlie with blunt force. The sorrow had the weight of a lost century to it, and it overwhelmed him.

"It's Charlie?" Grace asked.

"Yes." He squeezed her hand.

"Are you crying?"

"God, Grace..."

"It'll be fine." Grace folded her other hand over his. The solace, which Charlie intended to offer, was now his for the taking; Grace patted his hand. "I get very sore. I think I fall out of bed." She forced a self-deprecating laugh but looked suddenly worried. "Will they put me in a crib? Or am I too old? Isn't it silly?"

The salt of his tears stung the dry skin at a corner of his mouth. Unable to stem the flow, Charlie held her hand and felt again the furious beat of her heart.

"What is it?" Grace pointed her eyes his way, but they were cloudy.

"It's George."

"I never liked that name," Grace said. "I don't know why anyone would pick it. Who picked it?"

"Your son." Charlie was familiar with this story of hers. Grace had disliked her father-in-law, George F. Spaulding, whom she found insufferable and cruel; she had been displeased when his son named his only child, Charlie's best friend, George F. Spaulding II.

"Old George was full of himself. He had three sons and one daughter. I don't think he liked girls. Isn't that right?"

"Yes."

"The girl was only nine. He decided she was spoiled. Sent her to school at a Belgian convent." Grace paused to catch her breath. "A steamship. No governess accompanied her. Two years off from home at nine years of age. A long time ago, but my God, what kind of father does that?"

"A poor one." Charlie wanted to keep her talking; the oldest stories were still fresh for her.

"Old George got himself appointed Ambassador. To France, wasn't it? Didn't serve long. Six months. You'd have thought he'd made King. Full of himself. Wanted to be addressed as 'Ambassador.' 'The Honorable.' Stuffed shirt. Didn't like children. Why would you name a child after him?" Grace had never forgiven her son that.

"What was your father's name?" Charlie knew the story and wanted to keep it on track.

"Walter. He loved children. Ha! There was a time, I'd been raising rather a riot, and my mother sent him into my room. To spank me. Well, of course, he couldn't possibly do it. He'd never lift a hand to a child. My father."

"Walter."

"Is that a good name?"

"Yes."

"Would you give the name to a child?"

"Yes. Although I might have to call a girl 'Grace.'"

"Is that name in fashion?"

"It was never out."

"Oh. The other name?"

"George?"

"There was young George. Is he younger than you?"

"Same age."

"Are you his friend? He has some of the loveliest friends."

"I'm Charlie."

Grace groaned with delight. "Charlie? 'Cholly?'" Her delight at this recognition played across her face in the broadest of strokes. "Oh, Cholly! Have you been by the summer place? Are they planting the garden?"

"It's fall."

"Oh. Do we plant bulbs then? Or dig them up? I don't remember. Is that silly?"

Grace talked a while longer about gardens and fell asleep, a hand dangling over the side of the bed. Charlie held the other hand and, upon leaving, tucked it under the covers. The subject of George having not recurred, Charlie decided to leave it like that. He wouldn't take George away from Grace.

Outside, the wind ripped through the trees. Newly fallen leaves littered the sidewalk and crackled underfoot. Having failed to keep George safe, a mission Grace had once assigned him, Charlie was now charged with burying him. That evening at the mortuary, before setting off for the airport, he'd tried to imagine a fitting remembrance, a tribute to his dearest friend. He had spent long minutes pushing a pen across a legal pad, only to be frustrated. He would, once he had pursued whoever killed Joe and George, return to the task, but he had found himself, pen in hand and frozen in time. All he could think of were the years that George and he had spent together when they were young. The words that came to mind, which seemed to lead nowhere, were simple. "When the nights were long.."

37

The First District of the Federal Reserve occupies a handsome building overlooking renovated wharves on the Boston waterfront. Charlie had arranged an afternoon meeting there with a Vice President of the District Bank and made sure that Milton Greene of the OCC was also invited. Twenty miles south of the city, the skyscrapers visible on the horizon, Charlie reached Ray McLean from his car and told him of the meeting.

"I don't know what the bank watchdogs can do," the detective cautioned. "I don't think we got anything to incriminate the bank or its people."

"There's a hell of a lot of money sitting in Rhode Island."

"The money's on shore."

"So whose money is it?"

"It doesn't matter, not if the scam is offshore. We can't police that. You think the Swiss ever found a dollar so dirty they couldn't open an account with it?"

"It's not over, Ray."

"Maybe."

"The medical examiner in Dade County thinks George died five weeks ago. I was followed a week ago."

McLean exhaled hard. "Shit."

"I got a gun in the trunk."

"Jesus, Charlie. Leave it there. This is awful personal for you. I don't know where it's going. The goddamn problem is somebody's pretty much gotten away with it. The money's been salted away, right? The guy I want is the knife-happy bastard. Somebody's fond of the knife. Let's tack something on his ass, and I'll be okay with it."

"It doesn't stop there."

"Hey, listen, I'm real sorry about your friends. Real shame. George is the guy who took us out to play golf, right? Hit a few balls sideways and laughed about it. Damn rare. I'm sorry, man. Real sorry. But damnit, you be careful."

Charlie next tried Lucy at work but was told that she was home for the day. "A death," her secretary explained. "She's taking it awful hard." Someone else must have reached Lucy with the news about George because Charlie hadn't been able to.

He had managed to speak with Julia, earlier in the day. She'd gone to Vermont, in case Martin tried to get word to her there, and she'd called Charlie at a prearranged time from a payphone: there was no cell service and, as yet, no landline at her house. Julia had howled in protest when told of George, her shriek agonizing, a world ripping apart. "And Martin?" she'd asked, when words no longer failed. "George – I'm sick about George, and I'm so sorry for you. But Martin? What do we do now? Does any of it matter?"

The reflection of clouds floated across the brilliant glass of Boston's skyscrapers as Charlie neared downtown. He turned off Route 3 onto the Turnpike, made a quick exit, and drove to a parking lot on Newbury St. Lucy had a condo in Back Bay on Marlborough Street, a block and a half from the Public Garden. She answered the intercom and buzzed him through the entrance.

Lucy's apartment was on the top floor of the converted townhouse, where she waited on the landing for Charlie to climb the stairs. "This year is for shit," she said, when he came into view, half a flight below her. "This year is pure shit-on-shit, or have I said that lately?"

Reaching the landing, he opened his arms and wrapped her in a hug. "Who told you?"

"Quad. He called late last night. And Julia called a little while ago. Looking for you." Lucy pushed her uncombed hair behind her ears and led Charlie into her apartment. "She was so upset. We had ourselves a good long cry."

"I'm sorry."

"She was terrified. She said she'd spoken to you. She said if I talked to you to make you get bodyguards, police. Goddamnit, Charlie, you're not going to do anything rash?"

"Relax." He put his hand on Lucy's arm to calm her. "Your friend helped me get a meeting with the banking authorities. In an hour. I don't know how far I can push them."

"That's all? It's just a meeting?"

"Yeah."

Lucy studied him, then held onto the lapels of his coat. "A little while ago when I was talking to Julia? It reminded me of the summer we graduated. How crazy in love she was. You, too. Wild, huh? What you remember." She brushed a little lint from his coat and pulled away. "And now this. I can't handle any more heartache. I called Daddy and told him he was going to have a remission. That's what we all need, goddamnit. A remission."

Charlie had a cup of coffee with her and left for his meeting, walking to Arlington Street to catch a cab at the Ritz Carlton. The ride was so short and the day so beautiful that he felt foolish for not walking the whole way. It might have been faster. Boston was a city laid out long before the invention of the automobile, and the downtown grid didn't favor the perpendicular. Traffic was sluggish. Five minutes before the meeting was scheduled to start, the cab crawled to a stop in front of the office tower at 600 Atlantic Avenue. The Federal Reserve Bank.

Charlie found his way to the fourteenth-floor office of the District's Vice President, who was flanked by an executive assistant. Milton Greene, John Stuart Robbins' supervisor at the OCC, stood to shake hands and handled the introductions. Once everyone was seated, the Vice President summarized a conversation he'd had a day earlier with Ray McLean: the Providence Police Detective indicated that the death of a bank examiner might be linked to trouble at First Federal Bank of Rhode Island. Evidence, the Vice President announced, was "spotty."

"I invited the bank to have its representatives here," he continued. "I thought, given some of the allegations flying about, they should have a chance to address them."

Charlie was furious that the bank had been notified. "One of their senior officers was murdered. This isn't-"

"They declined," the Vice President interrupted. "According to them, this officer is a good friend of yours, and you have some personal vendetta."

"It is personal," Charlie admitted, "and it may become a vendetta, but at the moment the bank ought to be under your microscope."

"There's a question of jurisdiction, a problem you might consider since I'm told you're a state attorney. Our charter is even narrower than yours. We examine banks, not homicides."

Charlie turned his appeal on Milton Greene. "One of the examiners who worked for you is dead. So's his lover."

"We want to help," Greene said, checking the reactions of the senior officials, "if possible."

"We know the examiner covered Rhode Island." Charlie ticked off the successive points on his fingers. "We know he examined the bank. We know he repeatedly phoned someone at a co-op in New York, the same number the bank's Senior Vice President frequently called. We know the examiner had a lot of cash when he died."

"It wouldn't be appropriate for you to review the bank's files," Greene said, leaning back in his chair and lifting a thick folder from a desk. "But I can tell you the bank doesn't have a Category Four loan. Which is how we'd type an otherwise unsecured loan on an uninsured barn that was on fire."

"What about the bank's loan to Multimedia? A thirty-four-mil-lion-dollar catastrophe?"

The District Vice President stabbed the air with a finger. "That loan was performing, as of its last review."

"Let me guess. Robbins assisted in that review."

"Mr. Robbins can't defend himself against this sort of supposition."

"Neither can George Spaulding. He made the loan, and he's dead, too."

"If we can stick to the file..?" The Vice President signaled Milton Greene to hand it to him. "These are the facts. Although the loan's term was extended, the interest was continuously paid."

"You're telling me the loan is current?"

"Yes."

"How does Multimedia do it? They've been broke for months. It's in the newspapers. They haven't paid salaries. You're telling me they paid interest?"

"Apparently."

"No." Charlie was adamant. "I sat in a meeting with their lawyers. They were claiming default, some bullshit technicality, and refusing their take-out obligations. They were sticking the bank with a worthless negative to a godawful film. A thirty-four-million-dollar write-off."

"At last report," the Vice President interjected, "that loan may be syndicated. Which would substantially dilute the risk to this bank."

"Who in his right mind would want a piece of it? Christ, I'll tell you who. The banker in Chile who's helping syndicate it has a lot of his own money deposited at First Federal."

"Mr. Sanderson, it's not our job to evaluate the portfolio of a foreign bank. Naturally, if an American bank unloads a significant loan, we review the transaction."

"You can't let this bank unload the loan."

"Why not?" The Vice President was incredulous. "If, as you say, it's worthless-"

"Because that's what driving this whole damn thing. Somebody doesn't want the loan to fail. What happens if your examiners decide it's worthless?"

Milton Greene took up Charlie's point. "It's a fair question. A bank this size can't stand that kind of hit on its capital."

"And what's the government do?" Charlie insisted. "Seize the bank?"

The Vice President coughed with displeasure. "The verb 'seize' implies a hostile action. It's rarely hostile. The RTC is extinct. Lots of banks cooperate and are given a chance to boost capital and work through the difficulty."

"Yeah," Milton Greene deferred, then looked at Charlie. "Although a hit that size would be crippling. Of course, other things could cause the government to step in."

"Like what? A run on the bank?"

Milton Greene smiled. "You look a little young to remember the Depression."

"So what happens if the bank is seized?"

"The accounts are frozen. They're insured, of course, up to a hundred thousand dollars, but we'd need to identify the owners."

"If the owners wanted to be identified, they wouldn't have gone to the trouble of setting up shell entities offshore." Charlie faced the Vice President. "I'm talking about companies whose world headquarters are post office boxes in Panama and The Cayman Islands. I've identified eight or nine checking accounts with sixty million dollars in them, and they're tied to trust accounts with God knows how much more. The lawyer who formed these companies is dead. The trustee who signed on these accounts is dead. The banker who serviced them is dead. So's your bank examiner. Anybody who could identify the owners has been murdered."

For the first time the Vice President looked impressed. "If this is true, why haven't you approached the Justice Department?"

"Because almost all of it happened offshore. Because it'll take a long time to establish conclusive proof of ownership. All I've got is a cryptic addendum to a will and a bunch of fat accounts."

"In other words, a great deal of conjecture?" The Vice President put a finger to his chin, as if to underplay the sarcasm.

"Conjecture? Goddamnit, this is conjecture: Your bank examiner saw something, maybe a funny interest payment. A third-party making payments to keep the loan afloat. That would do it, right? Your bank examiner wonders what's going on, so he asks the guy fronting the money, who gives him a half-plausible explanation and a ten-thousand-dollar bag of cash."

"Jesus." Upset, Milton Greene uncrossed his legs and leaned forward.

Charlie appealed to him. "It could happen, right? With Robbins?"

Greene's shrug was an acknowledgement, if not an unequivocal endorsement. Charlie turned to the senior official. "Look, if this bank gets rid of this loan, it's free of its handcuffs, and everything goes away. Accounts get shuffled and moved and hidden. This is dirty money."

The Vice President held up a hand, a stop-traffic gesture. "Certainly, there are undesirable people who prefer American currency and markets to their own," he said, in a tone of real sympathy. "But we can't rewrite banking rules to trip them up."

"You're telling me there's no way to interfere with the bank's sale of the loan?"

"If, as it appears, an independent transaction takes place, no. I'm sorry. You'll have to slay this bull in some other ring."

Charlie stood up and walked to the picture window. Two gulls drifted past, riding an updraft on an unseasonably warm day and mocking the height with infrequent flaps of lazy wings. Much of the harbor was visible, and the ocean as well, gray and glittering beyond the islands and the breakwaters.

Grunting as he rose from a low couch, Milton Greene joined Charlie by the window. His towering frame slumped towards the view as his voice rose in gentle mimicry. "'*Idiot Summer*.' That's what Robbins used to call days like these. He had a grandmother, Hungarian or something. Mangled the language. Thought this weather was '*Idiot Summer*.' He could do impersonations, sometimes pretty funny. '*Dot's God's tooth*.'"

"He bled to death. His carotid arteries were slashed."

"God. I don't know if he screwed up. But..?."

"The banking procedures," Charlie said. "Maybe you could explain them..?"

The meeting lasted another ten minutes, while Charlie received a briefing on the Federal Reserve's role as the clearing house for the nation's banks, the safeguards that were established, the reserve requirements, the situations that might unleash government intervention. When he left, Charlie thanked the officials for their time and took an elevator to the lobby.

Outside, no cab was in sight. The walk wasn't much more than a mile, so Charlie cut over to State Street, which ran north through the financial district. He could continue down Court Street, branch off at Tremont, and clear his head with a stroll across Boston Common and the Public Garden.

Distracted, he found himself crossing a street against the light, a bus driver refusing to yield and stranding him between lanes until a police car slowed. The cop behind the wheel shook a finger in gentle reproach and let him pass. Charlie had almost reached Province Street, the mansard roof of the old City Hall visible in one direction, the concrete-and-glass top floor of the new City Hall visible in the other, when he noticed a man run down the intersecting street and pause at the corner to catch his breath. The man removed a Red Sox cap that didn't fit and used a thick forearm to dry his forehead.

A bakery truck was parked at a nearby meter. As Charlie walked past the truck's empty cab, he stepped on the running board for a clear view of the driver's side mirror, with its round and magnified inset. A hundred feet behind him, on the sidewalk across the street, a man in a maroon windbreaker and fishing cap loped forward. The bill of the man's cap shielded his eyes, but he was unmistakable. Charlie was furious at his own inattention. The men who had pursued him in New York and Grenada had been told of the meeting at the Federal Reserve, and he was now flanked by other assassins. One of them was carrying a knife that he was highly skilled at using.

38

Charlie jumped off the running board and picked up his pace, but the sidewalk was walled-in by construction fencing, slabs of plywood that rose on the edge of a giant rip in the earth, twenty-feet-deep. One of the pursuers remained behind him on the sidewalk across the street; the other hovered up ahead by a newsstand, also on the far sidewalk. A third man, fat dreadlocks hanging over muscular shoulders, came running out of an intersecting alley and past the newsstand; at the tip of the second man's head, he hurried north, towards Tremont. Charlie stepped off the curb and into the street. He walked alongside the traffic and kept looking both ways, indecisive about jaywalking, and continued that way. It was obvious to anyone watching that he was about to cross the street to the same side that the three men were on.

The gambit worked, the three men holding their positions on the far sidewalk, till Charlie reached the intersection with Tremont, where he returned to the curb, as if waiting for the light, then took off, sprinting in the opposite direction. Car horns blared as his pursuers bolted after him. Charlie hoped to find police or a crowd of people near Government Center, but the sidewalk was mostly deserted, a lonely vendor hawking pretzels, a homeless man seated on the hood of an air vent. He only looked over his shoulder once: the man in the fishing cap had passed his accomplices and was fifteen yards behind. Charlie wouldn't outrun him.

A street musician's horn blurted out of a subway entrance, which Charlie went flying into, taking the stairs into the Government Center subway station five steps at a time. He dodged the musician, who was blocking the bottom of the stairs, and kept to the station's first level, running down a tunnel toward turnstiles and hurdling them. He took the first turn-off and had reached the platform before he spotted a sign that told him which platform he'd arrived at. GREEN LINE. NORTHBOUND - LECHMERE.

Powered by an overhead line, the Green Line trains ran at platform level, with the tracks for the train wheels recessed in the platform's asphalt. A low partition separated the southbound tracks from the northbound tracks. Prepared to vault the barrier, if necessary, Charlie ran into the center of the station and peered down both tunnels; no train was visible. He spun around when a woman screamed. A long-bladed knife in hand, the man in the fishing cap was rushing him. One of his companions was circling towards the closest staircase.

Charlie raced into the nearest tunnel, running south down the northbound tracks. Forty feet into the tunnel, a dim bulb on a side wall threw off a small circle of light in the arc of the tunnel's curve; the train rails, recessed, disappeared in the darkness, invisible curbs to trip over. Charlie kept a hand on the side of the tunnel to space himself and sprinted down the thin lane between the wall and the rail. The hand steadied him when he tripped on a discarded bottle. Up ahead, a sudden bolt of light illuminated an elevated walkway, but he could hear other footsteps, close behind his own, and the walkway's ledge was too narrow to be anything other than a trap.

The rattle of the tracks, the tremor of the ground, the unexpected blast of air: a train was behind the light, which swept towards him. Charlie ran towards the train's headlight, its beacon eye-level and blinding, and shielded his eyes until the last moment, when he flattened himself against the wall. Four cars long, the subway train rumbled past. In the flash of passing faces, Charlie saw no sign of alarm, of recognition by a passenger that a man was trapped beneath them, pancaked against the wall of the subway's tunnel.

In the flicker of light from the train's well-lit windows, he caught sight of a shadow under a fishing cap. Even in the instant that the man in the cap was pinned to the wall, his shadow slithered along it. Charlie hurried off, running towards a tiny blur of light, a bulb a hundred yards ahead that offered a clue to the tunnel's gradual curve. He heard a terrible screech explode in the tunnel behind him, the grate of metal grinding on metal: the train in a panic stop. Another sound, not quite drowned out by the train's long slide, also chased Charlie: a howl, he thought.

By the time he reached the light, the end of the tunnel was visible, a hundred and fifty yards further down the line. He could see now, so he lengthened his stride and burst into the Green Line platform in Park Street Station, skipping over the rails and scrambling through an arch into a long passageway, where he ducked into the first stairwell and bounced off a passenger who had ridden up the escalator. Charlie leapt onto the staircase. Someone shouted as the man in the fishing cap collided with another passenger getting off the escalator.

The staircase dropped sharply to a Red Line platform. Halfway down it, the stairs were obstructed by two students, bent over to pick up books that had tumbled out of a backpack. Charlie jumped over the handrail onto the stainless-steel ramp that separated the stairs from the escalator and skid past the students, then hopped back onto the stairs and stumbled into the Red Line station.

At Park Street Station, where one could switch lines, the Red Line tunnels burrowed beneath those of the Green Line. Unlike the trains on the Green Line, the Red Line trains ran through a deep trough and drew their electricity from a live third rail. Unless there was an exit at the far end of the platform, Charlie was trapped by the wide trough that ran the length of it.

He raced down the platform till he could see the revolving door at the far end, caged in bars and padlocked. CLOSED, the sign read. He spun to watch the man in the fishing cap. The knife firmly in hand, the man was trotting alongside the wall, daring Charlie to try to double back between him and the subway's trough. Nearby, two bystanders made themselves small, flattening themselves against the filthy tiles behind their bench. Charlie looked at the trough and the platform on the far side of it; he had no more than a four-step approach to the fourteen-foot broad jump.

Charlie tried to leap across the trough, but his shoe skidded as he jumped. His front foot came up short, his toe catching the far wall, his shin slamming into the edge. He twisted his body with the fall, the momentum carrying him over the trough, his back crashing onto the opposite platform, where he lay beside the trough; little trails of fire shot up his lower leg as the man in the fishing cap stepped to the trough and checked both ways: no trains were coming.

Catlike, the man crouched next to the trough and dropped into it, then bounded across the tracks towards his prey. He stepped on the third rail, as if to pounce out of the trough from it but was suddenly frozen in place. The man hung in that pose, his foot mysteriously stuck to the third rail, until the violence of his electrocution lifted and toppled him. He landed in a heap on the rail, the current sizzling and snapping through his lifeless body before a loud pop dimmed the station's lights and sounded an alarm. A siren wailed, but the tunnels grew quiet, the power cut to their trains.

The noise slowly increased, first footsteps, then shouts and screams. Charlie saw a chubby man in an MBTA uniform barrel down the stairs onto the center platform. Across the trough the second attacker held the Red Sox cap in front of his face as he turned around, bullied his way past a woman, and charged up the slow-crawling escalator.

Charlie sat up, flexed his leg, and rubbed a hand over the sore shin. Nothing was broken. By the time the first cop arrived, he was on his feet. The man in the trough hadn't moved. His protruding tongue was held by the clench of his teeth; his fishing cap lay beside a rail. A knife was still in his hand.

It took eight hours for police to identify the man in the trough and one of his accomplices. Although the guy in the Red Sox cap had escaped, the man with the dreadlocks was rescued from the Green Line tunnel, where he had tripped while chasing Charlie. As the train approached, the man had cleared the track of everything save the front half of his right foot; this part of his body the train claimed. The rest of him, a police detective remarked, was being held in a criminal ward at a Boston Hospital.

Excited, Ray McLean drove to Boston and waited with Charlie while fingerprints were sent off for IDs. "I'll tell you one thing about that asshole with the knife," McLean said. "The dumb fuck didn't know Boston. Walks through a Red Line tube. Welcome to Beantown."

Once the medical examiner's report on the man in the fishing cap arrived, McLean leafed through it. "Look here. Our surgeon had another scalpel." McLean passed the report to Charlie. The deceased had kept a second knife in a sheath above his left ankle. The medical examiner suggested that this knife's metal had made contact with the third rail, since the shape of the blade had been etched into the skin.

Charlie was too impatient to be interested in the details. With the day shift gone, Boston Police Headquarters was becoming tomb-like, the few remaining officers periodically fetching cups of bitter, reheated coffee from a squad room. One of the attackers had gotten away. Whoever was responsible had time to start cleaning up after himself.

It was almost midnight when the man with the dreadlocks was identified. Until an interpreter could be found who spoke *patois*, the peculiarly Haitian mélange, the police couldn't interview him. However, his fingerprints identified him as Claude France, a former policeman from Haiti who'd been deported twice from American shores. He had prior convictions and no valid visa.

Within twenty minutes of the first break, the FBI produced a substantial dossier on the deceased, whose given name was Simon Digonier. Although he had a green card and a valid American passport, Digonier was presumed to have at least two other passports and a variety of aliases. He'd been arrested several times, if not convicted, in the twelve years that he'd been in the States. For twenty years prior to his emigration, he'd served as a Sergeant in Haiti's secret police, where he earned the nickname *Denduquin*. "Dent du requin". Shark Tooth. Both Amnesty International and Human Rights Watch were pressing for a trial, in Port-au-Prince, of Digonier and several of his notorious cohorts from the *Tonton Macoute*.

"'Shark Tooth,'" McLean marveled. "You can imagine the kind of monster that earns that nickname."

Ostensibly, Digonier worked as a chauffeur for Rumson Cay Development, which listed a New York City address on its payroll tax forms. 580 Park Avenue. The company had, Charlie knew, large accounts at First Federal Bank of Rhode Island. The person whom George had fingered as the owner of these accounts, Jean deVillieres, had been the Minister of State Security under both Duvaliers, Papa Doc and Baby Doc. As such, he'd been in charge of the secret police.

Interpol had files with mug shots of twelve former members of the *Tonton Macoute*. Charlie recognized Raul Cedric, the third attacker, instantly. Despite a boxer's puffiness under the eyes and a nose broadened by repeated fractures, his light brown skin gleamed with the photographer's flash. He, too, had a criminal record acquired in the ten years that he'd been in the States.

Charlie thanked the officers who had stayed late and found a pay phone near the end of a corridor. He fished coins out of a pocket before turning to McLean, who had tagged along.

"Give me a moment."

"Yeah." Misunderstanding, McLean held his ground.

Charlie shooed him away. "A bigger moment."

While McLean retreated thirty feet down the corridor, Charlie pulled a list of phone numbers from his pocket and dialed Marion Huntley in Dayton. She answered on the second ring and sounded relieved that he'd called. "I heard about George. God, Charlie, it doesn't seem real, none of it, not yet. When's it gonna seem real?"

"I've got some of it figured out. Even so.."

"I want the bastards who did this. You got it figured out? Well, that's all I want. The bastards who got Joe."

"Will you help?"

"What?"

"I've got an idea. Stop me if you don't like it." He proceeded to review the accounts to which Joe Turlik was known to be signatory and to outline his plan. Marion Huntley pledged her cooperation before Charlie hung up.

Amused, McLean shuffled back down the hall. He looked at the phone, hanging on its hook, then at Charlie. "Who was that?"

"Wrong number."

"What don't I know?"

"I may need you to help get some warrants."

"Those names I'll need."

"You'll get them."

"So what're we thinking? You get attacked by a few Haitians because..?"

"They work for Jean deVillieres. He's got a fancy place on Park Avenue and a ton of money in the Rhode Island bank. He's protecting his accounts. His friends' accounts, too."

"Where is the bugger?"

"He's probably careful to have some alibi."

"I don't give a damn. It was sloppy, him sending those knife-happy fuckers after you."

"It was really sloppy for a guy who was once in charge of the secret police."

"In Haiti? Think what the bastard stole. Gold teeth, dead men's passbooks. Can you tie him to the money?"

"Not if he has a chance to move it back offshore. That's what they'll do, as soon as they can. Shuffle everything."

"I don't know from banking, but some asshole lawyer is already trying to get our friend Foot-and-a-Half out of custody. He called for information. Offered the theory the dreadlock guy's not chasing you in the subway, he lives there. Homeless. Pure victim. With a Glock in his belt."

"Nine-millimeter?"

"Nasty little gun. You know the guy skips bail. Doesn't even hang around to sue the transit authority for his missing toes... I realize, of course, you're not planning anything. But if you were, how big is the bomb?"

Charlie shrugged. The wall surrounding the pay phone was covered with scribbled numbers, a few of which recurred in the same handwriting: crossed sevens, nines sloped forward. Somebody used the wall as a phonebook.

"I could call my wife." McLean interrupted Charlie's reverie. "She says she still appreciates it, a call, even this frigging late. But she's a great sleeper, a talent she has. So I honest-to-God never know - should I call her?" McClean lifted his eyes to Charlie's. "You're worrying about someone. Who is she?"

"It's a mess," Charlie said. "Her brother owns the damn bank."

"I'm sure you know what you're doing. I take it she's fallen on your side of the fence."

"She has."

"Then she's at the same risk you are."

39

er name's Julia," Charlie told McLean. "She's got this place she's fixing up in Vermont. Doesn't even have a phone yet. It'd be hard to track her there. I think she's safe."

"For how long?"

"If my idea works, things should come to a head quickly."

"And if not?"

"I can't even think about it." Charlie shuddered. "Somebody put a crater in my life, and I don't want that son-of-a-bitch slipping away."

On the drive to Providence, Charlie tuned in a radio station playing a string of hits. He needed the pure energy of the music, the pulse of the rock-n-roll, to stay awake till he reached the city limits, where he checked into a Holiday Inn. Shortly before eight a.m., he grabbed a cup of coffee in the lobby, walked to a nearby Hertz office, and rented a sport sedan with tinted windows. If people were still after him, they'd be chasing a moving target.

Charlie returned to the hotel to transfer the rifle to the rental car's trunk and was at the state capitol by nine, which was when the Attorney General liked to be briefed on the day ahead. Vicari's secretary broke off her recitation at the sight of Charlie walking into the office. Working on a donut, Peter Vicari didn't speak until he had finished it, daintily wiping his mouth with a napkin. "Vacation's over?"

"Not quite. Who's sitting in Criminal Court today?"

The secretary handed Vicari a schedule. "Okay," he said, running a finger down a column, "Judge Hood and Judge Modesto. Ernie Modesto, new appointment, not the swiftest river in our tributary system."

"I'll try Hood."

"What do you need?"

"Search warrants. Providence Police."

"I heard the damnedest story, not twenty minutes ago. Something about you and the Boston subway. *'Hang down your head, Tom Dooley.'*" Vicari turned to his secretary, who was half his age, and sang the next lyric. "'*Hang down your head and cry.*' It's a song. From when we were young."

"If you say so."

"What is this?" Vicari frowned at Charlie. "Boston? A chase? What?"

"Boston Police are on it. It all ties to the Newport bank."

"We're not trained for this." Vicari waited for a reply, then continued. "What's new with your friend? I haven't heard."

Charlie kept his voice level; he wanted no hint of emotion to erode the Attorney General's support in case it was needed. "Somebody got to George before I could. He's dead."

"Oh..? Uhh.." Vicari stuttered through his effort at condolence before finally murmuring, "Damn! Damnit, what a shame."

Ray McLean was waiting for Charlie by Criminal Court, where they secured a search warrant. McLean was at First Federal Bank of Rhode Island by noon, presenting the warrant to a flabbergasted Anderson Wells. Charlie doubted that Wells had any knowledge of the real owners of the suspect accounts, but as the bank's President he was in the way. McLean gave Wells a choice: either Wells and the bank's operations manager could agree to be in McLean's office in Providence at 9:30 a.m. the following morning, or McLean and a host of detectives would descend upon the bank and sort through countless documents.

"Damn, I can imagine how embarrassing that'd be," McLean apologized. "Police all over, interrupting things everywhere in the bank. Customers wondering *what-the-hell?* 'Course, we can probably straighten this out quietly."

It was raining hard, the water pooling in the roadside ditch, by the time Charlie got to Four Winds. He wondered where and when Martin would make landfall. Even if Martin could handle the rough seas, he wouldn't be able to stay away for long; his cellphone wouldn't work well, if at all, offshore. He wouldn't trust anyone but himself to save his bank, his fortune, his life.

Charlie let himself into the mansion, then flipped on half a dozen lights. No one would search the estate: George was dead. Joe, however, wasn't dead, at least not officially, and Charlie wanted to be in Newport for Joe's brief resurrection.

Charlie spent a long night on the cracked, stiff leather of the couch in the front office. The two-note bellow of a foghorn woke him, the sound rumbling up the shore from a lighthouse a mile away. The rain had quit, and the fog was lifting by the time he'd made himself his second cup of instant coffee. He checked the fax machine's supply of paper and called Marion Huntley, who promised to send him every document needed.

At precisely nine a.m. Charlie phoned the First Federal Bank of Rhode Island and requested Anderson Wells; Mr. Wells, his secretary said, was out of the office that morning. Fifteen minutes later, Charlie called the bank again, this time requesting the employee who operated the bank's wire desk. Beth had said that Joe Turlik, though he was authorized to initiate wire transfers by fax, had probably confirmed the transactions by phone.

Well-scrubbed by his travels, Joe's accent had lacked strong influences, save for an inclination towards the nasal that Charlie associated with the Great Lakes. Vowels tended to be dropped entirely, or to be flat and to drag out the consonants that trailed them. Words like "can't" sounded like "canned". The other consistent pattern of Joe's speech had been his habit of starting more sentences than he finished.

As his call was put through, Charlie expelled what breath he had in his lungs. Short of breath, his voice rose into his nose, a tone that aided his impersonation.

The bank employee came on the line with a breezy "Hello?"

"This Michael?"

"Yeah."

"Joe Turlik here."

"Yes, sir."

"Look, we got funds to transfer today, you'll be getting wire instructions soon, right?, these are big numbers. Very important. I want you on top of it."

"Yes, sir, Mr. Turlik."

"We got anxious people, nobody wants his wire lost on a desk or sitting in a fax tray. Seven accounts. You got my phone number?"

"Uhh, .. it's .."

"On the cover sheet. Top of the auth'rizations."

"Right."

"A problem? - you call. Otherwise, let's do 'em this morning, while the other bank has its wire desk open."

"Yes, sir.

"Appreciate it." Charlie pronounced the phrase "appreeshuh't." The other thing memorable about Joe were his manners; he had been effusive with praise and thanks. "Great. That's great. *Thank you.*"

"No problem."

After hanging up, Charlie called Marion Huntley and told her to fax the first order for the bank in Newport to Four Winds. If anyone at the bank called her house and asked for Joe, she was to claim that he was on another line and would call back. She'd relay the message to Charlie and let him return the call.

Marion Huntley used the blank forms that the bank supplied. The first transfer by wire authorization was typical of the ones that would follow. Charlie reviewed the order that Marion had signed and sent, and then faxed it to the bank:

Duncan R. Smith

FIRST FEDERAL BANK OF RHODE ISLAND

Date:_10-10-95 **DOMESTIC FUNDS TRANSFER ORDER**

ORIGINATOR INFORMATION
ORG NAME_Island Principal Management Trust_____
ADDRESS_#12 Boat St., Georgetown, Grand Cayman, C.I.
ACCOUNT TYPE_checking_____
ACCOUNT NUMBER_015-667289_____

BENFICIARY INFORMATION
BNF NAME_United Way, Manhattan_____
ACCOUNT NUMBER_22465-89700_____

BENEFICIARY BANK INFORMATION
BBL NAME_Chase Manhattan Bank_____
ADDRESS_50 E. 58th St., N.Y., N.Y. 10012_____
ABA ROUTING NUMBER_100102076_____

TRANSACTION AMOUNT
$4,500,000.00 Four million, five hundred thousand dollars

Joseph L. Turlik

Authorized Signature

Marion Huntley had been right about her ability to forge her husband's signature; her signature was indistinguishable from any of Joe's that Charlie had seen. Thirty minutes after receiving the first order, the bank completed the wire transaction. Though the ownership of Island Principal Management Trust was hidden by layers of paper, George's addendum had identified the owner to be Teddy Jenks, the former Prime Minister of the Bahamas, now living in Manhattan in splendor that might puzzle his fellow citizens. Mr. Jenks' unwitting gift, four and a half million dollars to the Manhattan branch of the United Way, would not be the last charitable transfer of the day.

Through the generosity of Rumson Cay Development, Jean deVillieres donated six million dollars, also to the United Way. Joe Turlik would have cherished this munificence and the irony of his own role in it; the bank signature cards for the Rumson Cay account listed Joe as the company's C.F.O.

By noon, more than thirty-eight million dollars had been transferred to the suddenly swollen bank account of the Manhattan branch of the United Way. The Senior Vice President who supervised the debited checking accounts was dead, and the bank's President and its operations manager were nowhere to be found. Michael, the employee who staffed the wire desk, was about to process the seventh and final order, which called for a further five million to be wired from his bank and credited to the United Way's account, when he received a call from an official at the Federal Reserve.

Michael did not entirely understand what was happening, except that he was ordered to forego further transfers from any account. The thirty-eight million dollars wired out of the bank that morning not only far exceeded the bank's reserves on hand, the amount constituted a major run on bank deposits. One of the peculiarities of banking that Michael would, in the weeks that followed, better comprehend was the mechanics by which a bank with two hundred million dollars in current deposits only needed cash reserves of six million of those dollars. Alerted of the Newport bank's sudden insolvency by a computer that tracks inter-bank transactions, the officer at the Federal Reserve explained that the bank would have to close within the hour. Bank assets would be frozen. By Monday, a team of bank examiners would be in Newport to conduct a complete review of assets and liabilities. The hope was, the officer said, that the bank might eventually survive the crisis.

Charlie had set off the kind of bomb that the bank, through the elimination of the troubled loan from its balance sheet, had been diligently working to defuse. He was certain that the bank's largest clients lacked plausible explanations for their accumulations of wealth, and now considerable attention would be paid to their accounts, the real ownership of which would need to be sorted out. The hundreds of millions of dollars in the trust accounts, though technically off the balance sheet, would also attract scrutiny.

Charlie didn't leave Newport until he had driven past First Federal Bank of Rhode Island and seen the large notice posted inside prematurely locked doors: CLOSED. Satisfied, he drove to a small bridge from which he dropped George's fax machine into the ocean. George's fax number, not Marion Huntley's, would appear on all the transfer requests. He continued to Providence, where Ray McLean was sitting on Charlie's back porch.

The detective got to his feet and greeted Charlie with an exaggerated yawn. "Thought you had a watchdog."

"She's on loan." Roxy was still with Quad and Erica.

"You see 'em?"

"Yeah." Charlie had noticed one of the detectives staking out his block.

"Hell of an interview this morning." McLean grinned. "The bank President and his officer? They were nice enough to stop by."

"What'd they say?"

"They complained... Said I took five minutes to ask each question... Said I talked .. too .. slow."

"Did you?"

"Depends. Maybe. If they were in a hurry. You think they were in a hurry?"

"I think they are now."

"Got a hunch?"

"When did they leave?"

"Wells got paged. About twelve-fifteen. I couldn't refuse him a phone call. God, I had him three hours in a room, and they were threatening to walk out, claiming I was wasting their time, can you imagine? Anyhow, Wells starts arguing with some lackey on the phone, says it's not possible, says '*it's absolutely preposterous!*' You get the picture. Wells in a fit of lockjaw."

"And?"

"Wells made another call."

"To whom?"

"I don't know for sure, except he called the guy 'Martin.' Anyhow, this time Wells didn't do much talking, he did more listening. Then he and his colleague lit out."

"That call?" Charlie said. "Can we find out the number that was dialed, track the call, see where Martin Hoffman is?"

"It'd take a while and maybe then some. First off, I'd have to pull records from the phone company." McLean fiddled with the ends of his tie. "Charlie? What am I missing?"

"There's a rumor. The bank may be in some trouble. The Feds closed it down today."

"So?"

"Best guess?"

"Yeah."

"All hell's going to break loose."

40

McLean considered the prospect and leaned on the doorframe. "I can protect you. If you stay put."

"I should be okay," Charlie said, as he unlocked his back door and led McLean inside. "I'll lay low, go to Vermont, stay with Julia. See what happens at the bank."

"What will happen? You got that figured?"

"No. It's out of my hands. I sent a memo to the Justice Department. We'll see what they stir up."

"I'll leave somebody here." McLean glanced out a window at the backyard. "See if anybody's still stirred up at you."

"Thanks." Charlie hurried upstairs and packed. Ten minutes later, he was back in his rented car, careful to weave through a few one-way alleys in case anyone was trying to pursue him. Once he turned onto the interstate, the traffic was clogged, the pace painfully slow. Charlie thought of Julia, alone at her farm. She'd be worried about him - and about her brother. At least Martin had been cautioned of the bank's closure; maybe he'd do himself the favor of disappearing for a while longer.

The traffic improved when Charlie took the new highway to Hartford, then branched north to the Massachusetts Turnpike. Not far from the New York State border, he got off the Turnpike at Route 7, paid the toll, and headed north. He continued for half a mile before pulling into a small gas station, tucked into a clearing in the Berkshire forest and closed for the night, where he spent a few minutes waiting and watching. He didn't see anyone who might be following him, so he swung back onto the road.

The night was dark, a sickle of a moon hung low in a clear sky. Few cars were on the roads. Even in the towns, a set of headlights was visible a long way off. Charlie tracked various vehicles with his rear-view mirror: the van with one light out, the car with the yellow fog lamps, the driver who refused to switch off his brights. All of them turned off the road or fell away as Charlie sped through the wooded hills to the Vermont state line.

Several miles past Bennington, two hundred yards short of Julia's driveway, a turn-out had been fashioned by the operator of a long-abandoned fruit stand. Thistles, knee-high and sparse, grew in the lot that separated the road from the dilapidated stand. Two things were momentarily apparent to Charlie in the sweep of his headlights: a car-wide swath had been cut through the thistles; something metallic gleamed beside the collapsing wall of the shack, then a red reflection of a taillight. A car was hidden just off the road in a spot not far below Julia's house.

Charlie stepped on the gas and drove past her farm. The field next to the road was striped by furrows, the dirt recently turned and black as soot. Up on the rise where the house stood, a dim lamp on the front porch beckoned. Charlie rounded the next two corners before veering off the road onto a dirt drive that bisected a neighbor's orchard. He circled past some trees, parked his car behind a stack of apple crates, and got the rifle from the trunk. He could slip over the hill to the farmhouse.

That summer, Julia had shown Charlie a trail that wove through the woods: the prior owner of her property had credited a horse that was fond of the neighbor's apples with cutting the trail. Charlie hustled to the edge of the orchard and pushed into the thick border of brambles, using the butt of his rifle to plow a course. Once he was out of the brambles and under the pine and maple trees, the brush thinned out, but the progress was slow until he found the trail. Four feet wide, it traced a series of rocky outcrops; rainwater had dug narrow gullies in well-trodden ruts between the exposed rocks.

Charlie raced along the path, cutting through the woods to a clearing behind the farmhouse, where he knelt behind a bush. In the near distance a dog barked, but broke off, as if the night chill that had settled upon the woods had settled it, too.

Charlie kept well out of sight, concerned that with the temperature dropping, the clouds of his breath could be seen by anyone watching the property. He followed the stand of trees around the house and all the way down close to the road where, on the near side of Julia's driveway, the dew had crystallized into frost on a patch of grass. Newly imprinted in the frost's sheen, a set of footprints looped from the road towards the house and back again.

Something moved on the far side of the driveway and the plowed field beyond, a shadow creeping along the far side of the fence rails. Charlie knew that an animal with four feet would have moved faster, would have kept lower, would have moved with some better combination of grace and stealth. Someone in a crouch was advancing on the house.

The trees provided cover for Charlie, who doubled back behind the house. At the base of the rear wall a square of plastic sheeting covered a pile of construction equipment, mostly paint cans and trays, with a tall ladder laid across the sheeting to anchor it. Thirteen feet off the ground, in the middle of the back wall, the painters had left a window cracked open in a second-floor room.

A squirrel carelessly scooted out of the woods across the yard to a woodpile, which it lazily crisscrossed, until the dog resumed barking out by the road. After surveying the outbuildings and the edge of the woods, Charlie made his rush. He hoisted the ladder, which clinked against the back wall, and scampered up it. New, the window slid open noiselessly. He reached inside and laid the rifle on the floor, then boosted himself through the window. He didn't see the gun until it was put to the side of his head.

"Jesus, Charlie." Martin Hoffman kept the muzzle of the handgun to Charlie's temple. "You could use the front door."

"Martin?"

"That was you today? All that money sent out of the bank? It'll sort itself out. In time."

"Your clients won't give you time."

Martin took a deep breath; he looked exhausted, a cheek twitching beneath sunken eyes. "I'm sure, if you'd asked them yesterday, they wouldn't have expected to give so much money away today. However, when we reverse the transactions-"

Charlie felt the gun quivering against his head, the tremor of Martin's hand, and wondered if Martin had ever held a gun before. "What're you thinking?" Charlie asked. "Goddamnit, where's Julia?!"

"A dog started barking half an hour ago. I made her hide in the cellar. Just in case. It wasn't smart, you coming here."

"They didn't follow me. They don't even know I'm here. They must've followed you."

In a slow acknowledgment, Martin turned to the window and looked at the backyard. "Jesus," he whispered, "I've had my secretary send packages here. They must've picked up on it. You're certain?"

"Yes."

"How many are there?"

"I don't know. There's a car down the road. Somebody's out front by the pasture."

"They didn't see you?"

"I'd be dead if they had."

"The trouble you made-"

"It isn't me they want. Not anymore."

With his free hand Martin closed and locked the window. "I need your rifle," he said, bending and lifting the weapon from the floor. "Julia's car is locked in the barn. Join her in the cellar. Keep her safe. They're not looking for either of you, and workmen are due in the morning. You'll be okay if I make a noisy exit."

"Martin?" Charlie was interrupted by a noise from outside: a branch cracking underfoot.

Martin retreated from the window. "I'll call the police from town," he promised, before prodding Charlie down the staircase and into the center hall closet. The cellar could be reached by the closet's back door, which Martin had disguised by hanging coats on its hooks and putting boxes of supplies across its bottom. Charlie slid the obstructions out of the way, then unbolted the door.

Martin used his gun to nudge Charlie into the darkness, where Charlie bumped his head on the low, steeply angled ceiling. His feet found the plank stairs, as the door closed behind him and the bolt slid into place. He felt his way down the stairs to the basement floor, where he heard Julia, her sharp inhales, before he saw her, the outline of her feet in the blue glow of the pilot light for the water heater. Frightened, she retreated, her feet sliding back into a hidden recess.

"Julia?"

She swept forward, grabbing his shoulders with her hands, and clung to him tightly enough to smother the convulsions that shook her. Overhead Martin's shoes clumped through the house. "Damn him. What's he doing?"

Charlie put a finger to her lips to hush her. "Someone's outside," he explained, turning towards the far end of the cellar. Next to the other set of stairs, which led outside, a shadow crossed a narrow casement window; a board creaked on top of the storm-cellar doors.

Julia backed into the recess behind the water heater, while Charlie inched along the back wall of the cellar until he came to the partition that blocked off the coal bin. He slipped around the partition, sliding his feet forward cautiously, the coal old and brittle, and loud if a foot inadvertently sent pieces scattering across the floor. He felt what he was looking for before he saw it, the handle of the coal shovel bumping against his thigh, the cellar's best makeshift weapon. Rolling down the pile as he extracted the blade of the shovel, cubes of coal came to rest against his feet, which buttressed further sliding.

The wood groaned as the storm door panels were pried apart, the shaft of a screwdriver sawing between them, the rotten wood popping loose an interior latch that dinged on the cellar's concrete floor. A storm door was slowly raised to reveal a man squatting against the backdrop of the sky. Charlie recognized him. Raul Cedric closed the door panel behind him as he ducked down the steps into the cellar. He kept his gun pointed in front of him. The advantage Charlie had, that his eyes had better adjusted to the dark, would quickly be lost. Upstairs, a door slammed, and Martin stomped across the front porch. Cedric paused, eight feet from Charlie.

Cedric turned to the casement window, but a trickle of coal slipped off the pile and over Charlie's feet. Four or five lumps of coal skittered across the floor. Cedric spun towards Charlie, who leapt forward, swinging the shovel as hard as he could, bringing it down and across Cedric's right arm. The shaft of the shovel broke, and Cedric fumbled his gun. Fragile and dry, the shaft snapped at a point a foot above the blade, which bounced off Cedric's chest and clanged on the floor. As Cedric tried to grip the gun, Charlie lunged forward with what was left of the shovel's handle. Sharp as a spear, the shaft impaled Cedric high in the abdomen and drove him backwards, Charlie pushing him all the way to the stairs. Cedric grabbed at the stake, dropping his gun as he toppled onto the stairs that led outside. He landed hard, under the full weight of Charlie's tackle, long slivers of wood piercing an intestinal wall and a lung.

Charlie gave the shovel handle a final thrust, then scrambled around the floor until he located the gun. Cedric writhed wildly on the steps, trying to extract the handle, but the jagged wood had fish-hooked his flesh. Unable to free himself, Cedric got to his feet and lumbered up the steps. He flung a storm door open and stumbled through it. Moments after the storm door slammed shut behind him, a couple of gunshots felled Cedric. He dropped to his knees, his shoulders pitching backwards before recoiling, his body folding over the shovel handle and collapsing onto a side. Charlie got a glimpse of the fall, Cedric's lifeless body rolling into view through the casement window, Martin holding George's .22 and jumping into his car in the background. Anxious to latch the storm door panels, Charlie grabbed an old aluminum pole and stuck it through the metal loops of the interior door handles.

Outside, Martin started his engine and raced it; thrust into gear, his car sent gravel spraying as it sped down the drive. A volley of gunfire erupted by the road, the odd percussion of different weapons lending a beat to the racket. Tires squealed on asphalt amidst more gunshots. After a brief lull, a second car fishtailed onto the road.

In the cellar Julia struck a match from a pack that she'd discovered in a drawer, but her hands shook so badly that the flame blew out. She struck another match and then another, and with their light Charlie crossed into the coal bin; high on the back wall was a chute, the gate of which had long ago been nailed shut. The chute led out back, where bushes had overgrown the path that once allowed the coal truck access. Charlie used the blade of the coal shovel to pry nails loose from the hinged gate but stopped when a distant burst of gunfire echoed through the hills, the reverberations making it difficult to separate and number the shots. Julia started to cry and groaned at the sound of one last retort, a dull *thump*.

Charlie slid back down the coal pile and joined Julia, who was slumped against a table and shaking fiercely. He had found a chair for her by the time they heard the first siren. Other sirens followed, their wails converging on a spot a mile east of the farm. The flicker of revolving lights, some blue, some red, played across the dusty panes of the casement window until it seemed that half of Vermont's emergency vehicles had shown up. Sirens howled erratically, the new cars on the scene blaring their arrival, until Julia couldn't take it anymore: she wept uncontrollably, her head buried in her lap.

Charlie crossed to the coal bin and scrambled up the pile; he lowered the chute's gate and wiggled through the aperture. Once outside, he propped the gate back in place. Careful to release the steam of his breath into his open collar, he was slithering past the evergreen bushes that hid him when a car came charging up the drive, its high beams flooding the farm with light.

41

B y the time Charlie made his way around the house, a spotlight on the patrol car was shining on the front door, which a Vermont State Trooper approached. Charlie hailed the trooper and carefully stepped into the beam of light.

"A shooting down the road," the trooper called out. "You live here?"

"It's my friend's house. Someone was shot here, too." The trooper retreated towards his car and unholstered his gun. "I'm a deputy state attorney," Charlie added.

The trooper got back in his car to summon extra units, then entered the house through the front door, which Martin had left unlocked. Charlie followed and brought Julia upstairs. Faint, she sat on the floor of the living room, her back to the wall, her knees to her chest.

The front yard crackled with the static of police radios when Charlie stepped back outside. He was joined by the first trooper on the scene, who left a group huddled around the body of Raul Cedric. "Got no pulse," the trooper said, with a flick of his head in Cedric's direction. "He got some kind of wooden stake in him. Like a vampire, is it?"

A senior officer wandered over, and Charlie briefed him on what had happened, then drove with the other trooper to the spot down the road where the final shooting had taken place. The BMW had drifted off the road, hopped a ditch, and skidded to a stop against the low remains of a stone wall. Martin Hoffman was doubled over in the driver's seat.

A local sheriff accompanied Charlie back to the vehicle and showed him a leg and a chest wound on Martin's body, both saturated with blood. "He must've been hit before he lost control," the sheriff surmised. "Somebody caught him here and put a quick end to it." A coup de grace had been administered: the bullet's messy exit from Martin's right temple had splattered the roof and whatever glass hadn't been shattered. Charlie's knees wobbled as he made the I.D.

The sheriff pointed out multiple bullet holes in a rear window panel, their circumference expanding upon exit; they'd been made by bullets fired from within the car. "The victim got off his shots," he said. George's .22 lay beside Martin. Its load of long, hollow-point bullets was mostly spent.

"Who are we missing?" The sheriff's eyes tracked the road south.

"You want to contact N.Y.P.D.," Charlie said. "A Manhattan precinct."

At nine the following morning, Jean deVillieres returned to his Park Avenue co-op after having been treated at a city hospital for a gunshot wound that he attributed to a foiled robbery attempt. Police were waiting. He'd been wounded by a narrow gauge, hollow point bullet, identical to the type that had killed Raul Cedric. The driver for deVillieres, another former officer from the *Tonton Macoute*, had been cut by flying glass; he claimed that his boss's car had been stolen earlier that morning.

"They'll find the car," McLean predicted, when he heard the excuse. "They'll find the car, and they'll nail this fucker deVillieres and all his Haitian gangsters, and best-of-all they'll do it somewhere else, with this asshole thoughtful enough to cross state lines. I'm gonna send him a thank-you note for making it so I don't even get called at his trial."

Charlie figured, correctly, that the extensive charges filed against deVillieres, in Federal and State courts, would frustrate any efforts to stage a quiet withdrawal of money from the Newport bank. The layers of ownership of the offshore trusts and corporations, painstakingly crafted, resisted a simple unraveling. That Tuesday, notified by the Justice Department of the existence of suspicious accounts frozen at the First Federal Bank of Rhode Island, four countries filed suit in Federal Court, using "sudden enrichment" laws, to recover hundreds of millions of dollars stolen from national treasuries by civil servants who had amassed inexplicable fortunes. Haiti, Panama, Chile and Indonesia filed first. Within the month they were joined by Honduras, Paraguay, Grenada, and the Bahamas, all of them seeking some of the more than five hundred million dollars that had been parked in deposit and trust accounts at the Rhode Island bank.

Charlie tracked the developments wearily. Glad as he was that money would find its way back into some of the pockets from which it had been picked, he was concerned about Julia, whose grief seemed to ricochet through a maze of emotions: disbelief, anger, guilt, profound sorrow. It was Thanksgiving weekend before she let go of the notion that she might have been able to save her brother. "I used to think," she told Charlie, "that all of us had pivotal moments which defined us. I know I was changed, in ways you can't ever entirely undo, by the summer we had together. And then I look at Martin's life, and I can't find anything like that summer. I can't find the moment that might've changed him."

"You can't blame yourself."

"Then neither can you. You can't feel responsible for George. You can't keep asking yourself '*If not me, who?*'. That'll be our agreement - we won't blame ourselves."

"Easier said than done?"

"Easier said than done."

Beth Spangler stayed in touch with Charlie and had his favorite take on the fortunes of the bank in Newport. Its deposit base substantially diminished, First Federal Bank of Rhode Island was quickly taken over by a large regional bank. Beth declined the offer to transfer her employment to the regional bank. "This new bank," Beth said, "they'll cut costs and close our beautiful office in Newport. They'll farm us out, one by one, to branches they put in different supermarkets. I'll be running my own entire branch bank, right there in the deli section of the supermarket, slopping up tubs of potato salad when things are slow at my counter. Me, a bank teller with a hairnet. No goddamn thank you. I want to work for somebody I love. Shit, I only worked for three people my whole life, and two of 'em were petty and mean. Selfish, screaming bastards. George always looked out for me, always took the time, the little things. I know there'll never be another George, he's pure class, but I'm gonna look anyhow. I'm gonna find some boss I love. I miss him terribly. You, too, huh?"

"Yeah."

"What're you gonna do? With George? I mean, it wouldn't be like him to have funeral plans. He'd make a joke of it. Give him the Viking special. Burning boats, right? Or donate himself to science." Beth gasped. "You wouldn't do that...? Charlie?"

42

The snow hadn't stuck. Nearly a foot had fallen a week earlier, and its slow melt had muddied most of the footpaths around the property. Incongruous on the floors of marble and herringbone oak, plastic runners had been laid through the rooms at Four Winds open to the public, but the prospective buyers walked everywhere except on the runners as they inspected the furniture and objects on display. As executor, Charlie had arranged the estate sale. A portion of the sum realized, along with the proceeds of an insurance policy, would help care for George's son, Walter, through his college years.

George's closest friends had been admitted to the sale half an hour before the public and had bought items dear to them: Lucy purchased a watercolor someone had once done of the estate's water garden, Charlie a bureau from his old quarters in the maids' wing. With the sale underway, and a crowd of people scurrying throughout the house, Charlie gathered his friends and led them outside.

Lucy was with them, but stopped at the sight of a stranger, snooping through shrubs by the back terrace. "Only five shopping days left," Lucy announced, in a voice noticeably absent of Christmas cheer, and pointed the stray shopper back towards the house.

"God," Erica moaned, as the woman disappeared inside the house. "I'm glad George didn't have to see this."

Lucy shook her head. "Me, too." It had been a rough five weeks: they had all attended a memorial service for Joe in Ohio and a service for George in Newport. Charlie had accompanied Julia to Martin's otherwise private burial.

"Where's Jennifer?" Julia asked Lucy. "I thought she was coming today."

"She got a better offer at the last minute. Some new guy called." Lucy shrugged and took Julia's arm. "She wanted me to buy you a wedding gift today." Julia's wedding with Charlie, planned for the first week of the new year, gave all of them there the lovely distraction of something to look forward to. "She said to ask if she was too old to be a flower girl."

"She's not too old." Julia winked. "Neither are you."

"I'm holding out for a better offer. I want to be the godmother." Lucy was thrilled, and admittedly a bit jealous, that Julia was eleven weeks pregnant.

Charlie started walking across the terrace and signaled the others to follow. "Hey boss?" Quad called after him, "where are you taking us?"

When Charlie didn't answer, they dutifully followed him across the back lawn to the bluff that dropped to the Women's Tee. Charlie climbed down the slippery rocks and helped the others descend: Julia, Lucy, Erica, and Quad. At the base of the ledge, where the horizontal shelf tucked into the vertical wall, a sheet was pinned to the ground by loose rocks. Lucy pointed at it. "What?"

Charlie tugged the sheet aside. A shallow shaft had been drilled by a jackhammer through the thin turf into a vein of bedrock, the hole barely wide enough to accommodate the black metal urn that sat beside it. A shallow tub, full of stiffening concrete, was on the other side of the grave.

"George?" Lucy knelt beside the urn and touched it.

"This can't be legal," Quad said. "The Zoning Board? Does anybody know?"

"Just us. People think the ashes were scattered at sea. I told the workmen we were putting in a flagpole." Charlie bent to the concrete and mixed it, as well as he was able, with a trowel that had been left beside it. Finished, he nodded at the urn. "Who wants to..?"

"You do it." Lucy handed the urn to Charlie, who put a knee to the ground and gently lowered the urn into the shaft. Before standing, Charlie reached into a pocket, brought out a golf ball, and placed it on top of the urn.

Lucy found a flowering weed that grew in a crevice. She broke off its purple blossom and dropped it into the shaft. After a pause in which no one else came forward, Julia scooped up a little loose earth and bent over the grave. She sprinkled the dirt in, said a silent prayer, and crossed herself before rising. As she backed away, Charlie and Quad tilted the tub.

The tub took a few minutes to empty. The trowel was caked with drying concrete, which itself was thickly studded with cinders to darken its mix. Once the shaft was packed, the group disguised the top by embedding it with small rocks and clumps of dirt. Within a few weeks, should anyone climb down to the ledge, it would be impossible to spot the grave.

"Are you going to say something?" Lucy's question sounded like an order.

Charlie, in a struggle to find his voice, listened to the surf. He felt, keenly, that George should be well and eloquently remembered, yet he could barely bring himself to begin, let alone finish, a eulogy, because George was gone too damn soon, and the bitter truth of that sentiment clouded all others.

"I haven't been able to figure this moment out," Charlie began. "I do know George would want us to have fun, to laugh at ourselves because we were in college for four incredible years when the world got stood on its head. I guess the world keeps getting stood on its head, that's the main thing I've learned since, that and the fact we're really lucky if we have people in our lives who, in passing, leave holes we'll never fill." Charlie paused and looked back at the mansion, the roof of which could be seen: a long patch of tar snaked across cracked tiles. "I used to wonder why he tried so hard to hang onto this place, this goddamn glorious white elephant. I think the biggest reason was to share it with us." Charlie turned to the grave. "George, goddamnit, we hate that you're gone. We'll miss you. We love you."

Lucy gave up trying to wipe away her tears, which flowed hard and fast. She hugged Charlie, then Julia, and started back up the rocks. With Erica holding tight to his arm, Quad stepped up to Charlie. "Anything I can do," he said. "Let me know. Anything. I'll help anyway I can, you know it, right?"

Charlie nodded, and Quad and Erica made their way back up the rocks. Once they were gone, Charlie dragged the crumpled sheet farther off to the side of the grave. An old golf club was lying on the ground, a five iron with a rusted steel shaft; it had been stuck in an umbrella stand at Four Winds as long as anyone could remember. "One more thing," Charlie told Julia, as he picked up the club. "For George." He took his coat off and set it down, then reached into a trouser pocket and dropped a golf ball on the ground.

The frayed leather grip irritated the dry, cold skin of Charlie's fingers, but he raised the old club over his head and swiveled his shoulders to loosen up. He dug the soles of his feet into the earth to prevent slipping, worked through the mechanics of a swing in slow motion, and addressed the ball. His stroke fluid, he caught the golf ball near the apex of the downswing. Even in the chill air, the ball climbed quickly, spinning through a light breeze and trailing a long arc until it dropped into the ocean.

"What would George say?" Julia asked. "'Nice shot, partner?'"

"He'd tell me I under-clubbed myself or hit it fat. He'd tell me I needed a mulligan - my last respects stunk. He wouldn't let go of the joke till he had me."

Julia smiled, but her heart wasn't much in it. She watched as Charlie tossed the club over the edge of the Women's Tee; the iron bounced off a rock and disappeared into gray foam.

Julia stepped closer to the edge and stared out to sea: aimless, a tangled raft of drifting wood and seaweed wove with the currents out past the reach of the surf, a black patch in a slow twirl, half-sunk, unsinkable. The ocean swelled under the weed-tangle without disturbing it, then rose and broke towards the shore. One of the waves, in a sudden leap, slapped the cliff beneath them.

To Charlie it seemed a hundred years since he and George had dangled their feet over this edge and, at age fourteen, imagined perfect girlfriends. George's recurring fantasy had involved "a poor girl. I mean *really damn poor.* So smart she's never even dreamed of the social bullshit. From West Virginia, from the hills or hollows or whatever-in-hell they got down there, and so beautiful no one state can hold her. She lives on the road! I'll have to quit school to go with her. Buy a gypsy wagon. No more boarding school assholes, not the good teachers, not the pricks. A whole new world."

Charlie wondered if George, who had been clever enough to conjure his escape, would ever have made good on it, had the chance presented itself. Charlie doubted it.

A glimpse of Julia made him glad that he couldn't recall his own dreamed-up lover: the meagerness of his boyhood fantasy would embarrass him. He could not have imagined a woman of Julia's strength, nor would he have had the years to appreciate the breadth of her passions. The sense of wonder that he sometimes felt in her presence was unknown to him back then; even if it had been grasped, his capacity for astonishment would not have seemed likely to survive into middle age. It did.

A week after the shootings, having waited till there was some break in the events that consumed them, Julia told Charlie that she was pregnant. She had not expected it; she offered no excuses. Sure of herself, she merely wanted his reaction. Which was immediate.

The wind kicked up a light tail of seawater, blown up and off a crest. Pungent as brine, the mist drifted over them and clung to their faces, a salt-and-vinegar wash. A corner of the unfolded sheet flapped itself flat, suddenly pasted to the wet earth. Julia glanced back at the sheet, then at the house as she approached Charlie.

"Will you come back? Once it's gone?"

"Probably not."

Julia opened her overcoat and embraced him inside its thick woolen flaps. Charlie huddled with her, his arms slipping around her back, her breath moist and warm on his neck, the freshwater scent of her hair stilling his disquieted senses. He brought her close, belly to belly, hips to hips, until it seemed to him that he could feel something stirring, new life within her. He knew that it was early for such sensations, yet in the press of their flesh, his abdomen to hers, he imagined the slightest pulse. A third current. Another life, long denied. Their life.

Lucy, in her excitement at first hearing the news, had put it best. "God, Charlie!" she teased. "You two are having a baby? You got a late start. Some long nights ahead of you."

THE END

AFTERWORD

I recognize that fraternities and sororities are under broad attack for gender specificity, exclusivity, excessive partying, etc., none of which I champion, and as the novel notes the idea of hazing was particularly repugnant when "hell nights" were staged by and for those lucky enough to have college deferments that postponed or spared us Vietnam. Also, I have no quarrel whatsoever with campus clubs (social, dining, residential) that are multi-gender, though in my era I think the females may have been spared the constant presence of the males' greater immaturity.

That said, at college I was lucky enough to find a great group of guys with whom I dined, lived, socialized, and played sports. Some people I continued to see often. Other of those friendships survived, intact, after a few decades of career- and family-building separation. I don't know what the most recent survey may show, but multiple surveys at my university have shown that students who belong to fraternities and sororities get better grades than their peers, graduate with a seemingly greater attachment to their school, and go on to become vastly bigger donors. I can't speak for members of any other "Greek" entity, and members of mine have not been spared tragedy or failure, nor did we always conduct ourselves as well as we should have, but I am proud of what so many have accomplished and given and the standards that were set all those years ago.

ABOUT THE AUTHOR

Duncan grew up in Buffalo, NY, and spent his early summers 30 miles north on the lower Niagara River. He moved to Los Angeles where he wrote film and tv scripts for years, then ran a small business while writing some novels and plays on the side. He and his wife Kathy Hallberg – an entertainment lawyer – raised two wonderful daughters there and now split their time between Florida and an old family summer house on the Niagara River. He often writes about characters or events from Buffalo and environs. One can learn more about him and his work at his website, www.duncanrsmith.com.

The author greatly appreciates his readers and hopes that, should you like a book, you will give it a positive review on Amazon and social media and recommend it to friends. Word of mouth – yours – is very important for my work.

Thanks,
Duncan

OTHER NOVELS BY DUNCAN R. SMITH

Jumpers

The House On The River

TOXIN (in progress)

Made in the USA
Columbia, SC
10 April 2022

58784474R00193